A TEXT BOOK OF

SURVEYING - II

FOR

Semester – II

Second Year Degree Course in Civil Engineering

As Per New Revised Syllabus of North Maharashtra University, Jalgaon, June 2013

A. S. SHELAR

B.E. Civil, M.Tech. (Town & Country Planning),
Senior Lecturer, Civil Engg. Deptt.,
Cusrow Wadia Institute of Technology,
PUNE - 1

Dr. S. T. MALI

B.E. Civil, M.E. (Construction Management), Ph.D.
Assistant Professor, Civil Engg. Deptt.,
STE's Sinhgad College of Engineering,
Vadgaon (Bk.) PUNE

U. S. PATIL

B.E. Civil, M. Tech (Construction Management),
Associate Professor, Civil Engg. Deptt.,
Bharati Vidyapeeth's Group of Institutes Technical Campus,
College of Engineering,
Lavale, PUNE - 43

NIRALI PRAKASHAN
ADVANCEMENT OF KNOWLEDGE

N3085

SURVEYING - II (S.E. CIVIL - SEMESTER II - NMU) ISBN 978-93-83971-23-7

Second Edition : January 2016

© : **Authors**

Published By :

NIRALI PRAKASHAN

Abhyudaya Pragati, 1312, Shivaji Nagar,

Off J.M. Road, PUNE – 411005

Tel - (020) 25512336/37/39, Fax - (020) 25511379

Email : niralipune@pragationline.com

☞ DISTRIBUTION CENTRES

PUNE

Nirali Prakashan : 119, Budhwar Peth, Jogeshwari Mandir Lane, Pune 411002, Maharashtra
Tel : (020) 2445 2044, 66022708, Fax : (020) 2445 1538
Email : bookorder@pragationline.com, niralilocal@pragationline.com

Nirali Prakashan : S. No. 28/27, Dhyari, Near Pari Company, Pune 411041
Tel : (020) 24690204 Fax : (020) 24690316
Email : dhyari@pragationline.com, bookorder@pragationline.com

MUMBAI

Nirali Prakashan : 385, S.V.P. Road, Rasdhara Co-op. Hsg. Society Ltd.,
Girgaum, Mumbai 400004, Maharashtra
Tel : (022) 2385 6339 / 2386 9976, Fax : (022) 2386 9976
Email : niralimumbai@pragationline.com

☞ DISTRIBUTION BRANCHES

JALGAON

Nirali Prakashan : 34, V. V. Golani Market, Navi Peth, Jalgaon 425001,
Maharashtra, Tel : (0257) 222 0395, Mob : 94234 91860

KOLHAPUR

Nirali Prakashan : New Mahadvar Road, Kedar Plaza, 1st Floor Opp. IDBI Bank
Kolhapur 416 012, Maharashtra. Mob : 9850046155

NAGPUR

Pratibha Book Distributors : Above Maratha Mandir, Shop No. 3, First Floor,
Rani Jhanshi Square, Sitabuldi, Nagpur 440012, Maharashtra
Tel : (0712) 254 7129

DELHI

Nirali Prakashan : 4593/21, Basement, Aggarwal Lane 15, Ansari Road, Daryaganj
Near Times of India Building, New Delhi 110002
Mob : 08505972553

BENGALURU

Pragati Book House : House No. 1, Sanjeevappa Lane, Avenue Road Cross,
Opp. Rice Church, Bengaluru – 560002.
Tel : (080) 64513344, 64513355,Mob : 9880582331, 9845021552
Email:bharatsavla@yahoo.com

CHENNAI

Pragati Books : 9/1, Montieth Road, Behind Taas Mahal, Egmore,
Chennai 600008 Tamil Nadu, Tel : (044) 6518 3535,
Mob : 94440 01782 / 98450 21552 / 98805 82331,
Email : bharatsavla@yahoo.com

niralipune@pragationline.com | www.pragationline.com

Also find us on ⨍ www.facebook.com/niralibooks

PREFACE TO SECOND EDITION

We are glad to note that the Second Edition of the book received an overwhelming response from the Engineering Students Community, compelling us to bring out its Second Edition with a very short period. Second Edition has been updated by providing additional matter, exercises and university question papers. We sincerely hope that his second edition will also be warmly received by all concerned.

Valuable suggestion from our esteemed readers to improve the text will be most welcome and highly appreciated.

22-1-2016   **Authors**

Pune

PREFACE TO FIRST EDITION

It gives us an immense pleasure to present this book on **'Surveying-II'** to the Students of Second Year of Degree in Civil Engineering. This book is written strictly as per the new revised syllabus of North Maharashtra University, Jalgaon.

One of the main concerns of Civil Engineer is survey work either in stage of planning or execution of different types of Civil Engineering Projects. He/she shall be well acquainted with the principles, concepts, facts and procedures in surveying. With this knowledge and skills, he/she will be able to develop or select and use appropriate techniques and instruments to establish controls, locate details, measure distances and directions, reduce positions, areas, volumes etc. during the survey for construction or maintenance or repair or extension of various civil engineering works in different roles.

The text book has been thoroughly prepared according to five units as per revised curriculum of 2013. An attempt is made to give due justice to the use of modern equipments in routine survey activities. The authors with their professional and academic experience have taken all efforts to present the text in lucid manner. The theoretical matter has been explained with number of diagrams and illustrations supported by solved examples.

In the preparation of this book we owe greatly to the authors and publishers of various books and the literature on all kind of survey equipments and techniques by various manufacturers.

We are thankful to our colleagues, friends and family members for their valuable assistance by variety of ways during the preparation of this book.

We sincerely thank to Shri. Dineshbhai K. Furia, Shri. Jigneshbhai C. Furia, Shri. M.P. Munde and the entire team of Nirali Prakashan namely Mr. Santosh Bare, Mrs. Prachi Sawant and Mrs. Manasi Pingle for their keen interest in publishing this book in attractive form in very short time.

We hope that the book will be well received by the students as well as the teaching faculty. We will like to welcome any kind of suggestions for the improvement of contents of this book.

January 2014 — *Authors*

PUNE

SYLLABUS

Unit I : GEODETIC SURVEYING   (08 Hours, 16 Marks)

(a) Objects, Methods in geodetic surveying.

(b) Triangular figure, Strength of figure, Classification of triangulation system.

(c) Selection of stations, Intervisibility of height of stations towers, Signal and their classification.

(d) Phase of signals, Satellite station and Reduction to centre, Eccentricity of signals.

(e) Base line measurement, Apparatus used, Base net, Equipment used for base line measurement, Extension of a base.

Unit II : TRIANGULATION ADJUSTMENTS   (08 Hours, 16 Marks)

(a) Kinds of errors, Laws of weights.

(b) Determination of the most probable values of quantities, The method of least squares, Indirect observations on independent quantities, Normal equation, Conditioned quantities.

(c) The probable error and its determination, Distribution of error to the field measurements.

(d) Method of correlates, Station adjustment and figure adjustment.

(e) Adjustment of a geodetic triangle, Figure adjustment of a triangle, Calculation of spherical triangle.

(f) Adjustment of geodetic quadrilateral, Adjustment of a quadrilateral with a central station by method of least squares.

Unit III : PHOTOGRAMMETRY   (08 Hours, 16 Marks)

(a) Objects, Applications of various fields, Terrestrial photogrammetry (only general idea) and aerial photogrammetry.

(b) Aerial camera.

(c) Comparison of map and vertical photograph.

(d) Vertical tilted and oblique photographs.

(e) Concept of principal point, nadir point, Isocentre, Horizon point and Principal plane.

(f) Scale of vertical photograph, Computation of length and height from the photograph.

(g) Relief displacement on vertical photograph.

(h) Flight planning, Ground control, Radial line method.

(i) Mirror and lens stereoscopes.

Unit IV : HYDROGRAPHIC SURVEYING   (08 Hours, 16 Marks)

(a) Objects, Establishing control, Shore line Survey, River surveys.

(b) Soundings, Tide gauges, Equipment for taking soundings, Signals.

(c) Nautical sextant, Measuring horizontal and vertical angles with the neutical sextant.

(d) Sounding party, Ranges making the soundings, Methods of locating the soundings, Reduction of soundings.

(e) The three point problem and methods of solution.

Unit V : REMOTE SENSING   (07 Hours, 16 Marks)

(a) Basic principles, Importance, Scope.

(b) Sensors used in remote sensing, Platforms.

(c) Applications of remote sensing of Civil Engineering.

Use of advance electronics instruments in surveys :

(a) Study and use of various electronics equipments like EDM and Total station.

CONTENTS

•••

GEODETIC SURVEYING

1.1 INTRODUCTION

1.1.1 Definitions of Some Terms

(i) Geodesy :

It is defined as 'the branch of science related to the Earth's surface and deals with ascertaining the shape of the earth, and determination of geodetic co-ordinates of the various points on the earth, taking the curvature of the earth into account'. Such points serve as *'controls'* for carrying out triangulation, trilateration or transverse surveys.

(ii) Topological (or Physical) Surface :

It is the existing surface of the Earth and is very irregular in nature and as such it cannot be defined mathematically and is of no use for computations of co-ordinates to determine the positions of the points on the surface of the Earth.

(iii) Geoid :

The earth is usually referred as a 'geoid' i.e. it is a surface drawn in such a way that it is everywhere normal to the gravitational force. However, due to variations of masses within the earth, it is irregular in shape and thus needs large number of parameters to define it in mathematical form. It is the surface obtained, if all the water of oceans is allowed to flow into the continents i.e. it is an imaginary mean sea level surface having earth like shape.

(iv) (Reference) Spheroid :

In order to carry out computations of geodetic co-ordinates accurately, it is necessary to assume or adopt that shape of the earth that nearly fits the shape of the earth i.e. the geoid at that place. Since the surface of the earth is different for different countries, each country will have its own 'reference spheroid' . Computations of geodetic co-ordinates for a country will be based upon such 'reference spheroid' adopted by that country.

Fig. 1.1 illustrates the topographical surface, geoid and (reference) spheroid. At point C, normals to both geoid and spheroid are drawn. The angle Δ between these two normals is called as deviation of the vertical. If these two normals coincide, the value of Δ will be equal to zero. The best fitting spheroid is one that gives minimum deviation of the vertical.

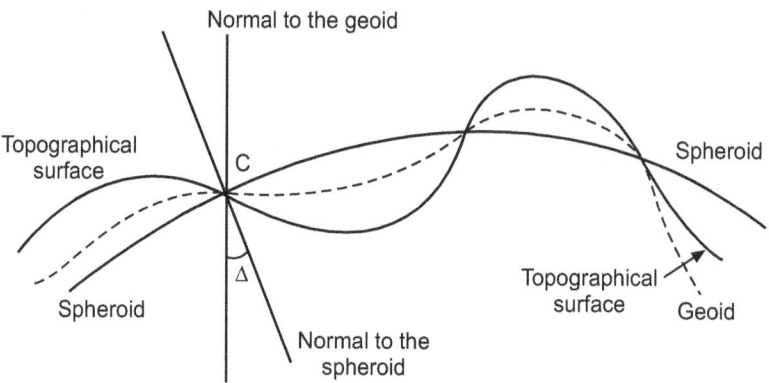

Fig. 1.1

(v) International Spheroid :

As the 'reference spheroid' for each country will be different, the magnitudes of semi-major and semi-minor axes for such spheroids will be different and for the computations of global co-ordinates, such reference spheroids will be of no use. In order to overcome this difficulty, a particular reference spheroid common for the entire earth is assumed and all countries will carry out computations of geodetic co-ordinates based on such a spheroid called as 'International spheroid'.

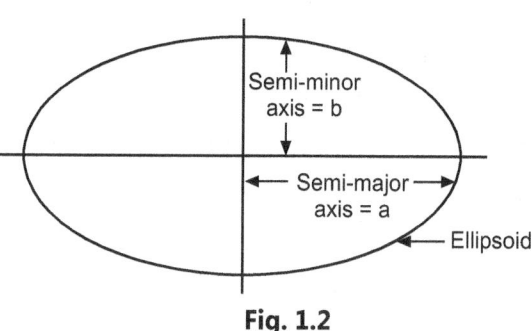

Fig. 1.2

The semi-major and minor axes of such an international spheroid are assumed as 6378.388×10^3 metres and 6356.91194×10^3 metres respectively.

Due to the rotation of the earth, it has taken the shape of an oblate spheroid as shown in Fig. 1.2.

The flattening of spheroid, $\quad f = \dfrac{a-b}{a} = \dfrac{6378.388 \times 10^3 - 6356.91194 \times 10^3}{6378.388 \times 10^3}$

$$= 0.0033667$$

or $\qquad \dfrac{1}{f} = 297 \text{ (approximately)}$

A nautical mile is defined as 'the distance measured on the arc of great circle that subtends an angle of 1 minute at the centre of the earth'.

$$\therefore \quad \text{One nautical mile} = \frac{\text{Circumference of great circle arc}}{360° \times 60}$$

$$= \frac{2\pi R}{360° \times 60} \text{; if } R = 6371 \text{ km for the earth}$$

$$= \frac{2 \times 3.142 \times 6371}{360° \times 60}$$

$$= 1.86 \text{ km}$$

(vi) Definition of Geodetic Surveying :

'Geodetic Surveying' is defined as 'that branch of surveying which accounts for the curvature of the earth, as the area to be covered is large and the distances to be measured are also very long'.

(vii) Object of Geodetic Surveying :

The main object of *'Geodetic Surveying'* is to establish *'Horizontal Controls'* and that of *'Geodetic levelling'* is to fix *'Vertical Controls'* throughout the area with the highest degree of precision. Thus, Geodetic Surveying and levelling aims at establishing a three-dimensional control (i.e. latitude, longitude and elevation above M.S.L.) network over the entire given area. As the accuracy desired in this type of work is very high, the surveying instruments to be used should be very precise and the surveying methods should also be very accurate. Geodetic surveying is usually carried by the Government agency e.g. in India, it is carried by the Survey of India Department, a Central Government agency with their head quarters at Dehrodon (U.P.)

(viii) Relative and Absolute Position of a Point :

In order to represent a true picture of the surveyed portion of the earth, it is necessary to know the absolute position of at least one of the points in terms of *'latitude'* and *'longitude'*. The conventional method of locating the position of a given point is to determine its *'relative position'* i.e. the position of the point is determined relative to the preceding known point. i.e. Assuming the position of the first point arbitrarily on the drawing paper, the position of the next point is determined from its known length and direction is measured from the first point. In such cases as the absolute position of none of the points is known, the surveyed portions cannot be shown on the surface of the earth. It is therefore, necessary to determine the absolute position of at least one point in the surveyed portion, in terms of latitude and longitude, so that the surveyed portion of the ground can be shown exactly on the surface of the earth.

1.2 METHODS OF ESTABLISHING HORIZONTAL CONTROLS

The horizontal controls in Geodetic surveying are established by the following methods :

(a)   Triangulation.

(b)   Precise theodolite traversing.

(c)   Trilateration.

(d)   Triangulateration (i.e. Triangulation + Trilateration).

(e)   Precise E.D.M. traversing.

(a)   Triangulation :

The conventional method of Geodetic surveying is *triangulation* and is based on the simple trigonometrical principle that "in any triangle if the length of one side and all the three angles are known, the lengths of the remaining sides can be computed by the application of sine rule". This method consists of selecting and establishing suitable triangulation stations that form well-conditioned triangles, in the entire area to be surveyed. Such stations when connected systematically form a chain of well-conditioned simple or double triangles or quadrilaterals, polygons etc.

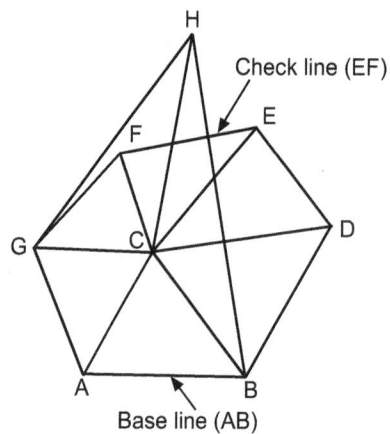

Fig. 1.3 : Triangulation survey

Thus in a triangulation survey, the length of one line AB of triangle ABC, [Fig. 1.3] is called as *Base line* and all the included angles are measured and then by the application of sine rule the lengths of the sides BC and CA are computed. These lines BC and CA then serve as base lines for the triangles BCD and ACG respectively. The included angles of these two triangles are then measured and by application of sine rule, the lengths CD and BD of triangle BCD and CG and GA of triangle ACG are computed. The procedure is then repeated to extend the triangle that covers the whole area. In order to have check over the accuracy, the length of one side of the last triangle CEF is also measured and compared with its computed length. Such a line (say EF) is known as *check line*. The apexes of triangles are termed as *'triangulation stations'*, the whole figure being known as *'triangulation system'* or '*triangulation figure*'. The main purpose of triangulation survey is to provide exact location of horizontal controls, the detailed survey of the area thereafter is carried out as usual either by plane tabling or theodolite traversing. The triangulation method was first suggested by Mr. Snell (Dutchman) in 1615.

The drawback of this system is that there is tendency of accumulation of errors of lengths and azimuths, as the length and azimuth of every line is based on the length and azimuth of the preceding line. By providing, '*subsidiary bases*' at suitable intervals, the accumulation of errors in lengths can be controlled and to minimise the errors in 'azimuth' of the stations, observations to celestial bodies (i.e. *astronomical observations*) for determination of azimuth are made at intervals. Such triangulation stations, at which astronomical observations are taken to check the accuracy of computed azimuth, are known as *Laplace stations*.

Triangulation is suitable in case of open, hilly country where long sights are possible. However, in case of very flat or densely wooded country, triangulation becomes difficult and very expensive.

Thus, the 'Geodetic triangulation' serves the following purposes :

(i)　It helps in determining the size and shape of the earth by carrying out observations for longitude, latitude and gravity.

(ii)　It provides accurately located system of primary horizontal controls on which less precise system of triangles i.e. '*Secondary controls*' can be established. These secondary controls in turn serve as a framework for further *cadastral, topographical, engineering* surveys to be carried out.

(iii)　It helps in fixing the centre line, shafts and terminal points for the long tunnels.

(iv)　It enables the fixing of centre line and abutments of very long bridges across wide rivers.

(v)　It also helps in providing horizontal ground controls required in aerial surveying.

(b)　Precise Theodolite Traversing :

In case of very flat or densely wooded country, where *triangulation* is not possible, *precise theodolite traversing* can be adopted. The drawback of this method is that the accumulation of error becomes much more as compared to triangulation. Moreover for large areas this method becomes inconvenient and time consuming.

(c)　Trilateration :

In recent years, with the introduction of *Electronic distance measuring instrument* (E.D.M.) the entire procedure of *conventional triangulation* is replaced by *trilateration*. A *Trilateration system* consists of a series of connected triangles, covering the entire area to be surveyed, in which the lengths of all the sides of triangles are measured with high degree of precision by an Electronic Distance Measuring Instrument. Occasionally directions or angles of certain survey lines are also observed to determine their azimuths. The entire field procedure of trilateration is similar to triangulation with the difference that there are no angular measurements but only linear measurements are to be carried with the help of EDM instruments. The accuracy obtained in linear measurements with an EDM instrument is much more as compared to triangulation system. Moreover, the time required for completing the survey work is also much less as compared to triangulation. The other advantages are that the manpower required for this survey is less, there is automatic recording of the field data and it can also be stored in data bank. However, the initial investment for the purchase of an EDM instrument is very high and there are no effective easy checks over the accuracy of the trilateration survey work.

(d) Triangulateration :

This method is a suitable combination of *triangulation* and *trilateration* systems that results in greater accuracy of the work. In this system, the lengths of all the sides and all angles of all triangles are measured with the help of modern *'Electronic Distance Meter'*. Thus, there are effective and easy checks available over the accuracy of the work. In short, triangulateration system combines the advantages of both triangulation and trilateration systems and is thus superior to triangulation or trilateration. However, there is high initial capital expenditure involved in the purchase of the most modern Electronic Distance Meter (called as *Total station*).

(e) Precise E.D.M. Traversing :

The drawbacks of precise theodolite traversing are overcome by using an Electronic Distance Measuring Instrument. This is the most accepted method of establishing horizontal controls in Geodetic surveying. Mistakes that are likely to occur in observations, measurements and computations by using a theodolite can be overcome by using an Electronic Distance Meter with a built-in vertical sensor (called as Total station).

The merits of this system over other systems are :

(i)   No necessity of thorough reconnaissance survey of the area to be surveyed.

(ii)   No problem of selection of suitable triangulation station and to ascertain their intervisibility etc.

(iii)   No necessity of selecting any 'satellite station' that may be required in triangulation survey.

(iv)   No necessity of selecting a suitable site for the measurement of base line required in triangulation survey.

(v)   Selection of suitable traverse stations and establishing traverse network is much easier as compared to triangulation system.

As the measurement of distances by an Electronic Distance Meter is going to be very costly, the conventional method of 'Geodetic surveying' by triangulation will be the most effective method of establishing horizontal controls and is thus discussed in details hereinafter.

1.3 TRIANGULATION FIGURES (OR SYSTEMS)

A *triangulation figure* is defined as 'a group or system of triangles arranged in such a way that any figure has only one side common to each of the preceding and following figures'. The triangulation system usually consists of any one or combination of the following :

(a) Chain of single triangles
(b) Chain of double triangles
(c) (Braced) Quadrilaterals
(d) Centered figures or triangulation system with central stations.

(a) Chain of Single Triangles (Fig. 1.4) :

This system is used while setting out control points for a narrow width of long length e.g. route surveys. The system is rapid and thus economical. However, as the number of geometrical conditions to be satisfied are relatively small, it is not preferred for primary triangulation work. As it is not possible to get the solution of triangles by two independent routes, it lacks in effective checks over the accuracy of the work. To reduce the excessive accumulation of errors (in this system), it is necessary to have more check lines and at times astronomical observations are to be taken to have a check over the accuracy of computed azimuths.

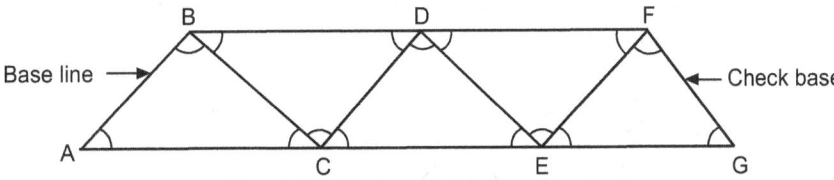

Fig. 1.4 : Chain of single triangles

(b) Chain of Double Triangles (Fig. 1.5) :

If the area to be covered by Geodetic surveying spreads in North-South and East-West directions, then it is not possible to cover the area by a chain of single triangles. In such cases a chain of double triangles is recommended.

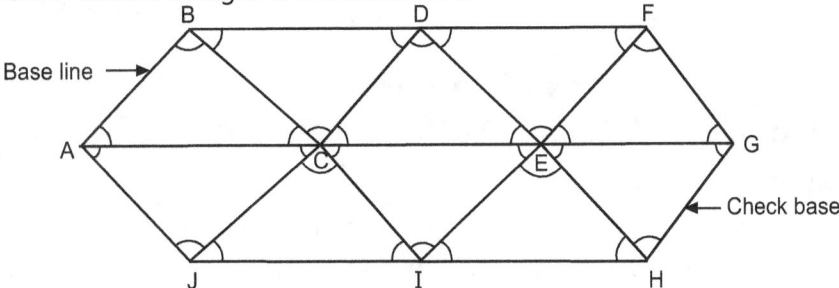

Fig. 1.5 : Chain of double triangles

(c) Braced Quadrilaterals (Fig. 1.6) :

A four sided figure i.e. quadrilateral with four corner stations and observation made along both the diagonals, without any central station, is known as 'braced quadrilateral'. In this system the number of conditions to be satisfied are much more as compared to the first two systems and hence it forms the best figure or system. This system is said to be most accurate as the computed lengths of the sides can be worked out with different combinations of sides and angles. This system is generally preferred for long, narrow areas.

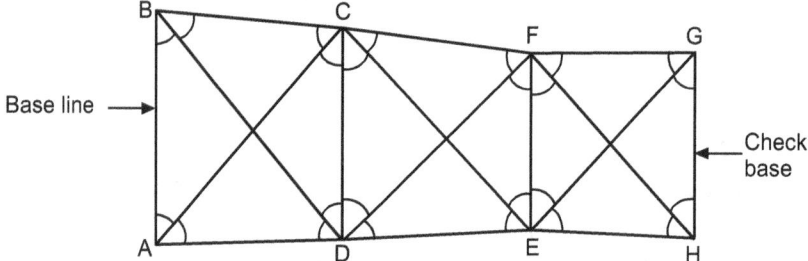

Fig. 1.6 : Braced quadrilaterals (without central station)

(d) Centered Figures (or Triangulation system with central stations) (Fig. 1.7) :

A triangulation system consisting of triangles, quadrilaterals, pentagons, hexagons etc. with central station is called centered figures. The method, which is generally used to cover large areas in a flat country, gives satisfactory results. Moreover, this system provides desired checks on computation works. However, the progress of the survey work is affected due to more number of settings of the instrument. Polygon system is generally adopted for long, wide areas.

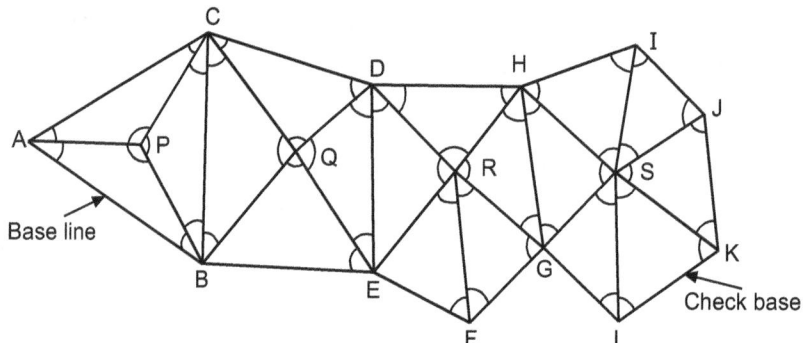

Fig. 1.7 : Centered figures

1.4 CRITERIA FOR THE SELECTION OF BEST TRIANGULATION FIGURE OR SYSTEM

The factors to be considered while selecting a particular figure are :

(a) It should be possible to carry out the computation work for the selected figure through two independent routes.

(b) Both the routes, if not at least one of the selected figure, should be well-conditioned.

(c) The triangles (in a chain of single or double triangles) should as far as possible be equilateral.

(d) The figures with minimum number of stations with maximum number of conditions should be preferred.

(e) The arrangement of the figures should be such that the progress of the work is satisfactory and the desired accuracy in computation work is obtained.

(f) The lengths of the sides of the selected figure should not be too small or too long.

(g) A complicated figure resulting in more than twelve conditions should be avoided (as the computation work becomes difficult).

1.5 TRIANGULATION FRAME WORK OF AN EXTENSIVE LARGE AREA

The triangulation frame work of a large country can be carried out by any one of the following methods :

(a) Grid iron system of triangulation or

(b) Central or centered system.

(a) Grid Iron System of Triangulation (Fig. 1.8) :

Fig. 1.8 : Grid iron system (of frame work)

While carrying out triangulation survey of large extensive area, it is usual practice to lay the primary triangulation in two series of chain of triangles, approximately at right angles to each other, one series being laid approximately along the meridian i.e. North-South and other series along East-West. The area enclosed between two series being further filled by second and third order triangulation systems. The countries adopting this system are France, India, Spain and Austria.

(b) Central or Centered System (Fig. 1.9) :

This system adopted in Great Britain (U.K.), consists of a network of primary triangulation extending outwards in all directions from the initial base line, passing through the centre of the country.

This system adopted in Great Britain (U.K.), consists of a net.

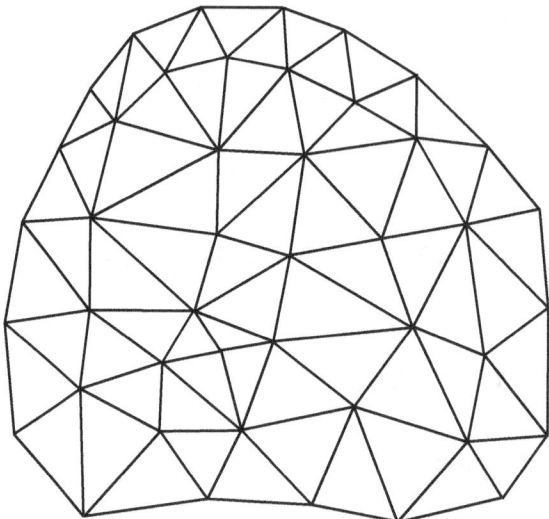

Fig. 1.9 : Central or centered system (of frame work)

1.5.1 Strength of Figure

In addition to the method and precision used in making observations, the accuracy of triangulation system also depends upon shape of the triangulation figures. The accuracy of shape is measured in terms of the strength of figure. To achieve desired degree of precision while establishing triangulation system, the strength of figure plays an important role.

Evaluating the strength of figure (as per US Coast and Geoditic Survey) :

If the computations are carried from known side through a single chain of triangles, the expression for square of probable error (L^2) which would be in the sixth place of logarithm of any side is

$$L^2 = \frac{4}{3} \cdot d^2 \cdot R$$

where   d = Probable error of an observed direction is sec.

R = Strength of figure = $\left(\dfrac{D-C}{D}\right) \cdot \Sigma\, (\delta_A^2 + \delta_A \cdot \delta_B + \delta_B^2)$

where   D = Number of directions observed (forward and backward) excluding those along known side

C = Number of conditions to be satisfied in each figure

= (n' − s' + 1) + (n − 2s + 3)

where   n' = Number of lines observed in both directions (including known side) s' = Number of stations occupied

n = Total number of lines (including known side)

s = Total number of stations

δ_A, δ_B = Difference per sec. in sixth place of log of the sine of the distance angles A and B respectively.

Distance angles are the two angles opposite to the known and required sides. The third angle is called as *azimuth angle*.

For different values of angles A and B, the values of $(\delta_A^2 + \delta_A \cdot \delta_B + \delta_B^2)$ for a triangle can be referred from standard table available. When figures of a triangulation net are other than single angles, more than one route can be used to calculate the required side. In that case symbol R_1 is used to indicate the strength of figure through the best route and R_2 for the second best route.

1.6 BEST SHAPED WELL-CONDITIONED TRIANGLES

Any triangulation system or figure essentially consists of triangles (and hence the name *triangulation*). The triangles should be so arranged that any error in the measurement of horizontal angles will have least effect on the lengths of its computed sides. Such triangles are then called as 'Well-conditioned triangles' in which no angle will be less than 30° and no angle will be more than 120°. In any triangle, the length of one side will always be known from computation of adjacent triangle. In order that, the error in computed lengths of the other two sides should have least effect on the accuracy, they should as far as possible be equal in length i.e. the triangles in the network should be isosceles having base angles as 56° 14' approximately.

Proof : Refer to the triangle ABC [Fig. 1.10]. Let a, b, c be the three sides, c (i.e. AB) being known and a and b (approximately of equal length) to be computed from the measured angles A, B, C.

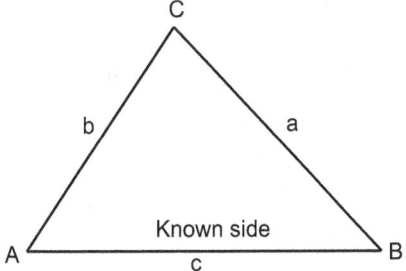

Fig. 1.10 : Best shaped well-conditioned triangle

As the lengths a and b are equal,

$\therefore$ $\angle A = \angle B$ ($\because$ Isoceles triangle)

Applying sine rule,

$$\frac{a}{\sin A} = \frac{c}{\sin C}$$

$\therefore$
$$a = \left(\frac{\sin A}{\sin C}\right) \cdot c \quad\quad ... (1.1)$$

Now, if $\quad\quad \delta a_1$ = Error in the computed side a, due to δA error in the measurement of angle A,

then differentiating the above equation (1.1) partially w.r.t. A, we get

$$\delta a_1 = \frac{c}{\sin C} (\cos A. \, \delta A) \quad\quad ... (1.2)$$

Now, dividing equation (1.2) by equation (1.1), we get

$$\frac{\delta a_1}{a} = \frac{\cos A}{\sin A} \cdot \delta A = \cot A \cdot \delta A \qu\quad ... (1.3)$$

Now, if $\quad\quad \delta a_2$ = Error in the computed side a, due to δC error in the measurement of angle C,

then differentiating the above equation (1.1) partially w.r.t. C, we get

$$\delta a_2 = -\frac{\cos C \sin A}{\sin^2 C} \times c \cdot \delta C \quad\quad ... (1.4)$$

$\therefore$ Dividing equation (1.4) by equation (1.1),

$$\frac{\delta a_2}{a} = -\frac{\cos C}{\sin C} \cdot \delta C = -\cot C \cdot \delta C$$

Assuming, δA equal to $\delta C = \pm \alpha$ i.e. probable errors in the measurement of angles, then

$$\begin{bmatrix} \text{Probable fraction error} \\ \text{in the length of side a} \end{bmatrix} = \frac{\delta a}{a}$$

$$= \pm \alpha \sqrt{\cot^2 A + \cot^2 C}$$

But $\quad\quad A + B + C = 180 \quad\quad (\because \text{ Sum of measurement of D is } 180°)$

$\therefore \quad\quad C = 180 - (A + B)$

$$= 180 - 2A \quad\quad \left(\because A = B\right)$$

$\therefore \quad\quad \frac{\delta a}{a} = \pm \alpha \sqrt{\cot^2 A + \cot^2 2A}$

For minimum value of $\frac{\delta a}{a}$, $\cot^2 A + \cot^2 2A$ should be minimum.

$\therefore$　Differentiating $(\cot^2 A + \cot^2 2A)$ w.r.t. A and equating to zero, we get

$$4\cos^2 A + 2\cos^2 A - 1 = 0$$

i.e.　　　　　　　　　　　　$A = 56° 14'$ approximately.

However, in practice, the angles are taken equal to $60°$. Thus, the best shape of the well conditioned triangle is an equilateral one. It may be noted that, for the change in given angles, the changes in sines of small angles are much more as compared to changes in sines of large angles.

1.7 CLASSIFICATION OF VARIOUS TRIANGULATION SYSTEMS

The classification is based on the degree of accuracy with which the length and azimuth (true bearing) of the lines of the triangulation are worked out. It is classified as

(a)　Primary or first order triangulation;

(b)　Secondary or second order triangulation; and

(c)　Tertiary or third order triangulation.

(a)　Primary or First Order Triangulation :

Primary or the first order triangulation is the highest grade of triangulation and is adopted for determining the shape and figure of the earth surface and to establish precise horizontal controls to which second order triangulation may be referred. In this, the area covered is very large i.e. practically the whole country is covered and as no external checks, except by astronomical observations are possible, all necessary precautions are to be taken in their observations (linear and angular) and subsequent reductions. Most modern refined instruments are to be used for this type of work. The standard specifications of primary triangulation are given in the tabular form in the Article 1.8.

(b)　Secondary or Second Order Triangulation :

The secondary or second order triangulation consists of establishing number of control points at closer intervals inside the framework of primary triangulation. The triangles formed (in secondary triangulation) are smaller in size as compared to primary triangulation. The instruments and methods adopted are inferior to primary work. The standard specifications for this type of work are given below in a tabular form.

(c)　Tertiary or Third Order Triangulation :

The tertiary or third order triangulation consists of establishing number of control points inside the framework of secondary triangulations and such controls serve as basis for further detailed and topographical surveys. The standard specifications for tertiary triangulation are shown in the tabular form in Article 1.8.

1.8   THE STANDARD SPECIFICATIONS FOR TRIANGULATION SYSTEMS IN TABULAR FORM

Table 1.1

Description of specification	Primary or 1st order	Secondary or 2nd order	Tertiary or 3rd order
1. Average length of base line	5 to 25 km	2 to 5 km	1.5 to 3 km
2. Length of sides	20 to 160 km	10 to 60 km	1.5 to 10 km
3. Average triangle of closure	Upto 1 second	3 seconds	6 seconds
4. Maximum triangle of closure	Upto 3 seconds	8 seconds	12 seconds
5. Actual error in base line	1 in 5,00,000	1 in 2,00,000	1 in 80,000
6. Probable error in base line	1 in 10,00,000	1 in 5,00,000	1 in 2,50,000
7. Permissible discrepancy between two measures	8 mm/km	15 mm/km	25 mm/km
8. Probable errors in computed distance	1 in 55,000 to 1 in 25,00,000	1 in 20,000 to 1 in 50,000	1 in 5,000 to 1 in 20,000
9. Probable errors in azimuth obtained astronomically	0.5 seconds	2.5 seconds	5 seconds

Note :   The methods and instruments used for primary, secondary and tertiary triangulation do not differ much. However, more observations are required to be taken for establishing primary controls as compared to establishing secondary controls and similarly for establishing secondary controls as compared to establishing tertiary controls.

1.9 GENERAL PROCEDURE OF TRIANGULATION SURVEY

1.9.1 Introduction

The first step in carrying out triangulation survey is to divide the entire given area into suitable triangulation figures. Next step is to measure the length and azimuth (i.e. *true bearing*) of one side of the (first) triangle and also to fix the positions of the end points of this line in terms of latitude and longitude. Horizontal angles at all stations are then measured by one second theodolite and after making station and figure adjustments, the lengths and azimuths of the remaining sides are computed. To have a check over the accuracy, the length of the last line of the triangulation figure is also measured which should be same as its computed length. The above procedure (of triangulation survey) is thus divided into the following steps :

(A)   Reconnaissance survey of the entire area.

(B)   Errection or construction of signals and towers.

(C) Measurement of base line.

(D) Measurement of horizontal angles.

(E) Astronomical observations for the determination of azimuth, latitude and longitude, at intervals.

(F) Computations - angles adjustments, length computations, base reduction.

1.9.2 Reconnaissance Survey

Procedure :

Careful study of the existing toposheets and the preliminary physical inspection of the entire area to be surveyed is to be carried out to ascertain the best possible locations for triangulation stations and the best possible site for the base line. This requires great skill, experience and judgement on the part of the chief surveyor. As the economy and accuracy of the whole work depends upon the reconnaissance, it should include the following :

(a) Thorough examination of country to be surveyed

(b) Selection of the best possible site for the base line.

(c) Selection of most suitable positions for triangulation stations

(d) Determination of intervisibility and the heights of stations.

(e) Collection of information as regards accessibility, communication, food, water and shelter problems.

Instruments Required :

The instruments commonly used for reconnaissance survey are :

(a) A sextant or theodolite for measurements of angles.

(b) Prismatic compass for direction observations.

(c) Aneroid barometer to ascertain elevations.

(d) Steel tape for measurement of distances.

(e) Ladders, ropes etc. for climbing tall trees.

(f) Drawing materials, drawing board etc.

Criteria for Selection of Suitable Triangulation Stations :

The factors to be considered while selecting triangulation stations are :

(a) The selected triangulation stations should be intervisible. To satisfy this requirement, the stations are generally selected on highest portion of ground i.e. on the tops of hills in the area.

(b) The selected triangulation stations should form well-conditioned triangles.

(c) The length of sight between the selected triangulation stations should not be too large to create the problems of inaccurate bisection of signals nor too small to create the errors of eccentricity and bisection.

  (d) The selected stations should be freely accessible.

  (e) Selection of stations in wooded country should not result in excessive cost of clearing, cutting of trees etc.

  (f) The selected stations as far as possible be in commanding position so that it may be possible to select them as controls - for subsidiary triangulation surveys.

Classification of Triangulation Stations :

  The triangulation stations may further be classified as *'main', 'subsidiary'* and *'satellite stations'*.

  (a) The *'main triangulation'* stations serve the purpose of horizontal controls and in continuing the triangulation network.

  (b) The *'subsidiary triangulation'* stations are used for providing additional rays to the intersected points on the ground.

  (c) *Satellite stations* are the stations selected very near to the true stations when the true stations cannot be occupied and also to solve the problems of intervisibility.

Intervisibility and Height of Stations :

  In order that the selected triangulation stations should be intervisible, there should not be any intervening obstruction to the line of sight. The intervisibility of selected stations can be ascertained by direct observation through field glasses or binoculars either from the ground level or tree-tops or ladders. However, if the selected triangulation stations are at long distance and the difference in elevations between them is less, certain computations are to be made considering the curvature of the earth, the height of the intervening obstructions etc. to ascertain the intervisibility of two triangulation stations. Accordingly, either the height of instrument or the height of signal or both will have to be raised to solve the problem of intervisibility.

  Factors affecting height of instrument and signal : The factors on which the height of the instrument and signal depends are as follows :

  (a) The distances between the selected triangulation stations.

  (b) The relative elevations of selected triangulation stations and

  (c) The profile of the intervening ground.

  (a) The distance between the selected triangulation stations : If there is no intervening obstruction to the line of sight, the distance of the visible horizon from a station of known elevation (above datum) is calculated by using the formula,

$$h = (1 - 2m)\frac{D^2}{2R}$$

where   h = Height of station above datum;

      D = Distance from the station to the visible horizon;

      R = Mean radius of the earth (6371 km) and

      m = Coefficient of refraction, the value being taken as 0.07 for sights over land and 0.08 for sights over water bodies i.e. sea.

Taking m = 0.07 and substituting D and R in their proper units, the above formula simplifies to

$$h = 0.0673 \, D^2$$

where h is in metres, and D is in kilometres.

(b) Relative elevations of triangulation stations : The formula $h = 0.0673 \, D^2$ can also be used to determine the required elevation of a station at a distance, so that it can be visible from other station whose elevation is known.

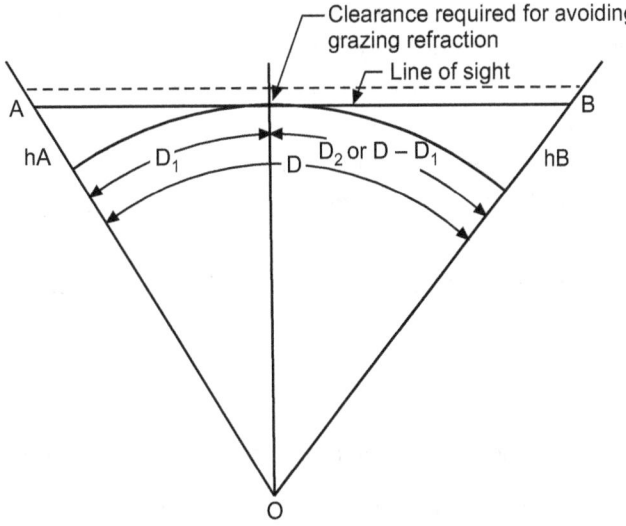

Fig. 1.11

Referring Fig. 1.11, Let

D = Known distance between two stations A and B = $D_1 + D_2$

D_1 = Distance from the ground point A to the point of tangency

D_2 = Distance from the ground point B to the point of tangency

h_1 = Known elevation of ground point A.

h_2 = Required elevation above datum at B.

Then using the above equation, $h_1 = 0.0673 \, D_1^2$, h_1 being known,

$$\text{the distance, } D_1 = \sqrt{\frac{h_1}{0.0673}} = 3.853 \sqrt{h_1}.$$

After calculating D_1, $D_2 = D - D_1$.

Then again using the same formula,

Required elevation at B = $h_2 = 0.0673 \, D_2^2$.

The elevation of the ground at B (which is already known) can be compared with the required elevation at B to ascertain whether the station B is to be elevated or not, and accordingly the height of scaffold at B is worked out.

In practice, however, to avoid the effect of grazing refraction (i.e. the line of sight should not graze the surface at the point of tangency) the line of sight should preferably be 2 to 3 m above the ground surface.

(c) The profile of the intervening ground : If there are any intervening peaks in between the triangulation stations, it is necessary to determine their positions and elevations. The elevations of the (proposed) line of sight at such peaks are then determined and are compared with the elevations of existing peaks to ascertain whether the line of sight clears or fails to clear the intervening obstructions.

The procedure of solving such field problems is illustrated in the following examples. There are two methods of solving the problem. The first method is based upon the theory explained above in (b) and (c). The second method as suggested by Capt. G.T. McCaw is as follows :

(d) Captain G. T. McCaw's solution : The method suggested by Capt. G. T. McCaw is as follows :

Referring to the Fig. 1.12, let

(i) $2s$ = Distance between two triangulation stations A and B.

(ii) $s + x$ = Distance of the obstruction (peak) at C measured from A.

(iii) $s - x$ = Distance of the obstruction (peak) at C measured from B.

(iv) h_1 = Elevation of triangulation station A above datum.

(v) h_2 = Elevation of triangulation station B above datum.

(vi) h = Elevation of the line of sight at obstruction (peak) at C.

(vii) ξ = Zenith distance of B from triangulation station A.

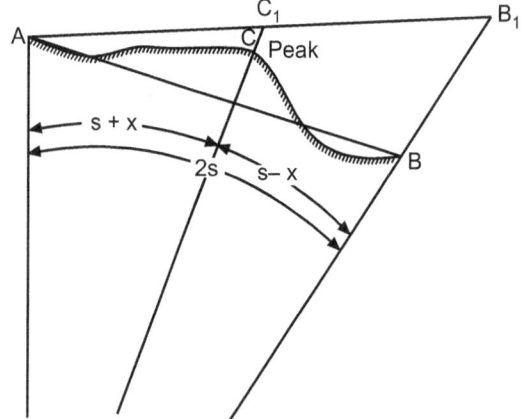

Fig. 1.12 : Capt. G.T. McCaw's solution

The expression for the elevation of line of sight at the obstruction (peak) at C as given by Capt. G. T. McCaw's is :

$$h = \frac{1}{2}(h_2 + h_1) + \frac{1}{2}(h_2 - h_1)\frac{x}{s} - (s^2 - x^2)\,cosec^2\,\xi\left(\frac{1 - 2m}{2R}\right)$$

Note :

(i) The zenith distance of B from A being approximately equal to $90°$, the value of $cosec^2\,\xi$ is taken as unity, else it can be computed by the expression

$$cosec^2\,\xi = \left[\frac{(h_2 - h_1)^2}{4s^2} + 1\right]$$

(ii) The value of $\left(\dfrac{1 - 2m}{2R}\right) = 0.0673$,

where m = coefficient of refraction and R = mean radius of earth (i.e. 6371 km).

where x, s and R are taken in km and h_1 and h_2 are in m.

Triangulation Station Marks :

The triangulation stations are permanently marked with bronze or copper plates on the ground. The name of the station and the year in which it is set is also written on the plates. These stations are generally marked on permanent objects such as solid firm rock or large embedded stones or concrete pillars specially prepared for these purposes. In order to identify these triangulation marks easily, either a vertical pole or a tall signal tower is erected centrally. Two or three prominent reference marks are established near the (true) triangulation station. Azimuth mark is also to be established at short distance away from the triangulation station when a tall signal tower is erected at the triangulation station.

1.9.3 Towers, Signal and Their Classification

Signals :

A signal is any object erected to define the exact position of the triangulation station to be observed. The qualities of good signals are as follows :

(a) It should be conspicuous i.e. clearly visible from a long distance against any background.

(b) It should be capable of correctly centered over the given triangulation station.

(c) It should be possible to bisect the centre of the signal accurately.

(d) (As far as possible) it should be free from phase or at the most it should exhibit very little phase.

Types of Signals :

The various types of signals commonly used are classified as :

(a) Non-luminous or Day light (opaque) signals.

(b) Luminous or sun signals.

(c) Night signals.

(a) Non-luminous or Day light signals : They are used during day time and are made of timber poles, or targets etc. They are generally used for short sights upto a distance of 30 km. Round pole signals (Fig. 1.13), usually painted alternate black and white, are supported on a tripod vertically above the station mark. These are suitable for sights upto 6 km.

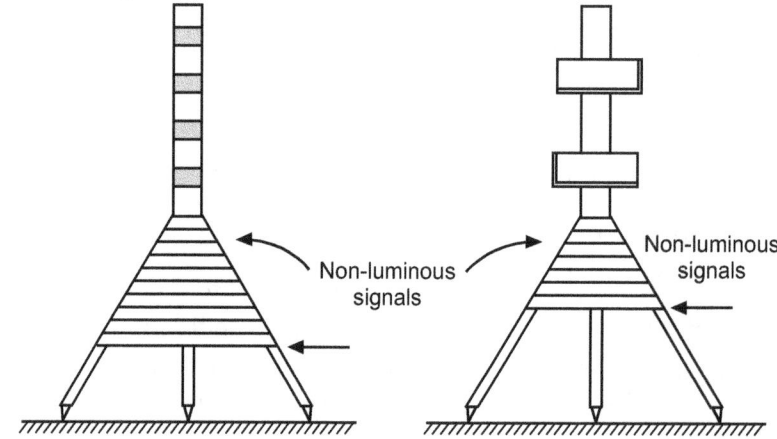

Fig. 1.13 : Timber pole signal   **Fig. 1.14 : Target type signal**

A target signal (Fig. 1.14), made up of pole, carries two square or rectangular targets fixed at right angles to each other. These signals are made of clothes stretched over wooden frames. Other types of signals used are Pole and Bush type (Fig. 1.15) and Becon type (Fig. 1.16).

Fig. 1.15 : Pole and bush signal   **Fig. 1.16 : Becon signal**

(b) Luminous or sun signals : These are generally used for sights exceeding 30 km and make use of sun's rays. These signals reflect the sun's rays towards the observer's station and are called as *Heliotropes* and *Heliographs*.

Heliotropes and Heliographs : It consists of circular plane mirror that reflects the sun's rays and is provided with a line of sight that transmits the reflected light towards the observer's station. The mirrors are capable of rotating in horizontal and vertical plane through $360°$. At first the heliotrope is accurately centered over the given triangulation station and the line of sight is adjusted by the assistant (to the surveyor) towards the distant observer's station. From the observer's station flashes are then sent to enable the assistant to establish the exact direction of sight. As the sun is a moving object (actually it is not the sun, but the earth that moves), it is necessary to adjust the mirror of the heliotrope towards the sun. The use of heliotrope is recommended when the signal station is situated in plains and the observation station is on a hilly ground. The modern trend is to use such luminous signals especially when the non-luminous signals cannot be seen clearly due to fog and haze.

(c) Night signals : These are mainly used while observing the angles of triangulation system during night time. They may be :

1. Oil lamps with parabolic reflectors or Capital collimators for sights less than 80 km and

2. G. T. McCaw's Acetylene gas lamps for sights even upto 80 km.

1.9.4 Phases of Signals (in Non-luminous Signals)

It may be defined as the error introduced in bisecting the centre of the signal (due to its apparent displacement) which is partly in shadow and partly in light. If at the time of observation, the sky is clear and the sun's rays are at right angles to the observer's direction, the error is maximum. The magnitude of this error can very well be determined in case of cylindrical signals according to :

(a) When an observation is made on the bright portion of cylindrical signal and

(b) When an observation is made on the bright line of the signal.

(a) When observation is made on the bright portion of signal : Refer to Fig. 1.17 (i).

Let O be the position of observer,

      A be centre of the cylindrical signal in plan,

      B be the mid-point of the curved bright portion CD,

α   be the phase correction,

α_1 and α_2 be angles which the extremities of the visible portion i.e. C and D make with the line OA,

θ   be the angle made by the sun's direction with OA,

D   be the distance of the signal from the observer's station i.e. OA, and

r   be radius of the cylindrical signal.

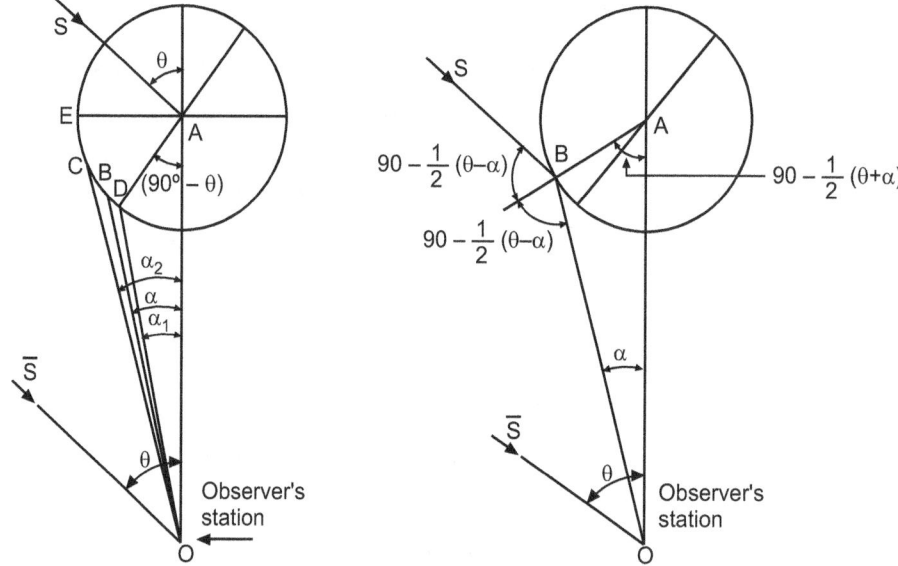

(i) When centre of bright portion of signal is bisected

(ii) When observation is made on the bright line

Fig. 1.17 : Phase of signal

Obviously,

$$\alpha \;=\; \text{Phase correction} \;=\; \alpha_1 + \frac{1}{2}(\alpha_2 - \alpha_1)$$

$$=\; \alpha_1 + \frac{1}{2}\,\alpha_2 - \frac{1}{2}\,\alpha_1 \;=\; \frac{1}{2}(\alpha_1 + \alpha_2)$$

For triangle OAE,

$$\tan \alpha_2 \;=\; \frac{AE}{OA} \;=\; \frac{r}{D} \;\text{ or } \alpha_2 \approx \frac{r}{D} \text{ radians (for small angles)}$$

and

$$\alpha_1 \;=\; \frac{r \sin (90 - \theta)}{D} \;=\; \frac{r \cos \theta}{D} \text{ (radians)}$$

Thus putting the values of α_1 and α_2 in the equation for phase correction, we get

$$\alpha = \frac{1}{2}\left[\frac{r \cos\theta}{D} + \frac{r}{D}\right]$$

$$= \frac{1}{2}\left[\frac{r}{D}(1 + \cos\theta)\right]$$

$$= \frac{\left[r \cos^2\frac{\theta}{2}\right]}{D} \text{ (radians)} = \frac{r \cos^2\frac{\theta}{2}}{D \sin 1''} \text{ (in seconds)}$$

Putting the value of $\sin 1'' = \dfrac{1}{206265}$

∴   Phase correction, $\alpha = \left[\dfrac{(206265)\, r \cos^2\frac{\theta}{2}}{D}\right]$ (in seconds)

In the figure 1.17, the sign of phase correction is negative to the observed horizontal angle.

(b) When observation is made on the bright line : [Fig. 1.17 (ii)]

In the figure, the observation is made against the bright line formed by the reflected ray SBO. Thus, OB becomes the line of sight along which observation is taken.

Then phase correction $= \angle\ BAO = \alpha$

Now SB and SO are parallel

∴ $\angle\ SBO = 180° - (\theta - \alpha)$

∴ $\angle\ ABO = 180° - \dfrac{1}{2}\ \angle\ SBO$

$$= 180° - \frac{1}{2}\left[180 - (\theta - \alpha)\right]$$

$$= 90° + \frac{1}{2}(\theta - \alpha)$$

∴ $\angle\ BAO = 180° - (\alpha + \angle\ ABO)$

$$= 180° - \left[\alpha + 90 + \frac{1}{2}(\theta - \alpha)\right]$$

$$= 90 - \frac{1}{2}(\theta + \alpha)$$

$$= 90 - \frac{1}{2}\theta$$

Neglecting α which is very small as compared to θ,

$$\therefore \quad \alpha = \frac{r \sin\left(90 - \frac{1}{2}\theta\right)}{D} \text{ radians}$$

$$\therefore \quad \alpha = \left[\frac{r \cos\frac{1}{2}(\theta)}{D}\right] \text{ (in radians)}$$

$$\therefore \quad \alpha = \frac{r \cos\frac{1}{2}\theta}{D \sin 1''} \text{ (in seconds)}$$

$$\text{writing } \sin 1'' = \frac{1}{206265}$$

$$\therefore \text{ Phase correction, } \quad \alpha = \left[\frac{(206265) \times r \cos\frac{1}{2}\theta}{D}\right] \text{ (in seconds)}$$

Points to be noted :

(i) The phase effect is commonly seen in case of cylindrical signals and square masts.

(ii) In case of target signals, the phase error is due to shadow of the upper target that falls upon the lower one. To eliminate the phase error, it is advisable to use a single target and set it normal to the line of sight at the time of observations.

(iii) The sign of phase correction depends upon the relative positions of the sun and the signal bisected.

1.9.5 Towers

When elevation of triangulation station is such that other stations can be bisected without elevating the instrument, then it is known as *ground station*. A tower is a structure constructed over a triangulation station to support the instrument and the observation party. The main purpose of tower is to elevate either the instrument station or signal station. The tower consists of two independent parts, the inner one supports the instrument whereas the outer one supports the observation party and the signal. The inner and outer structures are constructed independent of each other so that any movement of the outer structure will not be transferred to the inner structure. They are to be properly braced. Towers may be constructed of timber, masonry or steel. If the height of the tower to be constructed is small (say 40 to 50 m), masonry structures are preferred. Timber scaffolds are preferred when the height of tower exceeds 50 m.

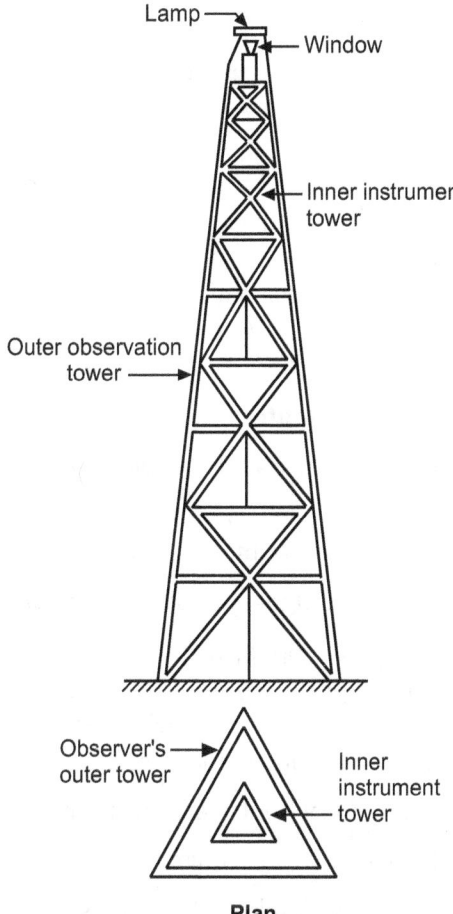

Fig. 1.18 : Bilby steel portable tower

Steel towers made up of light sections are easily portable. They can be very easily erected and dismantled quickly. Such steel towers are known as *Bilby Towers;* (Fig. 1.18). Their height varies from 35 to 50 m with a becon 3 m higher. The total weight of such towers is about 3 tonnes and can be erected with the help of five persons within 5 hours. They are named after Mr. J. S. Bilby, its original designer of United States coast and Geodetic survey.

1.9.6 Measurement of Horizontal Angles

Introduction :

The accuracy of the computed sides of triangulation depend upon how accurately the horizontal angles and base line is measured. The horizontal angles should be measured very precisely by using highly refined instruments. While measuring horizontal angles, the surrounding atmosphere should be clear and the refraction effect should be minimum. The suitable timings for measurement of horizontal angles is in the morning from 7 to 9.30 a.m. and in the afternoon from 4 p.m. onwards.

Instruments Required for Measurements :

Highly precise theodolites are used for this work. In the past, theodolites with large diameter horizontal circles upto 90 cm were used for geodetic triangulation work. Subsequently these theodolites were replaced by micrometer theodolites having diameter of horizontal circle varying from 15 cm to 30 cm. Recently, micrometer theodolites are also replaced by double reading type of theodolites with glass circle diameter varying from 8 to 10 cm. The least count of such theodolites for horizontal as well as vertical circles is 1 second direct and upto $(1/10)^{th}$ of a second by estimation. The well-known manufacturers of such 1 second theodolites are **Zeiss** (East and West Germany), Wild (Switzerland), Asia Pentax (Japan).

Special Features of One Second Theodolites :

The special features of the modern double reading type of theodolites with optical micrometer are :

(a)　They are small, compact and very light.

(b)　The circles are made of glass and the graduations are even and much finer.

(c)　The mean of the readings on opposite sides of the circles can be read directly through the additional eye-piece provided by the side of the main telescope and thus there is no necessity of observer moving around the instrument for taking circle readings. This results in saving in the observation time.

(d)　The instrument being closed from outside, is dust proof and water proof.

(e)　Adjustment of the micrometer is not required.

(f)　Instrument can be electrically illuminated and thus night observations can also be taken.

Types of Theodolites :

The theodolites used for triangulation survey of higher order are :

(a)　The repeating theodolites with double vertical axis, and

(b)　The direction theodolites with single vertical axis.

(a)　The repeating or double vertical axis type of theodolite : As the name suggests, it has double vertical axis i.e. two centres and two horizontal clamps and is provided with verniers with a least count varying from 20 seconds to 5 seconds. The most common 20 seconds vernier theodolite is an example of "repeating theodolite".

(b)　The direction theodolite with single vertical axis : It is provided with single vertical axis and the rotation of the instrument about this axis is controlled by single horizontal clamp and slow motion or tangent screw. To read the fractional parts of the smallest divisions of graduated horizontal or vertical circle, optical micrometers are provided. The instrument is generally used for the first or second order triangulation work.

Methods of Observation of Angles :

The methods commonly adopted for measurement of horizontal angles in triangulation survey are :

(a) Method of repetitions and

(b) Method of directions (or Reiteration method or method of series).

Generally, the first method is preferred in case of second or third order triangulation, whereas in case of first order the second method is used.

(a) Method of repetitions : Where the degree of accuracy desired in the measurement of horizontal angles is finer than that is possible with the least count of the vernier, the method of repetition is used. In this method, the horizontal angle is measured three times with face left and three times with face right keeping the vernier reading at the end of each measurement unchanged. Thus, the final reading in the first set becomes the initial reading in the next set and so on. Thus, there is mechanical addition of angles several times. The required mean horizontal angle with face left is then found out by dividing the final reading by the number of repetitions.

Similarly, mean horizontal angle with face right is also found out. The mean of these two means is the required horizontal angle.

The following errors are eliminated by the method of repetition :

1. By reading both the verniers every time the errors arising due to eccentricity of verniers and centre is eliminated.

2. By taking face left and face right observations every time, the errors due to line of collimation and trunnion axis, not being in adjustment, are eliminated.

3. By reading on different parts of the circle for each observation, the error due to improper graduations is eliminated.

4. By bisecting the same object number of times, the error due to bisection and improper centering may be eliminated.

(b) Method of direction (or reiteration method) : When round of angles at a particular station (as is the usual case in triangulation) are to be measured, the method of reiteration is adopted. The angles at the triangulation station are measured in succession in clockwise direction and finally the 'horizon is closed' to check the accuracy of measurements. It may be noted that the final reading after closing the horizon should be same as the initial reading that was recorded to start with. The same procedure is then repeated, this time rotating the telescope in counter-clockwise direction. Thus, the same angle is measured twice (once in clockwise and once in counter-clockwise). The face is then changed and the above procedure is repeated to obtain two more values of the same angles. i.e. In all four values of each angle are obtained which completes one set of observations. The above procedure is then repeated with different initial settings of the horizontal circle i.e. In the first set initially if it was at $0°$, it should now be 360/mn, where m is the number of verniers or micrometers (which are usually two) and n is the number of sets. The procedure is then repeated for the second set and so on. It is obvious that, larger the number of sets, greater will be degree of precision. Generally with one second direction theodolite eight sets are required for first order triangulation, the number of sets for second order and third order triangulation being six and four respectively. Mean of all such angles of different sets will be observed values of the respective angles.

The following errors are eliminated by the method of reiteration :

(a) Eccentricity errors of vertical axis and micrometers are eliminated by reading all the micrometers every time.

(b) By taking face left and face right observations every time, the errors due to line of collimation and trunnion axis not being in adjustment are eliminated.

(c) By reading on different parts of the circle, the errors due to improper graduations are eliminated.

(d) The errors of back lash, slip due to defective clamps and friction in moving parts are eliminated by changing the swing of the telescope i.e. by rotating the telescope in clockwise and anticlockwise direction.

(e) Errors of imperfect bisection and scale readings are eliminated by taking more number of observations.

(f) Mean of all such observed values results in minimising the personal observational errors.

1.10 MEASUREMENT OF BASE LINE

Introduction :

The most important operation in triangulation survey is the accurate measurement of selected base line. As the accuracy of computed sides of the triangulation system entirely depends upon the accuracy of measurements of base line and the horizontal angles, these measurements must to be carried out with the highest degree of precision. The length of the base line varies with the grade of triangulation system (which may be first, second or tertiary). For the entire triangulation system of our country (i.e. India) ten bases were used. The lengths of the nine bases chosen varied from 10.4 km to 14.1 km, whereas the length of the tenth base was about 2.73 km.

Selection of Base Line Site :

As the accuracy of the base line measurement mainly depends upon its site conditions, the following points need special attention while selecting the site for the base line.

(a) The selected site should be on a fairly level ground. If this is not possible, it should be on uniformly or gently sloping ground, with slope not exceeding 1 in 10 to 1 in 15.

(b) The selected site should be free from all obstructions throughout its length. Site clearance, if required, should be cheap.

(c) The ends (i.e. extremities) of the selected base line should be mutually intervisible at ground level.

(d) The nature of the ground should be smooth and firm. (i.e. unyielding).

(e) It should be possible to form well conditioned triangles on the selected base line.

(f) The selected site should permit further extension of base line (in both directions).

The length of the base line for fairly accurate results should approximately be equal to half the average lengths of sides of the main triangulation system.

Base Net :

Base net is defined as a system of triangles that connects base line to the main triangulation scheme.

Base Measuring Appliances :

These appliances can be divided into :

(a) Rigid bars (also called short-length methods), and

(b) Flexible appliances (also called long-length methods).

(a) Rigid bars :

In the past, when invar tape was not introduced, the rigid bars were used for measurement of base line. They may be

(i) Contact apparatus where the base bar ends are placed in successive contacts e.g. Embeck Duplex apparatus.

(ii) Optical apparatus in which the lengths engraved on the bars are observed by microscopes. e.g. Iced bar apparatus.

(iii) Compensating base bars are rigid bars, designed to maintain constant length under varying temperature conditions by combining two or more than two metals. e.g. Colby's apparatus.

(iv) Bimetallic and non-compensating base bars where two rigid measuring bars act as a bimetallic thermometer e.g. German system Bessel's apparatus or French system Borda's rod or U.S. Coast and Geodetic survey's Emibeck Duplex apparatus.

(v) Mono-metallic rigid base bars where the temperature is always kept constant at the melting point of ice. e.g. Russian system Struve's Bar or Woodward ice bar apparatus.

(vi) Colby's apparatus (Fig. 1.19) which was used in India for the measurement of ten bases in Great Trigonometric survey was designed by Maj. Gen. Colby in the 19th Century. The apparatus entirely eliminates the effect of variation of temperature on the measuring unit. It consists of two bars, each of 3 m (10 ft.) length, one made of steel and other made of brass, rivetted together at the centre of their length. The coefficients of linear expansion of the two metals are arranged in 3 : 5 proportion.

As shown in the Fig. 1.19, the horizontal distance AA' is 3 m (i.e. 10 ft). The distance AB (= A'B') to the junction with the steel is made equal to $3/5^{th}$ of the distance AC (= A'C') to the brass junction. Now, if due to variation in temperature, the distance BB' of steel bar B_1B_1' changes by amount say e, the distance CC' of the brass bar will change to C_1C' i.e. $3/5^{th}$ of e. Thus, there is no alteration of the positions of the points A and A'. The brass bar is coloured with special paint so as to make it equally susceptible to variation of temperature as that of steel bars.

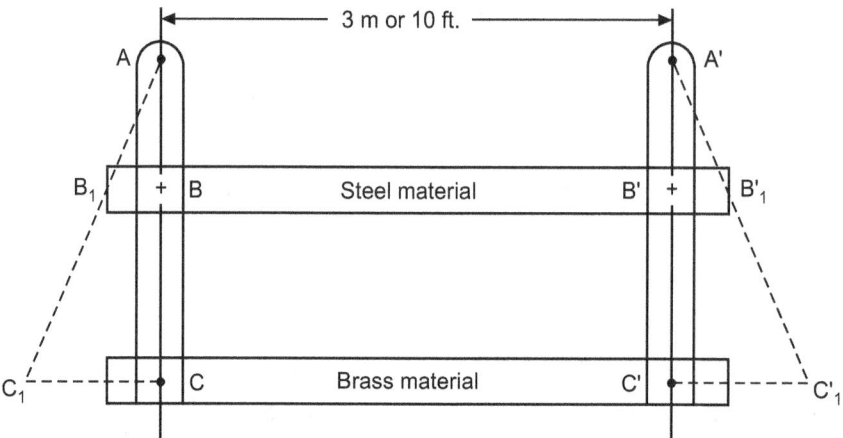

Fig. 1.19 : Colby's (rigid bar) apparatus

(b) Flexible apparatus (or Long length methods) :

Tapes or Wires :

The limitations of rigid bar apparatus which measure only the short distances are overcome by the use of flexible apparatus, consisting of tapes or wires (of steel or invar) of length 20 to 100 m.

Merits of Flexible Apparatus :

The merits of this type over rigid bar type are :

1. As the length of flexible apparatus is more than the rigid bar, and it can be hung clear of the ground on supports, thus the limitations of choice of suitable site conditions are overcome.

2. The cost of this type of apparatus is less than rigid bar.

3. The method is simpler and quicker and thus the cost of the survey is less.

4. Longer base lines and more check bases are possible with the flexible type of apparatus.

Types of Flexible Apparatus :

The flexible apparatus may be either a standardised (steel or invar) tape or a Hunter's short base.

(a) Standardised steel or invar tapes : Standardised steel or invar tapes vary in length from 20 to 100 m and are used for precise geodetic work.

Invar was first discovered by Dr. Guillaume (from France) in 1896. Invar tapes are made of steel and 36% nickel and have the lowest coefficient of expansion. To avoid measurement of distances by tape on uneven ground, they are supported on trestles and stretched between the supports by applying constant pull. In order to avoid variation in the length of the tape due to temperature changes, the exact temperature during measurements is recorded and temperature correction is applied accordingly. As the tape is standardised in the factory at certain temperature and pull and as these ideal conditions are never met in practice, necessary corrections for temperature and pull are to be applied to the measured base line.

(b) Hunters short base : (Fig. 1.20) It consists of a steel tape of total length 88 yards (i.e. 264 ft.) made up of four sections joined together, each section being one Gunter's chain length (i.e. 66 ft.). At the time of measurements, the whole tape (i.e. short base) is stretched and supported at the ends by the tripods. Intermediate two legged supports, at each Gunter's chain length are also provided. There are two targets provided at the end supports.

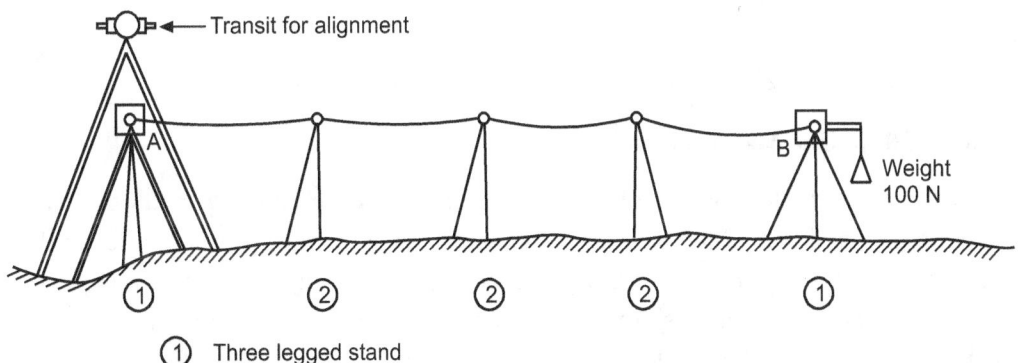

① Three legged stand
② Two legged stand

A and B are two targets (one in red and other in green colour)

Fig. 1.20 : Base measuring apparatus : Hunter's short base

Theodolites are set up at the starting and end points to check the alignment and are also used for measurement of angles in case the base line is to be extended. Measurements are generally carried out on cloudy day or during night time to minimise the effect of variation of temperature on the base measuring apparatus. All other necessary corrections are then applied to the measured base line. For easy identification, one end of the apparatus is painted red colour and the other end with green colour. To make tape horizontal during measurements, a weight of about 100 N is applied at one end.

Equipments for Base Line Measurements :

The following equipments are required for the base line measurements :

(a) Three standardised tapes out of which one is used for field measurements and other two to be used for standardising the field tape at specified intervals.

(b) One steel tape for spacing of tripods, stakes etc.

(c) Straining device, rear and forward marking stakes or tripods.

(d) Spring balance, weights, pulleys etc.

(e) Six thermometers, four to be used for measuring temperature and other two for standardisation.

Field work :

The field work of base line measurements is usually carried out as follows :

(a) Setting out party consists of two surveyors and number of assistants who will set the measuring tripods in proper alignment and at correct intervals, in advance of the measurements, and

(b) Measuring party comprising of two observers, a recorder, a levelling instrument man and staff-men who will carry out actual measurements.

Procedure of Base Line Measurements :

The first step is to clear all the obstructions along the base line and to divide it into convenient sections of 1 to 1.5 km in length and to accurately align it by using a transit. The next operation is the placing of measuring tripods, by the setting out party, in alignment and then the actual measurements are started. The actual base line measurement can then be carried out by any one of the following methods :

(a) Jaderin's method (Fig. 1.21) : The method suggested by Jaderin's consists of setting the measuring tripods at a distance of about one tape length, the tape being stretched inbetween the two straining tripods to which weights are attached. The pull applied is recorded by means of a spring balance. The zero of the tape is made to coincide with the mark on the rear tripod and the reading of the tape is taken against a similar mark on the forward tripod. Alignment of the tape and the levels at the top of tripod are taken to ascertain the difference in levels between the supports. The tape hanging in the catenary has a uniform tension throughout. In order to make the tape horizontal or to avoid excessive sag in the tape, the pull applied should be more than twenty times the weight of the steel (or invar) tape. The mean temperature of the tape during measurement is determined by thermometers. The process is continued till the other end of the base line is reached.

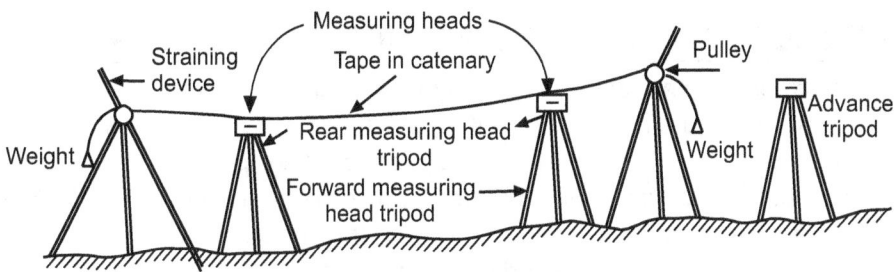

Fig. 1.21 : Jaderin's method

(b) Wheeler's base line apparatus method (Fig. 1.22) : In this method, the rear marking and forward marking stakes are fixed at a distance of about one tape length along the base line, their top being about 0.6 m above the ground level. The tape is supported in-between by supporting stakes at suitable intervals. For applying uniform tension (*i.e.* pull) weights are attached to the other end of the straining tripod. The supports are either set to have uniform slope between them or are arranged at the same level. The rear end of the tape coincides with mark on the rear tripod. After applying tension, reading of the tape is taken against the mark on the forward marking tripod. The temperature of the tape is observed at its beginning, middle and end, and the mean of these three temperatures is the average temperature during measurement. The procedure is continued till the other end of the base line is reached.

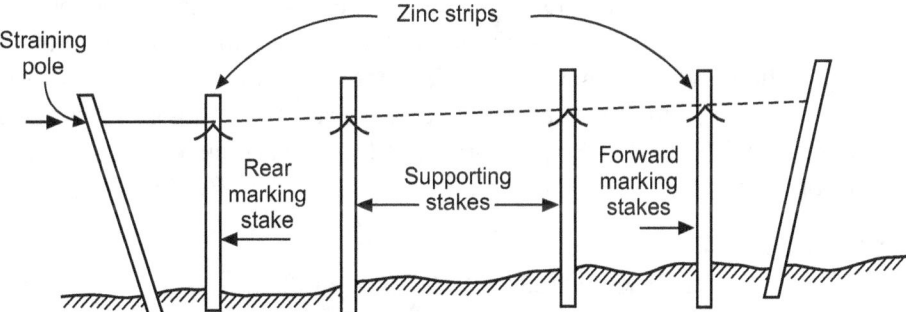

Fig. 1.22 : Base line measurement : Wheeler's base measuring apparatus

Tape Corrections (to be applied to measured length of the base line) :

As the base line measurements are not always made under ideal standardised conditions, it is necessary to apply following corrections :

1. Correction for standardisation i.e. for absolute length.
2. Correction for temperature variation.
3. Correction for tension or pull.
4. Correction for catenary or sag.
5. Correction for vertical alignment or slope.
6. Correction for horizontal alignment.
7. Correction for height above m.s.l or Reduction to m.s.l.

1.11 SATELLITE STATION AND REDUCTION TO CENTRE

One of the criteria for the selection of triangulation stations is that they should be visible from a long distance and should form well conditioned triangles. In order to fulfill these requirements, objects such as towers, church, spires, flag poles etc. are selected as triangulation stations. However, angle observed at such station cannot be occupied later as an instrument stations. In such a case, a subsidiary station called as a *'satellite station'* or *'eccentric'* or *'false station'* is established near the principal or true station (that could not be occupied). All the angles are then measured from the satellite station to other triangulation stations with the same precision as would have been taken from the true station. The angles measured from the satellite station are then reduced to the true station i.e. reduced to what they would have been had the true station occupied. This operation is commonly termed as *Reduction to centre*. The distance of the satellite station from the true station, called *Eccentric distance*, may be computed either by direct measurements, by tacheometry or by triangulation. Referring to Fig. 1.23 (a), let A, B and C be the triangulation stations, out of which station B being a tower or church spire, could not be occupied. S is the satellite station selected near to the true station B, the distance BS being d. Angles CAB and ACB have been already observed from triangulation station A and C, but angle ABC could not be observed as it was not possible to occupy station B. The simplest way of solving the triangle ABC will be from the two known angles CAB and ACB. The third angle will obviously be equal to 180 - sum of the two known angles. But this will be the value obtained by computations and not from observations. In order to strengthen the fix, it is desirable to get the value of the third angle (i.e. ABC) which depends upon the observation. To get such value, the theodolite is set up at the satellite station S, selected very near to the true station B and the angles ASC (θ) and CSB (γ) are observed and the required true angle is then computed as follows :

Obviously

$$\angle\ ABC\ =\ 180 - (\angle\ CAB + \angle\ ACB)$$

1. Now in triangle ABC, the angles CAB and ACB are already known by theodolite observations and knowing the length AC by computations from adjacent triangle, the lengths of sides AB and BC can be computed by the sine rule *i.e.*

$$\frac{BC}{\sin CAB}\ =\ \frac{CA}{\sin ABC}$$

$$\therefore \qquad BC\ =\ a\ =\ \frac{b \sin CAB}{\sin ABC}$$

Also $\qquad \dfrac{AB}{\sin ACB}\ =\ \dfrac{CA}{\sin ABC}$

$$\therefore \qquad AB\ =\ c\ =\ \frac{b \sin ACB}{\sin ABC}$$

2. Now applying sine rule to triangles BAS and BCS, we get

$$\sin x = \frac{BS \sin ASB}{AB} = \frac{d \sin (\theta + \gamma)}{c}$$

∴ ∠x is known.

and $\qquad \sin y = \dfrac{BS \sin CSB}{BC} = \dfrac{d \sin \gamma}{a}$

∴ ∠y is known.

3. As the eccentric distance d is very small as compared to the distances between triangulation station i.e. BA and BC, the angles x and y are going to be very small and therefore we may write

$$x \text{ (in seconds)} = \frac{\sin x}{\sin 1"}$$

$$= \frac{d \sin (\theta + \gamma)}{c \sin 1"}$$

$$= 206265 \times \frac{d \sin (\theta + \gamma)}{c}$$

and $\quad y \text{ (in seconds)} = \dfrac{\sin y}{\sin 1"}$

$$= \frac{d \sin \gamma}{a \sin 1"}$$

$$= 206265 \times \frac{d \sin \gamma}{a}$$

4. Thus, knowing the values of x, y, the required true angle B (i.e. ABC) can be determined as follows :

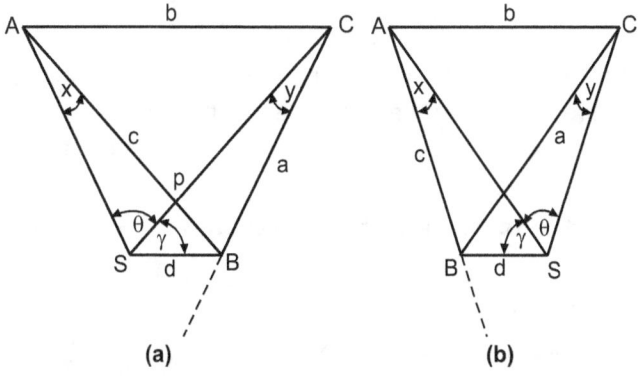

(a)   (b)

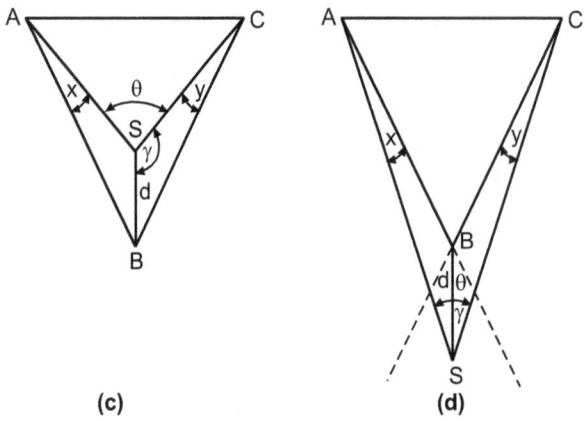

(c)   (d)

Fig. 1.23 : Four different positions of satellite station

$\angle$ APC, an exterior angle of triangles ASP and CBP can be written down as :

$$\angle \text{ APC } = \angle \text{ ASP} + \angle \text{ SAP} = \theta + x$$

and $\angle$ APC $= \angle$ PSB $+ y = B + y$

$\therefore$ Equating the two values of $\angle$ APC,

$$\theta + x = B + y \text{ or } B = \theta + x - y$$

$\therefore$ True angle ABC $= B = \left[\theta + \dfrac{d \sin (\theta + \gamma)}{c \sin 1''} - \dfrac{d \sin \gamma}{a \sin 1''} \right]$

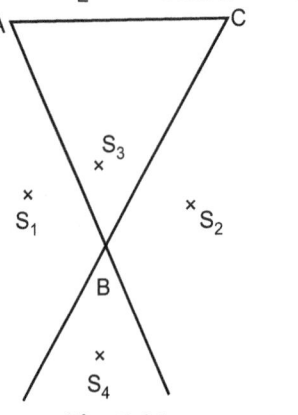

Fig. 1.24

This expression for true angle is valid for one position of satellite station selected to the left of true station. There are three other possible positions of satellite station with respect to true station. The Fig. 1.24 shows four different positions of satellite station with respect to true station.

(a) Satellite station S_1 to the left of true station B : (i.e. between CB produced and AB). Refer Fig. 1.23 (a).

In this case, as already proved,

True angle, ABC $= B = \theta + x - y$

(b) Satellite station S_2 to the right of true station B : (i.e. between AB produced and CB). Refer Fig. 1.23 (b).

Here, True angle, ABC $= B = \theta - x + y$

(c) Satellite station S_3, inside the triangle ABC : Refer Fig. 1.23 (c).

Here, True angle, ABC $= B = \theta - x - y$

(d) Satellite station S_4, Fig. 1.23 (d) outside the triangle ABC : i.e. within AB and CB produced.

Here, True angle, ABC $= B = \theta + x + y$

Measurement of Round of Angles from a Satellite Station :

When round of angles are observed from the satellite station, the corrections x, y are computed by assuming the line joining eccentric station to the true station as meridian. The observed angles are then reduced to this assumed meridian and the required corrections are then calculated by using the formula,

$$\text{Correction in seconds} = \frac{d \sin \theta}{D \sin 1''}$$

where
D = Distance of the observed station from the true station

d = Eccentric distance

θ = Observed angle reduced to assumed meridian.

The sign of correction is same as that of sin θ. Referring to Fig. 1.25, let S and B be satellite station and true station respectively and let B, C, D, E and F be the observed directions and θ_1, θ_2, θ_3 and θ_4 be their respective directions reduced to assumed meridian SB. Let x_1, x_2, x_3 and x_4 be respective corrections to the observed directions C, D, E and F respectively and let their distances from the true station B be D_1, D_2, D_3 and D_4 respectively.

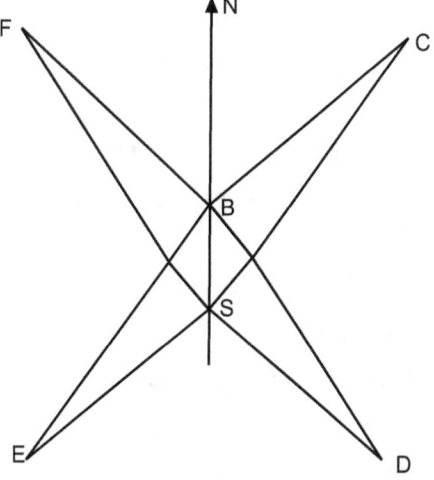

Fig. 1.25 : Round of angles from satellite station

Then the corrections are obtained by the formula

$$x_1 \text{ (in seconds)} = \frac{d \sin \theta_1}{D_1 \sin 1''}$$

$$x_2 \text{ (in seconds)} = \frac{d \sin \theta_2}{D_2 \sin 1''} \text{ and so on.}$$

The signs of the corrections will be same as those of $\sin \theta$. It is advisable to avoid satellite stations in first order triangulation. However, in second or third order triangulation, sometimes it may be necessary to select such stations.

Eccentricity of Signal :

When observations are made upon a signal (erected at the satellite station) which is eccentric (i.e. out of centre of main stations) then the observed angles are to be corrected. The method of applying corrections to the observed angles is similar to that of satellite station. Referring to the Fig. 1.23 (a), the signal for the true station B is say at S, then the angles observed from triangulation station A and C i.e. $\angle$ CAS and $\angle$ ACS have to be corrected by x and y respectively, found out by formulae,

$$x = \frac{d \sin (\theta + \gamma)}{c \sin 1''} \quad \text{and} \quad y = \frac{d \sin \gamma}{a \sin 1''}$$

1.12 EXTENSION OF BASE LINE

Introduction :

Usually the length of the base line is small (10 to 20 km) as compared to the lengths of the sides of triangles, because it is not always possible to secure a favourable site for a longer base and measurement of longer base lines becomes very expensive. The usual procedure is to measure a short base line and extend it by forming well conditioned triangles. The group of triangles required to be established for extension of base line is called as *Base net*.

The following points are to be considered while selecting a particular method for extension of base :

(a)   Avoid small angles opposite to the known side.

(b)   Select sufficient number of redundant lines to have more than two side equation within the figure.

(c)   Select the quickest method of extension with less number of stations.

Methods of Extending the Base Line :

There are two methods of extending the base line :

(a)   Forward method.

(b)   Alternate method.

(a) Forward method : (Fig. 1.26 (a)) :

1.   Let AB be the base line to be extended to C, D and so on.

2.   Let P and Q be two stations selected on either side of AB so as to form well conditioned triangles and are visible from extremities of the base line.

3.   With the theodolite now set up at stations A, B, C, P and Q, the angles at each of triangles ABP, ABQ, BCP, BCQ, ACP and ACQ are measured very accurately.

4.   Now in triangles ABP and ABQ, the length AB and all included angles are known. Thus applying sine rule, the lengths of sides AP, BP and AQ, BQ can be calculated. Similarly from the triangles BCP and BCQ, knowing the lengths of sides BP and BQ by computation and all included angles, the length of the side BC can be obtained by two independent methods. Now, from triangles ACP and ACQ, knowing lengths AP and AQ, and all included angles, two independent values of AC can be calculated. Knowing AC, BC will be equal to AC – AB, thus two more values of the BC are obtained. The average of the four values of BC (each obtained independently) will be the required length of the BC extended. The above procedure is repeated to extend the base to D etc.

(b) Alternate method : (Fig. 1.26 (b)) :

This is another method that is commonly adopted for the extension of base line. Let AB be the short base. Select two points C and D on either side of AB and measure the angles at each of the points A, B, C and D and by applying sine rule compute two values of CD independently. The average of the two will be taken as the length of CD, the new base line. Then again selecting two more points E and F on either side of CD and measuring all included angles at C, D, E and F, two values of EF can be obtained. The average of these two values will be the required length of the extended base EF. This new base EF can further be extended to say GH in the same manner. The accuracy of the extended base depends upon proper selection of subsidiary stations C, D, E, F etc. that necessarily form well conditioned triangles.

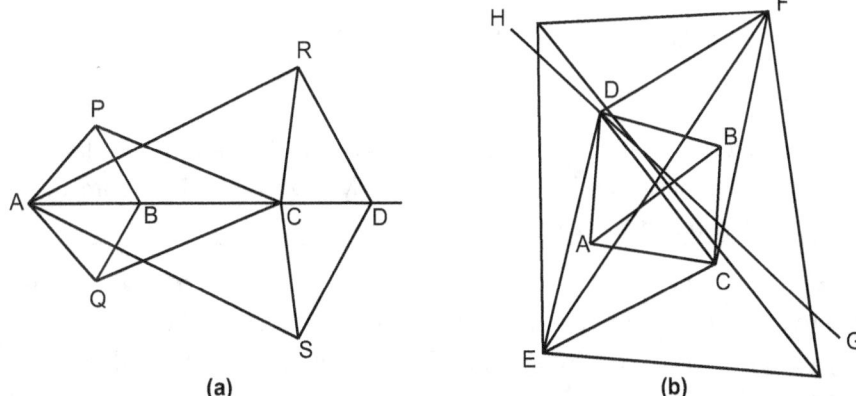

(a)   (b)

Fig. 1.26 : Extension of base

SOLVED EXAMPLES

Example 1.1 : Two triangulation stations A and B are 60 km apart and have elevations 240 m and 280 m respectively. The intervening ground may be assumed to have a uniform elevation of 200 m. Ascertain the intervisibility of A and B.

Solution. : Refer to Fig. 1.27.

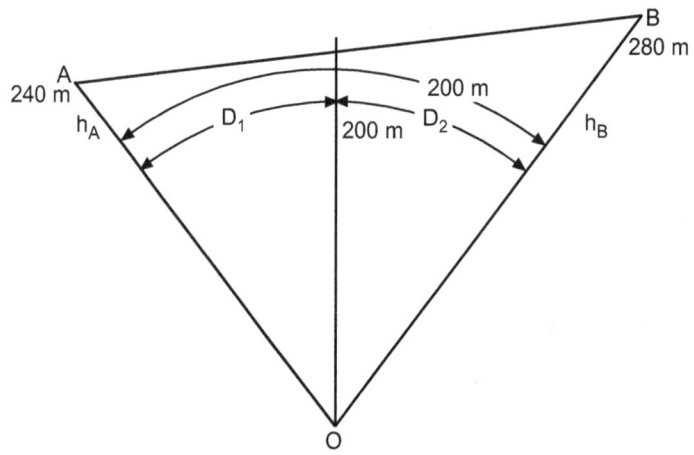

Fig. 1.27

$$h_1 = 240 - 200 = 40 \text{ m} = 0.0673 \, D_1^2$$

∴ $$D_1 = \sqrt{\frac{40}{0.0673}} = 24.37 \text{ km}$$

∴ $$D_2 = D - D_1 = 60 - D_1 = 60 - 24.37 = 35.63 \text{ km}$$

∴ $$h_B = 0.0673 \, D_2^2 = 85.44 \text{ mm}$$

∴ Elevation of line of sight = 200 + 85.44 = 285.44 m

But the elevation of B is 280 m.

Since the elevation of station B i.e. 280 m is less than the elevation of line of sight i.e. 285.44 m, the two stations A and B are not mutually intervisible. Therefore the minimum height of scaffold required at B = 285.44 − 280 = 5.44 m.

Example 1.2 : Two triangulation stations A and B are 42 km apart and have elevations of 279 and 276 m respectively. Find the minimum height of signal required at B so that the line of sight may not pass nearer the ground than 3 m. The intervening ground may be assumed to have a uniform elevation of 252 m.

Solution : Refer to Fig. 1.28.

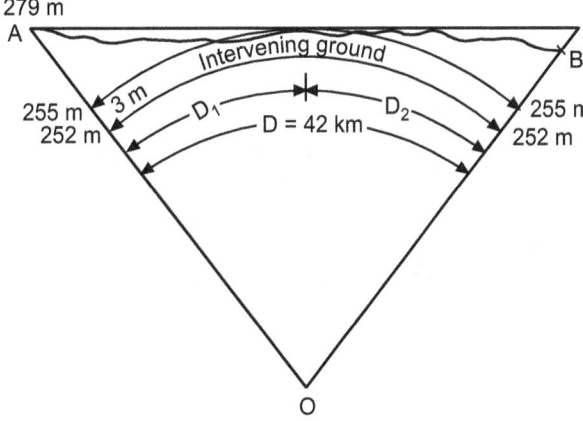

Fig. 1.28

The elevation of the intervening ground = 252 m (given).

The elevation of the line of sight = 252 + 3 = 255 m, this is assumed as datum level.

∴   The elevation of station A above this datum = Elevation of A − 255

$$= 279 - 255 = 24 \text{ m} \qquad \text{(say } h_1\text{)}$$

∴   The distance of the point of tangency corresponding to this height h_1 of 24 m is

$$24 = 0.0673 \, D_1^2$$

∴ $$D_1^2 = \frac{24}{0.0673}$$

or $$D_1 = \sqrt{\frac{24}{0.0673}} = 18.884 \text{ km}$$

∴ $$D_2 = D - D_1 = 42 - 18.884 = 23.116 \text{ km}$$

∴   The corresponding elevation h_2 to this distance to the point of tangency is,

$$h_2 = 0.0673 \, D_2^2 = 0.0673 \times (23.116)^2 = 35.9611 \text{ m}$$

∴   The line of sight at B will have the elevation

$$= 255 + 35.9611 = 290.9611 \approx 290.96 \text{ m}$$

But the elevation of the ground station B = 276 m (given)

∴   Minimum height of signal required at B

$$= 290.96 - 276 = 14.96 \text{ m}$$

Example 1.3 : Two triangulation stations A and B, 110 km apart, have altitudes of 422 m and 704 m respectively. The intervening peak C, 74 km from A has the altitude of 477 m.

Ascertain if A and B are intervisible. If necessary, find the minimum height of scaffolding required at B, so that the line of sight has atleast 3 m clearance anywhere along the path.

Solution : Refer to Fig. 1.29.

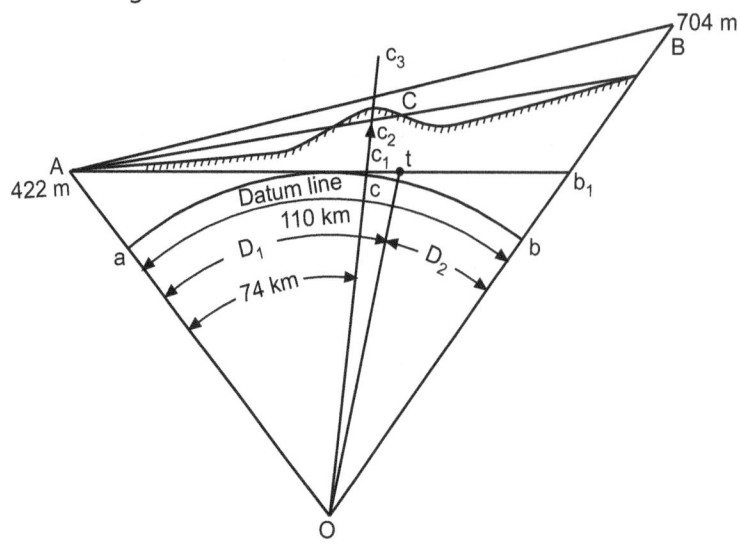

Fig. 1.29

From the ground station A, draw a line tangential to the datum line cutting at point t. Then the distance to the point of tangency = At = D_1.

$\therefore$ $\qquad\qquad\qquad\qquad$ h_1 = 0.0673 D_1^2

OR $\qquad\qquad\qquad\qquad$ 422 = 0.0673 D_1^2

$\therefore$ $\qquad\qquad\qquad\qquad$ $D_1 = \sqrt{\dfrac{422}{0.0673}}$ = 79.1860 km

$\therefore$ $\qquad\qquad\qquad\qquad$ D_2 = 110 − D_1 = 30.8140 km

But $\qquad\qquad\qquad\qquad$ ac = 74

$\therefore$ $\qquad\qquad\qquad\qquad$ tc = 79.1860 − 74 = 5.1860

$\therefore$ $\qquad\qquad\qquad\qquad$ cc_1 = 0.0673 × (tc)^2 = 1.810 m

and $\qquad\qquad\qquad\qquad$ bb_1 = 0.0673 D_2^2 = 0.0673 × (30.8140)^2 = 63.9011

$\therefore$ $\qquad\qquad\qquad\qquad$ b_1B = bB − bb_1 = 704 − 63.9011 ≈ 640.09

Now, by the principle of similar triangles,

$$\frac{c_1c_2}{b_1B} = \frac{Ac_1}{Ab_1}$$

$\therefore$ $\qquad\qquad\qquad\qquad$ $c_1c_2 = \dfrac{Ac_1}{Ab_1} \times b_1B$

$$= \frac{74}{110} \times 640.09$$

$$\approx 430.61 \text{ m}$$

Now, the elevation of line of sight at the intervening peak at C is,

$$cc_2 = cc_1 + c_1c_2 = 1.810 + 430.61 = 432.42$$

But the actual elevation of the peak at C = 477 m (given)

∴   Line of sight fails to clear the obstruction at peak C by

$$477 - 432.42 = 44.58 \text{ m}$$

Now, in order that the line of sight should have clearance of 3 m anywhere, its elevation at the obstruction should be (44.58 + 3) m above peak C = 47.58 m.

Now using principle of similar triangles,

The elevation of line of sight at B should be raised by

$$= 47.58 \times \frac{110}{74} = 70.727 \text{ m}$$

∴   Minimum height of scaffold required at B = 70.727 m

Example 1.4 : Solve the Example 1.3 by Capt. G.T. McCaw's method.

Solution : The above example can also be solved by Capt. G.T. McCaw's solution is explained below.

G.T. McCaw's formula stated below enables to find the elevation of the line of sight at the intervening (obstruction) peak C.

The formula is :

$$h = \frac{1}{2}(h_2 + h_1) + \frac{1}{2}(h_2 - h_1)\frac{x}{s} - (s^2 - x^2) \cosec^2 \xi \left(\frac{1 - 2m}{2R}\right)$$

where   h = Elevation of the line of sight at the intervening peak or obstruction

         h_1 & h_2 = Elevations of stations A and B respectively.

         2s = The horizontal distance between the two stations

         s + x = The horizontal distance of the obstruction at C from A

         s − x = The horizontal distance of the obstruction at C from B

         $\cosec^2 \xi$ = 1.00; and

$$\left(\frac{1 - 2m}{2R}\right) = 0.0673$$

In the example,

2s = 110 km, ∴ s = 55 km, s + x = 74, ∴ x = 19 km, s − x = 36, h_1 = 422 m; h_2 = 704 m

$\therefore$ $h = \frac{1}{2}(704 + 422) + \frac{1}{2}(704 - 422) \times \frac{19}{55} - (74 \times 36 \times 1 \times 0.0673)$

$= 563 + 48.70 - 179.287 = 432.413 \approx 432.42$

$=$ Elevation of the line of sight at the obstruction C.

But the actual elevation of peak at C = 477 m (given)

$\therefore$ Line of sight fails to clear the obstruction at peak C by 477 − 432.42 = 44.58 m

In order that the line of sight should have clearance of 3 m anywhere, its elevation at obstruction should be (44.58 + 3) m above peak at C = 47.58 m

Now, by using principle of similar triangles, the elevation of the line of sight at B should be raised by

$$= \frac{47.58 \times 110}{74} = 70.727 \text{ m}$$

Example 1.5 : The altitudes of two proposed stations A and C, 105 km apart, are respectively 214 m and 1072 m above the datum. The heights of two raised tops B and D on the profile between A and C are 357 m and 653 m respectively, the distance AB and AD being 38 km and 72 km.

Ascertain if A and C are intervisible and if necessary, determine a suitable height for a scaffold at C, given that A is a ground station. The line of sight must be clear from the ground by atleast 3 m.

Solution : Refer to Fig. 1.30.

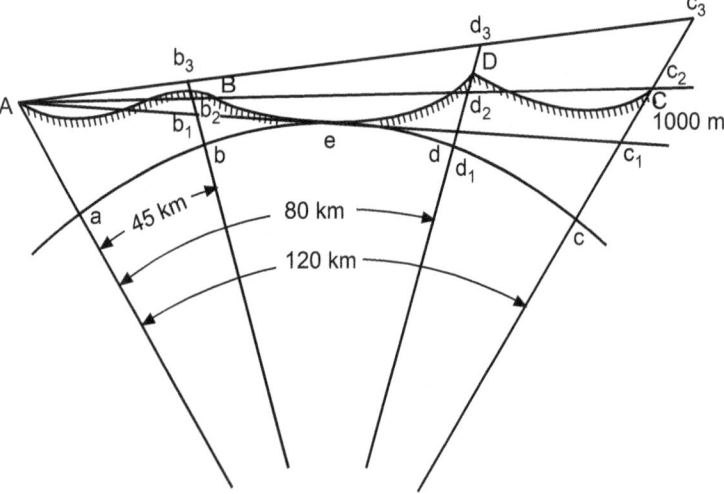

Fig. 1.30

Let ae = Distance to the visible horizon = D_1

$\therefore$ h_1 = $0.0673\ D_1^2$

$\therefore$ ae = $\sqrt{\dfrac{214}{0.0673}}$

$\therefore$ ae = 56.37 km

$\therefore$ be = 56.37 – 38

       = 18.37 km

$\therefore$ bb_1 = $0.0637 \times (18.37)^2$

       = 22.73 m

Similarly, de = 72 – 56.37

       = 15.63 m

$\therefore$ dd_1 = $0.0673 \times (15.63)^2$

       = 16.45 m

and cc_1 = $0.0673 \times (105 – 56.37)^2$

       = 159.27 m

and c_1c = 1072 – 159.27

       = 912. 73 m

By the principle of similar triangles,

$\therefore$ d_1d_2 = $912.73 \times \dfrac{72}{105}$

       = 625.872 m

$\therefore$ $d_1d_2 + dd_1$ = 625.872 + 16.45

       = 642.32 m

But the elevation of station D = 653 m

$\therefore$ Line of sight fails to clear obstruction at D.

Similarly, b_1b_2 = $912.73 \times \dfrac{38}{105}$

       = 330.32 m

$\therefore$ $b_1b_2 + bb_1$ = 330.32 + 22.73

       = 353.05 m

But the elevation of station B = 357 m

$\therefore$ The line of sight fails to clear the obstruction at B.

$\therefore$ Stations A and C are not intervisible.

For D : d_2d_3 = 653 – 644.32 + 3

       = 13.68 m

$\therefore$ Height of scaffold at C = $13.68 \times \dfrac{105}{72}$ = 19.95 m

For B : b_2b_3 = 357 – 353.05 + 3

                           = 6.95 m

∴   Height of scaffold at C = $6.95 \times \dfrac{105}{38}$ = 19.2 m

∴   The height of scaffold at C = 19.2 m (maximum of the two)

Example 1.6 : Two triangulation stations A and B, 120 km apart, have elevations 200 m and 1000 m respectively. The intervening peaks C and D are at 45 km and 80 km away from A have elevations 265 m and 525 m respectively. Ascertain, if A and B are intervisible or not. If not, find the height of scaffolding required at B, so as to make them intervisible. The line of sight should no where be less than 3 m above the surface of ground.

Solution :

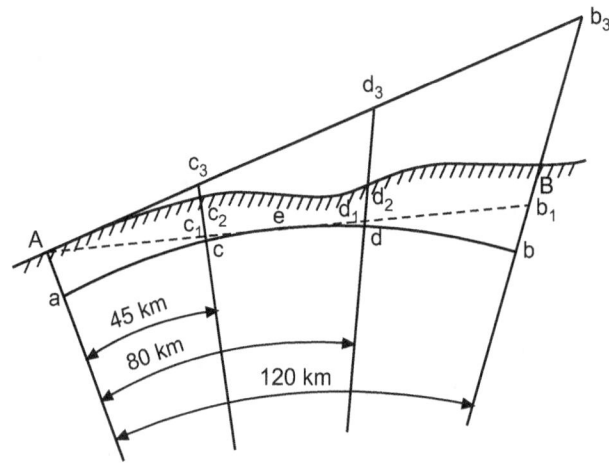

Fig. 1.31

Let   Ae = Distance of the visible horizon = D_1

∴ h_1 = $0.0673\, D_1^2$

∴ D_1 = Ae = $\sqrt{\dfrac{200}{0.0673}}$

∴   Ae = 54.48 km

∴   ce = 54.48 – 45

                                        = 9.48 km

                                 ed = 80 – 54.48

                                        = 25.52 km

and   eb = AB – Ae

∴   eb = 120 – 54.48

                                        = 65.52 km

Similarly, de = 80 – 54.51

                                    = 25.49 km

$\therefore$ dd_1 = 0.0673 $(25.52)^2$

                                    = 43.83 m

But,   Elevation of B = 1000 m

$\therefore$ b_1B = Bb – bb_1

                                    = 1000 – 289.12

                                    = 710.38 m

Now, by the principle of similar triangles Ac_1c_2, Ad_1d_2 and Ab_1B

$$d_1d_2 = 710.38 \times \frac{80}{120}$$

                                    = 473.58 m

Elevation of line of sight at D= Elevation of d_2

                $d_1d_2 + dd_1$ = 473.58 + 43.83

                                    = 517.41 m

  But,   Elevation of station D = 525 m

$\therefore$ Line of sight fails to clear obstruction at D.

$\therefore$ d_2D = 525 – 517.41

                                    = 7.59 m

Similarly, c_1c_2 = 710.38 $\times \frac{45}{120}$

                                    = 266.39

$\therefore$ Elevation of line of sight at 'C'

                                    = $c_1c_2 + cc_1$

                                    = 266.39 + 6.053

                                    = 272.44 m

But, Elevation of station at station C is 265 m.

Therefore, line of sight clears the peak C.

Hence, stations A and B are not intervisible.

Let Ad_3 be the new height of sight, such that

                Dd_3 = 3 m (minimum)

Hence $\qquad d_2d_3 = d_3D + d_2D$

$$= 3 + 7.56$$

$$= 10.56 \text{ m}$$

Hence $\qquad Bb_3 = d_2d_3 \cdot \dfrac{AB}{Ad_2}$

$$= 10.56 \times \dfrac{120}{80}$$

$$= 15.84 \approx 15.9 \text{ m}$$

Hence minimum height of scaffolding at B = 15.9 m

Example 1.7 : Two triangulation stations P and Q are at elevations of 200 m and 995 m respectively. The distance of Q from P is 105 km. If the elevation of a peak M at a distance of 30 km from P is 301 m, determine whether Q is visible from P or not. If not, what would be the height of signal required at Q so that these stations will be intervisible ?

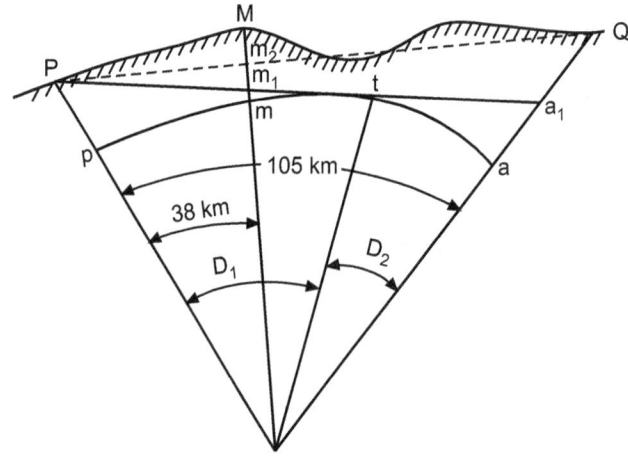

Fig. 1.32

Solution :

$$h_1 = 0.0673 \, D_1^2$$

$$200 = 0.0673 \, D_1^2$$

$\therefore \qquad D_1 = \sqrt{\dfrac{200}{0.0673}} = 54.51 \text{ km}$

$\therefore \qquad D_1 = 105 - D_1$

$$= 105 - 54.51$$

$$= 50.49 \text{ km}$$

But $\qquad$ pm $= 38$

$\therefore \qquad$ mt $= 54.51 - 38 = 16.51$ km

$\therefore \qquad mm_1 = 0.0673 \times (mt)^2$

$\qquad = 0.0673 \times (16.51)^2$

$\qquad = 18.34$ m

Now $\qquad qq_1 = 0.0673 \, D_2^2$

$\qquad = 0.0673 \times (50.49)^2$

$\qquad = 171.56$ m

$q_1Q = qQ - qq_1$

$\qquad = 995 - 171.56$

$\qquad = 823.44$

Now, by the principle of similar triangles,

$$\frac{m_1m_2}{q_1Q} = \frac{pm_1}{pq_1}$$

$\therefore \qquad m_1m_2 = \dfrac{pm_1}{pq_1} \times q_1Q$

$\therefore \qquad m_1m_2 = \dfrac{38}{105} \times 823.44$

$\qquad = 298.006$

Now, the elevation of line of sight at the intervening peak at M is

$\qquad mm_2 = mm_1 + m_1m_2$

$\qquad = 18.34 + 298.006$

$\qquad = 316.34$

But actual elevation of the peak at M $= 301$ m

$\qquad$ Fails to clear the peak $= 301 - 316.34$

$\qquad = 15.34$

But $\qquad m_2m_3$ minimum $= 15.34 + 3$

$\qquad = 18.34$ m

$\therefore \qquad$ Minimum height of scaffolding or signal Q_3Q

$$= m_2 m_3 \cdot \left(\frac{PQ}{pm_2}\right)$$

$$= 18.34 \left(\frac{105}{38}\right)$$

$$= 50.67 \text{ m}$$

Example 1.8 : The altitude of two proposed stations A and B 140 kms aparts are respectively 605 m and 1180 m. The altitude of two points C and D on the profile between them are respectively 595 m and 940 m. The distance being AC = 80 km and AD = 120 km. Determine whether A and B are intervisible or not ? If not, determine the height of target to be erected at B, so that the line of sight should no where be less than 2 m above ground surface.

Solution :

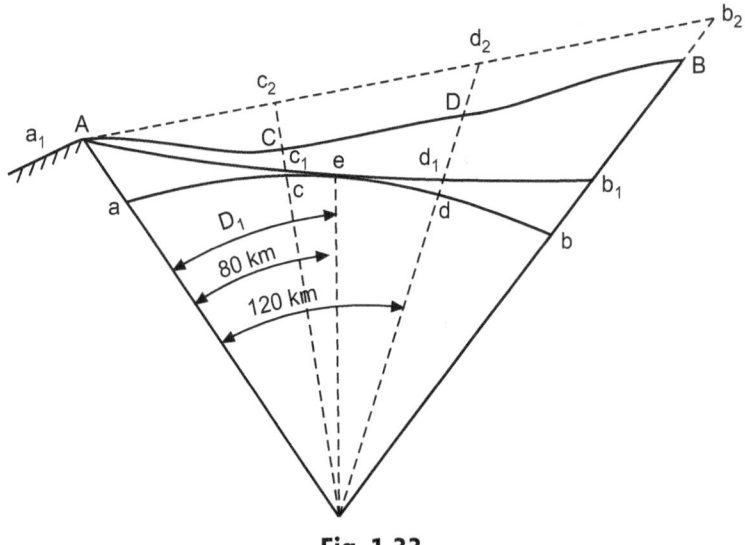

Fig. 1.33

Distance of A from visible horizon.

$$h_1 = 0.0673 \, D_1^2$$

$\therefore$
$$D_1 = A_e = \sqrt{\frac{605}{0.0673}} = 94.81 \text{ km}$$

$\therefore$
$$d_2D = 940 - 936.32 = 3.68 \text{ m}$$

Similarly,
$$\frac{C_1C_2}{b_1B} = \frac{80}{140}$$

$\therefore$
$$C_1C_2 = \frac{80}{140} \times 1042.56 = 595.74 \text{ m}$$

$\therefore$ Elevation of line of sight at C

$$= cc_1 + c_1c_2$$

$$cc_1 = 0.0673 \, (ce)^2$$

$$= 0.0673 \, (14.81)^2$$

$$= 14.76 \text{ m}$$

∴ Elevation of light of sight at C

$$= 14.76 + 595.74 = 610.5 \text{ m}$$

But elevation of C = 595 m. Therefore, line of sight clears the peak at C.

∴   A and B are intervisible.

Now, Let Ad_3 be the new height of sight, such that

$$Dd_3 = 2 \text{ m}$$

∴ $d_2d_3 = d_3D + d_2D$

$$= 2 + 3.68 = 5.68 \text{ m}$$

$$ce = 94.81 - 80 = 14.81 \text{ km}$$

$$ed = 120 - 94.81 = 25.19 \text{ km}$$

and $eb = AB - Ae$

$$= 140 - 94.81$$

$$= 45.19 \text{ km}$$

$$dd_1 = 0.0673 \, (25.19)^2$$

$$= 42.70 \text{ m}$$

$$\text{Elevation of B} = 1180 \text{ m}$$

∴ $b_1B = Bb_1 - bb_1$

$$bb_1 = 0.0673 \, (45.19)^2 = 137.43 \text{ m}$$

∴ $b_1B = 1180 - 137.43 = 1042.56 \text{ m}$

By the principle of similar triangle; In $\Delta \, Ac_1c_2$, $\Delta \, Ad_1d_2$ and $\Delta \, Ab_1B$,

$$\frac{d_1d_2}{b_1B} = \frac{120}{140}$$

∴ $d_1d_2 = 1042.56 \times \dfrac{120}{140} = 893.62 \text{ m}$

Now, elevation of line of sight at D,

$$= dd_1 + d_1d_2$$

$$= 42.70 + 893.62 = 936.32$$

$$\text{But elevation of D} = 940 \text{ m}$$

∴   Line of sight fails to clear obstruction at D.

Hence,

$$Bb_3 = d_2d_3 \cdot \frac{AB}{Ad_2}$$

$$= 5.68 \times \frac{140}{120} = 6.62 \text{ m}$$

$$\approx 6.7 \text{ m}$$

∴   Minimum height of scaffolding at B = 6.7 m.

Example 1.9 : Two proposed stations A and B are 105 km apart. The elevation of A is 300 m and elevation of B is 885 m. The intervening obstructions are situated at C and D, 40 km from A and D is 81 km from A. The elevation of C and D are respectively 320 m and 622 m, ascertain if A and B are intervisible or not, if necessary find by how much amount the station B is to be raised so that the line of sight should no where be less than 2 m above the surface of the ground.

Solution :

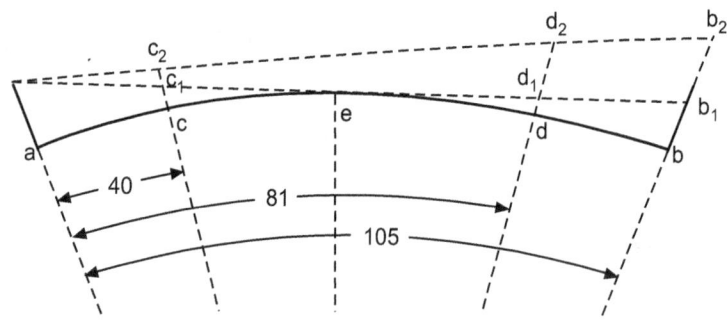

Fig. 1.34

Distance of A from visible horizon h_1

$$h_1 = 0.0673 \, D_1^2$$

$$300 = 0.0673 \, D_1^2$$

∴

$$D_1 = Ae = \sqrt{\frac{300}{0.06735}} = 66.74 \text{ m}$$

$$ce = 66.74 - 40 = 26.74 \text{ km}$$

$$ed = 81 - 66.74 = 14.26 \text{ km}$$

and

$$eb = 105 - 66.74 = 38.26 \text{ km}$$

We can calculate,

$$cc_1 = 0.0673 \, (66.74 - 40)^2 = 48.15 \text{ m}$$

$$dd_1 = 0.0673 \, (81 - 66.74)^2 = 13.09 \text{ m}$$

$$bb_1 = 0.0673 (105 - 66.74)^2 = 98.51 \text{ m}$$

$\therefore$

$$Bb_1 = \text{elevation of B} - bb_1$$
$$= 885 - 98.51 = 786.48 \text{ m}$$

$$c_1c_2 = \frac{786.48}{105} \times 40 = 299.61 \text{ m}$$

Now,   R.L. of c_2 = 299.61 + 48.15 = 347.73 m

But   R.L. of c = 320 m

Therefore, line of sight is not obstructed etc.

Now,

$$d_1d_2 = \frac{786.48}{105} \times 81 = 606.7$$

$\therefore$ R.L. of d_2 = $dd_1 + d_1d_2$
$$= 13.69 + 606.7 = 620.40 \text{ m}$$

But   R.L. of D = 622 m

$\therefore$ Line of sight is obstructed at D.

Abstraction = 622 – 620.4 = 1.65 m

R.L. of d_3 = 622 + 2 = 624 m

Now,   624 – 620.4 = 3.60 m

$\therefore$ Height of scaffolding required at B

$$= b_2b_3 = \frac{3.60}{81} \times 105 = 4.67 \text{ m}$$

Example 1.10 : There are two stations A and B at elevations of 200 m and 1000 m respectively. The distance between A and B is 100 km. If the elevation of a peak P at a distance of 40 km from A is 300 m. Show that station A and B are intervisible.

Solution :

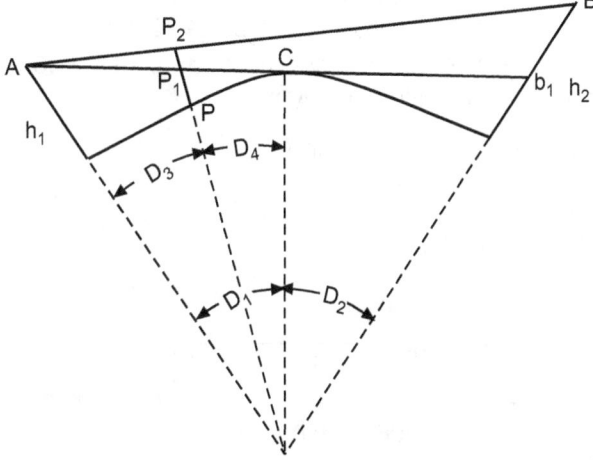

Fig. 1.35

$$h_1 = 0.0673\ D_1^2$$

$$200 = 0.0673\ D_1^2$$

$$\therefore \qquad D_1 = \sqrt{\dfrac{200}{0.0673}} = 54.51\ km$$

i.e. Distance between A and C = 54.51 km.

$$D_4 = \text{Distance between C and P}$$

$$= 54.51 - 40 = 14.51\ km$$

$$PP_1 = 0.0673 \cdot D_4^2 = 0.0673\ (14.51)^2 = 14.16\ m$$

$$\text{Distance, CB} = D_2 = 100 - 54.51 = 45.49\ km$$

$$\therefore \qquad bb_1 = 0.0673\ (45.49)^2 = 139.49\ m$$

$$\text{Height, } Bb_1 = 1000 - 139.49 = 860.51\ m$$

From similar, $\triangle\ AP_2P_1$ and ABb_1

$$P_2P_1 = \dfrac{860.51}{100} \times 40 = 344.20\ m$$

$\therefore$　Elevation of line of sight at

$$P_2 = PP_1 + P_2P_1 = 14.16 + 344.20 = 358.36\ m$$

As elevation of P (300 m) is less than elevation of line of sight at P_2, hence line of sight clears the obstruction.

Example 1.11 : Observations were taken from the triangulation station "O" to the polished cylindrical objects of diameter 0.2 m and having centres at A and B. A' and B' are the points on periphery of A and B towards the left of A and B, where the bright line from station O was seen to bisect. A'OB' is observed to be 59° 23' 45" and distances OA and OB were 15 km and 18 km respectively. If sun rays makes an angle of 50° 0' 0" with OA and of 60° 30' with OB, find the corrected value of $\angle$ AOB.

Solution : For observation made to station A,

$$\theta_A = 50° \text{ and } D_A = 15000\ m$$

$\therefore$　　　　Phase correction $= \alpha_A$

and　　　　　　$$\alpha_A = \left(\dfrac{206265 \cdot r \cdot \cos \dfrac{\theta_A}{2}}{D_A} \right) sec$$

$$= \dfrac{206265 \times 0.1 \times \cos \dfrac{50}{2}}{15000} = 1.25"$$

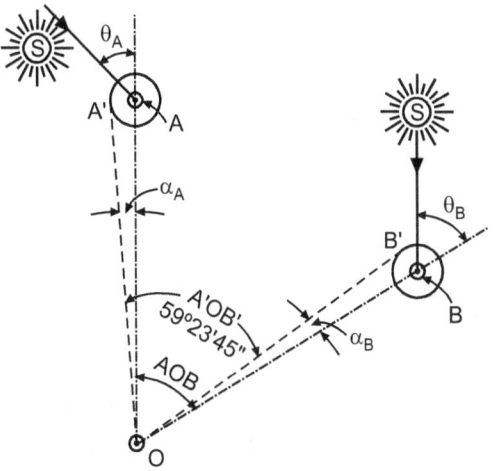

Fig. 1.36

For observation made to station B, $\theta_B = 60° 30'$, $D_B = 18000$ m

∴　　　Phase correction $= \alpha_B$

and

$$\alpha_B = \left(\frac{206265 \cdot r \cdot \cos \dfrac{\theta_B}{2}}{D_B} \right) \sec$$

$$= \frac{206265 \times 0.1 \times \cos \dfrac{60° 30'}{2}}{18000} = 0.99"$$

∴　　　$\angle AOB = \angle A'OB' - \alpha_A + \alpha_B$　　　　$[\because\; A'OB' - \alpha_A = AOB'$

$= 59° 23' 45' - 1.25" + 0.99"$　　　　$\&\; AOB' + \alpha_A = AOB]$

$= 59° 23' 44.74"$

Angle corrected from phase correction.

Example 1.12 : A polished metal cylindrical signal 0.80 m in diameter was situated at a distance of 12.75 km from the inst. station The sun rays made an angle of 72° 30' with the line joining the centre of the signal to the triangulation station. Compute the phase correction. Derive the expression you use.

Solution : Radiation of signal, r = 0.4 m, Distance to signal, D = 12750 m, $\theta = 72° 30'$

Assuming observation is made on bright portion

$$\text{Phase correction, } \alpha = \frac{206265 \cdot r \cdot \cos^2 \dfrac{\theta}{2}}{D}$$

$$= \frac{206265 \times 0.4 \times \cos^2 36° 15'}{12750} = 4.21"$$

Assuming observation is made on bright line

$$\text{Phase correction, } \alpha \; = \; \frac{206265 \cdot r \cdot \cos \dfrac{\theta}{2}}{D}$$

$$= \; \frac{206265 \times 0.4 \times \cos 36° \, 15'}{12750} \; = 5.22"$$

Example 1.13 : From an eccentric station E, 14.25 m to the west of main station B, following angles were measured :

$\angle$ BEC = 78° 25' 32",　　$\angle$ CEA = 56° 30' 20"

The stations E and C are on the opposite sides of the line AB. Reduce the angles to centre B, if AB and BC are 5368.2 m and 4682.3 m respectively.

Solution : Refer Fig. 1.37.

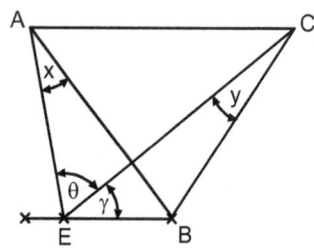

Fig. 1.37

In Δ AEB,　　　　　θ　=　56° 30' 20"

　　　　　　　　　　　γ　=　78° 25' 32"

and　　　　　　　　　BE　=　14.25 m

　　　　　　　　　　　AB　=　5368.2 m

$\therefore$　Applying sine rule

$$\sin x \; = \; \frac{14.25 \times \sin (56° \, 30' \, 20" + 78° \, 25' \, 32")}{5368.2}$$

$\therefore$　　　　　　　　　　x　=　5' 27.63"

Similarly,　　　　　　$\sin y \; = \; \dfrac{14.25 \times \sin 78° \, 25' \, 32"}{4682.3}$

$\therefore$　　　　　　　　　　y　=　10' 14.98" $\approx$ 10' 15"

Now true angle B can be obtained as following :

　　　　　　　　B + y　=　θ + x　　　　　$\therefore$　B = θ + x – y

$\therefore$　　　　　　　　　　B　=　56° 30' 20" + 6' 27.63" – 10' 15"

　　　　　　　　　　　　　=　56° 47.63" · 63 – 10' 15"

$\therefore$　　　　　True angle　=　56° 26' 32 . 63"

Example 1.14 : In a triangle ABC, station C was a church spire. A satellite station S was selected 15 m from C inside the triangle ABC. From S the angles CSA and ASB were measured and found to be 140° 30' 22" and 85° 30' 29" respectively. The lengths AC and BC was known to be 3600 m and 2748 m respectively. Compute the angle ABC.

Solution : Refer Fig. 1.38.

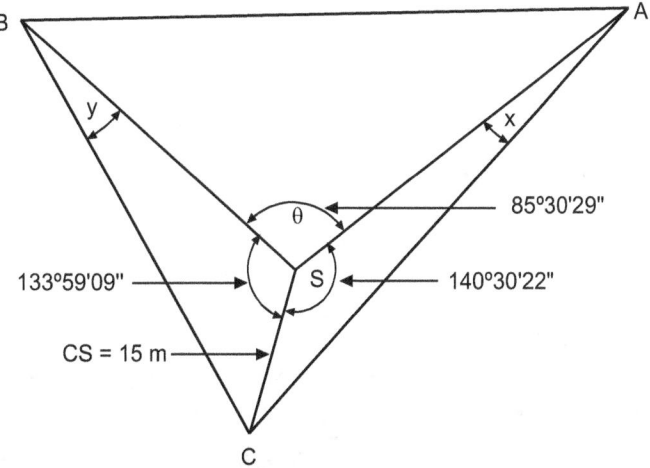

Fig. 1.38

Given : CS = d = 15 m,

$$\angle CSA = 140° 30' 22"$$
$$\angle ASB = 85° 30' 29"$$
$$\text{Length AC} = 3600 \text{ m}$$
$$\text{Length BC} = 2748 \text{ m}$$

Let angles ∠ CSA = x, ∠ CBS = y

From Δ CSA, applying sing rule, we have

$$\frac{\sin x}{CS} = \frac{\sin C\hat{S}A}{AC}$$

∴
$$\sin x = \frac{CS \sin CSA}{AC}$$

∴
$$\sin x = \frac{15 \sin 140° 30' 22"}{3600}$$

∴
$$x = 9' 6.6"$$

Similarly to find y, we have

$$\angle A\hat{S}B + \angle ASC + \angle CSB = 360°$$

∴
$$\angle CSB = 360° - 140° 30' 22" - 85° 30' 29"$$

$\therefore$ $C\hat{S}B = 133°\ 59'\ 9''$

$\therefore$ $\dfrac{\sin y}{15} = \dfrac{\sin CSB}{2748}$

$\therefore$ $\sin y = \dfrac{(15 \times \sin 133°\ 59'\ 9'')}{2748}$

$\therefore$ $y = 0°\ 13'\ 30.1''$

Here $\theta = 85°\ 30'\ 29''$

$\therefore$ We have $ACB + x + y = \theta$

$\therefore$ $\angle ACB = \theta - x - y$

     $= 85°\ 30'\ 29'' - 0°\ 9'\ 6.6'' - 0°\ 13'\ 30.1''$

$\therefore$ $\angle ACB = 85°\ 7'\ 52.3''$

Example 1.15 : Directions were obtained from a satellite station S 2.25 m from triangulation station A. The following results were obtained.

Station	Observed direction	Distance from A
A	00° 00' 00"	–
B	38° 45' 00"	2000 m
C	90° 15' 00"	1750 m

What would have been the value of angle CAB if the instrument had been set up at A.

Solution : Refer Fig. 1.39.

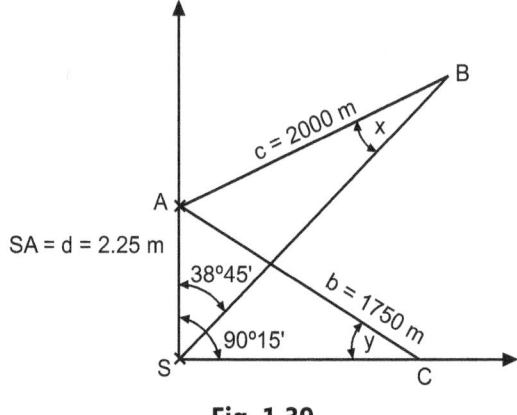

Fig. 1.39

$\angle OAB = $ Exterior angle of triangle BAS

$= \angle ASB + \angle ABS$

$= 38°\ 45'\ 00'' + x''$

$$\angle\, OAC \;=\; \text{Exterior angle of triangle ASC}$$

$$=\; \angle\, ASC + \angle\, ACS$$

$$=\; 90°\ 15'\ 00'' + y''$$

$$x'' \;=\; \frac{d \sin \gamma}{c \sin 1''}$$

$$x'' \;=\; \frac{d \sin (38°\ 45')}{2000 \times \dfrac{1}{206265}}$$

$$=\; \frac{2.25 \times \sin 38°\ 45'}{2000} \times 206265$$

∴ $x'' = 145.24'' = 2'\ 25.24''$ ... (i)

Similarly, $y'' = \dfrac{2.25 \times \sin (90°\ 15')}{1750} \times 206265$

∴ $y'' = 265.19'' = 4'\ 25.19''$ ... (ii)

∴ $\angle\, OAB = 38°\ 45'\ 00'' + x$

$$=\; 38°\ 45'\ 00'' + 2'\ 25.24''$$

$$=\; 38°\ 47'\ 25.24''$$

and $\angle\, OAC = 90°\ 15'\ 00'' + y$

$$=\; 90°\ 15' + 4'\ 25.18''$$

$$=\; 90°\ 19'\ 25.19''$$

Obviously, $\angle\, CAB = \angle\, OAC - \angle\, OAB$

$$=\; 90°\ 19'\ 25.19'' - 38°\ 47'\ 25.24''$$

$$=\; 51°\ 31'\ 59.95''$$

∴   The required angle

         CAB $= 51°\ 31'\ 59.95'' = 51°\ 32'\ 00''$

Example 1.16 : Directions were observed from a satellite station S, 2.18 m from station A and the following results were obtained :

Station	Observed direction	Distance from A
A	0° 0' 0"	–
B	39° 13'	2340.3 m
C	92° 46'	2040.7 m
D	169° 28'	1852 m
E	264° 44'	2445 m

Correct the observed directions to those which would have been measured if transit had been set up at station A. (converted to S.I. system).

Solution : Fig. 1.40.

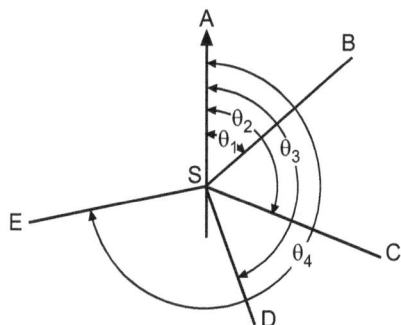

Fig. 1.40

$\therefore \qquad \alpha_1 = \dfrac{d \sin \theta}{D \sin 1''}$

where

d = Eccentric distance

θ = Observed angle reduced to the assumed meridian i.e. SA

D = Distance from the true station to be observed station

$\therefore \qquad \alpha_1 = \dfrac{d \sin \theta}{D \sin 1''}$

$\therefore \qquad \alpha_1 = \dfrac{2.18 \times \sin (39°\ 13')}{2340.3} \times 206265$

$\qquad = \dfrac{2.18 \times 0.6322 \times 206265}{2340.3}$ seconds

$\qquad = \dfrac{2.18 \times 0.6322 \times 206265}{2340.3 \times 60}$ minutes

$\qquad = 2'\ 1.4''$

Corrected observed direction = 39° 13' 0"

$$\begin{array}{r} + 0\ \ 2'\ 1.4'' \\ \hline 39°\ 15'\ 1.4'' \end{array}$$

$\therefore \qquad \alpha_2 = \dfrac{d \sin \theta_2}{D \sin 1''}$

$\qquad = \dfrac{2.18 \times \sin 92°\ 46'}{2040.7 \times 60} \times 206265$ minutes

$\qquad = \dfrac{2.18 \times \cos 2°\ 46'\ (0.9989)}{2040.7 \times 60} \times 206265$ minutes

$\qquad = 3.664$ minutes

$\qquad = 38\ 40''$

Corrected observed direction

$$= 92° 46' + 3' 40''$$

$$= 92° 49' 3' 40''$$

$$\therefore \qquad \alpha_3 = \frac{2.18 \times \sin (169° 28') \times 206265}{1852 \times 60}$$

$$= \frac{2.18 \times \sin 10° 32' \times 2.6265}{1852 \times 60}$$

$$= 0.7394 \text{ min}$$

$$= + 44.4 \text{ seconds}$$

$\therefore$ Corrected observed direction = 169° 28' 44.4"

$$\therefore \qquad \alpha_4 = \frac{2.18 \times \sin 264° 44' \times 206265}{2445 \times 60}$$

$$= -\frac{6.54 \times \sin 84° 44' \times 206265}{7335 \times 60}$$

$$= -3' 3.1'' \, (-ve)$$

$\therefore$ Observed correct direction = 264° 44' − 3' 3.1" = 264° 40' 56.9"

THEORETICAL QUESTIONS

1. Define 'Geodetic surveying' and state the object of Geodetic surveying.

2. What is a horizontal control ? Explain in brief the various methods of establishing horizontal controls.

3. Explain in brief the various triangulation figures commonly adopted and compare its merits and demerits.

4. Distinguish between :

   (a) Relative co-ordinates and Absolute co-ordinates.

   (b) Triangulation station and Laplace station.

   (c) Base line and Check base.

5. State the classification and norms of various triangulation systems.

6. Explain briefly the procedure of carrying out triangulation survey.

7. State how triangulation stations are classified.

8. Distinguish between triangulation and precise traversing. State when you will recommend them.

9. Explain the concept of intervisibility and height of triangulation station with neat sketches.

10. Explain Capt. G. T. McCaw's method of ascertaining the intervisibility of two triangulation stations with an intervening peak in between them.

11. Write a note on triangulation station marks.

12. What is the purpose of triangulation in Geodetic surveying ? Explain with sketches the base figures and patterns generally adopted for triangulation network.

13. What are towers in Geodetic Surveying ? Explain Bilby towers.

14. State the methods of measurement of horizontal angles in triangulation survey. State the merits and demerits of each. What is the advantage of closing the horizon in the method of reiteration ? What errors are eliminated by such methods ?

15. What is a base net ?

16. Write short notes on :

    (a) Signals

    (b) Reduction to m.s.l.

    (c) Capt. G. T. McCaw's solution

    (d) Classification of triangulation systems

17. What is the purpose of triangulation ? With the aid of suitable sketches, explain the base figures and patterns generally adopted for triangulation networks.

18. Differentiate between primary, secondary and tertiary triangulation work.

19. How do you determine the intervisibility of triangulation station ?

20. What are the main features of modern theodolite ? Discuss any one brand of modern theodolite.

21. (a) What consideration weighs in deciding the location of triangulation station ?

    (b) What is the difference between the bearing and azimuth of line ?

22. Which triangulation network is better – Geodetic quadrilateral with braced diagonals or polygon with central station ? Why ?

23. Will the azimuth of a line increase or decrease, if you move along it Eastwards ?

24. Which triangulation network is better ?

    (a) Geodetic quadrilateral with braced diagonals or

    (b) Polygon with central station.

25. How would you determine the intervisibility of the triangulation station ?

26. Is triangulation a method of control survey ? Distinguish between a control survey and a detail survey and in the same context elaborate the fundamental principle of surveying.

27. (a) Under what circumstances, triangulation is preferable to traversing ?

    (b) Differentiate between 'grid iron system' and 'central system' of triangulation.

28. What is the purpose of triangulation ? With the aid of suitable sketches, explain the base figures and patterns generally adopted for triangulation network.

NUMERICAL PROBLEMS

1. Two triangulation stations A and B are 60 km apart and have elevations 240 m and 280 m respectively. The intervening ground may be assumed to have a uniform elevation of 200 m. Ascertain the intervisibility of A and B.

   Ans. : 285.39 m; 5.39 height of scaffold.

2. Two triangulation stations A and B are 60 km apart and have elevations of 240 m and 280 m respectively. Find the minimum height of signal required at B so that the line of sight no where be nearer the ground than 2 m. The intervening ground may be assumed to have a uniform elevation of 200 m.

   Ans. : 70.20 m.

3. Two triangulation stations A and B, 120 km apart, have elevations 145 m and 556 m above M.S.L. respectively. An intervening peak P, 72 km from A, has R.L. of 162 m. Ascertain whether B is visible from A. If not, find the minimum height of scaffolding at B so that the line of sight has a clearance of 3 m over the peak at P.

   Ans. : Fails to clear by 3 m, height of scaffold = 10 m.

4.   Elevations of two triangulation stations A and B, 106 km apart, are 132 m and 435 m respectively. A peak C, 80 km from station A, has an elevation of 222.50 m. A is a ground station. Ascertain if it is visible from B or not. Also find the minimum height of scaffolding at B, so that the line of sight has a minimum 3 m clearance anywhere.

Ans. : The line of sight fails to clear the obstructions by 1.80 m. Minimum height of scaffold at B = 6.36 m.

5.   The elevations of two triangulation stations A and B, 100 km apart, are 180 m and 450 m respectively. The intervening obstruction situated at C, 75 km from A has an elevation of 259 m. Ascertain if A and B are intervisible. If not, by how much B should be raised so that the line of sight must no where be less than 3 m above the surface of the ground, assuming A as the ground station ?

Ans. : 7.52 m.

UNIT II

TRIANGULATION ADJUSTMENTS

2.1 INTRODUCTION

The object of Geodetic surveying is to establish a *three-dimensional control*. In order to achieve this object certain linear and angular measurements are to be made. Even if these measurements are made with high degree of precision, some observational (i.e. personal) and instrumental errors are likely to occur. The assessment and distribution of these errors by adopting statistical techniques that forms important part in surveying, is included under "Theory of Errors".

2.2 CLASSIFICATION OF ERRORS

All measurements carried out in Surveying are not free from errors. Some of the common terms used in the theory of errors are as follows :

2.2.1 Definitions of Terms

(i) **(Surveying) Instrument :** It is a device used to determine the value or magnitude of a quantity (or variable) to be measured.

(ii) **Accuracy :** It is defined as 'closeness with which a reading taken with an instrument approaches the true value of the quantity or the variable being measured'. Thus, it refers to the degree of closeness (i.e. conformity) to the true value of the quantity being measured.

(iii) **Precision :** It is a measure of the reproducibility of the measurement i.e. having given a fixed value of a particular variable, a precision is a measure of the degree to which the successive measurement (that are carried out) differ from one another. In other words, precision refers to the degree of agreement within a group of measurements (carried out) or instruments (used).

(iv) **Resolution :** It is defined as 'the smallest change in the measured value of a quantity to which the measuring instrument will quickly respond'.

(v) **Error :** It can be defined as 'the deviation from the true value of the measured quantity or variable'. Several techniques may be adopted to minimize the effects of errors. e.g. while carrying out measurements, it is always advisable to record a series of observations instead of relying on a single observation or different instruments may be used to perform the same observation. However, it is to be clearly understood that even though these techniques (as stated above) ultimately tend to increase the precision of the measured quantity by minimizing environmental or random errors, they certainly cannot account for the instrumental errors (that may arise).

2.2.2 Types of Errors

No measurement can be carried out with cent per cent accuracy. It is important to first determine to what accuracy the measurements are to be carried out and how the various errors enter into the measurement. A close study of such errors is the first wise step in finding the various means and ways to reduce or eliminate them.

Errors arising from different sources are usually classified under the following three categories :

(i) Gross errors or mistakes i.e. human errors.

(ii) Systematic errors that are cumulative in nature.

(iii) Random errors or Accidental errors that are compensating with each other.

(a) Gross Errors :

Gross errors or mistakes are largely due to human error e.g. misreading the instrument, imperfect adjustment and improper application of instrument and also mistakes in computations. Thus, they arise mainly due to carelessness and inexperience on the part of the observer. They can certainly be avoided by taking proper precautions and care and by applying suitable checks and counter checks during linear and angular measurements.

(b) Systematic Errors :

Systematic errors are those errors that will have same magnitude and direction under similar conditions. These errors have constant character and may be positive or negative. If the magnitude and direction of this error remains same throughout, it is called 'constant error'. The causes of systematic errors may be natural, instrumental or observational. They obey certain mathematical and physical laws and are deterministic in nature. Thus, proper corrections can be calculated and applied to the observed quantities to reduce their effect. The following are some of the examples of this type of error.

(a) Incorrect length of tape i.e. which is either too long or too short.

(b) Imperfect markings on the instrument (i.e. unequal graduations).

(c) Temperature, humidity and atmospheric changes that affect accuracy of measurements, and due to change in refractive index.

(d) Personal errors which may be constant, counteracting or erratic. These are environmental errors that are due to conditions external to the measuring devices e.g. effect of changes in temperature, humidity and barometric pressures etc.

(c) Accidental (or Random) Errors :

These errors are due to causes that cannot be directly established because of random variations in the system of measurements or its parameters, e.g. the errors which occur due to imperfect human eye sight, improper manipulation of the instruments etc. and are somewhat uncontrollable and random in behaviour. These errors are present even after all known errors are eliminated. These errors may sometimes be positive and sometimes negative and thus are compensating in nature, an example of this type of error is pull to be applied to the measuring steel or invar tape during measurement so that its length will be exactly equal to its designated length, but the actual pull applied may be sometimes more and sometimes less than the standard pull and the error introduced will be compensating in nature. Thus, such errors obey the laws of probability. All errors, not falling in the first two types, are included in accidental or random errors.

When the measured value of a quantity is more or less than the true value of the quantity, the error is said to be positive or negative respectively and the correction will be negative or positive accordingly.

The errors that will be discussed hereinafter are all accidental (i.e. random) errors that will be applied to the quantities (linear or angular) which are corrected for gross mistakes and systematic errors.

The only effective method to get rid of random errors is by increasing the number of observations and by adoption of statistical methods to obtain the most probable values that are best approximations of the true values of the quantities under measurement.

2.3 DEFINITIONS OF COMMON TERMS

Definitions of some of the terms that will be referred to in the theory of errors are as follows :

(i)　Observed value of a quantity is that value which is obtained after applying corrections for all known errors.

(ii)　True value of a quantity is the one which is absolutely free from all known and unknown errors. This value is indeterministic as all the true errors are not known.

(iii)　Most probable value of quantity (M.P.V.) is the one which is very near to the true value than any other value. It is obtained from the several measurements on which it is based.

(iv)　True error is defined as 'the difference between the true value of the quantity and its observed value'. Since true value of a quantity cannot be obtained, true error cannot be found.

(v)　Residual error is defined as 'the difference between the most probable value of a quantity and its observed value'.

(vi)　Most probable error is defined as 'a quantity to be added to or subtracted from the most probable value of a quantity and it fixes the limits with which the true value of a quantity has a chance to lie'.

(vii) Independent quantity : The observed value of a quantity as defined above, may be independent or conditioned. A quantity which is independent of the values of other quantities i.e. it does not depend upon the value of any other quantity is known as an independent quantity. The best examples of such quantities are reduced levels of various bench marks.

(viii) Conditioned (or dependent) quantity is one that depends upon the values of one or more other quantities. e.g. sum of three angles of a plane triangle ABC to be equal to 180°.

i.e. A + B + C = 180° is a conditional equation that must be satisfied. Thus, any two angles may be taken as independent and the third angle as conditioned or dependent.

(ix)　Observations which denote the numerical values of measured quantities are further classified as direct observations and indirect observations.

(x)　Direct observations are those that are made directly upon a quantity whose value is to be determined.

(xi)　Indirect observations are those that are deduced from some functions of the quantities e.g. measurement of horizontal angle by the method of repetition.

(xii)　Observation equation is the one that establishes relation between the observed quantity and its numerical value.

(xiii) Conditional equation is one that expresses the relation that exists between several dependent quantities.

(xiv) Normal equation is an equation that incorporates the unknown quantity whose most probable value is to be determined. It is obtained by multiplying each observed equation by the product of the coefficient of the unknown and the weight of observation and then by adding the equations thus formed. The number of normal equations to be formed are same as the number of unknowns. The most probable values of the unknowns are then determined by solving these normal equations.

(xv)　Weight of an observation is a measure of its relative trust worthiness or precision as compared to other quantities. If an observation is given weight 3, it indicates that it is three times as much as an observation having weight 1. If all the observations are made with same precision and under similar conditions they are said to have equal precision or equal weight. Otherwise, different weights are to be assigned to the observations and are called weighted observations.

2.4 ACCIDENTAL ERRORS AND THEORY OF PROBABILITY

After all the mistakes and systematic errors are eliminated, the observations may still contain some accidental (i.e. random) errors that obeys the laws of probability (meaning possible variation due to chance). Some of the properties of accidental (i.e. random) errors are as follows :

(i)　Small errors are more frequent than large errors.

(ii)　Positive and negative errors (of the same size) are likely to occur with equal frequency i.e. there probability is equal.

(iii)　Very large errors are not possible i.e. they are improbable.

2.5 CURVE OF ERROR (I.E. PROBABILITY CURVE)

The relative frequencies of errors of different extents that are likely to occur are shown in the form of curve known as *probability curve* or *curve of error*. Such curve shown in Fig. 2.1, forms the basis for the determination of error. For high degree of accuracy, the nature of the curve will be thin having more height; whereas for low degree of accuracy, the curve is flatter and of small height.

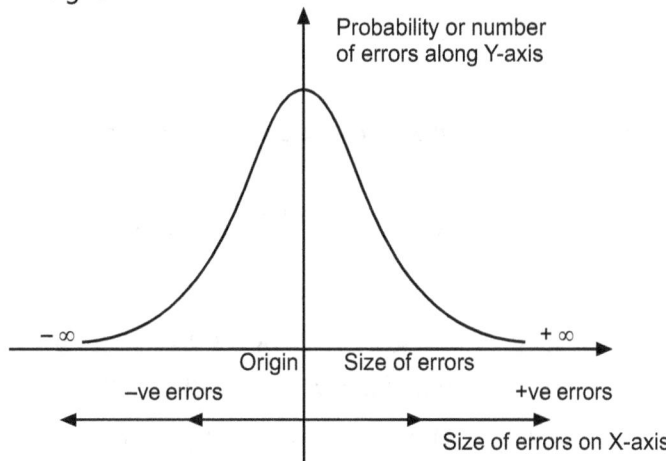

Fig. 2.1 : Probability curve or curve of error

2.6 FORMULAE FOR DETERMINATION OF PROBABLE ERRORS

The various formulae for probable error under different categories are given below :

(a) Direct Observations of Equal Weights :

(i) Probable error (p.e.) of single measurement (or observation) :

$$E_s = \pm 0.6745 \sqrt{\frac{\Sigma (v)^2}{n-1}}$$

where,

E_s = Probable error of single measurement or observation

Σv^2 = Summation of squares of residual error

v = Difference between any single observation and the average (or mean) of the series

n = Number of observations in series

(ii) Probable error of arithmetic mean (or average) of n measurements :

$$E_m = \frac{\sqrt{n}}{n} \times \text{Probable error of single measurement}$$

$$= \frac{\sqrt{n}}{n} \times 0.6745 \times \sqrt{\frac{\Sigma (v^2)}{n-1}} = 0.6745 \times \sqrt{\frac{(\Sigma v^2)}{n(n-1)}} = \frac{E_s}{\sqrt{n}}$$

where E_m = Probable error of the mean or average

and E_s = Probable error of single measurement

(b) Direct Observations of Unequal Weights :

    (i)   **The probable error of a single observation of weight equal to one :**

$$E_{s_u} = 0.6745 \times \sqrt{\frac{(\Sigma\, wv^2)}{n-1}}$$

    (ii)   **Probable error of any observation of weight w :**

$$p \cdot e = \frac{E_{s_u}}{\sqrt{w}}$$

    (iii)   **Probable error of weighted arithmetic average or mean :**

$$E_m = \frac{E_{s_u}}{\sqrt{\Sigma\, w}} = 0.6745 \times \sqrt{\frac{\Sigma\,(wv^2)}{\Sigma\, w\,(n-1)}}$$

where w = Weight of an observation

                      n = Number of times the observations are taken

            $\Sigma\, w$ = Sum of the weights of observations

and $\Sigma\, wv^2$ = Summation of the weighted squares of residual error

(c) Probable Error of a Sum :

Here probable error of measurement $= \sqrt{E_1^2 + E_2^2 + E_3^2 + \ldots\ldots + E_n^2}$, where E_1, E_2, E_3, $\ldots\ldots$ etc. are probable errors of n observations.

Example 2.1 : The following are six equally reliable and direct measurements of a base line.

702.0 m, 701.4 m, 701.8 m, 701.6 m, 701.5 m and 701.9 m

Calculate the most probable value and its probable error.

Solution :

Observed value	Arithmetic mean	Residual error	(Residual error)^2
702.00 m		+ 0.30	+ 0.09
701.40 m		− 0.30	+ 0.09
701.80 m		+ 0.10	+ 0.01
701.60 m	701.70 m	− 0.10	+ 0.01
701.50 m		− 0.20	+ 0.04
701.90 m		+ 0.20	+ 0.04
		$\Sigma v = 0$	$\Sigma v^2 = 0.28$

∴   Probable error of single observation

$$= 0.6745 \times \sqrt{\frac{\Sigma v^2}{n-1}} = 0.6745 \times \sqrt{\frac{0.28}{6-1}} = E_s = 0.1596$$

∴   Probable error of arithmetic mean

$$= \frac{E_s}{\sqrt{n}} = E_m = \frac{0.1596}{\sqrt{6}} = 0.06516$$

∴   Most probable value of the base line

$$= 701.70 \pm E_m = (701.70 \pm 0.06516) \text{ m}$$

Example 2.2 : Find the probable error in the area of a circle whose radius is 30 m ± 0.01 m.

Solution :   Area of circle $= x = \pi a^2$

∴ $e_x = e_a \cdot \dfrac{dx}{da}$

where, $e_a = \pm 0.01 \text{ m}$

     $x = \pi \times (30)^2 = 2827.5 \text{ m}^2$

∴ $\dfrac{dx}{da} = 2\pi x = 2 \times \pi \times 30$

∴ $e_x = e_a \cdot \dfrac{dx}{da} = 0.01 \times (2\pi \times 30) = 0.01 \times (2\pi \times 30)$

     $= 1.88$

∴   Probable error $= \pm 1.88 \text{ mm}$

Example 2.3 : The following are observed values of an angle.

Angle	Weight
40° 20' 20"	2
40° 20' 18"	2
40° 20' 19"	3

Find :
(i)   Probable error of single observation (of unit weight).
(ii) Probable error of weighted arithmetic mean.
(iii) Probable error of single observation of weight 3.

Solution :

Obs. Value	Weight, w	Obs. Value × Weight
20"	2	40"
18"	2	36"
19"	3	57"
	Σ w = 7	Σ (Obs. value × Weight) = 133"

Weighted arithmetic mean of the seconds reading of the observed angles = $133'' \div 7 = 19''$

Residual error for 1st observation = $v_1 = 20'' - 19'' = 1''$

Residual error for 2nd observation = $v_2 = 18'' - 19'' = -1''$

Residual error for 3rd observation = $v_3 = 19'' - 19'' = 0''$

Obs. No.	Weight, w	Residual error, v	v^2	$w \cdot v^2$
1.	2	1"	1	2
2.	2	–1"	1	2
3.	3	0	0	0
	$\Sigma w = 7$			$\Sigma (w \cdot v^2) = 4$

Now working out probable error (p.e.)

(i) Probable error (p.e.) of single observation of unit weight

$$= E_{su} = \pm 0.6745 \sqrt{\frac{\Sigma (w \cdot v^2)}{(n - 1)}}$$

Here = n = Number of observations = 3.

$\therefore$

$$E_{su} = \pm 0.6745 \sqrt{\frac{4}{(3 - 1)}} = \pm 0.6745 \sqrt{2} = \pm 0.95$$

(ii) Probable error (p.e.) of weighted arithmetic mean,

$$E_m = \pm 0.6745 \sqrt{\frac{\Sigma (w \cdot v^2)}{(\Sigma w) \cdot (n - 1)}}$$

$$= \pm 0.6745 \sqrt{\frac{4}{(7) \cdot (3 - 1)}} \pm 0.36$$

(iii) Probable error (p.e.) of single observation of weight 3.

We know probable error (p.e.) of single observation of weight w, $E_{sw} = \dfrac{E_{su}}{\sqrt{w}}$

Probable error (p.e.) of single observation of weight 3 = $E_{s3} = \dfrac{0.95}{\sqrt{3}} = 0.55$

2.7 MOST PROBABLE VALUE (M.P.V.)

The most probable value of a quantity is one which is very near to the true value than any other value. It has very bright chances of being true value than any other value.

(i) Rules for the Determination of Most Probable Values of Quantities :

(a) In case of direct observations of equal weights, the most probable value of a quantity is equal to the arithmetic mean or average of the observed values.

(b) In case of direct observations of unequal weights, the most probable value of a quantity is equal to the weighted arithmetic mean of the observed values.

The above two rules are based upon the *'principle of least squares'*.

(ii) Principle of Least Squares :

Case (a) Direct observations of equal precision (or weight) : The fundamental principle of the method of least squares states that in case of direct observations of equal precision (or weight), the most probable values of the quantities are those that render the sum of the squares of the residual errors to a minimum.

Let m = Required most probable value of a quantity and let $Z_1, Z_2, Z_3, \ldots$ upto Z_n be the observed values of quantities. Then residual error (e) for the above can be written as :

$$e_1 = m - Z_1$$
$$e_2 = m - Z_2$$
$$e_3 = m - Z_3$$
$$\text{----------------}$$
$$\text{----------------}$$
$$e_n = m - Z_n$$

Adding above results, it can be written as

$$e_1 + e_2 + e_3 + \ldots + e_n = n \cdot m - (Z_1 + Z_2 + Z_3 + \ldots + Z_n)$$

i.e.
$$\Sigma e = n \cdot m - \Sigma Z$$

or
$$m = \frac{\Sigma Z}{n} + \frac{\Sigma e}{n} \qquad \ldots (2.1)$$

But
$$\frac{Z_1 + Z_2 + Z_3 + \ldots + Z_n}{n} = \text{Arithmetic mean} = Z_m \text{ (say)}.$$

$\therefore$
$$\frac{\Sigma Z}{n} = Z_m \qquad \ldots (2.2)$$

$\therefore$ Putting the value of (2.2) in equation (2.1), we get,

$$m = Z_m + \frac{\Sigma e}{n} \qquad \ldots (2.3)$$

Now, if n i.e. number of observations are sufficiently large and e is kept very small because of precise measurements, then $\frac{\Sigma e}{n}$ becomes negligible with respect to Z_m.

Hence
$$m = Z_m = \text{Arithmetic mean} \qquad \ldots (2.4)$$

Thus, the arithmetic mean is the most probable value, provided the number of observations are very large.

Now let $r_1, r_2, r_3, \ldots, r_n$ are the residual errors, where residual error is the difference between the mean value and the observed values.

Then
$$\left.\begin{array}{l} r_1 = Z_m - Z_1 \\ r_2 = Z_m - Z_2 \\ r_3 = Z_m - Z_3 \\ \text{----------------} \\ \text{----------------} \\ r_n = Z_m - Z_n \end{array}\right\} \qquad \ldots (2.5)$$

Adding we have, $nZ_m - \Sigma Z = \Sigma r$

or
$$Z_m = \frac{\Sigma Z}{n} + \frac{\Sigma r}{n}$$

But
$$\frac{\Sigma Z}{n} = Z_m$$

$\therefore$
$$Z_m = Z_m + \frac{\Sigma r}{n}$$

i.e.
$$\frac{\Sigma r}{n} = 0$$

i.e. the summation of residual errors is zero.   ... (2.6)

Now if P is any value of the unknown other than the arithmetic mean (Z_m), then,

$$\left.\begin{array}{l} P - Z_1 = r_1' \\ P - Z_2 = r_2' \\ P - Z_3 = r_3' \\ \text{------------} \\ \text{------------} \\ P - Z_n = r_n' \end{array}\right\} \qquad ... (2.7)$$

Squaring the above equations and adding we have,

$$\Sigma r'^2 = nP^2 + \Sigma Z^2 - 2P \Sigma Z \qquad ... (2.8)$$

Similarly, squaring the equation (2.6) and adding, we have,

$$\Sigma r^2 = nZ_m^2 + \Sigma Z^2 - 2Z_m \Sigma Z \qquad ... (2.9)$$

Now writing $n \cdot Z_m = \Sigma Z$ in equation (2.9),

$$\Sigma r^2 = Z_m \Sigma Z - 2Z_m \Sigma Z + \Sigma Z^2$$
$$= \Sigma Z^2 - Z_m \Sigma Z$$
$$= \Sigma Z^2 - \frac{\Sigma Z}{n} \cdot \Sigma Z \qquad \left[\because \frac{\Sigma Z}{n} = Z_m\right]$$

$\therefore$
$$\Sigma r^2 = \Sigma Z^2 - \frac{\Sigma Z^2}{n}$$

or
$$\Sigma Z^2 = \Sigma r^2 + \frac{\Sigma Z^2}{n}$$

Putting this value in equation (2.8),

$$\Sigma r'^2 = \left[nP^2 + \left(\Sigma r^2 + \frac{\Sigma Z^2}{n}\right) - 2P \Sigma Z\right]$$

$\therefore$
$$\Sigma r'^2 = \Sigma r^2 + n\left[P^2 - 2P\frac{\Sigma Z}{n} + \frac{\Sigma Z}{n^2}\right]$$

$\therefore$
$$\Sigma r'^2 = \Sigma r^2 + n\left[P - \frac{\Sigma Z}{n}\right]^2$$

In the above equation, as the term $\left(P - \dfrac{\Sigma\,Z}{n}\right)^2$ is always positive, value of $\Sigma\ r^2$ will be always less than $\Sigma\ r'^2$ i.e. the sum of the squares of the residual errors found by using arithmetic mean is minimum, which is the fundamental principle of least squares.

2.8 ASSIGNMENT OF WEIGHTAGE TO AN OBSERVATION

Assuming that all the observations are carried out under more or less similar conditions, the following rules may be adopted for assigning weightages to the observations.

(i)   In case of angular observations, its weight varies directly with the number of observations made for the measurement of that angle.

(ii) In case of linear measurements (horizontal or vertical), the weights vary inversely as the lengths of various routes.

(iii) In case of angle measured a large number of times, its weight is inversely proportional to the square of probable error.

(iv) Corrections to the observed quantities are inversely proportional to their weights.

2.9 LAWS OF WEIGHTS

The laws of weights as established by the method of least squares are as follows :

Law (i) : The weight of the arithmetic mean of several observations of unit weight is equal to the number of observations.

Example 2.4 : The following are the values of the angle B, measured five times. Calculate its weight.

$$\angle B \ = \ 23°\ 12'\ 10''$$
$$\angle B \ = \ 23°\ 12'\ 12''$$
$$\angle B \ = \ 23°\ 12'\ 14''$$
$$\angle B \ = \ 23°\ 12'\ 08''$$
$$\angle B \ = \ 23°\ 12'\ 16''$$

∴   Arithmetic mean is 23° 12' 12" and as the number of observations are 5, the weight of arithmetic mean = 5.

Law (ii) : The weight of weighted arithmetic mean of several observations is equal to the sum of the individual weights of observation.

Example 2.5 : The weights of the weighted arithmetic means of observations are as follows. Calculate its weight.

$$\angle B \ = \ 41°\ 20'\ 10'' \qquad \text{Weight} \ = \ 1$$
$$\angle B \ = \ 41°\ 20'\ 11'' \qquad \text{Weight} \ = \ 2$$
$$\angle B \ = \ 41°\ 20'\ 14'' \qquad \text{Weight} \ = \ 4$$

∴　　Weight of weighted arithmetic mean

$$= \text{Sum of individual weights}$$

$$= 1 + 2 + 4 = 7$$

and Weighted arithmetic mean

$$= \frac{1}{7}\left[1 \times 41° \ 20' \ 10" + 2 \times 41° \ 20' \ 11" + 4 \times 41° \ 20' \ 14"\right]$$

$$= 41° \ 20' \ 11"$$

∴　　Weighted arithmetic mean is 41° 20' 11" and its weight is 7.

Law (iii) : In case two or more quantities are added algebraically, the weight of the algebraic result is equal to the reciprocal of the sum of the reciprocal of individual weights.

Example 2.6 : Let　　∠A　=　30° 30' 14"　　Weight　= 5

∠B　=　20° 10' 10"　　Weight　= 2

Then　　Weight of A + B = 50° 40' 24" $= \left[\dfrac{1}{\dfrac{1}{5} + \dfrac{1}{2}}\right] = \dfrac{10}{7}$

and　　Weight of A − B = 10° 20' 04" $= \left[\dfrac{1}{\dfrac{1}{5} + \dfrac{1}{2}}\right] = \dfrac{10}{7}$

Law (iv) : Weight of a quantity multiplied by a factor is equal to the weight of that quantity divided by the square of the multiplying factor.

Example 2.7 : If　　∠A　=　20° 12' 10"　　Weight　= 3

then　　Weight of 2 (A) 7= 40° 24' 20" $= \dfrac{3}{2^2} = \dfrac{3}{4}$

Law (v) : Weight of a quantity divided by a factor is equal to the weight of that quantity multiplied by the square of the dividing factor.

Example 2.8 : If　　∠A　=　93° 39' 42"　　Weight　= 4

then　　Weight of $\dfrac{A}{3}$ = 31° 13' 14" = $4 \times (3)^2$ = 36

Law (vi) : In case of equation multiplied by its (own) weight, the weight of the resulting equation will be the reciprocal of the weight of the equation.

Example 2.9 : Let　　A + B　=　100° 30' 20"　　Weight　= $\dfrac{2}{5}$

then　　Weight of $\dfrac{2}{5}$ (A + B) = 40° 12' 08" = $\dfrac{1}{\dfrac{2}{5}} = \dfrac{5}{2}$

Law (vii) : The weight of an equation remains same if all the signs of terms in equation are changed or even if the equation is added to or subtracted from a constant.

Example 2.10 : Let $A + B = 60° 10'$ Weight $= 2$

then   Weight of $180 - (A + B) = 119° 50' = 2$

2.10 MOST PROBABLE VALUES OF OBSERVED QUANTITIES (i.e. M.P.V.)

The various cases for which the M.P.V. are determined are as follows :

(i)   Direct observations of quantities of equal weights.

(ii)   Direct observations of quantities of unequal weights.

(iii) Indirect observations of quantities of equal weights.

(iv)   Indirect observations of quantities of unequal weights.

(v)   Dependent or conditioned quantities.

2.10 (i) Direct Observations of Quantities of Equal Weights

As per the principle of least squares, the most probable values of direct observations of equal weight are those that make the sum of the square of the residual errors to a minimum.

Let $Z_1, Z_2, Z_3, ..., Z_n$ be the observed values of the quantities and let M be the required most probable value of the quantity. Then the respective residual errors would be :

$$M - Z_1 = e_1$$
$$M - Z_2 = e_2$$
$$------- = ---$$
$$M - Z_n = e_n$$

Then as per the principle of least squares,

$$e_1^2 + e_2^2 + e_3^2 + ... + e_n^2 = \text{minimum}$$

$\therefore$ $(M - Z_1)^2 + (M - Z_2)^2 + ... + (M - Z_n)^2 = \text{minimum}$

For this value to be minimum, its differentiation w.r.t. M is to be equated to zero.

$\therefore$ $(M - Z_1) + (M - Z_2) + ... + (M - Z_n) = 0$

or $n \cdot M = (Z_1 + Z_2 + Z_3 + ... + Z_n)$

$\therefore$ Most probable value $= M = \left[\dfrac{Z_1 + Z_2 + Z_3 + ... + Z_n}{n}\right]$

i.e. the most probable value of the observed quantities (of equal weights) is equal to the Arithmetic mean of the observed quantities and the weight of the arithmetic mean is equal to n, the number of observations.

2.10 (ii) Direct Observations of Unequal Weights

As per the principle of least squares, the most probable value of observations of unequal weight (or precision) are those that make the sum of the weighted squares of residual errors to a minimum.

Let Z_1, Z_2, Z_3, ..., Z_n be the observed quantities of weights W_1, W_2, W_3, ..., W_n respectively.

Let m be the required most probable value of the observed quantities.

Then the respective residual errors would be

$$M - Z_1 = e_1$$
$$M - Z_2 = e_2$$
$$M - Z_3 = e_3$$
$$\text{----------------------}$$
$$\text{----------------------}$$
$$M - Z_n = e_n$$

∴   As per the principle of least squares,

$$W_1 e_1^2 + W_2 e_2^2 + W_3 e_3^2 + ... + W_n e_n^2 = \text{minimum}$$

$$W_1 (M - Z_1)^2 + W_2 (M - Z_2)^2 + W_3 (M - Z_3)^2 + ... + W_n (M - Z_n)^2 = \text{minimum}$$

∴   Differentiating and equating to zero (for minimum),

i.e. $W_1 (M - Z_1) + W_2 (M - Z_2) + W_3 (M - Z_3) + ... + W_n (M - Z_n) = 0$

or $M = \dfrac{W_1 Z_1 + W_2 Z_2 + W_3 Z_3 + ... + W_n Z_n}{W_1 + W_2 + W_3 + ... + W_n}$

i.e. The most probable value of the observed quantities of unequal weights will be equal to the weighted arithmetic mean of the observed values of quantities and weight of weighted arithmetic mean = Summation of the weights = $W_1 + W_2 + ... + W_n = \Sigma W$.

2.10 (iii) Indirect Observations of Equal Weights

In this case the most probable values of the unknowns are determined by the method of normal equations. In order to form a normal equation, multiply each of the observed equation by the algebraic coefficient of the unknown and add all such results.

Example 2.11 : Calculate the most probable value of angle A from the following :

(i)   A = 12° 10' 12"

(ii)   2A = 24° 20' 26"

(iii)   4A = 48° 40' 50"

Solution : First step is to form normal equation

∴ $1 \times (A) = 12° 10' 12"$

                      $2 \times (2A) = 48° 40' 52"$

                      $4 \times (4A) = 194° 43' 20"$

Adding $21 A = 255° 34' 24"$

∴ $A = 12° 10' 12.57"$

Example 2.12 : Determine the most probable values of the angles P and Q from the following observations :

$$P = 24°\ 12'\ 16''$$
$$Q = 32°\ 14'\ 20''$$
$$P + Q = 56°\ 26'\ 40''$$

Solution : The first step is to form normal equations in P and Q.

To form normal equation in P,

$$1 \times P = 24°\ 12'\ 16''$$
$$\underline{1 \times (P + Q) = 56°\ 26'\ 40''}$$

Adding $2P + Q = 80°\ 38'\ 56''$ Normal equation in A   ... (i)

To form normal equation in Q,

$$1 \times Q = 32°\ 14'\ 20''$$
$$\underline{1 \times (P + Q) = 56°\ 26'\ 40''}$$

Adding $P + 2Q = 88°\ 41'\ 00''$ Normal equation in B   ... (ii)

Thus, we have two unknowns and two equations which are to be solved as follows :

$$2P + Q = 80°\ 38'\ 56''$$
$$\underline{2P + 4Q = 177°\ 22'\ 00''}\quad \text{After multiplying equation (ii) by 2}$$

Subtracting $3Q = 96°\ 43'\ 04''$

∴ $Q = 32°\ 14'\ 21.33''$

∴ $2P = 80°\ 38'\ 56'' - 32°\ 14'\ 21.33''$
$$= 48°\ 24'\ 34.67''$$

∴ $P = 24°\ 12'\ 17.335''$

and $Q = 32°\ 14'\ 21.33''$

2.10 (iv) Indirect Observations of Unequal Weights

In order to form normal equation, multiply each of the observed equation by the product of the algebraic coefficient of the unknown and the weight of the observation and add all such results.

Example 2.13 : Calculate the most probable values of angles from the following :

$$P = 16°\ 10'\ 12'' \quad \text{Weight 1}$$
$$2P = 32°\ 20'\ 26'' \quad \text{Weight 2}$$
$$4P = 64°\ 40'\ 50'' \quad \text{Weight 4}$$

Solution : The first step is to form a normal equation

$$(1 \times 1)\ (P) = 16°\ 10'\ 12''$$
$$(2 \times 2)\ (2P) = 4\ (32°\ 20'\ 26'')$$
$$\underline{(4 \times 4)\ (4P) = 16\ (64°\ 40'\ 50'')}$$

Adding $73\ A = 1180°\ 25'\ 16''$

∴ $A = 16°\ 10'\ 12.548''$

Example 2.14 : Find the most probable values of angles A and B from the following observations :

$$A = 57° 25' 35" \quad \text{Weight 1}$$
$$B = 31° 23' 30" \quad \text{Weight 2}$$
$$A + B = 88° 48' 57" \quad \text{Weight 1}$$

Solution : Given :

$$A = 57° 25' 35" \quad \text{Weight 1}$$
$$B = 31° 23' 30" \quad \text{Weight 2}$$
$$A + B = 88° 48' 57" \quad \text{Weight 1}$$

Let C_1, C_2 be the corrections to be applied to angles A and B so that the most probable values of A and B will be

$$A = 57° 25' 35" + C_1$$
$$B = 31° 23' 30" + C_2$$

Now,   Actual sum of $A + B$ = 88° 49' 05"

But,   Observed sum = 88° 48' 57" (Given)

∴   Discrepancy = 8"

∴ By normal equation method,

$$C_1 = 0$$
$$2C_2 = 0$$
$$C_1 + C_2 = 8"$$

∴ Normal equation in C_1

$$C_1 = 0$$
$$\underline{C_1 + C_2 = 8"}$$

∴   Adding $2C_1 + C_2 = 8"$ ... (i)

  Normal equation in C_2

$$2C_2 = 0$$
$$\underline{C_1 + C_2 = 8"}$$

∴   Adding $C_1 + 3C_2 = 8"$ ... (ii)

Solving equations (i) and (ii),

$$2C_1 + C_2 = 8"$$

and $C_1 + 3C_2 = 8"$

∴ $2C_1 + C_2 = 8"$

∴ $\underline{2C_1 + 6C_2 = 16}$

∴ Subtracting, $-5C_2 = -8"$

∴ $C_2 = 1.6"$

∴　　Substituting in equation (ii), we get,

$$C_1 = 8'' - 3C_2$$
$$= 8'' - 3 \times 1.6''$$

∴　　　　　　　　$$C_1 = 3.2''$$

and　　　　　　　$$C_2 = 1.6''$$

∴　　Most probable values are

$$A = 57° 25' 35'' - C_1$$
$$= 57° 25' 31.8''$$
$$B = 31° 23' 30'' - C_2$$
$$= 31° 23' 28.4''$$

2.10 (v) Dependent or Conditioned Quantities

If in a given set of observations, there exists one or more conditional equations, then the most possible values of the unknowns can be found out by any one of the following methods :

Method 1 : The first step is to avoid the conditioned equations and then to form the normal equations of the unknowns as usual.

Method 2 : In this case, the observation equations are avoided first and then the unknown quantities are found out by any one of the following methods.

(a)　By the method of differences or corrections, and

(b)　By the method of correlatives or correlates.

(a) Method of Differences (or Corrections) :

As the number of unknowns go on increasing, the 'normal equation' method as explained above becomes tedious and difficult as the normal equations will have large unknowns. In such case, the solution of the problem by the method of corrections becomes easy i.e. the most probable values of these respective corrections are determined first and then the most probable values of the required quantities are found out by applying the above corrections.

Example 2.15 : Based on method of difference or corrections, adjust the angles of the triangle ABC from the following :

$$\angle A = 77° 14' 20'' \quad \text{Weight 4}$$
$$\angle B = 49° 40' 35'' \quad \text{Weight 3}$$
$$\angle C = 53° 04' 52'' \quad \text{Weight 2}$$

Solution : Method 1 : Let us write the condition as

$$A + B + C = 180°$$

∴　　　　　　　$$C = 180° - (A + B)$$

∴ $A + B = 180° - C$

                                $= 180° - 53° 04' 52"$

∴ $A + B = 126° 55' 08"$

∴   After eliminating the condition equation C, we have,

                    $\angle A = 77°14' 20"$ Weight 4

                    $\angle B = 49° 40' 35"$ Weight 3

                    $A + B = 126° 55' 08"$ Weight 2

Let C_A and C_B be the corrections to the angles A and B.

∴   The most probable values of A, B and A + B will be

                    $A = 77° 14' 20" + C_A$

∴ $C_A = 0$ Weight 4

                    $B = 49° 40' 35" + C_B$

∴ $C_B = 0$ Weight 3

and $A + B = 126° 54' 55" + C_A + C_B$

i.e. $126° 55' 08" = 126° 54' 55" + C_A + C_B$

∴ $C_A + C_B = 13"$ Weight 2

∴   We have, $C_A = 0$ Weight 4

                              $C_B = 0$ Weight 3

                    $C_A + C_B = 13"$ Weight 2

∴   Normal equation in C_A

                    $4C_A + 2C_A + 2C_B = 26$

i.e. $6C_A + 2C_B = 26$ ... (i)

                    Normal equation in C_B

                    $3C_B + 2C_A + 2C_B = 26$

i.e. $2C_A + 5C_B = 26$ ... (ii)

∴   Multiplying the equation (ii) by 3, and subtracting equation (i) from this product,
we have,

                    $6C_A + 2C_B = 26$

                    $\underline{6C_A + 15C_B = 78}$

            Subtracting $13C_B = 52$

∴ $C_B = 4"$

∴ $6C_A + 8 = 26$

∴ $C_A = 3"$

∴   The most probable values of A, B will be

$$A = 77° 14' 20'' + 3''$$
$$= 77° 14' 23''$$
$$B = 49° 40' 35'' + 4''$$
$$= 49° 40' 39''$$

∴

$$C = 180° - (A + B)$$
$$= 180° - (77° 14' 23'' + 49° 40' 39'')$$
$$= 180° - 126° 55' 02''$$
$$= 53° 04' 58''$$

Check : $A + B + C = 77° 14' 23'' + 49° 40' 39'' + 53° 04' 58''$
$$= 180° 00' 00''$$

Method 2 : The problem can also be solved by the laws of weights which states that the corrections are inversely proportional to their weights.

i.e.   Sum of $A + B + C = 179° 59' 47''$

But   the theoretical sum $= 180° 00' 00''$

∴   Discrepancy $= -13''$

∴   Correction $= +13''$

Let C_A, C_B, C_C be the corrections to the angles A, B, C respectively.

∴

$$C_A : C_B : C_C = \frac{1}{W_A} : \frac{1}{W_B} : \frac{1}{W_C}$$
$$= \frac{1}{4} : \frac{1}{3} : \frac{1}{2}$$
$$= 3 : 4 : 6 \quad \text{By L.C.M.}$$

∴

$$C_A = \frac{3}{13} \times 13'' = 3'' (+ve)$$

$$C_B = \frac{4}{13} \times 13'' = 4'' (+ve)$$

and

$$C_C = \frac{6}{13} \times 13'' = 6'' (+ve)$$

∴   The most probable values of A, B, C will be

$$A = 77° 14' 20'' + 3'' = 77° 14' 23''$$
$$B = 49° 40' 35'' + 4'' = 49° 40' 39''$$
$$C = 53° 04' 52'' + 6'' = 53° 04' 58''$$

Check : $A + B + C = 180° 00' 00''$

Example 2.16 : Example on method 1 : Adjust the following angles A, B, C at a station, the condition being A + B = C.

$$A = 50° 11' 25" \quad \text{Weight 6}$$
$$B = 20° 45' 19" \quad \text{Weight 4}$$
$$C = 70° 56' 54" \quad \text{Weight 1}$$

Solution : The first step is to avoid the conditional equation C by writing it equal to A + B.

∴

$$A = 50° 11' 25" \quad \text{Weight 6}$$
$$B = 20° 45' 19" \quad \text{Weight 4}$$
$$A + B = 70° 56' 44" \quad \text{Weight 1}$$

To form normal equation in A,

∴

$$6A = 301° 08' 30"$$
$$A + B = 70° 56' 54"$$

Adding $\qquad$ $7A + B = 372° 05' 24"$

To form normal equation in B,

$$4B = 83° 01' 16"$$
$$A + B = 70° 56' 54"$$

Adding $\qquad$ $A + 5B = 153° 58' 10"$

∴　　We have two equations and two unknowns, which can be solved to get the values of

$$A = 50° 11' 8.5"$$
$$B = 20° 45' 24.3"$$
$$C = 70° 56' 32.8"$$

Check : $\qquad$ $A + B = C$

Example 2.17 : Adjust the following station observations

$$A = 34° 18' 20.4" \quad \text{Weight 1}$$
$$B = 28° 32' 12.8" \quad \text{Weight 2}$$
$$C = 22° 48' 32.6" \quad \text{Weight 2}$$
$$A + B = 62° 50' 29.6" \quad \text{Weight 2}$$
$$A + B + C = 85° 39' 8.6" \quad \text{Weight 1}$$

Solution : By the method of corrections : Let C_A, C_B, C_C be the corrections to angles A, B, C respectively.

$\therefore$

$$C_A = 0 \qquad \text{Weight 1}$$
$$C_B = 0 \qquad \text{Weight 2}$$
$$C_C = 0 \qquad \text{Weight 2}$$
$$C_A + C_B = -3.6" \qquad \text{Weight 2}$$
$$C_A + C_B + C_C = +2.8" \qquad \text{Weight 1}$$

$\therefore$ Normal equation in C_A :

$$C_A = 0$$
$$2(C_A + C_B) = -7.20"$$
$$\underline{(C_A + C_B + C_C) = 2.8"}$$

Adding $\qquad 4C_A + 3C_B + C_C = -4.40"$ ... (i)

$\therefore$ Normal equation in C_B :

$$2C_B = 0$$
$$2(C_A + C_B) = -7.20"$$
$$\underline{(C_A + C_B + C_C) = +2.8"}$$

Adding $\qquad 3C_A + 5C_B + C_C = -4.40"$ ... (ii)

$\therefore$ Normal equation in C_C :

$$2C_C = 0$$
$$\underline{C_A + C_B + C_C = +2.8"}$$

Adding $\qquad C_A + C_B + 3C_C = +2.8"$ ... (iii)

$\therefore$ Equating (i) and (ii), both being equal to 4.40",

$\therefore \qquad 4C_A + 3C_B + C_C = 3C_A + 5C_B + C_C$

$\therefore \qquad C_A = 2C_B$

$\therefore$ Putting this value in (i), (ii) and (iii) above, we get,

$$8C_B + 3C_B + C_C = -4.40"$$

i.e. $\qquad 11C_B + C_C = -4.40"$

and $\qquad 2C_B + C_B + 3C_C = 2.8"$

i.e. $\qquad 3C_B + 3C_C = 2.8"$

$\therefore \qquad 33C_B + 3C_C = -13.2"$

and $\qquad \underline{3C_B + 3C_C = 2.8"}$

Subtracting $\qquad 30C_B = -16"$

$\therefore \qquad C_B = -\dfrac{16}{30} = -0.533"$

$\therefore \qquad 3 \times \dfrac{16}{30} + 3C_C = 2.80$

$\therefore \qquad C_C = -1.47"$

$\therefore \qquad C_A = -1.066"$

∴　　The most probable values of A, B and C are :

$$A = 34° 18' 20.4'' - 1.066'' = 34° 18' 19.334''$$

$$B = 28° 32' 12.8'' - 0.533'' = 28° 32' 12.267''$$

$$C = 22° 48' 32.6'' - 1.47'' = 22° 48' 31.13''$$

Example 2.18 : The following angles of different weights, close the horizon. Determine their M.P.Vs.

$$A = 69° 59' 30'' \quad \text{Weight 1}$$

$$B = 70° 59' 33'' \quad \text{Weight 2}$$

$$C = 71° 59' 33'' \quad \text{Weight 3}$$

$$D = 72° 59' 34'' \quad \text{Weight 4}$$

$$E = 73° 59' 35'' \quad \text{Weight 5}$$

Solution :　　　　　Sum　=　359° 57' 43''

But the theoretical sum　=　360° 00' 00''

∴　　　　Discrepancy　=　2' 17'' = 137''

∴　　　　Correction　=　+137''

∴ $C_A : C_B : C_C : C_D : C_E = \dfrac{1}{1} : \dfrac{1}{2} : \dfrac{1}{3} : \dfrac{1}{4} : \dfrac{1}{5}$

$$= 60 : 30 : 20 : 15 : 12$$

∴ 　　　$C_A = \dfrac{60}{137} \times 137 = +60''$

$$C_B = \dfrac{30}{137} \times 137 = +30''$$

$$C_C = \dfrac{20}{137} \times 137 = +20''$$

$$C_D = \dfrac{15}{137} \times 137 = +15''$$

$$C_E = \dfrac{12}{137} \times 137 = +12''$$

∴　　Most probable values are :

70° 00' 30'', 71° 00' 01'', 71° 59' 53'', 72° 59' 49'', 73° 59' 47''

Example 2.19 : Summation on adjustment : Adjust the angles at a station given below :

$$A = 42° 20' 10" \quad \text{Weight 2}$$
$$B = 22° 10' 12" \quad \text{Weight 1}$$
$$C = 14° 20' 14" \quad \text{Weight 3}$$
$$A + B = 64° 30' 24" \quad \text{Weight 2}$$
$$B + C = 36° 30' 30" \quad \text{Weight 1}$$

Solution : (I) By normal equation method :

To form the normal equation in A :

$$2 \times 1A = 2 \times (42° 20' 10") = 84° 40' 20"$$
$$2 \times 1 \times (A + B) = 2 \times (64° 30' 24") = 129° 0' 48"$$

Adding $\quad 4A + 2B = 213° 41' 8"$ ... (i)

To form normal equation in B :

$$1 \times 1 \times B = 22° 10' 12"$$
$$2 \times 1 \times (A + B) = 129° 0' 48"$$
$$1 \times 1 \times (B + C) = 36° 30' 30"$$

Adding $\quad 2A + 4B + C = 187° 41' 30"$ ... (ii)

To form normal equation in C :

$$3 \times 1 \times C = 3 \times (14° 20' 14") = 43° 0' 42"$$
$$1 \times 1 \times (B + C) = 1 \times (36° 30' 30") = 36° 30' 30"$$

Adding $\quad B + 4C = 79° 31' 12"$ ... (iii)

The normal equations formed are :

$$2A + B = 106° 50' 34" \qquad \text{... (iv)}$$
$$2A + 4B + C = 187° 41' 30" \qquad \text{... (v)}$$
$$B + 4C = 79° 31' 12" \qquad \text{... (vi)}$$

Subtracting equation (iv) from equation (v), we get,

$$3B + C = 80° 50' 56"$$
$$3B + 12C = 238° 33' 36" \text{ (Multiplying equation (vi) by 3)}$$

Subtracting $\quad -11C = -157° 42' 40"$

∴ $\quad C = 14° 20' 14.5"$

Putting value of C in equation (vi),

$$B + 4 \times (14° \ 20' \ 14.5") = 79° \ 31' \ 12"$$

$$\therefore \qquad\qquad B = 22° \ 10' \ 13.8"$$

Putting value of B in equation (iv),

$$2A + 22° \ 10' \ 13.8" = 106° \ 50' \ 34"$$

$$A = 42° \ 20' \ 10.1"$$

$\therefore$　　Most probable values will be :

$$A = 42° \ 20' \ 10.1"$$
$$B = 22° \ 10' \ 13.8"$$
$$C = 14° \ 20' \ 14.5"$$
$$A + B = 64° \ 30' \ 23.9"$$
$$B + C = 36° \ 30' \ 28.3"$$

(II)　Method of correction : The above problem can be solved by the method of corrections. Let C_A, C_B and C_C be corrections for angles A, B, C respectively.

$A + C_A = 42° \ 20' \ 10"$		Weight 2
$B + C_B = 22° \ 10' \ 12"$		Weight 1
$C + C_C = 14° \ 20' \ 14"$		Weight 3
$A + B \ (C_A + C_B) = 64° \ 30' \ 24"$		Weight 2
$B + C + (C_B + C_C) = 36° \ 30' \ 30"$		Weight 1
$C_A = 0$		Weight 2
$C_B = 0$		Weight 1
$C_C = 0$		Weight 3
$C_A + C_B = +2"$		Weight 2
$C_B + C_C = +4"$		Weight 1

To form normal equation in C_A :

$$2C_A = 0$$
$$2 \ (C_A + C_B) = +2 \times 2" = +4"$$

Adding　$\overline{\qquad\qquad 4C_A + 2C_B = +4"}$

$$2C_A + C_B = +2" \qquad\qquad\qquad ... (i)$$

To form normal equation in C_B :

$$1 \times C_B = 1 \times 0 = 0$$
$$2 \ (C_A + C_B) = +2 \times 2" = +4"$$
$$1 \ (C_B + C_C) = +1 \times 4" = +4"$$

Adding　$\overline{\qquad 2C_A + 4C_B + C_C = +8"} \qquad\qquad\qquad ... (ii)$

To form normal equation in C_C :

$$3 \times C_C = 0$$

$$1 (C_B + C_C) = 4"$$

Adding　　　　$C_B + 4C_C = +4"$　　　　　　　　　　... (iii)

The equations formed are :

$$2C_A + C_B = +2"$$　　　　　　　　　　... (i)

$$2C_A + 4C_B + C_C = +8"$$　　　　　　　　　　... (ii)

$$C_B + 4C_C = +4"$$　　　　　　　　　　... (iii)

Subtracting equation (ii) from equation (i),

$$3C_B + C_C = +6"$$

$$3C_B + 12C_C = 12 \text{ (Multiplying equation (iii) by 3)}$$

∴　　　　Subtracting　　　　$-11C_C = -6"$

$$C_C = \pm 0.54"$$

Putting value of C_C in equation (iii),

$$C_B + 4 \times 0.54 = 4"$$

$$C_B = 1.84"$$

Putting value of C_B in equation (i),

$$2C_A + 1.84" = 2"$$

$$C_A = 0.16"$$

Thus $C_A = 0.16"$, $C_B = 1.84"$, $C_C = 0.54"$

∴　　　The most probable values are :

$$A = 42° 20' 10.16"$$

$$B = 22° 10' 13.84"$$

$$C = 14° 20' 14.54"$$

$$A + B = 64° 30' 24"$$

$$B + C = 36° 30' 28.38"$$

Example 2.20 : Find most probable value of the angels A, B and C of a triangle ABC from the following observations. (Use method of differences)

∠ A = 65° 15' 30"　　　　Weight = 3

∠ B = 51° 11' 25"　　　　Weight = 2

∠ C = 63° 32' 34"　　　　Weight = 4

Solution : Let us write the condition as

$$A + B + C = 180°$$

$$\therefore \qquad C = 180° - (A + B)$$

$$\therefore \qquad A + B = 180° - C = 180° - 63° 32' 34"$$

$$\therefore \qquad A + B = 116° 27' 26"$$

After eliminating the condition equation C, we have

$$\angle A = 65° 15' 30' \text{ weight} = 3$$

$$\angle B = 51° 11' 25" \text{ weight} = 2$$

$$\angle A + \angle B = 116° 27' 26" \text{ weight} = 4$$

Let C_A and C_B be the corrections of angle A and B.

The MPVS of A, B and A + B will be

$$A = 65° 15' 30" + C_A \qquad \therefore C_A = 0 \text{ weight} = 3$$

$$B = 51° 11' 25" + C_B \qquad \therefore C_B = 0 \text{ weight} = 2$$

and $$A + B = 116° 26' 55" + C_A + C_B$$

i.e. $$116° 27' 26" = 116° 26' 55" + C_A + C_B$$

$$\therefore \qquad C_A + C_B = 31" \text{ weight} = 4.$$

$\therefore$ Three equations are as :

$$C_A = 0 \text{ weight} = 3$$

$$C_B = 0 \text{ weight} = 2$$

$$C_A + C_B = 31 \text{ weight} = 4$$

$\therefore$ Normal equation in C_A

$$7C_A + 4C_B = 124 \qquad\qquad\qquad \dots \text{(i)}$$

and normal equation in C_B

$$4C_A + 6C_B = 124 \qquad\qquad\qquad \dots \text{(ii)}$$

Solving equation (i) and (ii)

$$C_A = 9.54" \text{ and } C_B = 14.31"$$

$\therefore$ Most probable values of A, B and C.

$$A = 65° 15' 30" + 9.54" = 65° 15' 39.54"$$

$$B = 51° 11' 25" + 14.31" = 51° 11' 39.31"$$

and $$C = 180 - (A + B)$$

$$= 180 - (65° 15' 39.54" + 51° 11' 39.31")$$

$$= 62° 33' 41.15"$$

Check : $\angle A + \angle B + \angle C = 180°$

(b) Method of Correlates (or Correlatives) :

When there are large number of conditioned equations, the usual method of normal equations becomes labourious and difficult. In such cases, the method of correlates is used. The correlates (or correlatives) are the unknown multiples (or independent constants) that are used to determine the most probable values of unknowns.

Procedure :

(i)   Write down all the conditioned equations.

(ii)   To the above conditioned equations, include one or more equation of condition based upon the principle of least squares which states that the sum of the squares of the residuals (or residual errors) should be minimum.

(iii) Next step is to introduce probable corrections to be applied to the observed quantities say C_1, C_2, C_3 upto C_n.

(iv)   Now differentiate all the conditioned equations, including least square condition equation one by one and multiply each of the differentiated equation of conditions by unknown multipliers or independent constants say $-\lambda_1$, $-\lambda_2$, $-\lambda_3$, ..., $-\lambda_n$ and add up all the results of the conditioned equations, to the least square equation in differential forms (as already obtained above).

(v)   Now, rearrange the above result in terms of δC_1 ( ) + δC_2 ( ) + δC_3 ( ) + ... + δC_n ( ) and equate it to zero.

(vi)   As δC_1, δC_2, δC_3, ..., δC_n have definite values and are independent of each other, their coefficients must be equated to zero independently, thus getting the most probable value of the various corrections C_1, C_2, C_3, ..., C_n.

(vii) The above values of C_1, C_2, C_3, ..., C_n are then substituted in the conditioned equations. These equations, when solved, will enable us to find the values of correlates $-\lambda_1$, $-\lambda_2$, ..., $-\lambda_n$.

(viii) After getting the values of correlates $-\lambda_1$, $-\lambda_2$, ..., $-\lambda_n$, the most probable values of the corrections C_1, C_2, ..., C_n are found out (as usual).

(ix)   The above corrections are then applied to the respective observed angles to get the most probable values of the angles.

Example 2.21 : By method of correlates or correlatives : Determine the most probable values of the angles A, B and C of the triangle ABC from the following observations :

$$\angle A = 48° \ 14' \ 26''$$

$$\angle B = 57° \ 17' \ 48''$$

$$\angle C = 74° \ 27' \ 50''$$

Use method of correlates.

Solution :   Observed sum = 180° 00' 04"

But   The theoretical sum = 180° 00' 00"

∴   Discrepancy = 4"

and   Correlation = – 4"

Let C_A, C_B, C_C be the most probable values of corrections to A, B and C respectively.

Then $\quad\quad\quad\quad\quad\quad C_A + C_B + C_C = -4''$ ... (i)

By the least square principle, sum of weighted squares of residual errors should be zero.

i.e. $\quad\quad\quad\quad\quad\quad\quad \Sigma\, WC^2 = \text{Minimum}$

or $\quad\quad\quad\quad\quad\quad C_A^2 + C_B^2 + C_C^2 = \text{Minimum}$ ... (ii)

$\therefore\quad$ Differentiating (i) and (ii), we get,

$$\delta C_A + \delta C_B + \delta C_C = 0 \quad\quad\quad \text{... (iii)}$$

and $\quad\quad 2C_A \cdot \delta C_A + 2C_B \cdot \delta C_B + 2C_C \cdot \delta C_C = 0$

i.e. $\quad\quad\quad C_A \cdot \delta C_A + C_B \cdot \delta C_B + C_C \cdot \delta C_C = 0$ ... (iv)

Now equation (iii) is to be multiplied by $-\lambda$ and then to be added to equation (iv) and equated to zero.

$\therefore\ \delta C_A\,(C_A - \lambda) + \delta C_B\,(C_B - \lambda) + \delta C_C\,(C_C - \lambda) = 0$

i.e. $\quad\quad\quad\quad\quad\quad C_A - \lambda = 0$

$$C_B - \lambda = 0$$

$$C_C - \lambda = 0$$

$\therefore\quad\quad\quad\quad\quad\quad\quad C_A = C_B = C_C = \lambda$

But $\quad\quad\quad\quad\quad\quad\quad C_A + C_B + C_C = -4$

$\therefore\quad\quad\quad\quad\quad\quad\quad\quad\quad 3\lambda = -4$

or $\quad\quad\quad\quad\quad\quad\quad\quad\quad \lambda = -\dfrac{4}{3} = -1.33''$

$\therefore\quad\quad\quad\quad\quad\quad\quad\quad\quad C_A = -1.33''$

$$C_B = -1.33'' \text{ say } -1.34''$$

$$C_C = -1.33''$$

so that $\quad\quad\quad\quad\quad C_A + C_B + C_C = 4.00''$

$\therefore\quad$ The most probable values of the angles A, B and C are :

$$A = 48°\ 14'\ 26'' - 1.33''$$

$$= 48°\ 14'\ 24.67''$$

$$B = 57°\ 17'\ 48'' - 1.34''$$

$$= 57°\ 17'\ 46.66''$$

$$C = 74°\ 27'\ 50'' - 1.33''$$

$$= 74°\ 27'\ 48.67''$$

Check : $\quad\quad\quad\quad A + B + C = 180°\ 00'\ 00''$

Example 2.22 : Illustrative example by the method of correlates : The following are the observed values of angles in a triangle of a triangulation survey. Adjust the angles

$$A = 87° 35' 11.1''\ \ \text{Weight 1}$$
$$B = 43° 15' 17.00''\ \ \text{Weight 2}$$
$$C = 49° 09' 34.1''\ \ \text{Weight 3}$$

Solution : Observed sum of all the angles $= 180° 00' 2.2''$

But　　　　　　　　The theoretical sum $= 180° 00' 00''$

$\therefore$　　　　　　　　　　Discrepancy $= 2.2''$

$\therefore$　　　　　　　　　　Correction $= -2.2''$

If C_A, C_B, C_C are the corrections to the angles A, B, C respectively, then,

$$C_A + C_B + C_C = -2.2''　\qquad\text{... (i)}$$

By the principle of least squares,

$$\Sigma wC^2 = \text{Minimum}$$

i.e.　　　　$1\ (C_A)^2 + 2\ (C_B)^2 + 3\ (C_C)^2 = \text{Minimum}　\qquad\text{... (ii)}$

i.e.　　　　$C_A^2 + 2C_B^2 + 3C_C^2 = \text{Minimum}$

On differentiation of equations (i) and (ii) above,

$$\delta C_A + \delta C_B + \delta C_C = 0　\qquad\text{... (iii)}$$
$$C_A\,\delta C_A + 2C_B\,\delta C_B + 3C_C\,\delta C_C = 0　\qquad\text{... (iv)}$$

On multiplying the equation (iii) by $-\lambda$ and by addition to the equation (iv) above we get,

$$\delta C_A\,(C_A - \lambda) + \delta C_B\,(2C_B - \lambda) + \delta C_C\,(3C_C - \lambda) = 0$$

The above equation will be valid, provided,

$$C_A - \lambda = 0$$
$$2C_B - \lambda = 0$$
$$3C_C - \lambda = 0$$

$\therefore$　　　　　　　　　　$C_A = \lambda$

　　　　　　　　　　　$C_B = \lambda/2$

　　　　　　　　　　　$C_C = \lambda/3$

But　　　　　$C_A + C_B + C_C = -2.2''$

i.e.　　　　　$\lambda + \dfrac{\lambda}{2} + \dfrac{\lambda}{3} = -2.2''$

or　　　　　$\dfrac{6\lambda + 3\lambda + 2\lambda}{6} = -2.2''$

$$\therefore \qquad \lambda\left(\frac{11}{6}\right) = -2.2''$$

$$\text{or} \qquad \lambda = \frac{-2.2'' \times 6}{11} = -1.2''$$

$$\therefore \qquad C_A = -1.2''$$

$$C_B = \frac{\lambda}{2} = -\frac{1.2}{2} = -0.60''$$

$$C_C = \frac{\lambda}{3} = -\frac{1.2}{3} = -0.40''$$

Check : $\qquad C_A + C_B + C_C = -(1.2'' + 0.60'' + 0.40'') = -2.2''$

$\therefore$ The most probable values of the angles are :

$$A = 87° \ 25' \ 11.1'' - 1.2''$$
$$= 87° \ 35' \ 9.9''$$
$$B = 43° \ 15' \ 17.00'' - 0.60''$$
$$= 43° \ 15' \ 16.40''$$
$$C = 49° \ 09' \ 34.1'' - 0.40''$$
$$= 49° \ 09' \ 33.7''$$

Check : $\qquad A + B + C = 180° \ 00' \ 00''$

Note : The above problem can also be solved by the following methods :

(i) Normal equation.

(ii) Method of differences or correction.

(iii) By laws of weights.

(i.e. corrections are inversely proportional to their weights).

2.11 TRIANGULATION ADJUSTMENTS

Introduction :

In triangulation survey, after the horizontal angles are measured, they are to be adjusted first to satisfy certain geometric conditions and are then to be used for the computations of the sides.

Geometrical Conditions :

The geometrical conditions to be satisfied may generally be classified under the following two categories :

(i) Station adjustment and

(ii) Figure adjustment.

2.11.1 Station Adjustment

Station adjustment consists of determining the most probable values of two or more angles observed at a station that satisfy geometric consistency. Such station adjustment may further be sub-divided into the following :

    (a)   When the angles closing the horizon are all of equal weights.

    (b)   When the angles closing the horizon are all of unequal weights.

    (c)   When several angles are measured independently and also in combination.

(a) When angles closing the horizon are of equal weights (Fig. 2.2) :

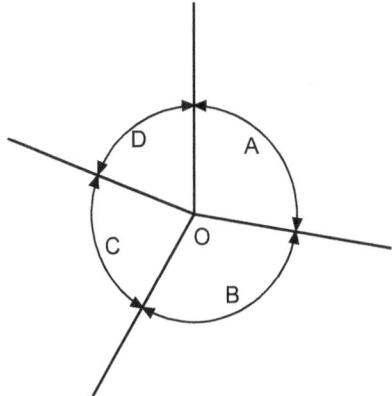

Fig. 2.2

The Fig. 2.2 shows four angles A, B, C and D observed at station O, closing the horizon, all of same weight.

Obviously, $A + B + C + D = 360°$

If not, find the discrepancy between the observed sum and theoretical sum and distribute it equally amongst all the four angles to obtain the most probable values of the observed angles.

(b) When the horizon is closed with angles of unequal weights :

If the observed sum of all the angles at a station is not equal to its theoretical sum (i.e. 360°), find the discrepancy and distribute the discrepancy amongst the observed angles inversely proportional to their weights to obtain the most probable values of the observed angles.

(c) When several angles at a station are measured independently and also in combination (Fig. 2.3) i.e. Summation Adjustment :

As shown in the Fig. 2.3, the angles A, B and C are measured independently and also in combination i.e. summation angles (A + B), (B + C) and (A + B + C) have also been measured. The most probable values of the angles are then determined by forming normal equations (for the unknown quantities) and then solving them as simultaneous equations.

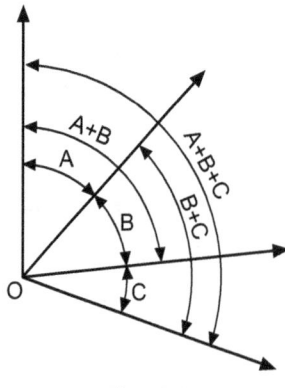

Fig. 2.3

Example 2.23 : Illustrative example on equal weights : The following angles, at a station O, closing the horizon were observed. Find their most probable values :

$$AOB = 85° 44' 30.75"$$

$$BOC = 100° 13' 41.26"$$

$$COD = 90° 34' 23.22"$$

$$DOA = 83° 27' 27.77"$$

Solution : The sum of the observed angles = 360° 00' 03"

whereas,　　　The theoretical sum = 360° 00' 00"

∴　　　　　　　　　　Discrepancy = 3"

∴　　　　　　　　　　Correction = –3"

Now, as all the angles are of equal weights (when no weights are given, it means they are of same precision or weight), the discrepancy is to be distributed equally amongst the four angles i.e. correction to each angle $= -\dfrac{3}{4} = -0.75"$

∴　　The most probable values of angles will be

$$\angle AOB = 85° 44' 30.75" - 0.75"$$
$$= 85° 44' 30.00"$$
$$\angle BOC = 100° 13' 41.26" - 0.75"$$
$$= 100° 13' 40.51"$$
$$\angle COD = 90° 34' 23.22" - 0.75"$$
$$= 90° 34' 22.47"$$
$$\angle DOA = 83° 27' 27.77" - 0.75"$$
$$= 83° 27' 27.02"$$

Check : $\begin{bmatrix} \text{Sum of all} \\ \text{adjusted angles} \end{bmatrix} = 360° 00' 00"$

Example 2.24 : Illustrative example on unequal weights (closing horizon) : Find the most probable values of the angles closing the horizon at a station, from the following observations :

$$\angle A = 110° \, 05' \, 58.9" \text{ Weight 2}$$
$$\angle B = 98° \, 45' \, 16.1" \quad \text{Weight 1}$$
$$\angle C = 72° \, 55' \, 30.7" \quad \text{Weight 3}$$
$$\angle D = 78° \, 13' \, 17.3" \quad \text{Weight 1}$$

Solution : The sum of the observed angles = 360° 00' 03"

But   The theoretical sum = 360° 00' 00"

∴   Discrepancy = 3"

∴   Total correction = − 3"

Observed sum is greater than theoretical sum and this total correction is to be distributed amongst observed angles inversely proportional to their weights.

i.e. If C_A, C_B, C_C and C_D are the corrections to the respective angles A, B, C and D, then,

$$C_A : C_B : C_C : C_D = \frac{1}{2} : \frac{1}{1} : \frac{1}{3} : \frac{1}{1}$$

$$= 3 : 6 : 2 : 6 \qquad \text{(By L.C.M.)}$$

∴
$$C_A = \frac{3}{17} \times 3 = 0.529$$

$$C_B = \frac{6}{17} \times 3 = 1.060$$

$$C_C = \frac{2}{17} \times 3 = 0.351$$

$$C_D = \frac{6}{17} \times 3 = 1.060$$

∴   The most probable values are :

$$A = 110° \, 05' \, 58.9" - 0.529"$$
$$= 110° \, 05' \, 58.371"$$
$$B = 98° \, 45' \, 16.1" - 1.06"$$
$$= 98° \, 45' \, 15.040"$$
$$C = 72° \, 55' \, 30.7" - 0.351"$$
$$= 72° \, 55' \, 30.349"$$
$$D = 78° \, 13' \, 17.3" - 1.06"$$
$$= 78° \, 13' \, 16.240"$$

Check : (After adjustment) A + B + C + D = 360° 00' 00"

2.11.2 Figure Adjustment

The determination of most probable values of the angles in any geometrical figure to satisfy the geometrical conditions is called the *figure adjustment*. Generally, figure adjustment involves one or more than one conditional equations. The various methods of determining the most probable values in such cases are already explained earlier. However, the method of correlates or correlatives being simpler, is to be preferred when there are large number of conditional equations.

The geometrical figures, commonly used in triangulation system are :

(a)   Plane and spherical triangles,

(b)   Braced quadrilaterals and

(c)   Polygons with centered figure.

2.12 ADJUSTMENT OF PLANE TRIANGLE

As the principle of Geodetic surveying is triangulation, i.e. dividing the area into suitable number of triangles, it is necessary to study the adjustment of such triangles. The only condition, the triangulation figure has to satisfy, is that the sum of the three angles of triangles should be equal to $180°$.

I.   Rules for Corrections :

The rules generally adopted for applying corrections to the observed angles are as follows :

Notations :

(i)   A, B, C $\rightarrow$ Observed angles

(ii) C_A, C_B, C_C $\rightarrow$ Corrections to respective angles to get M.P.V.

(iii) W_A, W_B, W_C $\rightarrow$ Weights of respective angles A, B, C.

(iv) E_A, E_B, E_C $\rightarrow$ Probable errors of A, B, C respectively

(v)   d $\rightarrow$ Total correction which equals the discrepancy between the observed sum and theoretical sum of angles.

(vi) n_A, n_B, n_C $\rightarrow$ Number of observations of angles A, B and C respectively.

Rule 1 : Equal weights - Equal corrections :

If the observed angles are of equal weights, the discrepancy (d) is to be distributed equally amongst all the three observed angles i.e. $C_A = C_B = C_C = \pm \dfrac{d}{3}$. Use plus sign for corrections, if the observed sum is less than the theoretical sum and minus sign if it is more than the theoretical sum.

Check : After adjusting the angles, their sum $A + B + C = 180°$

Rule 2 : Unequal weights - Inverse (weight) correction :

When the observed angles are of unequal weights, the discrepancy is to be distributed inversely proportional to their respective weights.

i.e.
$$C_A : C_B : C_C = \frac{1}{W_A} : \frac{1}{W_B} : \frac{1}{W_C}$$
$$= W_B W_C : W_C W_A : W_A W_B$$

∴
$$C_A = \frac{\dfrac{1}{W_A}}{\dfrac{1}{W_A} + \dfrac{1}{W_B} + \dfrac{1}{W_C}} \times d$$

$$= \left[\frac{W_B W_C}{W_A W_B + W_B W_C + W_C W_A} \right] \times d$$

Also,
$$C_B = \frac{\dfrac{1}{W_B}}{\dfrac{1}{W_A} + \dfrac{1}{W_B} + \dfrac{1}{W_C}} \times d$$

$$= \left[\frac{W_C W_A}{W_A W_B + W_B W_C + W_C W_A} \right] \times d$$

and
$$C_C = \frac{\dfrac{1}{W_C}}{\dfrac{1}{W_A} + \dfrac{1}{W_B} + \dfrac{1}{W_C}} \times d$$

$$= \left[\frac{W_A W_B}{W_A W_B + W_B W_C + W_C W_A} \right] \times d$$

Check :   (i) $C_A + C_B + C_C$ = Total correction to be applied.

           (ii)   After applying the above correction to the observed angles, the sum of the adjusted angles should be equal to 180°.

Rule 3 : Inverse (observation) corrections :

When the weights of observations are not assigned, the discrepancy is to be distributed inversely proportional to the number of observations.

i.e.
$$C_A : C_B : C_C = \frac{1}{n_A} : \frac{1}{n_B} : \frac{1}{n_C}$$

∴
$$C_A = \frac{\dfrac{1}{n_A}}{\dfrac{1}{n_A} + \dfrac{1}{n_B} + \dfrac{1}{n_C}} \times d$$

$$= \left[\frac{n_B \, n_C}{n_A \, n_B + n_B \, n_C + n_C \, n_A} \right] \times d$$

Also,
$$C_B = \frac{\dfrac{1}{n_B}}{\dfrac{1}{n_A} + \dfrac{1}{n_B} + \dfrac{1}{n_C}} \times d$$

$$= \left[\frac{n_C \, n_A}{n_A \, n_B + n_B \, n_C + n_C \, n_A} \right] \times d$$

and
$$C_C = \frac{\dfrac{1}{n_C}}{\dfrac{1}{n_A} + \dfrac{1}{n_B} + \dfrac{1}{n_C}} \times d$$

$$= \left[\frac{n_A \, n_B}{n_A \, n_B + n_B \, n_C + n_C \, n_A} \right] \times d$$

Check : (i) The sum of $C_A + C_B + C_C$ = Total correction

(ii) After applying the above corrections to the observed angles, their sum should be equal to $180°$.

Rule 4 : Inverse square correction :

The rule states that 'the corrections are in inverse proportion to the square of the number of observations'.

i.e.
$$C_A : C_B : C_C = \left(\frac{1}{n_A}\right)^2 : \left(\frac{1}{n_B}\right)^2 : \left(\frac{1}{n_C}\right)^2$$

$\therefore$
$$C_A = \left\{ \frac{\left(\dfrac{1}{n_A}\right)^2}{\left(\dfrac{1}{n_A}\right)^2 + \left(\dfrac{1}{n_B}\right)^2 + \left(\dfrac{1}{n_C}\right)^2} \right\} \times d$$

$\therefore$
$$C_B = \left\{ \frac{\left(\dfrac{1}{n_B}\right)^2}{\left(\dfrac{1}{n_A}\right)^2 + \left(\dfrac{1}{n_B}\right)^2 + \left(\dfrac{1}{n_C}\right)^2} \right\} \times d$$

and
$$C_C = \left\{ \frac{\left(\dfrac{1}{n_C}\right)^2}{\left(\dfrac{1}{n_A}\right)^2 + \left(\dfrac{1}{n_B}\right)^2 + \left(\dfrac{1}{n_C}\right)^2} \right\} \times d$$

Note : There is no or little mathematical justification for the above method.

Rule 5 : Probable error - square correction :

When the probable errors to each angle are known, then the corrections are directly proportional to the square of the probable errors.

$$C_A : C_B : C_C \ :: \ E_A^2 \ : \ E_B^2 \ : \ E_C^2$$

$\therefore$

$$C_A \ = \ \frac{E_A^2}{E_A^2 + E_B^2 + E_C^2} \times d$$

$$C_B \ = \ \frac{E_B^2}{E_A^2 + E_B^2 + E_C^2} \times d$$

$$C_C \ = \ \frac{E_C^2}{E_A^2 + E_B^2 + E_C^2} \times d$$

Rule 6 : Gauss's rule :

Gauss's rule is to be applied when the weights of observations are not directly given. However, if the residual error of each observation is known, its weight can be determined by using Gauss's rule.

i.e.   Weight of observations, $W \ = \ \dfrac{\left(\frac{1}{2} n^2\right)}{\Sigma v^2}$

where n = Total number of observations made for the observed quantity

        Σv^2 = Sum of the squares of residual errors (or residuals)

The residual error being the difference of mean observed value (M) and the observed value.

i.e. $\Sigma v^2 \ = \ (M - Z_1)^2 + (M - Z_2)^2 + \ldots\ldots + (M - Z_n)^2$

where M = Mean observed value of angles

and $Z_1, Z_2, \ldots, Z_n$ = Observations of the angles

Thus, $W_A \ = \ \dfrac{\frac{1}{2} n_A^2}{\Sigma v_A^2}$

$\therefore$ $\dfrac{1}{W_A} \ = \ \dfrac{\Sigma v_A^2}{\frac{1}{2} n_A^2} \ = \ K_A \ (\text{say})$

Similarly, $\quad W_B = \dfrac{\dfrac{1}{2} n_B^2}{\Sigma v_B^2}$

$\therefore \quad \dfrac{1}{W_B} = \dfrac{\Sigma v_B^2}{\dfrac{1}{2} n_B^2} = K_B \text{ (say)}$

and $\quad W_C = \dfrac{\dfrac{1}{2} n_C^2}{\Sigma v_C^2}$

$\therefore \quad \dfrac{1}{W_C} = \dfrac{\Sigma v_C^2}{\dfrac{1}{2} n_C^2} = K_C \text{ (say)}$

After the weights of observations are computed, the corrections being inversely proportional to their weights, can be computed as follows :

$$C_A : C_B : C_C = \dfrac{1}{W_A} : \dfrac{1}{W_B} : \dfrac{1}{W_C}$$

$$= K_A : K_B : K_C$$

$\therefore \quad C_A = \left(\dfrac{K_A}{K_A + K_B + K_C} \right) \times d$

$\quad C_B = \left(\dfrac{K_B}{K_A + K_B + K_C} \right) \times d$

$\quad C_C = \left(\dfrac{K_C}{K_A + K_B + K_C} \right) \times d$

The signs of corrections may be either positive or negative depending upon whether the sum of mean observed angles of triangle is less or more than 180°.

Example 2.25 : Illustrative example on Gauss's rule of triangulation adjustment :

Adjust the following angles of the triangle PQR from the following observations :

∠P = 37° 10' 12"	∠Q = 55° 31' 12"	∠R = 87° 18' 45"
∠P = 37° 10' 10"	∠Q = 55° 31' 15"	∠R = 87° 18' 43"
∠P = 37° 10' 11'	∠Q = 55° 31' 14"	∠R = 87° 18' 41"
∠P = 37° 10' 13"	∠Q = 55° 31' 11"	∠R = 87° 18' 44"
∠P = 37° 10' 14"		∠R = 87° 18' 42"

Solution :

Mean observed $\angle P = 37°10'\ 22"$	Mean observed $\angle Q = 55°\ 31'\ 13"$	Mean observed $\angle R = 87°\ 18'\ 43"$
$\Sigma\ v_P^2 = (0)^2 + (+2)^2 + (+1)^2 +$ $(-1)^2 + (-2)^2$ $= 0 + 4 + 1 + 1 + 4 = 10$	$\Sigma\ v_Q^2 = (+1)^2 + (-2)^2 + (-1)^2 +$ $(+2)^2$ $= 1 + 4 + 1 + 4 = 10$	$\Sigma\ v_R^2 = (-2)^2 + (0)^2 + (+2)^2 +$ $(-1)^2 + (+1)^2$ $= 4 + 0 + 4 + 1 + 1 = 10$
Number of observations, $n_P = 5$	$n_Q = 4$	$n_R = 5$
$\therefore$ Weight of observations $$W_P = \frac{\frac{1}{2}\,n_P^2}{\Sigma\ v_P^2}$$ $$= \frac{\frac{1}{2} \times (5)^2}{10}$$ $$= \frac{25}{20} = 1.25$$	$\therefore$ Weight of observations $$W_Q = \frac{\frac{1}{2}\,n_Q^2}{\Sigma\ v_Q^2}$$ $$= \frac{\frac{1}{2} \times (4)^2}{10}$$ $$= \frac{16}{20} = 0.8$$	$\therefore$ Weight of observations $$W_R = \frac{\frac{1}{2}\,n_R^2}{\Sigma\ v_R^2}$$ $$= \frac{\frac{1}{2} \times (5)^2}{10}$$ $$= \frac{25}{20} = 1.25$$
$K_P = \dfrac{1}{W_P} = 0.80$	$K_Q = \dfrac{1}{W_Q} = 1.25$	$K_R = \dfrac{1}{W_R} = 0.80$
Sum of observed mean angles = $37°\ 10'\ 12" + 55°\ 31'\ 13" + 87°\ 18'\ 43" = 180°\ 00'\ 08"$ $\therefore$ Correction = $-8"$		
$$C_P = \frac{K_P}{K_P + K_Q + K_R} \times d$$ $$= \frac{0.80}{0.80 + 1.25 + 0.80} \times 8$$ $$= \frac{0.80}{2.85} \times 8$$ $$= -2.246"$$	$$C_Q = \frac{1}{W_Q} = 1.25$$ $$= \frac{1.25}{0.80 + 1.25 + 0.80} \times 8$$ $$= \frac{1.25}{2.85} \times 8$$ $$= -3.508"$$	$$C_R = \frac{K_R}{K_P + K_Q + K_R} \times 8$$ $$= \frac{0.80}{0.80 + 1.25 + 0.80} \times 8$$ $$= \frac{0.80}{2.85} \times 8$$ $$= -2.246"$$
Check : $C_P + C_Q + C_R = -(2.246 + 3.508 + 2.246) = -8"$		
Most probable values of angles : $\angle P = 37°\ 10'\ 12"$ $\underline{\quad -2.246"\quad}$ $\therefore\ \angle P = 37°\ 10'\ 09.754"$	$\angle Q = 55°\ 31'\ 13"$ $\underline{\quad -3.508"\quad}$ $\therefore\ \angle Q = 55°\ 31'\ 09.492"$	$\angle R = 87°\ 18'\ 43"$ $\underline{\quad -2.246"\quad}$ $\therefore\ \angle R = 87°\ 18'\ 40.754"$
Check : $\begin{bmatrix} \text{Sum of most probable} \\ \text{values of angles} \\ \text{after adjustments} \end{bmatrix}$ $= 37°\ 10'\ 09.754" + 55°\ 31'\ 09.492" + 87°\ 18'\ 40.754"$ $= 180°\ 00'\ 00"$ which is same as the theoretical sum $180°\ 00'\ 00"$ $\therefore$ O. K.		

Example 2.26 : Find the most probable values of observed angles closing the horizon at station.

$$A = 120° 05' 58.9" \quad \text{Weight 2}$$

$$B = 88° 45' 16.1" \quad \text{Weight 1}$$

$$C = 72° 55' 30.7" \quad \text{Weight 3}$$

$$D = 78° 13' 17.3" \quad \text{Weight 1}$$

Solution : The sum of observed angles $= 360° 00' 3.0"$

But   Theoretical sum $= 360° 00' 00"$

∴   Discrepancy $= 3"$

∴   Total correction $= -3"$

As per the laws of weights, the corrections are inversely proportional to their weights.

If C_A, C_B, C_C and C_D are the corrections to the observed values of angles A, B, C and D respectively, then,

$$C_A : C_B : C_C : C_D = \frac{1}{2} : \frac{1}{1} : \frac{1}{3} : \frac{1}{1}$$

$$= 3 : 6 : 2 : 6 \qquad \text{(By L.C.M.)}$$

$$C_A = \frac{3}{17} \times 3" = \frac{9}{17} = 0.529"$$

$$C_B = \frac{6}{17} \times 3" = \frac{18}{17} = 1.0589"$$

$$C_C = \frac{2}{17} \times 3" = \frac{6}{17} = 0.353"$$

$$C_D = \frac{6}{17} \times 3" = \frac{18}{17} = 1.0589"$$

Check : $C_A + C_B + C_C + C_D = 3.0000"$

∴   The most probable values of angles are :

$$A = 120° 05' 58.9" - 0.5291" = 120° 05' 57.4809"$$

$$B = 88° 45' 16.1" - 1.0589" = 88° 45' 15.411"$$

$$C = 72° 55' 30.7" - 0.3531" = 72° 55' 30.3469"$$

$$D = 78° 13' 17.3" - 1.0589" = 78° 13' 16.2411"$$

Check : $A + B + C + D = 360° 00' 00"$

II. Computations of Sides of Triangle and Co-ordinates of Triangulation Stations :

If the sum of the observed angles of a triangle in triangulation system is not equal to 180º, the observed angles are to be adjusted by the application of the relevant rules as explained above. Once the observed angles are corrected, the lengths of the other sides of triangle can be computed, with the help of corrected angles and the known side, (which may be a base line or computed line) by application of 'sine rule' .

The next part is the computation of co-ordinates of other triangulation stations from the known co-ordinates of A, length AB and azimuth of AB. The procedure is as follows :

(i)   From the triangle ABC, the angles A and B and azimuth of AB being known, the azimuths of sides AC and BC can be computed.

(ii)   Knowing the length AB and its azimuth, its latitude and departures can be calculated.

(iii) The co-ordinates of station A being already known, the co-ordinates of station B can be found out from latitude and departure of line AB.

(iv)   The same procedure is then repeated to calculate the latitude and departure of BC and AC and co-ordinates of station C are calculated first from B and then from A to check the accuracy of the results. The co-ordinates of C obtained from B and A should agree with each other.

2.13 EFFECT OF EARTH'S CURVATURE ON SURVEYS

Due to the curved surface of the Earth, the following are two effects on surveys :

(i)   Spherical excess and   (ii) Convergence of meridians.

(i)   Spherical excess : When the area under survey is very large, the curvature of the earth is to be accounted for and thus the lines joining three points on the earth surface will not be a plane triangle, but a spherical triangle. The sum of the three angles of a spherical triangle will be always greater than 180° and the amount by which this exceeds 180° is known as 'spherical excess' (E_S).

(ii)   Convergence of meridians : Due to the spherical surface of the earth, the meridians drawn from different points on the surface of the earth will not be parallel to each other (except at the equator) but will converge and meet at the poles and is termed as 'convergence of meridians'. The difference between the force and back azimuth of a line will not be equal to 180°. The convergence i.e. the change in azimuth is the angle subtended between the true meridian passing through the point under consideration and the line drawn through this point parallel to the original reference line (i.e. meridian) passing through the origin or first point of the survey.

2.13.1 Spherical Excess

Introduction :

Whenever the area to be surveyed is very large, the line joining two triangulation stations will no longer be a straight horizontal line, but it will be a curved line and the triangle formed by such curved lines will not be a plane triangle, but it will be 'geodetic' or spherical triangle. Thus, spherical triangle is a triangle formed by three arcs of great circles. One of the distinguishing property of the spherical triangle is that the sum of the three angles is always greater than $180°$.

Definition of Spherical Excess :

The amount, by which this sum of angles of a spherical triangle exceeds $180°$, is called as 'spherical excess'. The spherical excess is about one second for every 197 sq. km. (approximate area covered on the ground).

Thus,   Spherical excess $= E_S = \left(\begin{array}{c}\text{Sum of three angles} \\ \text{of spherical triangle}\end{array}\right) - 180°$

The spherical excess can be determined by the formula

$$\left(\begin{array}{c}\text{Theoretical spherical} \\ \text{excess in degrees}\end{array}\right)^° = E_{S_T}^° = \frac{A \times 180°}{\pi R^2} \qquad \text{... (2.10)}$$

where A = Area of spherical triangle in sq. km.

R = Mean radius of the earth in km.

$$E_{S_T} \text{ (in seconds)} = \frac{A \times 180°}{\pi \times R^2} \times 3600 \text{ second} = \frac{(648000) \times (A)}{\pi R^2}$$

$$= \frac{A \times 206265}{R^2} = \left[\frac{A}{R^2 \times \dfrac{1}{206265}}\right]$$

But $\sin 1'' = \dfrac{1}{206265}$

$\therefore$ $E_{S_T} \text{ (in seconds)} = \dfrac{A}{R^2 \sin 1''}$ ... (2.11)

If the mean radius of earth is taken as 6370 km then,

$$E_{S_T} \text{ (in seconds)} = \left[\frac{\text{Area (in sq. km.)}}{197}\right] \qquad \text{... (2.12)}$$

After computing the spherical excess as stated above, the theoretical sum of the three angles of spherical triangle will be $180° + E_{S_T}$. The sum of the observed angles of spherical triangle $(A + B + C)$ is then compared with the $180° + E_{S_T}$ and the discrepancy (d) between the two is determined as follows :

$$d = \left(180° + E_{S_T}\right) - (A + B + C)$$

This is to be distributed amongst the three angles as per rules explained above.

The area of the spherical triangle (A) required in computing the theoretical spherical excess (E_{S_T}), is calculated by considering the triangle as approximately a plane one.

i.e.   Area of the triangle A $= \dfrac{1}{2}$ bc sin A   ... (2.13)

or $= \dfrac{1}{2} a^2 \dfrac{\sin B_a \sin C_a}{\sin A_a}$ ... [2.13 (a)] where ' a' (i.e. BC) is a known or measured side and A_a, B_a and C_a are the approximate plane angles of triangle ABC. Thus, having calculated the area of the spherical triangle by the above formula, theoretical spherical excess is determined and compared with the observed spherical excess and the discrepancy, if any, is distributed according to the rules explained earlier amongst the observed spherical angles to get the most probable values of the adjusted spherical angles.

Check : The sum of the adjusted spherical angles = 180° + E_{ST}

The corrected plane angles are then calculated by subtracting $1/3^{rd}$ the theoretical excess from each of the adjusted spherical angles.

Check : The sum of the corrected plane angles = 180°

Derivation of Formula for Spherical Excess (E_S) :

ABC is a spherical triangle having spherical angles α, β and γ.

The Fig. 2.4 shows a spherical triangle ABC formed by three arcs AB, BC and CA of three great circles, which divide the whole sphere into 8 parts, the four parts ABC, ACD, DCE and BCE in one semisphere are identical to the corresponding four parts in the other semisphere (seen from the other side).

Let R be the radius of the sphere, then its area = S = $4\pi R^2$.

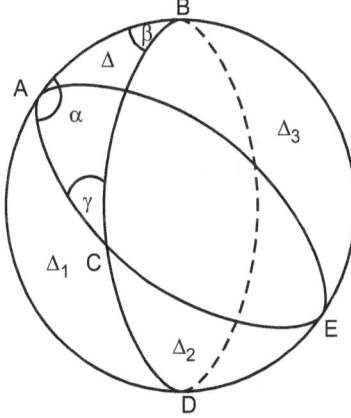

Fig. 2.4

Now denoting the areas of triangles ABC, ACD, DCE and BCE as Δ, Δ_1, Δ_2 and Δ_3 respectively, we may write,

$$\frac{\Delta + \Delta_1}{\angle \beta} = \frac{S}{360^\circ} \quad \text{or} \quad \Delta + \Delta_1 = \frac{\angle \beta}{360^\circ} \times S \qquad \text{... (2.14)}$$

$$\frac{\Delta + \Delta_3}{\angle \alpha} = \frac{S}{360^\circ} \quad \text{or} \quad \Delta + \Delta_3 = \frac{\angle \alpha}{360^\circ} \times S \qquad \text{... (2.15)}$$

and $$\frac{\Delta + \Delta_2}{\angle \gamma} = \frac{S}{360^\circ} \quad \text{or} \quad \Delta + \Delta_2 = \frac{\angle \gamma}{360^\circ} \times S \qquad \text{... (2.16)}$$

Summation of equations (2.14), (2.15) and (2.16) gives,

$$3\Delta + \Delta_1 + \Delta_2 + \Delta_3 = \frac{S}{360°}(\alpha + \beta + \gamma) \qquad ... (2.17)$$

But,

$$\Delta + \Delta_1 + \Delta_2 + \Delta_3 = \text{Area of semisphere} = \frac{S}{2} \qquad ... (2.18)$$

$\therefore$

$$2\Delta + \frac{S}{2} = \frac{S}{360°}(\alpha + \beta + \gamma)$$

or

$$2\Delta = \frac{S}{360°}(\alpha + \beta + \gamma) - \frac{S}{2}$$

$$= \frac{S}{360°}[(\alpha + \beta + \gamma) - 180°]$$

But by definition $[(\alpha + \beta + \gamma) - 180°]$ is spherical excess i.e. E_S

$$2\Delta = \frac{S}{360°}[E_S] = \frac{4\pi R^2 \, E_S}{360°}$$

On simplification,

$$E_S = \left[\frac{\Delta \times 180°}{\pi R^2}\right] \text{ in degrees}$$

But

$$\Delta = \text{Area of spherical triangle ABC} = A$$

$\therefore$

$$E_S = \frac{A \times 180°}{\pi R^2}$$

Then,

$$E_S \text{ (in seconds)} = \frac{A \times 180 \times 60 \times 60}{\pi R^2} \text{ seconds}$$

$$= \frac{A \times 648000}{3.142 \, R^2} \text{ seconds}$$

$\therefore$

$$E_S \text{ (in seconds)} = \frac{A}{R^2 \times \dfrac{1}{206265}} = \left[\frac{A}{R^2 \sin 1''}\right]$$

A_o', B_o', C_o' be the corrected spherical angles.

A_a, B_a, C_a be the approximate plane angles.

A_a', B_a', C_a' be the corrected plane angles.

Adjustments of Spherical Triangles :

(i) Sum up all the three observed spherical angles A_o, B_o and C_o and compare it with 180° and determine the discrepancy between these two which is the observed spherical excess $\left(E_{S_o}\right)$, including observational errors if any.

(ii) Subtract $\frac{1}{3}$rd E_{S_o} from each of the observed spherical angle to get the approximate plane angle A_a, B_a and C_a.

(iii)   Knowing approximate plane angles calculate the area of the triangles (A) by the formula stated above in 2.13 (a).

(iv)   Calculate the theoretical spherical excess by the formula

$$E_{S_T} \; = \; \left[\frac{A}{R^2 \sin 1''} \right] \text{(seconds)} \text{ as stated in (2.11) above.}$$

(v)   If the observed spherical excess E_{S_O} is same as the theoretical spherical excess E_{S_T}, no adjustment is necessary. Otherwise, find the difference between them $\left(\text{i.e. } E_{S_O} \text{ and } E_{S_T} \right)$ say ε.

(a)   Now if all the three angles are of equal weights, correct each of the observed angles A_O, B_O, C_O by applying the correction algebraically to get the corrected spherical angles (A_a', B_a', C_a').

In this case as all the angles are of equal weights, the difference between ($A_O + B_O + C_O$) and $180°$ includes error due to spherical excess and observational error.

(b)   However, if the observed spherical angles are of unequal weights,

(i)   Then after finding the difference between E_{S_T} and E_{S_O} i.e. ε, distribute the error ε, inversely proportional to their respective weights amongst the observed spherical angles, to get the corrected spherical angles A_O', B_O' and C_O'.

Check : Sum of ($A_O' + B_O' + C_O'$) $= 180° + E_{S_T}$

(ii)   The corrected plane angles A_a', B_a', C_a' are then computed by subtracting the $\frac{1}{3} E_{S_T}$ from the above corrected spherical angles.

Check : Sum of ($A_a' + B_a' + C_a'$) $= 180°$.

Computations for the Sides of a Spherical Triangle :

The methods used for the computations of sides of spherical triangle are :

(a)   Legendre's method,

(b)   Spherical trigonometry method,

(c)   Delambre's method.

(a) Legendre's Method (Fig. 2.5) :

If the sides are small as compared to the radius of sphere, then each of the corrected spherical angle can be diminished by $\frac{1^{\text{rd}}}{3}$ the spherical excess to get the corrected plane angles and then such triangle can be considered as plane triangle and the sides can be calculated by applying simple sine rule i.e. $\dfrac{\sin A_a'}{a} = \dfrac{\sin B_a'}{b} = \dfrac{\sin C_a'}{c}$. If ' a' is the known side from adjacent triangle, then the required sides b and c can be calculated by :

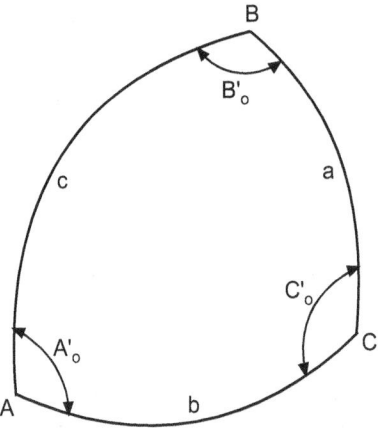

Fig. 2.5

The method is based on the Legendre's theorem, which states that in any spherical

$$b = \left[\frac{\sin B_a'}{\sin A_a'}\right] \times a$$

$$c = \left[\frac{\sin C_a'}{\sin A_a'}\right] \times a$$

(b) Spherical Trigonometry Method (Fig. 2.6) :

Let the corrected spherical angles be A_o', B_o', C_o' and the known side of the spherical triangle be BC i.e. 'a' . Also let α, β and γ be angles subtended at the centre (of the sphere) by the sides a, b and c respectively.

The computations are carried out as follows :

(i)   Since   arc length, a = R·α

∴ $\alpha = \dfrac{a}{R}$ (radians)

$$= \frac{a \times 180°}{\pi R}$$

where,   R = Mean radius of earth

(ii)   By the use of sine rule for spherical triangle, calculate the values of β and γ.

i.e. $\sin \beta = \dfrac{\sin \alpha \cdot \sin B_o'}{\sin A_o'}$

and $\sin \gamma = \dfrac{\sin \alpha \cdot \sin C_o'}{\sin A_o'}$

(iii)   After knowing β and γ, the required lengths AB (i.e. c) and CA (i.e. b) can be calculated by formulae :

$$AB = (c) = \frac{\pi R \gamma^\circ}{180^\circ}$$

and

$$CA = (b) = \frac{\pi R \beta^\circ}{180^\circ}$$

(c) Delambre's Method (Fig. 2.6) :

(i)   The method assumes that if the triangulation stations A, B and C are joined by the chords, the triangle formed will be a plane one. Now, central angle $\alpha^\circ = \dfrac{a \times 180^\circ}{\pi R}$.

(ii)   Calculate the length of the chord 'a' knowing the arc length 'a' and the central angle α.

i.e.   Chord length, a $= 2R \sin \dfrac{\alpha}{2}$

(iii)   Now from plane triangle ABC, knowing the chord length 'a' and the corrected plane angles A_a', B_a' and C_a', calculate the lengths of the remaining two chords b and c by applying simple sine rule.

Thus,   Chord length, b $=$ Chord length a $\times \dfrac{\sin B_a'}{\sin A_a'}$.

and   Chord length, c $=$ Chord length a $\times \dfrac{\sin C_a'}{\sin A_a'}$

(iv)   Now, knowing the chord b and c, calculate the corresponding central angles β° and γ° by the formulae :

$$\sin \frac{\beta^\circ}{2} = \frac{\text{Chord length b}}{2R}$$

and

$$\sin \frac{\gamma^\circ}{2} = \frac{\text{Chord length c}}{2R}$$

(v)   Having determined the values of β° and γ°, calculate the arc lengths b and c, by the formulae :

$$\text{Length of arc b} = \frac{\pi R \beta^\circ}{180^\circ}$$

and

$$\text{Length of arc c} = \frac{\pi R \gamma^\circ}{180^\circ}$$

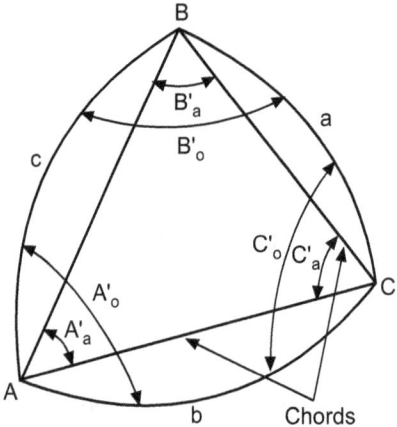

(i)　　A_o', B_o', C_o'　→　**Corrected spherical angles**

(ii)　　A_a', B_a', C_a'　→　**Corrected plane angles**

Fig. 2.6 : Computations of sides of spherical triangle

Example 2.27 : In a triangle ABC, in the mean latitudes of 40°, having sides AB = 19.2 km, AC = 25.4 km and angle BAC = 23° 54' 23", calculate the spherical excess. Take mean radius of the earth as 6400 km.

Solution : Using the formula for spherical excess,

$$E_S = \frac{A \times 180°}{\pi R^2}$$

where,　　A = Area of spherical triangle in sq. km.

∴.　　$$E_S = \left[\frac{\frac{1}{2} cb \sin \gamma}{R^2 \sin 1"} \right] \text{ seconds}$$

R = Mean radius of earth in km

= 6400 km

Substituting,　　$$= \frac{1}{2} \times \frac{19.2 \times 25.4 \sin 23° 54' 23"}{(6400)^2 \times \frac{1}{206265}}$$

= 0.497 seconds

Example 2.28 : The following values were recorded for a spherical triangle ABC, the individual measurements being equally precise.

$\angle A$ = 62° 28' 06"　　Weight 8

$\angle B$ = 57° 43' 36"　　Weight 6

$\angle C$ = 59° 48' 38"　　Weight 4

Spherical excess was known to be 7".

Find the corrected spherical angles.

Solution : Observed sum of spherical angles $= 180° 00' 20''$

Whereas the theoretical spherical excess (given) $= 7''$

∴   Discrepancy $= 20'' - 7'' = 13''$

Total correction $= -13°$ to be distributed inversely proportional to weights of observation.

i.e. $C_A : C_B : C_C = \dfrac{1}{W_A} : \dfrac{1}{W_B} : \dfrac{1}{W_C}$

$$= \dfrac{1}{8} : \dfrac{1}{6} : \dfrac{1}{4}$$

$$= 3 : 4 : 6 \qquad \text{(By L.C.M.)}$$

∴ $C_A = \dfrac{3}{13} \times 13'' = -3''$

$C_B = \dfrac{4}{13} \times 13'' = -4''$

$C_C = \dfrac{6}{13} \times 13'' = -6''$

∴   The corrected spherical angles are :

$A_O' = 62° 28' 03''$

$B_O' = 57° 43' 32''$

$C_O' = 59° 48' 32''$

Check : $A_O' + B_O' + C_O' = 180° 00' 07''$

Example 2.29 : The angles of a spherical triangle PQR are given below :

$\angle P = 49° 11' 13.2''$ Weight 1

$\angle Q = 74° 26' 34.8''$ Weight 3

$\angle R = 56° 22' 17''$ Weight 2

If the area of the above spherical triangle is 1764 sq. km., adjust the angles of above triangles. Take spherical excess equal to 1'' for every 196 sq. km. area.

Solution : (i) Observed sum of the spherical angles,

$P + Q + R = 180° 00' 05''$

(ii) $\left(\begin{array}{c}\text{Theoretical} \\ \text{spherical excess}\end{array}\right) = \dfrac{\text{Area of triangle}}{196.0}$

$$= \dfrac{1764}{196} = 9''$$

(iii)   Discrepancy $= 9'' - 5'' = 4''$

(iv)   The discrepancy of 4" is to be distributed inversely proportional to their weights.

$$\therefore \qquad C_P : C_Q : C_R = \frac{1}{1} : \frac{1}{3} : \frac{1}{2}$$

$$= 6 : 2 : 3 \qquad \text{(By L.C.M.)}$$

$$\therefore \qquad C_P = \frac{6}{11} \times 4" = +2.18"$$

$$C_Q = \frac{2}{11} \times 4" = +0.73"$$

$$\text{and} \qquad C_R = \frac{3}{11} \times 4" = +1.09"$$

Check : $C_P + C_Q + C_R = 4.00"$

$\therefore$ Adjusted spherical angles are :

$$P_C = 48° \ 11' \ 15.38"$$

$$Q_C = 74° \ 26' \ 35.53"$$

$$R_C = 56° \ 22' \ 18.09"$$

Check : Sum of adjusted spherical angles = 180° 0' 9"

Example 2.30 : Mean observed angles in a spherical triangle ABC were

$$\angle A = 48° \ 20' \ 27.2" \quad \text{Weight 2}$$

$$\angle B = 68° \ 17' \ 32.8" \quad \text{Weight 1}$$

$$\angle C = 63° \ 22' \ 15.4" \quad \text{Weight 3}$$

Length BC = 16.5 km

Assume the radius of earth to be 6400 km.

Calculate : (i) Spherical excess, (ii) Adjusted spherical angles, (iii) Adjusted plane angles.

Solution : (i) Add up all the observed spherical angles.

$\therefore$ Observed sum = A + B + C = 180° 00' 15.4"

(ii)   Subtract $\frac{1}{3}$ (15.4") i.e. 5.13", 5.13" and 5.14" from the observed spherical angles to get the approximate plane angles A_a, B_a and C_a.

$$\therefore \qquad A_a = 48° \ 20' \ 27.20" - 5.13"$$

$$= 48° \ 20' \ 22.07"$$

$$B_a = 68° \ 17' \ 32.80" - 5.13"$$

$$= 68° \ 17' \ 27.67"$$

$$C_a = 63° 22' 15.40" - 5.14"$$

$$= 63° 22' 10.26"$$

Check : $\quad A_a + B_a + C_a = 180° 00' 00"$

(iii) Calculate the area of the triangle ABC.

$$A = \frac{\frac{1}{2} a^2 \sin B_a \sin C_a}{\sin A_a}$$

$$= \frac{\frac{1}{2} (16.5)^2 \times \sin (68° 17' 27.67") \sin (63° 22' 10.26")}{\sin (48° 20' 22.07")}$$

$$= 151.324 \text{ sq. km.}$$

(iv) Theoretical spherical excess in seconds

$$= \left[\frac{A \times 180 \times 3600}{\pi \times R^2} \right]$$

$$= \left[\frac{151.324 \times 180 \times 3600}{\pi \times (6400)^2} \right]$$

$$= 0.76 \text{ seconds}$$

whereas the observed spherical excess (including observation error) = 15.4" seconds

$\therefore \qquad$ Discrepancy $= 15.4" - 0.76"$

$$= 14.64 \text{ seconds}$$

Now if C_A, C_B and C_C are the corrections to the observed spherical angles, then using the laws of weights, the corrections are inversely proportional to their weights.

$\therefore \qquad C_A : C_B : C_C = \dfrac{1}{2} : \dfrac{1}{1} : \dfrac{1}{3}$

$$= 3 : 6 : 2$$

$\therefore \qquad C_A = \dfrac{3}{11} \times 14.64 \text{ seconds}$

$$= 3.99 \text{ seconds}$$

$\qquad C_B = \dfrac{6}{11} \times 14.64 \text{ seconds}$

$$= 7.99 \text{ seconds}$$

and $\qquad C_C = \dfrac{2}{11} \times 14.64$

$$= 2.66 \text{ seconds}$$

Check : $\quad C_A + C_B + C_C = 14.64"$

∴   Corrected spherical angles are :

$$A_o' = 48° 20' 27.2" - 3.99"$$

$$= 48° 20' 23.21"$$

$$B_o' = 68° 17' 32.8" - 7.99"$$

$$= 68° 17' 24.81"$$

$$C_o' = 63° 22' 15.4" - 2.66"$$

$$= 63° 22' 12.74"$$

Check : $A_o' + B_o' + C_o' = 180° 0' 0.76"$

∴   Corrected plane angles $= \begin{bmatrix} \text{Corrected} \\ \text{spherical angles} \end{bmatrix} - \begin{bmatrix} \frac{1}{3}^{rd} \text{ of theoretical} \\ \text{spherical excess} \end{bmatrix}$

Now $\frac{1}{3}^{rd}$ of theoretical spherical angles are :

$$\frac{0.76}{3} = 0.25, 0.25 \text{ and } 0.26$$

$$A_a' = 48° 20' 23.21" - 0.25"$$

$$= 48° 20' 22.96"$$

$$B_a' = 68° 17' 24.81" - 0.25"$$

$$= 68° 17' 24.56"$$

$$C_a' = 63° 22' 17.4" - 0.26"$$

$$= 63° 22' 12.48"$$

Check : $A_a' + B_a' + C_a' = 180° 00' 00"$

Example 2.31 : Mean observed angles in a spherical triangle ABC were recorded as given below :

$$\angle A = 48° 20' 17.2" \quad \text{Weight 2}$$
$$\angle B = 68° 17' 32.8" \quad \text{Weight 1}$$
$$\angle C = 63° 22' 13.4" \quad \text{Weight 3}$$

Length of side BC was 59.508 km.

(i)   Find the spherical excess.

(ii)   Find adjusted spherical and plane angles.

(iii)   Compute the sides CA and AB of spherical triangle.

Solution : Sum of observed spherical angles,

$$A + B + C = 180° 00' 3.4"$$

$\therefore$ Approximate plane angles will be obtained by subtracting $\frac{1}{3}$ (3.4)" from each of the observed spherical angles.

$$A_a = 48° \; 20' \; 17.20" - 1.13"$$
$$= 48° \; 20' \; 16.07"$$
$$B_a = 68° \; 17' \; 32.80" - 1.13"$$
$$= 68° \; 17' \; 31.67"$$
$$C_a = 63° \; 22' \; 13.40" - 1.14"$$
$$= 63° \; 22' \; 12.26"$$

Check : $A_a + B_a + C_a = 180° \; 00' \; 00"$

$$A = \text{Area of triangle}$$
$$= \frac{1}{2} \times \frac{a^2 \sin B_a \sin C_a}{\sin A_a}$$
$$= \frac{1}{2} \times \frac{(59.508)^2 \times \sin (68° \; 17' \; 31.67") \times \sin (63° \; 22' \; 12.26")}{\sin (48° \; 20' \; 16.07")}$$
$$A = 1968.3763 \text{ sq. km.}$$

Theoretical spherical excess in seconds

$$E_{S_T} = \frac{A}{R^2 \sin 1"}$$
$$= \frac{1968.3763}{6370 \times \dfrac{1}{206265}}$$
$$= 10 \text{ seconds}$$

$\therefore$ $\text{Discrepancy} = 10" - 3.4" = 6.6"$

$$= \left(E_{S_T} - E_{S_O} \right)$$

which is to be divided amongst the observed angles inversely proportional to their weights. If C_A, C_B and C_C are the corrections to the angles A, B and C respectively, then,

$$C_A : C_B : C_C = \frac{1}{2} : \frac{1}{1} : \frac{1}{3}$$
$$= 3 : 6 : 2$$

$\therefore$ $C_A = \dfrac{3}{11} \times 6.6" = 1.8" \; (+ve)$

$C_B = \dfrac{6}{11} \times 6.6" = 3.6" \; (+ve)$

and $C_C = \dfrac{2}{11} \times 6.6" = 1.2" \; (+ve)$

Check : $C_A + C_B + C_C = 1.8" + 3.6" + 1.2" = 6.6"$

∴　　Adjusted spherical angles will be

$$A_0' = 48° 20' 19''$$

$$B_0' = 68° 17' 36.4''$$

$$C_0' = 63° 22' 14.6''$$

Check :　$A_0' + B_0' + C_0' = 180° 00' 10''$

∴　　Adjusted plane angles will be obtained by subtracting $\frac{1^{rd}}{3}$ (10") from each of the adjusted spherical angles.

$$A_a' = 48° 20' 15.67''$$

$$B_a' = 68° 17' 33.07''$$

$$C_a' = 63° 22' 11.26''$$

Check :　$A_a' + B_a' + C_a' = 180° 00' 00''$

Computations of sides i.e. CA and AB of spherical triangle ABC :

(a)　By Legendre's method : Here the spherical triangle is assumed as a plane triangle and taking adjusted plane angles, the lengths of CA and AB are computed by applying simple sine rule.

i.e.　　　　$$\frac{\sin A_a'}{a} = \frac{\sin B_a'}{b} = \frac{\sin C_a'}{c}$$

∴　　Here　　$$B_c = a = 59.508 \text{ km (given)}$$

$$b = \frac{59.508 \times \sin (68° 17' 33.07'')}{\sin (48° 20' 15.67'')}$$

∴　　　　$$b = 74.05 \text{ km}$$

and　　　　$$c = \frac{59.508 \times \sin (63° 22' 11.26'')}{\sin (48° 20' 15.67'')}$$

∴　　　　$$c = 71.204 \text{ km}$$

(b)　By spherical trigonometry method :

$$\alpha = \frac{a}{R} \times \frac{180}{\pi}$$

$$= \frac{59.508 \times 180}{6370 \times \pi}$$

$$= 0° 32' 6.61''$$

∴   Applying sine rule for spherical triangle and considering adjusted spherical angles, we get,

$$\beta = 0° \, 39' \, 55.98''$$

and

$$\gamma = 0° \, 38' \, 25.3''$$

∴

$$b = \frac{\beta \times R \times \pi}{180}$$

$$= 74.00 \text{ km}$$

and

$$c = \frac{\gamma \times R \times \pi}{180}$$

$$= 71.22 \text{ km}$$

(c)   By Delambre's method :

$$\alpha = \frac{a}{R} \times \frac{180}{\pi}$$

$$= 0° \, 32' \, 6.61'' \text{ (as above)}$$

∴

$$\text{Chord } a = 2R \sin \frac{\alpha}{2}$$

$$= 2 \times 6370 \times \frac{\sin (0° \, 32' \, 6.61'')}{2} = 59.49$$

∴

$$\frac{\sin A_a'}{\text{Chord } a} = \frac{\sin B_a'}{\text{Chord } b} = \frac{\sin C_a'}{\text{Chord } c}$$

∴

$$\text{Chord } b = 74.005 \text{ km}$$

$$\text{Chord } c = 71.2 \text{ km}$$

∴

$$\sin \frac{\beta}{2} = \frac{\text{Chord } b}{2R} = \frac{74.005}{2 \times 6370}$$

∴

$$\beta = 39' \, 56.34''$$

and

$$\sin \frac{\gamma}{2} = \frac{\text{Chord } c}{2R} = \frac{71.20}{2 \times 6370}$$

∴

$$\gamma = 38' \, 25.4''$$

∴

$$\text{Arc } b = \frac{\pi R \beta}{180} = \frac{\pi \times 6370}{180} \times 0.6656 = 74.00 \text{ km}$$

and

$$\text{Arc } c = \frac{\pi R \gamma}{180} = \frac{\pi \times 6370}{180} \times 0.6404 = 71.20 \text{ km}$$

Example 2.32 : The observed angles of a spherical triangle ABC are as follows :

$$\angle A = 58° 20' 22.2" \quad \text{Weight 1}$$

$$\angle B = 70° 22' 30.8" \quad \text{Weight 2}$$

$$\angle C = 51° 17' 17" \quad \text{Weight 3}$$

If the spherical excess was 1" for every 196.00 sq. km. area and the area of spherical triangle was known to be 980 sq. km, adjust the above spherical angles.

Solution : Observed sum of three angles of spherical triangle = 180° 00' 10"

Observed spherical excess = 10"

$$\text{Theoretical spherical excess} = \frac{\text{Area of triangle}}{196} = \frac{980}{196} = 5"$$

$\therefore$ Discrepancy = 10" − 5" = 5"

This discrepancy is to be distributed inversely proportional to the weights.

Let C_A, C_B and C_C be the corrections to angles A, B and C.

$$\therefore \qquad C_A : C_B : C_C = \frac{1}{1} : \frac{1}{2} : \frac{1}{3}$$

$$= 6 : 3 : 2$$

$$\therefore \qquad C_A = 5" \times \frac{6}{11} = 2.73"$$

$$C_B = 5" \times \frac{3}{11} = 1.36"$$

$$\text{and} \qquad C_C = 5" \times \frac{2}{11} = 0.91"$$

Since observed spherical excess is greater than theoretical spherical excess, the correction is to be subtracted from observed angles.

$\therefore$ Corrected spherical angles :

$$\angle A_C = 58° 20' 22.2" − 2.73"$$

$$= 58° 20' 19.47"$$

$$\angle B_C = 70° 22' 30.8" − 1.36"$$

$$= 70° 22' 29.44"$$

$$\angle C_C = 51° 17' 17" − 0.91"$$

$$= 51° 17' 16.09"$$

Check : $\angle A_C + \angle B_C + \angle C_C = 180° 0' 5"$

Example 2.33 : The angles of a spherical triangle PQR were observed as follows :

$$P \ = \ 87° \ 14' \ 39" \qquad \text{Weight 4}$$
$$Q \ = \ 39° \ 40' \ 48" \qquad \text{Weight 3}$$
$$R \ = \ 53° \ 04' \ 55" \qquad \text{Weight 2}$$

Find the values of the adjusted spherical angles, if the spherical excess is known to be 9".

Solution :

$$\text{Sum of observed spherical angles} \ = \ 180° \ 00' \ 22"$$

$\therefore$ Observed $E_S \ = \ 22"$

whereas   Theoretical $E_S \ = \ 9"$ (Given)

$\therefore$ Error $\ = \ 22 - 9 \ = \ 13"$

$\therefore$ Correction $\ = \ -13"$

If C_A, C_B and C_C are the corrections to the respective angles,

$$C_A : C_B : C_C \ = \ \frac{1}{4} \ : \ \frac{1}{3} \ : \ \frac{1}{2}$$

$$= \ 3 : 4 : 6$$

$\therefore$
$$C_A \ = \ \frac{3}{13} \times 13" \ = \ -3"$$

$$C_B \ = \ \frac{4}{13} \times 13" \ = \ -4"$$

and
$$C_C \ = \ \frac{6}{13} \times 13" \ = \ -6"$$

$\therefore$ Corrected spherical angles are :

$$87° \ 14' \ 36"$$
$$39° \ 40' \ 44"$$
$$53° \ 04' \ 49"$$

Therefore,   Sum $\ = \ 180° \ 00' \ 9"$

2.13.2 Convergence of Meridians

Introduction :

The surface of the earth is assumed to be roughly spheroid. If the survey extends to a limited small area, the Earth' s surface may be considered as flat, and the survey is called as *'Plane Surveying'*. However, if it extends over a considerable area, it is necessary to consider the curvature of the earth during surveying and is known as *'Geodetic Surveying'* and in such case spherical co-ordinates are to be computed to determine the position of points. It may be noted that due to the Earth' s curvature, straight line will constantly be changing its azimuth and a line with constant azimuth throughout its length is not a straight line, but a parallel of latitude. On the spheroid, the directions are referred to the meridian passing through the point under consideration. Due to the spherical shape of the earth, such meridians (also called as longitude lines) will not be parallel to each other, but will converge (i.e. meet) at the poles i.e. meridians converge at the poles.

Fig. 2.7 shows two points A and B on the surface of the Earth and P is the position of the north pole. AP and BP are the two meridians passing through A and B and meeting at the pole P. C is a point on the extension of the line AB. EF is the position of the terrestrial equator.

Let A_1A = Latitude of point A = θ_A

∴   Distance PA = $90 - \theta_A$

Similarly, BB_1 = Latitude of the point B = θ_B

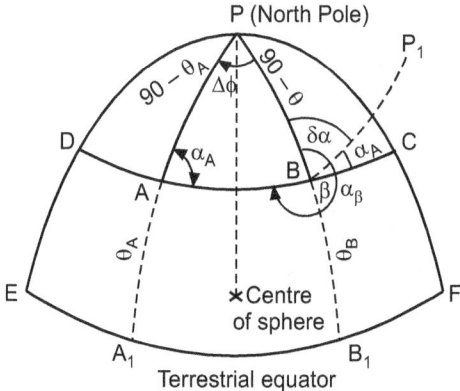

Fig. 2.7

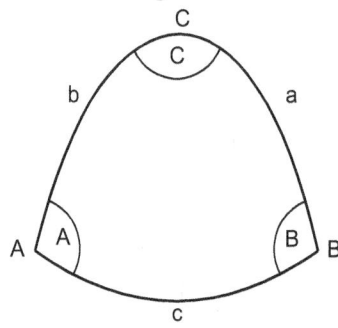

Fig. 2.8

Spherical triangle :

$$\tan\frac{(A + B)}{2} = \left[\frac{\cos\frac{1}{2}(a - b)}{\cos\frac{1}{2}(a + b)} \times \cot\frac{C}{2}\right]$$

∴   Distance PB = $90 - \theta_B$

Now, azimuth of AB measured at A = α_A and azimuth of BA measured at B = α_B.

Obviously from the figure, since AP is parallel to BP_1,

Azimuth of AB at A = $\angle$ PAB = α_A

and   Azimuth of AB at B = $180° - \angle$ PBA = $180° - \alpha_B$

$\therefore$ $\delta\alpha$ = Difference of these two azimuths

= $(180° - \angle$ PBA$) - \angle$ PAB

i.e.   Convergence of meridians,

$\delta\alpha$ = $180° - (\alpha_A + \alpha_B)$

i.e. due to the convergence of meridians AP and BP, the fore and back (i.e. reverse) azimuth of line AB do not differ exactly by 180° (as noticed in plane surveying) but they differ by 180° + $\delta\alpha$, the term $\delta\alpha$ being known as 'Convergence of meridians'.

Approximately, the value of $\delta\alpha$ (i.e. the convergence meridians) = (Difference of longitudes of A and B) × sine average of latitudes.

i.e. $\delta\alpha$ = $(\phi_B - \phi_A) \times \sin\left(\dfrac{\theta_A + \theta_B}{2}\right)$

= $\delta\phi \times$ sine of mean latitude

Bearing and Azimuth (of a survey line) :

(i)   Bearing of a line : Bearing of a line is its direction measured with respect to the plane of reference passing at each station and is drawn parallel to the origin of the survey. Thus, the fore and back bearings of a survey line always differ by 180°.

(ii)   Azimuth of a line : Azimuth of a line is its direction measured with respect to meridian passing through it i.e. measured with respect to the true north passing at that place. As the meridians drawn at different longitudes converge at the poles, the meridians passing through the beginning and end of the line will no longer be parallel and as such, the fore and back azimuth of the line will not differ by 180°.

As shown in the figure, BP_1 is a line drawn from B, parallel to the meridian AP passing through the origin of survey (i.e. A). Thus, the fore and back bearings of the line AB will differ exactly by 180°. However, the meridian drawn from B will be BP (which is not parallel to the meridian AP passing through the point A) and as such the fore and back azimuths of the line AB will not differ by 180°.

Expression for the Convergence of Meridians :

The Fig. 2.7 shows two points A and B on the surface of the earth whose respective co-ordinates are as stated below.

Point	Latitude	Longitude
A	θ_A	ϕ_A
B	θ_B	ϕ_B

∴ Difference of longitudes of these two points

$$= \phi_B - \phi_A = \delta\phi$$

Now, convergence of meridians,

$$\delta\alpha = 180° - (\alpha_A + \alpha_B)$$

In the spherical triangle PAB,

$$PA = 90° - \theta_A ; \quad PB = 90° - \theta_B$$

Now, using the formula from spherical triangle (Fig. 2.11),

$$\tan\frac{(A + B)}{2} = \frac{\cos\frac{1}{2}[(90° - \theta_B) - (90° - \theta_A)]}{\cos\frac{1}{2}[(90° - \theta_A) + (90° - \theta_B)]} \times \cot\frac{\delta\phi}{2}$$

$$(\because \angle APB = \phi_B - \phi_A = \delta\phi)$$

or

$$\cot\frac{1}{2}[180° - (A + B)] = \frac{\cos\frac{1}{2}(\theta_A - \theta_B)}{\cos\frac{1}{2}(180° - \theta_A - \theta_B)} \times \cot\frac{\delta\phi}{2}$$

$$= \frac{\cos\frac{1}{2}(\theta_A - \theta_B)}{\sin\frac{1}{2}(\theta_A + \theta_B)} \times \cot\frac{\delta\phi}{2}$$

But

$$180° - (A + B) = 180° - \left[\alpha_A + (360° - \alpha_B)\right]$$

$$= 180° - \left[\alpha_A + \{360° - (180° + \alpha_A + \delta\alpha)\}\right]$$

$$= 180° - \left[\alpha_A + 180° - (\alpha_A + \delta\alpha)\right] = \delta\alpha$$

∴

$$\cot\frac{1}{2}(\delta\alpha) = \frac{\cos\frac{1}{2}(\theta_A - \theta_B)}{\sin\frac{1}{2}(\theta_A + \theta_B)} \times \cot\frac{\delta\phi}{2}$$

or

$$\tan\frac{1}{2}(\delta\alpha) = \frac{\sin\frac{1}{2}(\theta_A + \theta_B)}{\cos\frac{1}{2}(\theta_A - \theta_B)} \times \tan\frac{\delta\phi}{2} \qquad \ldots (2.19)$$

Now, if the length AB is small as compared to the radius of the Earth, then approximately we may write,

$$\tan\frac{\delta\alpha}{2} \approx \frac{\delta\alpha}{2} \quad \text{and} \quad \tan\frac{\delta\phi}{2} \approx \frac{\delta\phi}{2}$$

∴   The above equation (2.19) reduces to

$$\frac{\delta\alpha}{2} = \left[\frac{\sin\frac{1}{2}(\theta_A + \theta_B)}{\cos\frac{1}{2}(\theta_A - \theta_B)}\right] \times \frac{\delta\phi}{2}$$

or

$$\delta\alpha = \frac{\sin\frac{1}{2}(\theta_A + \theta_B)}{\cos\frac{1}{2}(\theta_A - \theta_B)} \times \delta\phi$$

i.e. convergence of meridians = $\delta\alpha$

$$= \frac{\sin\frac{1}{2}(\theta_A + \theta_B)}{\cos\frac{1}{2}(\theta_A - \theta_B)} \times \delta\phi \qquad\qquad \text{... (2.20)}$$

Further if the value of $\theta_A - \theta_B$ is very small, $\left[\dfrac{\theta_A - \theta_B}{2}\right]$ will be still smaller and approximately the value of $\cos\frac{1}{2}(\theta_A - \theta_B)$ will be taken as unity.

Then

$$\delta\alpha = \left[\frac{\sin\frac{1}{2}(\theta_A + \theta_B)}{1}\right] \times \delta\phi \qquad\qquad \text{... [2.21 (a)]}$$

But $\dfrac{\theta_A + \theta_B}{2}$ = Average of two latitudes of A and B

and $\delta\phi$ = Difference of longitudes of A and B

∴   Convergence of meridians,

$$\delta\alpha = \left[\begin{matrix}\text{Sine average}\\\text{of latitude}\end{matrix}\right] \times \left[\begin{matrix}\text{Difference of}\\\text{longitude}\end{matrix}\right] \qquad\qquad \text{... [2.21 (b)]}$$

Example 2.34 : The following are the latitudes and longitudes of two stations C and D. Obtain the convergence of meridian through C to D.

Station	Latitude	Longitude
C	48° 40' 12" N	78° 30' 20" E
D	49° 01' 10" N	78° 55' 32" E

Solution :

1. **By exact method :**

$$\tan \frac{1}{2} C = \frac{\sin \frac{1}{2}(y_1 + y_2)}{\cos \frac{1}{2}(y_1 - y_2)} \cdot \tan \frac{(x_2 - x_1)}{2}$$

$$= \frac{\sin \frac{1}{2}(48° \ 40' \ 12" + 49° \ 01' \ 10")}{\cos \frac{1}{2}(48° \ 40' \ 12" - 49° \ 01' \ 10")} \cdot \tan \frac{(25' \ 12")}{2}$$

∴ Convergence of meridians,

$$C = 0° \ 18' \ 58.44"$$

2. **By approximate method :**

$$\left(\frac{\text{Convergence of meridians}}{2} \right) = \frac{C}{2} = \frac{\sin \frac{1}{2}(y_1 + y_2)}{\cos \frac{1}{2}(y_1 - y_2)} \cdot \frac{(x_2 - x_1)}{2}$$

$$= \frac{\sin \frac{1}{2}(48° \ 40' \ 12" + 49° \ 01' \ 10")}{\cos \frac{1}{2}(49° \ 01' \ 12" - 48° \ 40' \ 10")} \times \frac{0° \ 25' \ 12"}{2}$$

∴ $\left[\begin{array}{c} \text{Convergence of} \\ \text{meridians} \end{array} \right] = C = 0° \ 18' \ 58.43"$

3. **By approximate, approximate method :**

$$\left[\begin{array}{c} \text{Convergence} \\ \text{of meridian} \end{array} \right] = \sin(\text{Average of latitudes}) \times \text{Difference of longitudes}$$

∴ $C = \sin(48° \ 50' \ 41") \times (0° \ 25' \ 12")$

$$= 0° \ 18' \ 58.43"$$

Example 2.35 : Given the following latitudes and longitudes of two stations P and Q. Obtain the convergence of meridian through P and Q.

Station	Latitude	Longitude
P	40° 30' 10" N	70° 25' 40" E
Q	41° 56' 20" N	70° 50' 52" E

Solution :

1. By exact formula :

$$\text{Longitude difference} = (x_2 - x_1) = 0°\ 25'\ 12" = x_2 - x_1$$

$$\tan\frac{C}{2} = \frac{\sin\frac{1}{2}(y_1 + y_2)}{\cos\frac{1}{2}(y_1 - y_2)} \cdot \tan\frac{(x_2 - x_1)}{2}$$

$$= \frac{\sin\frac{1}{2}(82°\ 26'\ 30")}{\cos\frac{1}{2}(1°\ 26'\ 10")} \times \frac{0°\ 25'\ 12"}{2}$$

$$\therefore \qquad C = 0°\ 16'\ 36.43"$$

$$\therefore \qquad \begin{bmatrix}\text{Convergence}\\ \text{of meridian}\end{bmatrix} = 0°\ 16'\ 36.43"$$

2. By approximate formula :

i.e.
$$\frac{C}{2} = \frac{\sin\frac{1}{2}(y_1 + y_2)}{\cos\frac{1}{2}(y_1 - y_2)} \cdot \frac{(x_2 - x_1)}{2}$$

$$= \frac{\sin\frac{1}{2}(82°\ 26'\ 30")}{\cos\frac{1}{2}(1°\ 26'\ 10")} \times \frac{0°\ 25'\ 12"}{2}$$

$$\therefore \qquad C = 0°\ 16'\ 36.43"$$

$$\text{Convergence of meridian} = 0°\ 16'\ 36.43"$$

3. By approximate, approximate method :

$$\begin{bmatrix}\text{Convergence}\\ \text{of meridian}\end{bmatrix} = \sin(\text{Average of latitudes}) \times \text{Difference of longitudes}$$

$$= \sin(41°\ 13'\ 15") \times 0°\ 25'\ 12"$$

$$\therefore \qquad C = 0°\ 16'\ 36.35"$$

$$\therefore \qquad \begin{bmatrix}\text{Convergence}\\ \text{of meridian}\end{bmatrix} = C = 0°\ 16'\ 36.35"$$

Example 2.36 : Two points A and B have the following co-ordinates :

Station	Latitude	Longitude
A	52° 21' 14" N	93° 48' 50" E
B	52° 24' 18" N	93° 42' 50" E

Given the following values :

Latitude	1" of Latitude	1" of Longitude
52° 20'	30.42345 m	18.63816 m
52° 25'	30.42387 m	18.60312 m

Find the azimuth of B from A and of A from B and also find the distance AB.

Solution : It is an inverse problem.

1. Mean latitude of A and B $= \dfrac{52° \ 21' \ 14" + 52° \ 24' \ 18"}{2}$ $= 52° \ 22' \ 46"$

2. Value of 1" of latitude (m) for mean latitude, by interpolation $= 30.423682$
3. Value of 1" of longitude (n) for mean latitude, by interpolation $= 18.618771$
4. Difference in longitude, $\delta\phi \ = \ 0° \ 6' \ 0"$

   Using equation, $\delta\alpha \ = \ \delta\phi \cdot \sin$ (average of latitudes)

   $= \ 0° \ 6' \ 0" \sin (52° \ 22' \ 46")$

   $= \ 0° \ 4' \ 45.15"$

5. From equation,

$$\tan\left(\alpha + \frac{\delta\alpha}{2}\right) \ = \ \frac{n \ \delta\phi}{m \ \delta\theta}$$

$$\tan\left(\alpha + \frac{0° \ 4' \ 45.15"}{2}\right) \ = \ \frac{18.618771}{30.423682} \times \frac{0° \ 6' \ 0"}{0° \ 3' \ 4"}$$

∴ $\alpha \ = \ 50° \ 5' \ 33.71"$

∴   Azimuth of line AB at A $\ = \ 50° \ 5' \ 33.71"$

6. Azimuth of line BA at B $\ = \ \alpha + \delta\alpha$

   $= \ 50° \ 5' \ 33.71" + 0° \ 4' \ 45.15"$

   $= \ 50° \ 10' \ 18.8"$

7. Length of line AB :

   From equation, $\delta\theta \ = \ \dfrac{l \cos\left(\alpha + \dfrac{\delta\alpha}{2}\right)}{m}$

∴ $l \ = \ \dfrac{30.423682 \times 0° \ 3' \ 4"}{\cos\left(50° \ 5' \ 33.71" + \dfrac{0° \ 4' \ 45.15"}{2}\right)}$

   $= \ 2.4258 \ km$

From equation, $\delta\phi = \dfrac{l \sin\left(\alpha + \dfrac{\delta\alpha}{2}\right)}{n}$

$\therefore$ $l = \dfrac{18.618771 \times 0° \; 6' \; 0''}{\sin\left(50° \; 5' \; 33.71'' + \dfrac{0° \; 4' \; 45.15''}{2}\right)}$

$= 2.4258 \text{ km}$

Example 2.37 : Given the following co-ordinates of two stations A and B.

Station	Latitude	Longitude
A	54° 52' 10" N	83° 2' 30" E
B	54° 54' 24" N	83° 48' 10" E

Find the azimuth of line AB at A and azimuth of AB at B. Also find out length of line AB.

Geodetic Table :

Latitude	1" of Latitude in metres (m)	1" of Longitude in metres (n)
54° 50'	30.9234	17.8509
54° 55'	30.9238	17.8141

Solution : It is an inverse problem.

1. Mean latitude of A and B

$$= \frac{54° \; 52' \; 10'' + 54° \; 54' \; 24''}{2} = 54° \; 53' \; 12''$$

2. Value of 1" of latitude (n) for mean latitude,

By interpolation $= 30.92366 \text{ m}$

3. Value of 1" of longitude (n) for mean latitude,

By interpolation $= 17.826735 \text{ m}$

4. Difference in longitude

$\delta\phi = 0° \; 45' \; 40''$

Using equation $\delta\alpha = \delta\phi \times \sin \text{(Average of latitudes)}$

$= 0° \; 45' \; 40'' \sin (54° \; 53' \; 17'')$

$= 0° \; 37' \; 21.4''$

5. From equation

$$\tan\left(\frac{\alpha + \delta\alpha}{2}\right) = \frac{n\,\delta\phi}{m\,\delta\theta}$$

$$\tan\left(\alpha + \frac{0° 37' 21.4''}{2}\right) = \frac{17.826735}{30.923663} \times \frac{0° 45' 10''}{0° 2' 14''}$$

$\therefore \qquad\qquad\qquad\qquad \alpha = 84° 50' 22.6''$

Azimuth of line AB at A $= 84° 50' 22.6''$

6. Azimuth of line BA at B

$$= \alpha + \delta\alpha$$

$$= 84° 50' 22.6'' + 0° 37' 21.4''$$

$$= 85° 27' 44''$$

7. Length of line AB :

From equation $\delta\theta = \dfrac{l \cos\left(\alpha + \dfrac{\delta\alpha}{2}\right)}{m}$

$\therefore \qquad\qquad l = \dfrac{30.923663 \times 2' 14''}{\cos (84° 50' 22.6'' + 0° 18' 40.7'')}$

$l_{AB} = 13.616 \text{ km}$

From equation $\delta\phi = \dfrac{l \sin\left(\alpha + \dfrac{\delta\alpha}{2}\right)}{n}$

$l = \dfrac{17.826735 \times 0° 45' 40''}{\sin (84° 50' 22.6'' + 0° 40.7'')}$

$l_{AB} = 13.616 \text{ km}$

2.14 ADJUSTMENT OF A CHAIN OF TRIANGLES

Let there be a chain of triangles ABC, BCD and CDE as shown in Fig. 2.9. All the angles i.e. 1, 2, 3, ..., 14 measured at the various triangulation stations are of equal weights. The adjustment of such a figure is done in the following two steps :

(i)   Station adjustment and

(ii) Figure adjustment.

(i) Station Adjustment :

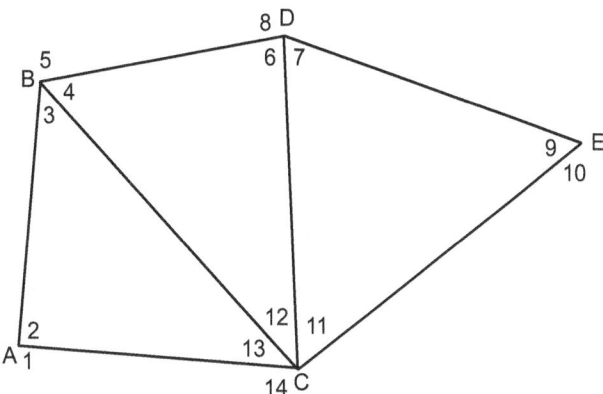

Fig. 2.9 : Adjustment of chain of triangles

The condition to be satisfied by the angles measured at various stations is that their sum should be equal to 360°.

i.e.　(a)　1 + 2　　　= 360°

　　　(b)　3 + 4 + 5　= 360°

　　　(c)　6 + 7 + 8　= 360°

　　　(d)　9 + 10　　= 360°

　　　(e)　11 + 12 + 13 + 14　= 360°

The discrepancy, if any, is to be distributed equally amongst all the angles at the triangulation station, as they are of same weight.

(ii) Figure Adjustment :

The adjusted values of the angles as stated above, are then taken for carrying out figure adjustments.

i.e.　For triangle ABC : 2 + 3 + 13　= 180°

　　　For triangle BCD : 4 + 6 + 12　= 180°

　　　For triangle CDE : 7 + 9 + 11　= 180°

The discrepancy, if any, in the above cases is adjusted by adding or subtracting $\frac{1}{3}^{rd}$ of the discrepancy from each of the three angles of the above triangles, if all observations are of same weights. However, if they are of different weights, the discrepancy is to be adjusted inversely proportional to their weights.

2.15 ADJUSTMENT OF TWO CONNECTED TRIANGLES

As shown in Fig. 2.10, CD is a side common to both triangles ACD and BCD. The six angles A, C' , C", B, D' and D" have been measured. In addition, two more angles ACB and ADB (i.e. summation angles) have also been measured.

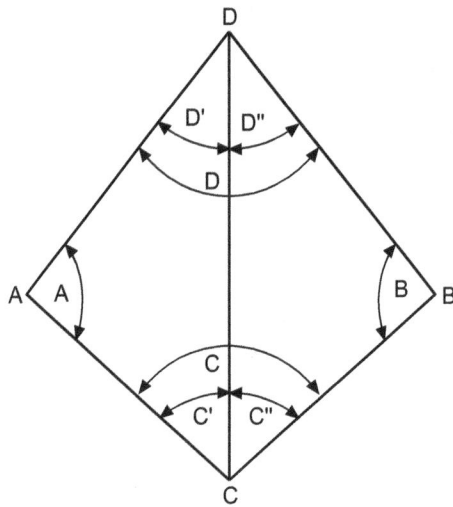

Fig. 2.10 : Two connected triangles adjustment

The conditions i.e. angle equations to be satisfied are as follows :

$$A + C' + D' = 180°$$

$$B + C'' + D'' = 180°$$

$$C = C' + C''$$

$$D = D' + D''$$

Thus out of eight unknowns, C' , C", D and D" are taken as independent unknowns, whereas the other remaining four A, B, C and D are called dependent as they can very well be determined by making use of conditional equations.

The most probable values of the angles can either be obtained by 'Normal equation method' or by 'Method of corrections' .

The procedure of normal equation method will be :

(1)   Express the four dependent unknowns A, B, C and D in terms of other four independent unknowns C' , C", D' and D".

i.e. $$A = 180° - C' - D'$$

$$B = 180° - C'' - D''$$

$$C = C' + C''$$

and $$D = D' + D''$$

Next form four normal equations for C' , C", D' and D" and solve them to get the most probable values.

2.16 ADJUSTMENT OF TRIANGLE WITH A CENTRAL STATION

Procedure :

ABC is a triangle with a central station O. The angles observed at stations A, B, C and O are denoted by θ_1, θ_2, θ_3, ..., θ_8 as shown in Fig. 2.11. The odd angles θ_1, θ_3, θ_5 which are to the left of the surveyor as he walks along the boundary of the figure i.e. AB, BC, CA always facing towards the central station O, are termed as "*Left hand angles*" and the even angles θ_2, θ_4, θ_6 to the right of the surveyor as "*Right hand angles*". The angles θ_7, θ_8, θ_9 at O are called *central angles*.

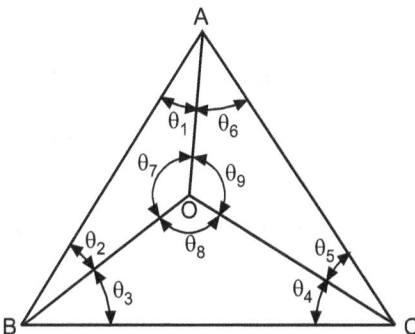

Fig. 2.11 : Adjustment of triangle with a central station

The conditional equations can be written as :

(i)　Apex angle condition i.e.　　$\theta_7 + \theta_8 + \theta_9 = 360°$

(ii)　Triangle condition i.e.　　$\theta_1 + \theta_2 + \theta_7 = 180°$

　　　　　　　　　　　　　　$\theta_3 + \theta_4 + \theta_8 = 180°$

　　　　　　　　　　　　　　$\theta_5 + \theta_6 + \theta_9 = 180°$

(iii)　Side equation i.e. product of sines of odd angles should be equal to the product of the sines of even angles.

i.e.　　　　$\sin \theta_1 \cdot \sin \theta_3 \cdot \sin \theta_5 = \sin \theta_2 \cdot \sin \theta_4 \cdot \sin \theta_6$

Proof : From $\triangle$ ABO,　　$AO = BO \cdot \dfrac{\sin \theta_2}{\sin \theta_1}$　　　　　　　　... (2.22)

From triangles ACO and BCO,

$$AO = CO \cdot \frac{\sin \theta_5}{\sin \theta_6}$$

But　　　　$CO = \dfrac{BO \sin \theta_3}{\sin \theta_4}$

∴　　　　$AO = BO \cdot \dfrac{\sin \theta_3 \cdot \sin \theta_5}{\sin \theta_4 \cdot \sin \theta_6}$　　　　　　　　... (2.23)

∴   Equating (2.22) and (2.23), we get,

$$BO \cdot \frac{\sin \theta_2}{\sin \theta_1} = \frac{BO \sin \theta_3 \cdot \sin \theta_5}{\sin \theta_4 \cdot \sin \theta_6}$$

Cancelling BO and cross multiplying we get,

$$\sin \theta_1 \cdot \sin \theta_3 \cdot \sin \theta_5 = \sin \theta_2 \cdot \sin \theta_4 \cdot \sin \theta_6$$

The above equation is known as side equation because it gives the relation between the three sides AO, BO and CO meeting at O.

Taking log on both sides we get,

$$\log \sin \theta_1 + \log \sin \theta_3 + \log \sin \theta_5 = \log \sin \theta_2 + \log \sin \theta_4 + \log \sin \theta_6$$

i.e. $\begin{bmatrix} \Sigma \text{ log sine of left hand} \\ \text{angles or odd angles} \end{bmatrix} = \begin{bmatrix} \Sigma \text{ log sine of right hand} \\ \text{angles or even angles} \end{bmatrix}$

i.e. $\Sigma \log \sin (\text{L.H.A.}) = \Sigma \log \sin (\text{R.H.A.})$

and is known as *"Log sine condition"*.

Adjustment :

Let C_{r_1}, C_{r_2}, C_{r_3}, ..., C_{r_9} be the corrections to the respective angles θ_1, θ_2, θ_3, ..., θ_9 to get the most probable values of angles and d_1, d_2, d_3, ..., d_9 be the tabular differences for 1" of log sin 1, log sin 2, log sin 3, ..., log sin 9 (obtained from seven figure log table).

∴   The above conditional equations in 'Correction form' would be :

(i) $C_{r_7} + C_{r_8} + C_{r_9} = \pm e_1 \text{ (say)}$

(ii) $C_{r_1} + C_{r_2} + C_{r_7} = \pm e_2 \text{ (say)}$

(iii) $C_{r_3} + C_{r_4} + C_{r_8} = \pm e_3 \text{ (say)}$

(iv) $C_{r_5} + C_{r_6} + C_{r_9} = \pm e_4 \text{ (say)}$

(v)   By log sine condition, we get,

$$d_1 C_{r_1} - d_2 C_{r_2} + d_3 C_{r_3} - d_4 C_{r_4} + d_5 C_{r_5} - d_6 C_{r_6} = \pm M \text{ (say)}$$

where M is expressed with the units of seventh decimal place of logarithms.

(vi)   By the principle of least square, we get,

$\Sigma v^2 = \text{minimum}$

i.e. $(C_{r_1})^2 + (C_{r_2})^2 + (C_{r_3})^2 + (C_{r_4})^2 + (C_{r_5})^2 + (C_{r_6})^2 + (C_{r_7})^2 + (C_{r_8})^2 + (C_{r_9})^2 = \text{minimum}$

Thus, the number of unknowns are nine, whereas the number of equations are only five, therefore the "method of correlates" or correlatives of unknown multipliers $\lambda_1, \lambda_2, \lambda_3$ etc. is to be used to determine the most probable values of the corrections C_{r_1}, C_{r_2}, C_{r_3}, ..., C_{r_9}. The adjusted angles are then worked out after applying the corrections C_{r_1}, C_{r_2}, C_{r_3}, ..., C_{r_9}.

2.17 ADJUSTMENT OF A GEODETIC QUADRILATERAL (i.e. Braced Quadrilateral)

Procedure :

In 'Geodetic Quadrilateral' , all (eight) angles are to be measured independently, observations being made along both the diagonals. If the quadrilateral is of small size, it is considered as a plane one. If, however, it is of large size, it is considered as geodetic and spherical excess (E_S) is calculated for the whole figure. If the work is of minor nature, then $\frac{1}{8}$ th of the spherical excess of quadrilateral is subtracted from each of the observed angle to get the corresponding plane angles.

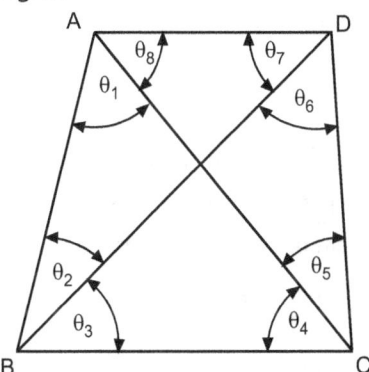

Fig. 2.12 : Adjustment of geodetic quadrilateral

The Fig. 2.12 represents quadrilateral ABCD in which all eight angles $\theta_1, \theta_2, \theta_3, ..., \theta_8$ are measured. The angles $\theta_1, \theta_3, \theta_5, \theta_7$ are called as *"odd angles"* or left hand angles and the angles $\theta_2, \theta_4, \theta_6, \theta_8$ are known as *"even angles"* or right hand angles. The various conditional equations to be satisfied are written down as follows :

(a) Angle equation :

$$\theta_1 + \theta_2 + \theta_3 + \theta_4 + \theta_5 + \theta_6 + \theta_7 + \theta_8 = 360° \qquad ... (2.24)$$
$$\theta_1 + \theta_2 = \theta_5 + \theta_6 \qquad ... (2.25)$$
$$\theta_3 + \theta_4 = \theta_7 + \theta_8 \qquad ... (2.26)$$

(b) Side equation :

$$\begin{bmatrix} \text{Product of sine of the odd} \\ \text{angles or left hand angles} \end{bmatrix} = \begin{bmatrix} \text{Product of sine of even} \\ \text{angles or right hand angles} \end{bmatrix}$$

i.e. 　　　$\sin \theta_1 \cdot \sin \theta_3 \cdot \sin \theta_5 \cdot \sin \theta_7 = \sin \theta_2 \cdot \sin \theta_4 \cdot \sin \theta_6 \cdot \sin \theta_8$

or taking logs,

$$\Sigma \text{ log sine of odd angles } = \Sigma \text{ log sine of even angles}$$

which is known as 'log sine condition'.

Proof : From $\triangle$ ABC, $AB = BC \cdot \dfrac{\sin \theta_4}{\sin \theta_1}$ ... (2.27)

and from $\triangle$ BCD, $BC = CD \cdot \dfrac{\sin \theta_6}{\sin \theta_3}$ ... (2.28)

$\therefore$ From equations (2.27) and (2.28),

$$AB = CD \cdot \frac{\sin \theta_4 \cdot \sin \theta_6}{\sin \theta_1 \cdot \sin \theta_3} \qquad \text{... (2.29)}$$

Similarly from $\triangle$ ABD, $AB = AD \cdot \dfrac{\sin \theta_7}{\sin \theta_2}$ ... (2.30)

and from $\triangle$ ADC, $AD = CD \cdot \dfrac{\sin \theta_5}{\sin \theta_8}$ ... (2.31)

$\therefore$ From equations (2.30) and (2.31),

$$AB = CD \cdot \frac{\sin \theta_5 \cdot \sin \theta_7}{\sin \theta_2 \cdot \sin \theta_8} \qquad \text{... (2.32)}$$

$\therefore$ From equations (2.29) and (2.32), equating the values of AB, we get,

$$\frac{\sin \theta_4 \cdot \sin \theta_6}{\sin \theta_1 \cdot \sin \theta_3} = \frac{\sin \theta_5 \cdot \sin \theta_7}{\sin \theta_2 \cdot \sin \theta_8}$$

$\therefore$ $\sin \theta_1 \cdot \sin \theta_3 \cdot \sin \theta_5 \cdot \sin \theta_7 = \sin \theta_2 \cdot \sin \theta_4 \cdot \sin \theta_6 \cdot \sin \theta_8$

or taking logarithm,

$$\begin{bmatrix} \Sigma \text{ log sine of odd angles} \\ \text{or left hand angles} \end{bmatrix} = \begin{bmatrix} \Sigma \text{ log sine of even angles} \\ \text{or right hand angles} \end{bmatrix}$$

Adjustment :

The adjustment of the quadrilateral can be carried out by any one of the following methods :

(a)   Rigorous method of least squares,

(b)   Approximate adjustment method, and

(c)   Equal shift method.

(a) Adjustment by the rigorous method of least squares :

Let C_{r_1} , C_{r_2} , C_{r_3} , ..., C_{r_8} be the corrections to the respective angles $\theta_1, \theta_2, \theta_3, ..., \theta_8$. Then the conditional equations 1, 2, 3 and 4 in "correction form" can be written down as :

$$Cr_1 + Cr_2 + Cr_3 + Cr_4 + Cr_5 + Cr_6 + Cr_7 + Cr_8 = \pm K_1 \qquad \text{... (2.33)}$$

$$\left(Cr_1 + Cr_2\right) - \left(Cr_5 + Cr_6\right) = \pm K_2 \qquad \text{... (2.34)}$$

$$\left(Cr_3 + Cr_4\right) - \left(Cr_7 + Cr_8\right) = \pm K_3 \qquad \text{... (2.35)}$$

and $\quad d_1 Cr_1 - d_2 Cr_2 + d_3 Cr_3 - d_4 Cr_4 + d_5 Cr_5 - d_6 Cr_6 + d_7 Cr_7 - d_8 Cr_8 = \pm M$ ... (2.36)

where $d_1, d_2, d_3, ..., d_8$ are the tabular differences for 1" of log sine 1, log sine 2 etc. and by the principle of least squares,

i.e. $(Cr_1)^2 + (Cr_2)^2 + (Cr_3)^2 + (Cr_4)^2 + (Cr_5)^2 + (Cr_6)^2 + (Cr_7)^2 + (Cr_8)^2 = \text{minimum}$ ... (2.37)

Thus there are eight unknowns and only five equations, therefore conventional method of solving equations becomes difficult and hence method of correlation is adopted.

∴　　　Differentiating the above equations (2.33), (2.34), (2.35), (2.36) and (2.37), we have,

$$\delta Cr_1 + \delta Cr_2 + \delta Cr_3 + \delta Cr_4 + \delta Cr_5 + \delta Cr_6 + \delta Cr_7 + \delta Cr_8 = 0 \qquad \text{... (2.38)}$$

$$\left(\delta Cr_1 + \delta Cr_2\right) - \left(\delta Cr_5 + \delta Cr_6\right) = 0 \qquad \text{... (2.39)}$$

$$\left(\delta Cr_3 + \delta Cr_4\right) - \left(\delta Cr_7 + \delta Cr_8\right) = 0 \qquad \text{... (2.40)}$$

$$\delta Cr_1 \, d_1 - \delta Cr_2 \, d_2 + \delta Cr_3 \, d_3 - \delta Cr_4 \, d_4 + \delta Cr_5 \, d_5 - \delta Cr_6 \, d_6 + \delta Cr_7 \, d_7 - \delta Cr_8 \, d_8 = 0$$
$$\text{... (2.41)}$$

$$\delta C_1 Cr_1 + \delta C_2 Cr_2 + \delta C_3 Cr_3 + \delta C_4 Cr_4 + \delta C_5 Cr_5 + \delta C_6 Cr_6 + \delta C_7 Cr_7 + \delta C_8 Cr_8 = 0$$
$$\text{... (2.42)}$$

Now multiplying the equations (2.38), (2.39), (2.40), (2.41) by $-\lambda_1, -\lambda_2, -\lambda_3$ and $-\lambda_4$ respectively and adding them to equation (2.42), and after equating the coefficients δCr_1, δCr_2, δCr_3, ..., δCr_8 to zero we have,

$$Cr_1 = \lambda_1 + \lambda_2 + d_1 \lambda_4$$

$$Cr_2 = \lambda_2 + \lambda_2 - d_2 \lambda_4$$

$$Cr_3 = \lambda_1 + \lambda_3 + d_3 \lambda_4$$

$$Cr_4 = \lambda_1 + \lambda_3 - d_4 \lambda_4$$

$$Cr_5 = \lambda_1 - \lambda_2 + d_5 \lambda_4$$

$$Cr_6 = \lambda_1 - \lambda_2 - d_6 \lambda_4$$

$$Cr_7 = \lambda_1 - \lambda_3 + d_7 \lambda_4$$

$$Cr_8 = \lambda_1 - \lambda_3 - d_8 \lambda_4$$

Substituting the values of C_{r_1}, C_{r_2}, C_{r_3}, ..., C_{r_8} as obtained above in the initial equations (2.33), (2.34), (2.35) and (2.36), we get,

$$8\lambda_1 + (d_1 - d_2 + d_3 - d_4 + d_5 - d_6 + d_7 - d_8)\lambda_4 = \pm K_1$$

$$4\lambda_2 + [(d_1 - d_2) - (d_5 - d_6)]\lambda_4 = \pm K_2$$

$$4\lambda_3 + [(d_3 - d_4) - (d_7 - d_8)]\lambda_4 = \pm K_3$$

$$\begin{bmatrix} (d_1 - d_2) + (d_3 - d_4) + (d_5 - d_6) + (d_7 - d_8)]\lambda_1 \\ + [(d_1 - d_2) - (d_5 - d_6)]\lambda_2 + [(d_3 - d_4) - (d_7 - d_8)]\lambda_3 \\ + [d_1^2 + d_2^2 + d_3^2 + d_4^2 + d_5^2 + d_6^2 + d_7^2 + d_8^2]\lambda_4 \end{bmatrix} = \pm M$$

Thus, there are now four equations and four unknowns (λ_1, λ_2, λ_3 and λ_4) and can be solved by normal equation method, thus knowing the values of λ_1, λ_2, λ_3 and λ_4. On substitution of these values in correction equations, the values of C_{r_1}, C_{r_2}, C_{r_3}, ..., C_{r_8} can be obtained. On applying these corrections to the observed angles, the adjusted or most probable values of the angles can be obtained.

(b) Approximate method of adjustment :

The method used for adjusting quadrilateral figures of moderate size or minor importance is approximate and less accurate as compared to the method of correlates.

The assumptions made in this are :

(i)   All the angles have been measured with equal precision i.e. they have equal weights and

(ii)   The angles have been corrected for spherical excess, if any. However, in obtaining the most probable values of the angles by this method, the important condition of "Least square principle" is not satisfied.

Method : Referring to the same Fig. 2.12, the conditional equation can again be written as :

$$\theta_1 + \theta_2 + \theta_3 + \theta_4 + \theta_5 + \theta_6 + \theta_7 + \theta_8 = 360° \qquad \text{... (2.43)}$$

(Figure adjustment)

$$\theta_1 + \theta_2 = \theta_5 + \theta_6 \text{ (Opposite angle condition) ... (2.44)}$$

$$\theta_3 + \theta_4 = \theta_7 + \theta_8 \text{ (Opposite angle condition) ... (2.45)}$$

and $\begin{bmatrix} \Sigma \text{ log [sine of odd angles} \\ \text{ or left hand angles]} \end{bmatrix} = \begin{bmatrix} \Sigma \text{ log [sine of even angles} \\ \text{ or right hand angles]} \end{bmatrix}$ ... (2.46)

If the above conditions are not satisfied, then the adjustment is carried in the following steps :

Step 1 : Station adjustment :

Add up all the observed angles at each station (i.e. A, B, C, D) and check for their sum which should be 360º. If not, find the discrepancy between the observed and theoretical sum and distribute it equally amongst all the concerned angles.

Step 2 : Figure adjustment :

The sum of all the eight angles θ_1, θ_2, ..., θ_8 (obtained after the station adjustment) of the quadrilateral should now be equal to 360°. If not, find the discrepancy between the observed and theoretical sum and correct each angle by adding or subtracting $\frac{1\text{th}}{8}$ of the discrepancy so as to make their sum equal to 360°.

Step 3 : Opposite angle adjustment :

The adjusted angles obtained after the step 2 are then checked to see whether :

$$(\theta_1 + \theta_2) - (\theta_5 + \theta_6) = 0$$

and
$$(\theta_3 + \theta_4) - (\theta_7 + \theta_8) = 0$$

If not, calculate the difference between them and divide it by four and apply this correction to the above angles with proper sign i.e. if $(\theta_1 + \theta_2)$ is greater than $(\theta_5 + \theta_6)$, the sign or correction will be negative for θ_1, θ_2 and positive for θ_5, θ_6. Similarly apply correction for θ_3, θ_4, θ_7 and θ_8.

Step 4 :

The angles adjusted after step no. 3 are then verified for side equation condition i.e. Σ log sine of odd angles (or left hand angles) should be same as the Σ log sine of even angles (or right hand angles). If not, find the discrepancy between them, say M. This discrepancy is to be distributed amongst all the eight angles as follows :

Let $\bar{\theta}_1$, $\bar{\theta}_2$, $\bar{\theta}_3$, ..., $\bar{\theta}_8$ be the observed angles so far adjusted (i.e. after step no. 3)

Let d_1, d_2, d_3, ..., d_8 be the tabular differences for 1" of log sin $\bar{\theta}_1$, log sin $\bar{\theta}_2$,... log sin $\bar{\theta}_8$.

Then correction to each of the eight angles is found by using the formula :

$$\text{Correction to the angle } \bar{\theta}_1 = \frac{d_1}{\Sigma d^2} \cdot M$$

$$\text{Correction to the angle } \bar{\theta}_2 = \frac{d_2}{\Sigma d^2} \cdot M$$

....

$$\text{Correction to the angle } \bar{\theta}_8 = \frac{d_8}{\Sigma d^2} \cdot M$$

where $\Sigma d^2 = d_1^2 + d_2^2 + ... + d_8^2$

and $M = \Sigma$ [log sine of odd angles] $- \Sigma$ [log sine of even angles] (numerical value)

The sign of correction will be negative to the left hand angles and positive to right angles if Σ log sine of odd angles or L.H.A. is greater than Σ log sine of even angles or R.H.A. and vice versa.

Note : In order to fulfill the side equation, the angles so far adjusted, will have to be modified. This modification may in turn disturb the earlier conditions satisfied. In such cases, the whole procedure of adjustment is to be repeated from the step 1 to the step 4 until the angles obtained after the last step do not disturb the earlier conditions already fulfilled.

The illustrative example based on the above method is as follows :

Example 2.38 : Illustrative example on adjustment of geodetic quadrilateral by approximate method :

Geodetic quadrilateral adjustment exercise (Fig. 2.13) :

Field Data Collected :

Round of angles at all the four stations A, B, C and D were measured with 'face left' in clockwise and anticlockwise direction and also 'face right' in clockwise and anticlock-wise direction with four separate different settings of horizontal circle each time i.e. each horizontal angle was measured 16 times and its mean is taken for computations.

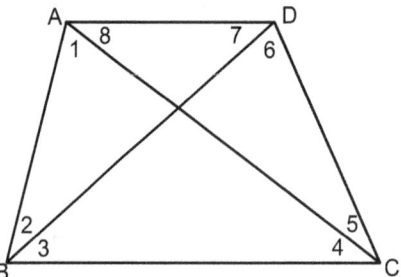

Fig. 2.13 : Geodetic quadrilateral adjustment exercise

Measured mean angles of 16 readings :

(1)   At station A :

$$\angle 1 \ = \ 64° \ 42' \ 55.44''$$
$$\angle 8 \ = \ 30° \ 23' \ 6''$$
$$\text{Ext. A} \ = \ 264° \ 53' \ 58''$$

Station adjustment :

Sum of observed angles = 30° 23' 6" + 64° 42' 55.44" + 264° 53' 58"

= 359° 59' 59.44"

Discrepancy = 360° – 359° 59' 59.44" = 0.56"

Correction = $\dfrac{0.56''}{3}$ = 0.187"

Corrected angles :   Ext. A'   =   264° 53' 58.187"

$\angle 1'$ =   64° 42' 55.627"

$\angle 8'$ =   30° 3' 06.187"

(2)   At station B :

$\angle 2$ =   36° 7' 11.25"

$\angle 3$ =   25° 18' 33.37"

Ext. B   =   298° 34' 16.25"

Sum of measured angles   =   360° 0' 0.87"

Discrepancy   =   360° − 360° 0' 0.87"   =   − 0.87"

$$\text{Correction} \ = \ \frac{-0.87"}{3} \ = \ -0.29" \text{ (negative)}$$

Corrected angles : $\angle 2'$ =   36° 7' 10.96"

$\angle 3'$ =   25° 18' 33.08"

Ext. B'   =   298° 34' 15.96"

(3)   At station C :

$\angle 4$ =   53° 50' 32.4"

$\angle 5$ =   53° 55' 57"

Ext. C   =   262° 13' 27"

Sum of observed angles   =   359° 59' 56.4"

Discrepancy   =   360° − 359° 59' 56.4"   =   3.6"

$$\text{Correction} \ = \ \frac{3.6"}{3} \ = \ 1.2" \text{ (Additive)}$$

Corrected angles : $\angle 4'$ =   53° 50' 33.6"

$\angle 5'$ =   43° 55' 58.2"

Ext. C'   =   262° 13' 28.2"

(4)   At station D :

$\angle 6$ =   56° 55' 8"

$\angle 7$ =   48° 46' 0"

Ext. D   =   254° 18' 51"

Sum of observed angles   =   359° 59' 59"

Discrepancy   =   360° − 359° 59' 59"   =   1"

$$\text{Correction} \ = \ \frac{1"}{3}$$

$$= \ 0.33", \ 0.34" \text{ and } 0.33"$$

Corrected angles :　　　$\angle 6'$　$= 56° 55' 8.33"$

$\angle 7'$　$= 48° 46' 0.34"$

Ext. D'　$= 254° 18' 51.33"$

Figure adjustment :

Condition :　$\angle 1' + \angle 2' + \angle 3' + \dots + \angle 8' = 360°$

Sum of observed angles　$= 359° 59' 26.32"$

Discrepancy　$= 360° - 359° 59' 26.32" = 33.68"$

Correction　$= \dfrac{33.68"}{3} = 0° 0' 4.2"$ (Additive)

Corrected angles :　　　$\angle 1"$　$= 64° 42' 59.83"$

$\angle 2"$　$= 36° 7' 15.17"$

$\angle 3"$　$= 25° 18' 37.29"$

$\angle 4"$　$= 53° 50' 37.8"$

$\angle 5"$　$= 43° 56' 2.4"$

$\angle 6"$　$= 56° 55' 12.54"$

$\angle 7"$　$= 48° 46' 4.55"$

$\angle 8"$　$= 30° 23' 10.4"$

Opposite angle correction conditions :

$\angle 1" + \angle 2" = \angle 5" + \angle 6"$　　　　　　　　　　　... (i)

$\angle 3" + \angle 4" = \angle 7" + \angle 8"$　　　　　　　　　　　... (ii)

Taking equation (i),　　L.H.S.　$= \angle 1" + \angle 2" = 100° 50' 15"$

R.H.S.　$= \angle 5" + \angle 6" = 100° 51' 14.95"$

Discrepancy　$= 0° 0' 59.95"$

Correction　$= \dfrac{59.95"}{4} = 0° 0' 14.99"$

which is additive for $\angle 1"$ and $\angle 2"$ and subtractive for $\angle 5"$ and $\angle 6"$

∴　Corrected angles :　$\angle 1'''$　$= 64° 43' 14.82"$

$\angle 2'''$　$= 36° 7' 30.15"$

$\angle 5'''$　$= 43° 55' 47.42"$

$\angle 6'''$　$= 56° 54' 57.55"$

Taking equation (ii),   L.H.S. $= \angle 3'' + \angle 4'' = 79° 9' 15.09''$

R.H.S. $= \angle 7'' + \angle 8'' = 79° 9' 14.95''$

Discrepancy $= 0.14''$

Correction $= \dfrac{0.14''}{4} = 0.035''$

Correction is subtractive for 3" and 4" and additive for 7" and 8". Therefore corrected angles are :

$$\angle 3''' = 25° 18' 37.255''$$

$$\angle 4''' = 53° 50' 37.765''$$

$$\angle 7''' = 48° 46' 4.585''$$

$$\angle 8''' = 30° 23' 10.435''$$

Side equation correction :

Condition :

$$\sin 1''' \cdot \sin 3''' \cdot \sin 5''' \cdot \sin 7''' = \sin 2''' \cdot \sin 4''' \cdot \sin 6''' \cdot \sin 8'''$$

No.	Angle	log (sin n''' angle)	log (sin n''' + 1")	Diff. (d) xi	Corr. in sec.	Corrected angle
1"	64° 43' 14.82"	− 0.0437174	− 0.0437164	$d_1 = -1 \times 10^{-6}$	− 1.59"	64° 43' 13.23"
2"	36° 7' 30.16"	− 0.2294797	− 0.2294768	$d_2 = -2.9 \times 10^{-6}$	+ 4.61"	36° 7' 34.77"
3"	25° 18' 37.255"	− 0.3690424	− 0.3690424	$d_3 = -4.7 \times 10^{-6}$	− 7.47"	25° 18' 29.781"
4"	53° 50' 37.765"	− 0.0929049	− 0.0929033	$d_4 = -1.5364 \times 10^{-6}$	+ 2.443"	53° 40' 40.208"
5"	43° 55' 47.42"	− 0.1587801	− 0.1587779	$d_5 = -2.1765 \times 10^{-6}$	− 3.461"	43° 55' 43.959"
6"	56° 54' 57.55"	− 0.0768228	− 0.0768214	$d_6 = -1.3586 \times 10^{-6}$	+ 2.16"	56° 54' 59.71"
7"	48° 46' 4.585"	− 0.1237554	− 0.1237536	$d_7 = -1.7808 \times 10^{-6}$	− 2.8318"	48° 46' 1.753"
8"	30° 23' 10.435"	− 0.2959984	− 0.2959948	$d_8 = -3.5593 \times 10^{-6}$	+ 5.6599"	30° 23'16.095"
	Correction $= \dfrac{d}{\Sigma d^2 \times M}$		Σd^2 $= 5.62833 \times 10^{-11}$			359° 59' 59.51" $\approx 360° 00' 00''$ $\therefore$ O.K.

Where $M = \Sigma \log (\sin L) - \Sigma \log (\sin R) = -8.95 \times 10^{-5}$

(c) Adjustment by method of equal shifts (or Semi-rigorous method) :

In this method, the error in the angular measurements is to be divided equally amongst the three angles of a triangle.

Principle : The method of equal shift says that any shift which is required to fulfill the local equation as well as side equation should be same for each triangle of the polygon.

The conditional equations to be satisfied for any closed polygon having a central station, are as follows :

(i)   Figure condition : The sum of the included angles of a triangle should be 180°.

(ii) Station or local condition : Round of angles at a station should be 360°.

(ii) Side equation or log sine condition :

i.e. $\left[\begin{array}{c}\Sigma \log [\text{sine of odd angles} \\ \text{or left hand angles}]\end{array}\right] = \left[\begin{array}{c}\Sigma \log [\text{sine of even angles} \\ \text{or right hand angles}]\end{array}\right]$

The computation work for equal shift method is carried out as follows :

(1)   Determine the total corrections to be applied to each triangle.

(2)   Correct each central angle of a triangle by one-third of the corrections for that triangle.

(3)   The summation of all the central angles should be equal to 360° to fulfill the station condition.

(4)   The side equation i.e. log sine condition should be satisfied.

(5)   The sum of angles of any triangle should be 180°.

2.18 ADJUSTMENT OF A GEODETIC QUADRILATERAL HAVING A CENTRAL STATION

In Fig. 2.14, Q is a central station of a geodetic quadrilateral ABCD. The angles measured at A, B, C, D and Q are denoted by θ_1, θ_2, ..., θ_{12} and are corrected for spherical excess, if any.

The various conditions of equation may be written as :

(i) $\theta_1 + \theta_2 + \theta_9 = 180°$

(ii) $\theta_3 + \theta_4 + \theta_{10} = 180°$

(iii) $\theta_5 + \theta_6 + \theta_{11} = 180°$

(iv) $\theta_7 + \theta_8 + \theta_{12} = 180°$

(v) $\theta_9 + \theta_{10} + \theta_{11} + \theta_{12} = 360°$

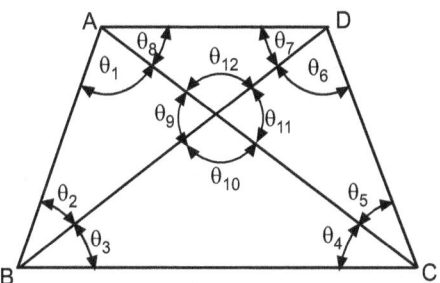

Fig. 2.14 : Quadrilateral with a central station

Now, if C_{r_1}, C_{r_2}, C_{r_3}, ..., $C_{r_{12}}$ are the various corrections to be applied to the angles θ_1, θ_2, θ_3, ..., θ_{12} respectively, then the above equations can be rewritten as :

$$C_{r_1} + C_{r_2} + C_{r_9} = \pm K_1 \qquad \qquad ... (2.47)$$

$$C_{r_3} + C_{r_4} + C_{r_{10}} = \pm K_2 \qquad \qquad ... (2.48)$$

$$C_{r_5} + C_{r_6} + C_{r_{11}} = \pm K_3 \qquad \qquad ... (2.49)$$

$$C_{r_7} + C_{r_8} + C_{r_{12}} = \pm K_4 \qquad \qquad ... (2.50)$$

$$C_{r_9} + C_{r_{10}} + C_{r_{11}} + C_{r_{12}} = \pm K_5 \qquad \qquad ... (2.51)$$

By log sine condition,

$$d_1 C_{r_1} - d_2 C_{r_2} + d_3 C_{r_3} - d_4 C_{r_4} + ... + d_8 C_{r_8} = \pm M \qquad \qquad ... (2.52)$$

and by the principle of least squares,

$$(C_{r_1})^2 + (C_{r_2})^2 + (C_{r_3})^2 + (C_{r_4})^4 + ... + (C_{r_{12}})^2 = \text{minimum} \qquad \qquad ... (2.53)$$

$\therefore$ Differentiating the above equations (2.47), (2.48), (2.49) , (2.50) , (2.51), (2.52) and (2.53), we have,

$$\delta C_{r_1} + \delta C_{r_2} + \delta C_{r_9} = 0 \qquad \qquad ... (2.54)$$

$$\delta C_{r_3} + \delta C_{r_4} + \delta C_{r_{10}} = 0 \qquad \qquad ... (2.55)$$

$$\delta C_{r_5} + \delta C_{r_6} + \delta C_{r_{11}} = 0 \qquad \qquad ... (2.56)$$

$$\delta C_{r_7} + \delta C_{r_8} + \delta C_{r_{12}} = 0 \qquad \qquad ... (2.57)$$

$$\delta C_{r_9} + \delta C_{r_{10}} + \delta C_{r_{11}} + \delta C_{r_{12}} = 0 \qquad \qquad ... (2.58)$$

and $d_1 \delta C_{r_1} - d_2 \delta C_{r_2} + d_3 \delta C_{r_3} - d_4 \delta C_{r_4} + ... + d_8 \delta C_{r_8} = 0 \qquad \qquad ... (2.59)$

and $C_{r_1} \delta C_1 + C_{r_2} \delta C_2 + C_{r_3} \delta C_3 + ... + C_{r_{12}} \delta C_{12} = 0 \qquad \qquad ... (2.60)$

Now multiply equations (2.54) to (2.59) by $-\lambda_1, -\lambda_2, -\lambda_3, -\lambda_4, -\lambda_5$ and $-\lambda_6$ respectively and add the results to the equation (2.60). Now equating the coefficients of $\delta C_{r_1}, -\delta C_{r_2}, \ldots$ $\delta C_{r_{12}}$ to zero, we get,

$$C_{r_1} = \lambda_1 + d_1 \lambda_6$$

$$C_{r_2} = \lambda_1 - d_2 \lambda_6$$

$$C_{r_3} = \lambda_2 + d_3 \lambda_6$$

$$C_{r_4} = \lambda_2 - d_4 \lambda_6$$

$$C_{r_5} = \lambda_3 + d_5 \lambda_6$$

$$C_{r_6} = \lambda_3 - d_6 \lambda_6$$

$$C_{r_7} = \lambda_4 + d_7 \lambda_6$$

$$C_{r_8} = \lambda_4 - d_8 \lambda_6$$

$$C_{r_9} = \lambda_1 + \lambda_5$$

$$C_{r_{10}} = \lambda_2 + \lambda_5$$

$$C_{r_{11}} = \lambda_3 + \lambda_5$$

$$C_{r_{12}} = \lambda_4 + \lambda_5$$

On substitution of the above values of $C_{r_1}, C_{r_2}, \ldots, C_{r_{12}}$ in original equation, we get,

(a) $3\lambda_1 + \lambda_5 + \lambda_6 (d_1 - d_2) = C_{r_1}$

(b) $3\lambda_2 + \lambda_5 + \lambda_6 (d_3 - d_4) = C_{r_2}$

(c) $3\lambda_3 + \lambda_5 + \lambda_6 (d_5 - d_6) = C_{r_3}$

(d) $3\lambda_4 + \lambda_5 + \lambda_6 (d_7 - d_8) = C_{r_4}$

(e) $\lambda_1 + \lambda_2 + \lambda_3 + \lambda_4 + 4\lambda_5 = C_{r_5}$

(f) $\left\{ \begin{array}{l} \lambda_1 (d_1 - d_2) + \lambda_2 (d_3 - d_4) + \lambda_3 (d_5 - d_6) + \lambda_4 (d_7 - d_8) \\ + \lambda_6 \left[(C_{r_1})^2 + (C_{r_2})^2 + (C_{r_3})^2 + (C_{r_4})^2 + (C_{r_5})^2 + (C_{r_6})^2 + (C_{r_7})^2 + (C_{r_8})^2 \right] \end{array} \right\} = C_{r_6}$

Now we have six equations and six unknown multipliers $\lambda_1, \lambda_2, \ldots, \lambda_6$. On substitution of these values in the equation for $C_{r_1}, C_{r_2}, \ldots, C_{r_8}$, we get the values of the various $C_{r_1}, C_{r_2}, \ldots, C_{r_8}$. After applying these corrections to the respective angles $\theta_1, \theta_2, \ldots, \theta_8$, we get the adjusted angles i.e. M.P.V. of angles.

Example 2.39 : Determine the most probable values of the angles A, B and C of a triangle ABC from the following observed angles and the respective probable errors of measurements

$$A = 64° 12' 40" \pm 3"$$
$$B = 55° 14' 23" \pm 2"$$
$$C = 64° 33' 21" \pm 4"$$

Solution :　Sum of three angles $= 184° 0' 24"$

Discrepancy $= 4° 0' 24"$

Hence, each angle is to be decreased and the error of $4° 0' 24"$ is to be distributed in proportion to the square of the probable error.

Let C_1, C_2 and C_3 be the corrections to be applied to A, B and C respectively,

$$C_1 : C_2 : C_3 = (3)^2 : (2)^2 : (4)^2 = 9 : 4 : 16 \qquad \text{... (i)}$$

Also $\qquad C_1 + C_2 + C_3 = 4° 0' 24" \qquad \text{... (ii)}$

From equation (i),

$$C_2 = \frac{4}{9} \cdot C_1 \quad \text{and} \quad C_3 = \frac{16}{9} \cdot C_1$$

Substituting these values of C_2 and C_3 in equation (ii), we get

$$C_1 + \frac{4}{9} C_1 + \frac{16}{9} C_1 = 4° 0' 24"$$

$$C_1 \left(1 + \frac{4}{9} + \frac{16}{9} \right) = 4° 0' 24"$$

$$C_1 \left(\frac{29}{9} \right) = 4° 0' 24"$$

$$C_1 = 4° 0' 24" \left(\frac{9}{29} \right) = 1° 14' 36.4"$$

Now, $\qquad C_2 = \frac{4}{9} C_1$

$$= \frac{4}{9} (1° 14' 36.4")$$

$\therefore \qquad C_2 = 0° 33' 9.52"$

and $\qquad C_3 = \frac{16}{9} C_1 = \frac{16}{9} (1° 14' 36.4")$

$\therefore \qquad C_3 = 2° 12' 38"$

Check : $\qquad C_1 + C_2 + C_3 = 1° 14' 36.4" + 0° 33' 9.52" + 2° 12' 38"$

$$= 4° 0' 24"$$

Hence, the corrected angles are,

$$A = 64° \, 12' \, 40'' - 1° \, 14' \, 36.4'' = 62° \, 58' \, 3.6''$$

$$B = 55° \, 14' \, 23'' - 0° \, 33' \, 9.52'' = 54° \, 41' \, 13''$$

$$C = 64° \, 33' \, 21'' - 2° \, 12' \, 38'' = 62° \, 20' \, 43''$$

$$\text{Sum} = 180° \, 00' \, 00''$$

Example 2.40 : The observations closing the horizon at a station are as follows :

$$\angle A = 24° \, 22' \, 18.2'' \quad \text{weight} \quad 1$$

$$\angle B = 30° \, 12' \, 24.4'' \quad \text{weight} \quad 2$$

$$\angle A + \angle B = 54° \, 34' \, 49.2'' \quad \text{weight} \quad 3$$

$$\angle C = 305° \, 25' \, 15.5'' \quad \text{weight} \quad 2$$

$$\angle B + \angle C = 335° \, 37' \, 37.00'' \quad \text{weight} \quad 3$$

Find most probable values of angles A, B and C.

Solution : Let C_A, C_B and C_C be the corrections of angles A, B and C respectively.

Then the most probable values of A, B and C are

$$A = 24° \, 22' \, 18.2'' + C_A \qquad\qquad\qquad \text{... (i)}$$

$$B = 30° \, 12' \, 24.4'' + C_B \qquad\qquad\qquad \text{... (ii)}$$

$$C = 305° \, 25' \, 15.5'' + C_C \qquad\qquad\qquad \text{... (iii)}$$

$$A + B = 54° \, 34' \, 42.6'' + C_A + C_B \qquad \text{[... by adding (i) and (ii)]}$$

$$B + C = 335° \, 37' \, 39.9'' + C_B + C_C \qquad \text{[... by adding (ii) and (iii)]}$$

Substituting these in the corresponding observation equations, we get the following reduced observation equations :

$$C_A = 0 \qquad\qquad \text{weight 1}$$

$$C_B = 0 \qquad\qquad \text{weight 2}$$

$$C_C = 0 \qquad\qquad \text{weight 2}$$

$$C_A + C_B = 6.6'' \qquad\qquad \text{weight 3}$$

$$C_B + C_C = -2.9'' \qquad\qquad \text{weight 3}$$

Normal equation for C_A :

$$C_A = 0$$
$$3C_A + 3C_B = 19.8"$$

Adding $4C_A + 3C_B = 19.8"$

Normal equation for C_B :

$$2C_B = 0$$
$$3C_A + 3C_B = 19.8"$$
$$3C_B + 3C_C = -8.7"$$

Adding $3C_A + 8C_B + 3C_C = 11.1"$

Normal equation for C_C :

$$2C_C = 0$$
$$3C_B + 3C_C = -8.7"$$

Adding $3C_B + 5C_C = -8.7"$

Hence, three normal equations are

$$4C_A + 3C_B = 19.8" \qquad \text{... (iv)}$$

$$3C_A + 8C_B + 3C_C = 11.1" \qquad \text{... (v)}$$

$$3C_B + 5C_C = -8.7" \qquad \text{... (vi)}$$

Solving these simultaneously for C_A, C_B and C_C, we get

$$C_A = 4.54", \quad C_B = 0.55" \text{ and } C_C = -2.06".$$

Hence, most probable values of the angles are

$$A = 24° \ 22' \ 18.2" + 4.54" = 24° \ 22' \ 22.74"$$

$$B = 30° \ 12' \ 24.4" + 0.55" = 30° \ 12' \ 24.95"$$

$$C = 305° \ 25' \ 15.5" - 2.06" = 305° \ 25' \ 13.44"$$

Example 2.41 : Adjust the following angles closing the horizon.

P	110° 20' 48"	weight 4
Q	92° 30° 12"	weight 1
R	56° 12' 00"	weight 2
S	100° 57' 04"	weight 3

Solution : The sum of observed angles = 360° 00' 04".

But,   Theoretical sum = 360° 00' 00"

∴   Discrepancy = 4"

∴   Total correction = – 4"

As per the laws of weights, the corrections are inversely proportional to their weights. Let C_p, C_q, C_r and C_s are the corrections to the observed values of angles P, Q, R, S then

$$C_p : C_q : C_r : C_s \ = \ \frac{1}{4} : \frac{1}{1} : \frac{1}{2} : \frac{1}{3}$$

$$= \ 3 : 12 : 6 : 4$$

Now, $C_P \ = \ \dfrac{3}{25} \times 4" \ = \ 0.48"$

$$C_Q \ = \ \frac{12}{25} \times 4" \ = \ 1.92"$$

$$C_R \ = \ \frac{6}{25} \times 4" \ = \ 0.96"$$

and $C_S \ = \ \dfrac{4}{25} \times 4" \ = \ 0.64"$

Check : $C_P + C_Q + C_R + C_S \ = \ 4"$

∴   Most probable values of angles are :

P = 110° 20' 48" – 0.48" = 110° 20' 47.52"

Q = 92° 30' 12" – 1.92" = 92° 30' 10.08"

R = 56° 12' 00" – 0.96" = 56° 11' 59.04"

S = 100° 57' 04" – 0.64" = 100° 57' 3.36"

Check :   P + Q + R + S = 360° 00' 00"

Example 2.42 : The following observations towards three angles A, B and C were recorded at one station.

A = 82° 40' 12.5"   weight = 4

B = 45° 23' 09.3"   weight = 2

C = 120° 09' 45.6"   weight = 5

A + B + C = 248° 13' 04.0"   weight = 2

A + B = 128° 03' 19.2"   weight = 3

B + C = 165° 32' 56.5"   weight = 2

Find the most probable value of each angle by method of differences only.

Solution : Let C_A, C_B, C_C be the most probable corrections to A, B and C.

Then the most probable values of A, B and C are :

$$A = 82° \ 40' \ 12.5'' + C_A \qquad \text{... (i)}$$

$$B = 45° \ 23' \ 09.3'' + C_B \qquad \text{... (ii)}$$

$$C = 120° \ 09' \ 45.6'' + C_C \qquad \text{... (iii)}$$

$$A + B = 128° \ 03' \ 21.8'' + C_A + C_B \qquad \text{... (iv)}$$

adding equations (i) and (ii),

$$B + C = 165° \ 32' \ 54.9'' + C_B + C_C \qquad \text{... (v)}$$

adding equations (ii) and (iii),

and $\qquad A + B + C = 248° \ 13' \ 7.4'' + C_A + C_B + C_C \qquad \text{... (vi)}$

adding equations (i), (ii) and (iii)

Subtracting these from the corresponding observation equations, we get the following reduced observation equations :

$$C_A = 0 \qquad \text{weight 4}$$

$$C_B = 0 \qquad \text{weight 2}$$

$$C_C = 0 \qquad \text{weight 5}$$

$$C_A + C_B = -2.6'' \qquad \text{weight 3}$$

$$C_B + C_C = 1.6'' \qquad \text{weight 2}$$

$$C_A + C_B + C_C = -3.4'' \qquad \text{weight 2}$$

Normal equation for C_A :

$$4C_A = 0$$

$$3C_A + 3C_B = -7.8''$$

$$2C_A + 2C_B + 2C_C = -6.8''$$

$$\therefore \qquad 9C_A + 5C_B + 2C_C = -14.6$$

Normal equation for C_B :

$$2C_B = 0$$

$$3C_A + 3C_B = -7.8$$

$$2C_B + 2C_C = 3.2$$

$$2C_A + 2C_B + 2C_C = -6.8$$

$$5C_A + 9C_B + 4C_C = -11.4$$

Normal equation for C_C :

$$5C_C = 0$$

$$2C_B + 2C_C = 3.2"$$

$$\underline{2C_A + 2C_B + 2C_C = -6.8"}$$

$$2C_A + 4C_B + 9C_C = -3.6"$$

Hence, three normal equations are

$$9C_A + 5C_B + 2C_C = -14.6"$$

$$5C_A + 9C_B + 4C_C = -14.4"$$

$$2C_A + 4C_B + 9C_C = -3.6"$$

Solving these equations,

$$C_A = -1.32", \quad C_B = -0.6" \quad \text{and} \quad C_C = 0.16"$$

Hence, most probable values of A, B, C are

$$A = 82° 40' 12.5" - 1.32" = 82° 40' 11.18"$$

$$B = 45° 23' 9.3" - 0.6" = 45° 23' 8.7"$$

$$C = 120° 09' 45.6" + 0.16" = 120° 09' 45.76"$$

Example 2.43 : Following angles were recorded closing the horizon, around a station 'O'.

$$A = 45° 20' 10.5" \qquad \text{weight} = 1$$

$$B = 102° 36' 21.5" \qquad \text{weight} = 3$$

$$C = 90° 54' 43" \qquad \text{weight} = 2$$

$$D = 121° 08' 41" \qquad \text{weight} = 4$$

Find the corrected values of the following angles using any one method.

Solution : The sum of the observed angles = 359° 59' 56".

$$\text{The theoretical sum} = 360° 00' 00"$$

$$\therefore \qquad \text{Discrepancy} = 4"$$

$$\therefore \qquad \text{Total correction} = + 4"$$

Observed sum is less than theoretical sum and this total correction is to be distributed amongst observed angles inversely proportional to their weights.

If C_A, C_B, C_C and C_D are the corrections to the respective angles A, B, C and D then

$$C_A : C_B : C_C : C_D = \frac{1}{1} : \frac{1}{3} : \frac{1}{2} : \frac{1}{4}$$

$$= 12 : 4 : 6 : 3$$

$\therefore$

$$C_A = \frac{12}{25} \times 4 = 1.92"$$

$$C_B = \frac{4}{25} \times 4 = 0.64"$$

$$C_C = \frac{6}{25} \times 4 = 0.96"$$

and

$$C_D = \frac{3}{25} \times 4 = 0.48"$$

Check : $C_A + C_B + C_C + C_D = 4"$

$\therefore$ Most probable values are

$$A = 45° 20' 10.5" + 1.92" = 45° 20' 12.42"$$
$$B = 102° 36' 21.5" + 0.64" = 102° 36' 22.14"$$
$$C = 90° 54' 43" + 0.96" = 90° 54' 43.96"$$
$$D = 121° 08' 41" + 0.48" = 121° 08' 41.48"$$

Check :   Sum of A + B + C + D = 360° 00' 00"

Example 2.44 : Adjust the following angles closing the horizon :

$$A = 80° 30' 40" \text{ weight 1}$$
$$B = 100° 30' 12" \text{ weight 4}$$
$$C = 93° 15' 10" \text{ weight 3}$$
$$D = 85° 44' 10" \text{ weight 2}$$

Solution : The sum of observed angles = 360° 00' 12"

Theoretical sum = 360° 00' 00"

$\therefore$ Discrepancy = 12"

$\therefore$ Total correction = $-12"$

As observed sum is greater than theoretical sum, corrections can be distributed amongst observed angles inversely proportional to their weights.

$$C_A : C_B : C_C : C_D = \frac{1}{1} : \frac{1}{4} : \frac{1}{3} : \frac{1}{2} = 12 : 3 : 4 : 6$$

$\therefore$

$$C_A = \frac{12}{25} \times 12" = 5.76"$$

$$C_B = \frac{3}{25} \times 12" = 1.44"$$

$$C_C = \frac{4}{25} \times 12" = 1.92"$$

and

$$C_D = \frac{6}{25} \times 12" = 2.88$$

∴   Most probable values of angles are :

$$A = 80° \; 30' \; 40" - 5.76" = 80° \; 30' \; 34.24"$$

$$B = 100° \; 30' \; 12" - 1.44" = 100° \; 30' \; 10.56"$$

$$C = 93° \; 15' \; 10" - 1.92" = 93° \; 15' \; 8.08"$$

$$D = 85° \; 44' \; 10" - 2.88" = 85° \; 44" \; 7.12"$$

Check : A + B + C + D = 360° 00' 00"

Example 2.45 : Find most probable value of angle A and B from the following observations :

$$A = 60° \; 20' \; 36" \text{ weight } 2$$

$$B = 80° \; 30' \; 40" \text{ weight } 3$$

$$A + B = 140° \; 50' \; 57" \text{ weight } 4$$

Solution : There are two unknowns A and B and both are independent of each other, and there will be two normal equations.

Normal equations are formed as :

$$2A = 120° \; 41' \; 12"$$
$$4A + 4B = 563° \; 23' \; 48"$$

$$6A + 4B = 684° \; 05' \; 00" \text{ Normal equation for A}$$

Also,

$$3B = 241° \; 32' \; 00'$$
$$4A + 4B = 563° \; 23' \; 48"$$

$$4A + 7B = 804° \; 55' \; 48" \text{ Normal equation for B}$$

Hence two normal equations are

$$6A + 4B = 684° \; 05' \; 00" \qquad \qquad \text{... (i)}$$

$$4A + 7B = 804° \; 55' \; 48" \qquad \qquad \text{... (ii)}$$

Solving equation (i) and (ii)

$$12A + 8B = 1368° \; 10' \; 00"$$

$$12A + 21B = 2414° \; 47' \; 24"$$

$$+ \; 13B = + \; 1046° \; 37' \; 24"$$

∴

$$B = 80° \; 30' \; 28.24"$$

Substituting value of B in (i) we get

$\quad$ 6A+ 4 (80° 30' 28.24")= 684° 05' 00"

∴ $\qquad\qquad$ 6A $\ =\ $ 684° 05' 00" − 322° 01' 52.96"

∴ $\qquad\qquad$ 6A $\ =\ $ 362° 03' 7.04"

∴ $\qquad\qquad$ A $\ =\ $ 60° 20' 31.17"

Example 2.46 : Adjust the following angles closing the horizon.

$$\angle\ A\ =\ 60°\ 16'\ 43''\ \text{weight} = 4$$
$$\angle\ B\ =\ 110°\ 37'\ 09''\ \text{weight}\ = 1$$
$$\angle\ C\ =\ 140°\ 10'\ 27''\ \text{weight}\ =\ 2$$
$$\angle\ D\ =\ 48°\ 55'\ 32''\ \text{weight}\ =\ 3$$

Use any suitable method.

Solution : The sum of the observed angles $\ =\ 359°\ 59'\ 51''$

But $\quad$ The theoretical sum $\ =\ 360°\ 00'\ 00''$

∴ $\qquad\qquad$ Discrepancy $\ =\ -\ 0°\ 0'\ 9''$

∴ $\qquad\qquad$ Correction $\ =\ +\ 0°\ 0'\ 9''$

Observed sum is less than theoretical sum and this total correction is to be distributed among observed angles inversely proportional to their weights.

If $C_A,\ C_B,\ C_C$ and C_D are the corrections to the respective angles A, B, C and D,

then, $\qquad C_A : C_B : C_C : C_D\ =\ \dfrac{1}{4} : \dfrac{1}{2} : \dfrac{1}{2} : \dfrac{1}{3}$

$\qquad\qquad\qquad\qquad\qquad =\ 3 : 12 : 6 : 4$

∴ $\ $ Various corrections can be calculated as

$$C_A\ =\ \frac{3}{25} \times 9''\ =\ 1.08''$$

$$C_B\ =\ \frac{12}{25} \times 9''\ =\ 4.32''$$

$$C_C\ =\ \frac{6}{25} \times 9''\ =\ 2.16''$$

$$C_D\ =\ \frac{4}{25} \times 9''\ =\ 1.44''$$

∴ $\ $ Most probable values are −

$$\angle\ A\ =\ 60°\ 16'\ 43'' + 1.08'' = 60°\ 16'\ 44.08''$$
$$\angle\ B\ =\ 110°\ 37'\ 09'' + 4.32'' = 110°\ 37'\ 13.33''$$
$$\angle\ C\ =\ 140°\ 10'\ 27'' + 2.16'' = 140°\ 10'\ 29.16''$$
$$\angle\ D\ =\ 48°\ 55'\ 32'' + 1.44'' = 48°\ 55'\ 33.44''$$

Check : Sum of $\angle$ A + $\angle$ B + $\angle$ C + $\angle$ D = 360° 00' 00".

Example 2.47 : Find most probable values of angles A, B and C of a triangle from following observations :

$$\angle A = 80° 20' 12'' \text{ weight} = 3$$
$$\angle B = 52° 15' 35'' \text{ weight} = 2$$
$$\angle C = 47° 24' 18'' \text{ weight} = 4$$

Use any suitable method.

Solution : Problem can be solved by the laws of weights

sum of $\angle A + \angle B + \angle C = 180° 00' 05''$

But   the theoretical sum $= 180° 00' 00''$

∴   Discrepancy $= + 5''$

∴   Correction $= -5''$

Let C_A, C_B and C_C be the corrections to the angles A, B and C.

∴
$$C_A : C_B : C_C = \frac{1}{W_A} : \frac{1}{W_B} : \frac{1}{W_C}$$
$$= \frac{1}{3} : \frac{1}{2} : \frac{1}{4}$$
$$= 4 : 6 : 3$$

∴
$$C_A = \frac{4}{13} \times 5 = 1.54''$$
$$C_B = \frac{6}{13} \times 5 = 2.31''$$

and
$$C_C = \frac{3}{13} \times 5 = 1.15''$$

∴   Most probable values of A, B, C will be

A $= 80° 20' 12'' - 1.54'' = 80° 20' 10.46''$

B $= 52° 15' 35'' - 2.31'' = 52° 15' 32.69''$

C $= 47° 24' 18'' - 1.15'' = 47° 24' 16.85''$

Check :   A + B + C $= 180° 00' 00''$

Example 2.48 : Determine the MPV's of the angles A, B and C from the following observed value, by the method of difference.

$$\angle A = 39° 14' 15.3''$$
$$\angle B = 31° 15' 26.4''$$
$$\angle C = 42° 18' 18.4''$$
$$\angle A + \angle B = 70° 29' 45.2''$$
$$\angle B + \angle C = 73° 33' 48.3''$$

Solution : Let C_A, C_B and C_C be the most probable correction to angles A, B and C, then MPVs of angles A, B, C are :

$$\angle A = 39° 14' 15.3" + C_A$$

$$\angle B = 31° 15' 26.4" + C_B$$

$$\angle C = 42° 18' 18.4" + C_C$$

$$\angle A + \angle B = 70° 29' 41.7" + C_A + C_B \qquad [\because \text{ adding A and B}]$$

$$\angle B + \angle C = 73° 33' 44.8" + C_B + C_C \qquad [\because \text{ adding B and C}]$$

Subtracting these from corresponding observation equation,

$$
\begin{aligned}
C_A &= 0\\
C_B &= 0\\
\underline{C_C} &\underline{= 0}\\
C_A + C_B &= 3.5"\\
C_B + C_C &= 3.5"
\end{aligned}
$$

Hence, normal equation of C_A

$$
\begin{aligned}
C_A &= 0\\
\underline{C_A + C_B} &\underline{= 3.5"}\\
2C_A + C_B &= 3.5"
\end{aligned}
\qquad \ldots \text{(i)}
$$

Normal equation of C_B

$$
\begin{aligned}
C_B &= 0\\
C_A + C_B &= 3.5"\\
\underline{C_B + C_C} &\underline{= 3.5"}\\
C_A + 3C_B + C_C &= 7.0"
\end{aligned}
\qquad \ldots \text{(ii)}
$$

Normal equation of C_C

$$
\begin{aligned}
C_C &= 0\\
\underline{C_B + C_C} &\underline{= 3.5"}\\
C_B + 2C_C &= 3.5"
\end{aligned}
\qquad \ldots \text{(iii)}
$$

Substituting $C_C = \dfrac{(3.5 - C_B)}{2}$ in equation (ii)

$$C_A + 3C_B + \frac{3.5 - C_B}{2} = 7"$$

$$\therefore \quad 2C_A + 6C_B + 3.5 - C_B = 14"$$

$$\therefore \quad 2C_A + 5C_B = 10.5" \qquad \ldots \text{(iv)}$$

Solving equation (i) and (iv)

$$C_A = 9.625''$$
$$C_B = -1.75''$$
$$C_C = 2.625''$$

∴   MPVs of angle A, B and C are –

$$\angle A = 39° 14' 15.3'' + 9.625'' = 39° 14' 24.925''$$
$$\angle B = 31° 15' 26.4'' - 1.75'' = 31° 15' 24.65''$$
$$\angle C = 42° 18' 18.4'' + 2.625'' = 42° 18' 21.025''$$

Example 2.49 : Find the most probable values of angles A, B and C from following data : (Use method of difference).

$$A = 70° 34' 12.6'' \text{ Weight 3}$$
$$B = 55° 45' 8.2'' \text{ Weight 2}$$
$$C = 125° 15' 27.3'' \text{ Weight 4}$$
$$A + B = 126° 19' 25.5'' \text{ Weight 2}$$
$$B + C = 181° 00' 42.0'' \text{ Weight 2}$$
$$A + B + C = 251° 34' 41.4'' \text{ Weight 1}$$

Solution : Let C_A, C_B and C_C be the most probable corrections to A, B, C. Then the most probable values of A, B and C are :

$$A = 70° 34' 12.6'' + C_A \qquad\qquad \text{... (i)}$$
$$B = 55° 45' 8.2'' + C_B \qquad\qquad \text{... (ii)}$$
$$C = 125° 15' 27.3'' + C_C \qquad\qquad \text{... (iii)}$$
$$A + B = 126° 19' 20.8'' + C_A + C_B \qquad\qquad \text{... (iv)}$$

[By adding equation (i) and (ii)]

$$B + C = 181° 00' 35.5'' + C_B + C_C \qquad\qquad \text{... (v)}$$

[By adding (ii) and (iii)]

$$A + B + C = 251° 34' 48.1'' + C_A + C_B + C_C \qquad\qquad \text{... (vi)}$$

[By adding (i), (ii) and (iii)]

Substracting these from the corresponding observation equations.

$$C_A = 0 \quad \text{weight 3}$$
$$C_B = 0 \quad \text{weight 2}$$
$$C_C = 0 \quad \text{weight 4}$$
$$C_A + C_B = 4.7 \quad \text{weight 2}$$
$$C_B + C_C = 6.5 \quad \text{weight 2}$$
$$C_A + C_B + C_C = -6.7 \quad \text{weight 1}$$

Normal equation of C_A

$$3C_A \qquad\qquad = 0$$
$$2C_A + 3C_B \qquad = 9.4$$
$$\underline{C_A + C_B + C_C \quad = -6.7}$$
$$6C_A + 3C_B + C_C \quad = +2.7"$$

Normal equation of C_B

$$2C_B \qquad\qquad = 0$$
$$2C_A + 2C_B \qquad\quad = 9.4$$
$$2C_B + 2C_C \quad = 13.0$$
$$\underline{C_A + C_B + C_C \quad = -6.7}$$
$$3C_A + 7C_B + 3C_C \quad = 15.7$$

Normal equation of C_C

$$4C_C \quad = 0$$
$$2C_B + 2C_C \quad = 13.0$$
$$C_A + C_B + C_C \quad = -6.7$$
$$C_A + 3C_B + 7C_C \quad = 6.3$$

Solving normal equations simultaneously for C_A, C_B and C_C

$$C_A = +0.57"$$
$$C_B = -0.225"$$
$$C_C = -0.045"$$

Hence, most probable values of A, B and C are –

$$A = 70°\ 34'\ 12.6" + 0.57" = 70°\ 34'\ 12.03"$$
$$B = 55°\ 45'\ 08.2" - 0.225" = 55°\ 45'\ 07.975"$$
$$C = 125°\ 15'\ 27.3" - 0.045" = 125°\ 15'\ 27.255"$$

Example 2.50 : Four angles were measured around a station closing the horizon. The observed values are given below. Find most probable values of the angles using method of correlates only.

$$A = 75°\ 42'\ 20.3"\ \text{Weight 2}$$
$$B = 82°\ 36'\ 40.5"\ \text{Weight 4}$$
$$C = 120°\ 23'\ 15.2"\ \text{Weight 1}$$
$$D = 81°\ 17'\ 51.0"\ \ \text{Weight 4}$$

Solution : Observed sum of angles is :

$$A + B + C + D = 360° \ 00' \ 07''$$

$$\text{Theoretical sum} = 360° \ 00' \ 00''$$

$$\text{Discrepancy} = +07''$$

$$\therefore \qquad \text{Correction} = -07''$$

Let C_A, C_B, C_C and C_D be the corrections to the angles A, B, C, D.

$$\therefore \qquad C_A + C_B + C_C + C_D = -07'' \qquad \qquad \text{... (i)}$$

By the principle of least squares,

$$\sum W_C^2 = \text{minimum}$$

$$2C_A^2 + 4C_B^2 + 1C_C^2 + 4C_D^2 = \text{minimum} \qquad \qquad \text{... (ii)}$$

Differentiating equation (i) and (ii)

$$\delta C_A + \delta C_B + \delta C_C + \delta C_D = 0 \qquad \qquad \text{... (iii)}$$

$$2 \cdot C_A \cdot \delta C_A + 4 \cdot C_B \cdot \delta C_B + C_C \cdot \delta C_C + 4 \cdot C_D \cdot \delta C_D = 0 \qquad \qquad \text{... (iv)}$$

Multiplying the equation (iii) by $-\lambda$ and by adding to the equation (iv) above, we get

$$\delta C_A (-\lambda + 2C_A) + \delta C_B (-\lambda + 4C_B) + \delta C_C (-\lambda + C_C) + \delta C_D (-\lambda + 4C_D) = 0$$

The above equation will be valid provided

$$-\lambda + 2C_A = 0 \qquad \qquad \therefore C_A = \frac{\lambda}{2}$$

$$-\lambda + 4C_B = 0 \qquad \qquad \therefore C_B = \frac{\lambda}{4} \qquad \qquad \text{... (v)}$$

$$-\lambda + C_C = 0 \qquad \qquad \therefore C_C = \lambda$$

$$-\lambda + 4C_D = 0 \qquad \qquad \therefore C_D = \frac{\lambda}{4}$$

Substitute values of equation (v) in equation (i)

$$\frac{\lambda}{2} + \frac{\lambda}{4} + \lambda + \frac{\lambda}{4} = -07''$$

$$\therefore \qquad 2\lambda + \lambda + 4\lambda + \lambda = -28''$$

$$\therefore \qquad \lambda = -3.5''$$

$$\therefore \qquad C_A = -1.75''$$

$$C_B = -0.875''$$

$$C_C = -3.5''$$

$$C_D = -0.875''$$

∴   Most probable values of the angles are :

$$\angle A = 75° 42' 20.3" - 1.75" = 75° 42' 18.55"$$

$$\angle B = 82° 36' 40.5" - 0.875" = 82° 36' 39.625"$$

$$\angle C = 120° 23' 15.2" - 3.5" = 120° 23' 11.7"$$

$$\angle D = 81° 17' 51.0" - 0.875" = 81° 17' 50.125"$$

Example 2.51 : Determine the MPV's of the angles A, B and C of the triangle ABC from the following observed angles and the respective probable errors of measurements.

$$\angle A = 64° 12' 40" \pm 3"$$

$$\angle B = 55° 14' 23" \pm 2"$$

$$\angle C = 60° 33' 21" \pm 4"$$

Solution : Sum of the three angles of triangle ABC

$$\angle A + \angle B + \angle C = 180° 00' 24"$$

∴   Discrepancy $= + 24"$

∴   Each angle is to be reduced, and the error of + 24" is to be distributed in proportion to the square of the probable error. Let C_A, C_B and C_C be the corrections to be applied to the angles A, B and C respectively.

$$C_A : C_B : C_C = (3)^2 : (2)^2 : (4)^2 = 9 : 4 : 16 \qquad \text{... (i)}$$

Also, $C_A + C_B + C_C = 24"$ ... (ii)

∴ $C_B = \dfrac{4}{9} C_A$ and $C_C = \dfrac{16}{9} C_A$

Substituting these values of C_B and C_C in equation (ii)

$$C_A + \frac{4}{9} C_A + \frac{16}{9} C_A = + 24"$$

$$9C_A + 4C_A + 16C_A = 216"$$

$$29C_A = 216"$$

We get, $C_A = 7.45"$ (substantive)

$$C_B = 3.31 \text{ (substantive)}$$

$$C_C = 13.24 \text{ (substantive)}$$

Hence MPV's are –

$$\angle A \; = \; 64° \; 12' \; 40" - 7.45" \; = \; 64° \; 12' \; 32.55"$$

$$\angle B \; = \; 55° \; 14' \; 23" - 3.31" \;\; = \; 55° \; 14' \; 19.69"$$

$$\angle C \; = \; 60° \; 33' \; 21" - 13.24" \; = \; 60° \; 33' \; 7.76"$$

Hence, **Check :** 180°   00'   00"

Example 2.52 : Adjust the angles P, Q, R and S which close the horizon.

$$\angle P \; = \; 100° \; 30' \; 22" \text{ weight } 1$$

$$\angle Q \; = \; 80° \; 40' \; 10" \text{ weight } 2$$

$$\angle R \; = \; 90° \; 20' \; 08" \;\; \text{weight } 3$$

$$\angle S \; = \; 88° \; 29' \; 25" \;\; \text{weight } 4$$

Solution : The sum of observed angles $\; = \; 360° \; 00' \; 05"$

The theoretical sum $\; = \; 360° \; 00' \; 00"$

∴   Discrepancy $\; = \; 5"$

∴   Total correction $\; = \; -5"$

Observed sum is greater than theoretical sum therefore correction is negative.

As per the laws of weights, the corrections are inversely proportional to their weights. Let C_p, C_q, C_r and C_s be the corrections to the observed values of angles P, Q, R, S then,

$$C_p : C_q : C_r : C_s \; = \; \frac{1}{1} : \frac{1}{2} : \frac{1}{3} : \frac{1}{4} \; = \; 12 : 6 : 4 : 3$$

Hence, $C_p \; = \; \dfrac{12}{25} \times 5" \; = \; 2.40"$

$$C_q \; = \; \frac{6}{25} \times 5" \; = \; 1.20"$$

$$C_r \; = \; \frac{4}{25} \times 5" \; = \; 0.80"$$

$$C_s \; = \; \frac{3}{25} \times 5" = 0.60"$$

Check : $C_p + C_q + C_r + C_s \; = \; 5"$

∴   Most probable values of angles are :

$$P \; = \; 100° \; 30' \; 22" - 2.40" \; = \; 100° \; 30' \; 19.60"$$

$$Q \; = \; 80° \; 40' \; 10" - 1.20" \; = \; 80° \; 40' \; 8.80"$$

$$R \; = \; 90° \; 20' \; 08" - 0.80" \; = \; 90° \; 20' \; 7.20"$$

$$S \; = \; 88° \; 29' \; 25" - 0.60" \; = \; 88° \; 29' \; 24.40"$$

Check : P + Q + R + S = 360° 00' 00".

THEORETICAL QUESTIONS

1. Explain step by step, the procedure of adjustment of the observed spherical angles of the triangle.

2. State and briefly explain the laws of weights.

3. Explain with illustrations : Normal equation and rules for formulation of them.

4. Explain probable error and mean square error.

5. Distinguish clearly between the "most probable error" and the "probable error". What is the significance of each one of them ?

6. State and explain Gauss rule.

7. What is a side equation ? Derive an expression for the same in case of geodetic quadrilateral.

8. State the conditions of adjustments of a triangle with central station.

9. What do you mean by side equation ? Derive an expression for the same for a triangle with central station.

10. Explain how you will obtain the most probable values from the direct observations of unequal weights by the method of least squares.

11. Explain the principle of least squares. Starting from the principle of least squares show that the arithmetic mean is the most probable value, when a quantity is repeatedly measured.

12. Explain clearly theory of least squares as applied to the adjustment of survey measurements. Are there any assumptions involved in the method ?

13. (a) What is meant by the term side equation ?

    (b) State the equation of condition in each of the following cases :

    　　(i)　A polygon comprising the triangles having a common vertex.

    　　(ii)　Geodetic quadrilateral.

14. (i) What is a spherical triangle ?

    (ii) Write down the formula for spherical excess.

    (iii) What is the maximum value of spherical excess ? What happens to the spherical triangle in that case ?

15. Define the principle of least squares and explain how this law can be applied to get the most probable value of a quantity.

16. Differentiate between a plane triangle and a spherical triangle.

17. Explain clearly the following :

    (i) Geoid, (ii) Spheroid, (iii) International spheroid, (iv) Laplace station,

    (v) Topographical surface.

18. What is meant by convergence of meridians ? Show that the convergence of meridians is equal to the product of difference in longitude and sine average of latitude.

19. What are the effects of the curvature of the Earth on surveys ?

Show that change in azimuth in case of a long survey line is equal to the product of difference of longitudes at its ends and the sine of average latitudes at its ends.

NUMERICAL PROBLEMS

1. Six measures of the angle in seconds are :

27.5" , 26.22", 26.95", 27.08", 24.30", 27.85"

Compute the probable error of a single observation with unit weight and that of arithmetic mean.

Ans. : 0.34", Observed value = $26.59 \pm 0.34"$

2. Find the probable error in the supplement of an angle A = 86° 23' 13.2" $\pm 0.01"$

3. Adjust the angles α and β, observations of which give

$$\alpha = 10° 20' 10" \qquad \text{Weight 7}$$
$$\beta = 20° 30' 30" \qquad \text{Weight 8}$$
$$\alpha + \beta = 30° 50' 50" \qquad \text{Weight 2}$$

Ans. : $\alpha = 10° 20' 11.6", \ \beta = 20° 30' 32.8"$

4. Find the most probable values of angles A, B and C of a triangle ABC from the following observations by the method of a normal equation.

$$\angle A = 48° 14' 26"$$
$$\angle B = 57° 17' 48"$$
$$\angle C = 74° 27' 50"$$

Ans. : 48° 14' 24.67", 57° 17' 46.66", 74° 27' , 48.67"

5. Find the most probable values of angles A, B and C of a triangle ABC from the following observations :

$$\angle A = 56° 24' 36"$$
$$\angle B = 52° 12' 43"$$
$$\angle C = 71° 22' 45"$$

Ans. : 56° 24' 34.67", 52° 12' 41.67", 71° 22' 43.66"

6. Find the most probable values of the angles A and B from following observations :

$$\angle A = 47° 25' 35" \qquad \text{Weight 2}$$
$$\angle B = 21° 23' 30" \qquad \text{Weight 3}$$
$$\angle A + \angle B = 68° 48' 55" \qquad \text{Weight 4}$$

Ans. : A = 47° 25' 30", B = 21° 23' 27"

7. The observed values of A, B and C at a station are :

$$\angle A = 25° 10' 35.5''$$

$$\angle B = 47° 48' 18.8''$$

$$\angle C = 72° 58' 43.5''$$

Subject to the condition that A + B = C.

Determine the most probable values of A, B and C.

8. Formulate the normal equations in A, B and C from the following observations :

A = 25° 17' 10"	Weight 2
B = 28° 52' 13"	Weight 3
C = 42° 37' 49"	Weight 1
A + B = 54° 09' 20"	Weight 3
A + B + C = 96° 47' 14"	Weight 2

Ans. :   7A + 5B + 2C = 406° 35' 47"

5A + 8B + 2C = 442° 39' 06"

2A + 2B + 3C = 236° 12'15"

9. The angles of a spherical PQR were observed as follows :

P = 77° 14' 39"	Weight 2
Q = 49° 40' 48"	Weight 3
R = 53° 04' 55"	Weight 4

Find the values of adjusted spherical and plane angles if the spherical axis excess was known to be 9".

Ans. : (i) 77° 14' 33", 49° 40' 44", 53° 04' 52"

(ii) 77°14' 30", 49° 40' 41", 53° 04' 49"

10. Find the most probable value of angle A from the following equations :

2A = 30° 30' 31.00"	Weight 1
3A = 45° 45' 48.00"	Weight 2
4A = 61° 01' 00.00"	Weight 3

11. The following values were recorded for a triangle ABC, the individual measurement being equally precise.

A = 62° 28' 15"	6 observations
B = 56° 24' 39"	8 observations
C = 61° 07' 25"	6 observations

Find the corrected value of the angles if the spherical excess is known to be 10".

12. Compute the lengths of the triangle ABC from the following :

   (1)   Corrected spherical angle A = 78° 34' 01"   Weight 1

   (2)   Corrected spherical angle B = 50° 15' 30.3" Weight 1

   (3)   Corrected spherical angle C = 51° 10' 34.7" Weight 1

   Length AC = 4255630 m

13. Mean observed angles in a spherical triangle ABC were

$$\angle A \ = \ 48° 20' 27.2" \qquad \text{Weight 2}$$
$$\angle B \ = \ 68° 17' 32.8" \qquad \text{Weight 1}$$
$$\angle C \ = \ 63° 22' 15.4" \qquad \text{Weight 3}$$

   Assuming the radius of earth to be 6400 km, calculate :

   (i)   Spherical excess,

   (ii)   Adjusted spherical angles, and

   (iii)   Adjusted plane angles.

14. The following are the observed values of an angle :

Angle	Weight
40° 20' 20"	2
40° 20' 18"	2
40° 20' 19"	3

   Find (a) Probable error of single observation of unit weight.

   (b) Probable error of weighted arithmetic mean.

15. Find the most probable values of angles A and B from the following :

$$A \ = \ 62° 25' 17" \qquad \text{Weight 2}$$
$$B \ = \ 49° 12' 37" \qquad \text{Weight 3}$$
$$A + B \ = \ 111° 37' 22" \qquad \text{Weight 4}$$

   Ans. : 62° 25' 05", 49° 12' 23", 111° 37' 28"

16. Angles A, B and C close the horizon. Find their most probable values with the help of the following observations :

A	= 99° 45' 40"	Weight 2
B	= 127° 32' 30"	Weight 4
C	= 132° 42' 16"	Weight 3

   Ans. : $C_A = -12"$, $C_B = -6"$, $C_C = -8"$

17. The following are the angles of a plane triangle ABC, the individual measurement being uniformly precise :

$$\angle A = 77° 40' 43'' \qquad 8 \text{ observations}$$
$$\angle B = 49° 36' 35'' \qquad 4 \text{ observations}$$
$$\angle C = 52° 42' 51'' \qquad 2 \text{ observations}$$

Find the correct values of the angles.

Ans. : Corrections inversely proportional to their number of observations. The corrections are : $C_A = -\dfrac{9}{7}$, $C_B = -\dfrac{18}{7}$, $C_C = -\dfrac{36}{7}$

18. The following angles were measured at a station O, so as to close the horizon.

$$a = 83° 42' 28.8'' \qquad \text{Weight 3}$$
$$b = 102° 15' 43.3'' \qquad \text{Weight 2}$$
$$c = 94° 38' 25.3'' \qquad \text{Weight 4}$$
$$d = 79° 23' 23'' \qquad \text{Weight 2}$$

Find the most probable values of angles.

19. Find the most probable values of angles A and B and the summation angle (A + B) from the following observations :

$$A = 47° 25' 35.4'' \qquad \text{Weight 1}$$
$$B = 41° 23' 30.5'' \qquad \text{Weight 2}$$
$$A + B = 88° 48' 59.3'' \qquad \text{Weight 3}$$

Ans. :
$$A = 47° 25' 31.8''$$
$$B = 41° 23' 28.7''$$
$$A + B = 88° 49' 0.5''$$

20. The following are six, equally reliable and direct measurements of a base line :

702.0 m, 701.4 m, 701.8 m, 701.6 m, 701.56 m, 701.9 m

Calculate the most probable value and its probable error.

21. The angles of a plane triangle are measured as follows :

$$A = 79° 48' 52'' \qquad \text{Weight 4}$$
$$B = 42° 32' 17'' \qquad \text{Weight 1}$$
$$C = 57° 38' 54'' \qquad \text{Weight 2}$$

Find the adjusted values of A, B and C.

Ans. :
$$A = 79° 48' 51.57''$$
$$B = 42° 32' 15.29''$$
$$C = 57° 38' 53.14''$$

Check : $A + B + C = 180° 00' 00''$

22. Find the most probable values of the following angles closing the horizon :

$$P = 45° 23' 37" \qquad \text{Weight 1}$$
$$Q = 75° 37' 15" \qquad \text{Weight 2}$$
$$R = 125° 21' 21" \qquad \text{Weight 3}$$
$$S = 113° 37' 59" \qquad \text{Weight 3}$$

23. Find the most probable values of the angles A and B from the following data :

$$A = 42° 48' 36.6" \qquad \text{Weight 2}$$
$$B = 64° 37' 48.3" \qquad \text{Weight 3}$$
$$A + B = 107° 26' 28.5" \qquad \text{Weight 4}$$

Ans. :
$$A = 42° 48' 38.22"$$
$$B = 64° 37' 49.42"$$

24. The following are the mean values observed in the measurement of three angles A, B and C at one station :

$$A = 76° 42' 46.2" \qquad \text{Weight 4}$$
$$A + B = 134° 36' 32.2" \qquad \text{Weight 3}$$
$$B + C = 185° 35' 24.8" \qquad \text{Weight 2}$$
$$A + B + C = 262° 18' 10.4" \qquad \text{Weight 1}$$

Calculate the most probable values of angles.

25. Find the most probable values of angles of a spherical triangle ABC.

$$\angle A = 87° 14' 48" \qquad \text{Weight 4}$$
$$\angle B = 49° 40' 35" \qquad \text{Weight 3}$$
$$\angle C = 43° 04' 52" \qquad \text{Weight 2}$$

The spherical excess was known to be 0° 0' 2"

26. The following are the mean observed angles of a spherical triangle ABC :

$$\angle A = 40° 12' 27.2" \qquad \text{Weight 2}$$
$$\angle B = 78° 25' 32.8" \qquad \text{Weight 1}$$
$$\angle C = 61° 22' 15" \qquad \text{Weight 3}$$

If the length of the line BC = 15 km

Calculate : (i) Spherical excess, (ii) Adjusted spherical angles.

Assume mean radius of the earth = 6370 km

Ans. : 0.76", 40° 12' 23.3", 78° 25' 25.03", 61° 22' 12.41"

27. A survey was conducted from station P in latitude 53° 40' 30" N and longitude 125° 00' 18" W to a point Q of latitude 54° 04' 30" N and longitude 125° 21' 18" W. What would be the theoretical difference between the azimuth of the final line at Q determined astronomically and the bearing calculated by the co-ordinates from the meridian at P ?

    Ans. : 16' 57.6"

28. A station in latitude 47° 22' 40" N and longitude 00° 41' 10" E, the azimuth of the CD was 23° 44' 00". If the length of the line CD was 29.625 km, compute the latitude and longitude of station D and the back azimuth of the line from station D.

    Given :

Latitude	Length of 1" of latitude in metres	Length of 1" of longitude in metres
47° 30'	30.399	20.601
47° 35'	30.399	20.568

    Ans. : 47° 37' 30" N, 00° 50' 49" E and 203° 51' 10"

29. Calculate the azimuth of the line PQ at P and of the line PQ at Q and the length of the line PQ from the following data :

Station	Latitude	Longitude
P	54° 51' 30" N	92° 20' 30" E
Q	54° 54' 00" N	92° 58' 10" E

    Given :

Latitude	Length of 1" of latitude in metres	Length of 1" of longitude in metres
54° 50'	30.9234	17.8509
54° 55'	30.9238	17.8141

    Ans. : 83° 10' 37", 83° 41' 25.6", 40.5634 km

30. What is the direction of New York from London and of London from New York, on the great circle route ? What is the length of this route ? The geographic co-ordinates are as follows :

London	51° 30' N	0° 50' W
New York	40° 43' N	73° 59' W

    Radius of earth = 6367 km

31. A transverse is run from a station X, latitude 52° 10' 16" N, longitude 8° 56' 36" W to a station Y, latitude 52° 32' 48" N and longitude 9° 15' 18" W.

Calculate the direction and distance of the line XY at X and also at Y. Hence determine the convergence of meridians. Assume radius of earth = 6370 km.

Ans. : (i) θ = 0° 48' 37"

(ii)   xy = 90.08 km

(iii) α = 61° 58' 4.74"

(iv) $\delta\alpha$ = 0° 14' 48.46"

PHOTOGRAMMETRY

3.1 INTRODUCTION

The word "Photography' is formed from two Greek words 'Photos' and "Graphy' meaning drawing with the reflected light. Rays of light coming from the sun will be falling on different objects on the surface of the earth. The objects in turn will partly or wholly reflect these rays. If such reflected rays reach the emulsion of the camera film, the objects will be photographed. These photographs form the basis for obtaining information about the objects indirectly. Thus, photographic surveying may be defined as 'the art and science of obtaining valuable information i.e. size, shape and position of the objects from measurements and interpretation of their photographic images taken by keeping the camera on the ground or in the air', the former being called as "*Ground or Terrestrial photographic surveying*", and the latter as "*Aerial photographic surveying*" or "*Air survey*".

The various operations involved in photogrammetric or photographic surveying are :

(i)   Taking photographs of the area to be surveyed,

(ii)   Processing the photographs in the laboratory to obtain the photographic prints or images.

(iii)   Scrutinising the photograph prints to acquire the desired information or maps.

3.2 BROAD CLASSIFICATION

Photogrammetric surveying is further divided into two broad categories or areas as follows :

(a) Metric or Quantitative Photogrammetry which aims at determining the shapes, sizes, positions and elevations of the objects appearing on the photographic prints, and preparation of contour maps.

(b) Interpretative or Qualitative Photogrammetry that deals with analysing the photographic images to recognise and identify the objects and deduce their significance. It is a form or branch of 'Remote sensing' in which the black and white images are recorded on photographic emulsions that are sensitive to energy in the visible electromagnetic spectrum.

3.3 CHART SHOWING CLASSIFICATION OF PHOTOGRAMMETRIC SURVEYING

Photographic or photogrammetric surveying initially started with the ground or terrestrial photographic survey. With the invention of aeroplane by Wright Brothers in 1902, aerial photogrammetry has been developed. Recently, infrared and radar imagery systems, known as *Remote sensing* i.e. space photography, have been used for interpretative or qualitative analysis.

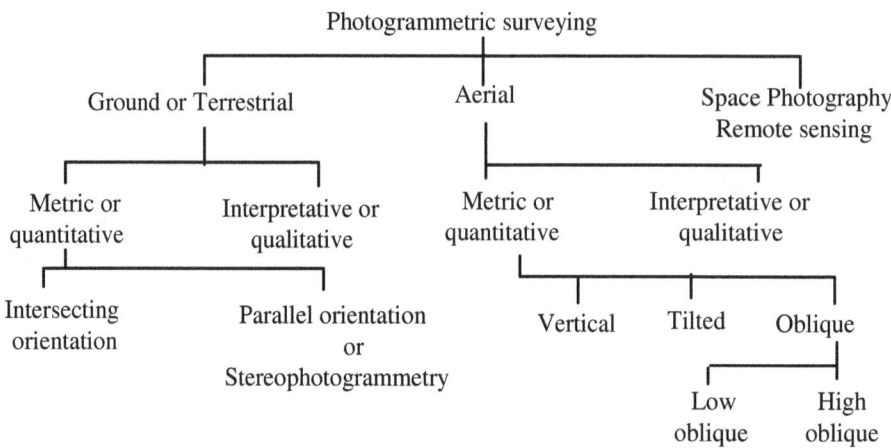

3.4 AERIAL PHOTOGRAMMETRY

3.4.1 Introduction

Aerial photogrammetry may be defined as 'the technique of obtaining reliable measurements from the photographs taken by keeping the camera in the aeroplane'. When these measurements are made in horizontal plane and plotted, a 2-dimensional picture of the ground is obtained. In addition, if the measurements made in vertical plane are also plotted systematically, a 3-dimensional picture of the ground is obtained. The aerial surveying, carried out on large scale during first world war in 1914, was mainly used for the military intelligence purposes. Subsequently, it was extensively used for carrying out reconnaissance and preliminary surveys of large Civil Engineering projects, such as catchment and command area surveys, route surveys etc.

The method is very rapid and mostly used for preparing small scale contour map of the area. However it is somewhat less accurate. In India, it is mainly carried out by Survey of India Department with their head quarters at Deharadoon. Certain private companies are also permitted by Survey of India Department to carry out aerial surveying.

3.4.2 Equipments Required for Aerial Surveying

The equipments required for aerial surveying are :

(i)　An aerial camera

(ii)　Air craft and

(iii)　Plotting machines.

(i) Aerial Camera [Fig 3.1 (a)] :

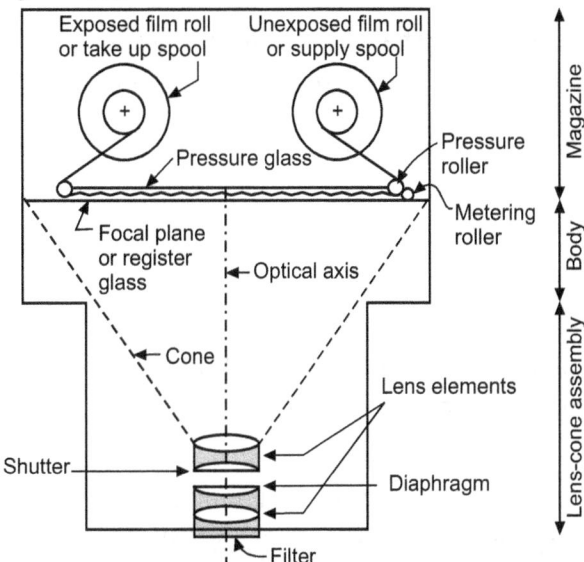

Fig. 3.1 (a) : Aerial camera

The aerial camera, which is of fixed focus type, should be highly precise. It may have a single or multiple lens system. The lens should be fast, with high speed shutter $\left(\frac{1}{100}^{th} \text{ seconds to } \frac{1}{1500}^{th} \text{ seconds}\right)$, high speed type emulsion and there should be sufficient space inside the camera to house the film rolls. The lenses used are classified according to the field angle as [Fig. 3.1 (b)].

   (i)   Superwide angle (upto 125°), with focal length f = 305 mm.

   (ii) Wide angle (upto 90°), with focal length f = 153 mm.

   (iii) Normal angle (upto 60°) with focal length f = 305 mm.

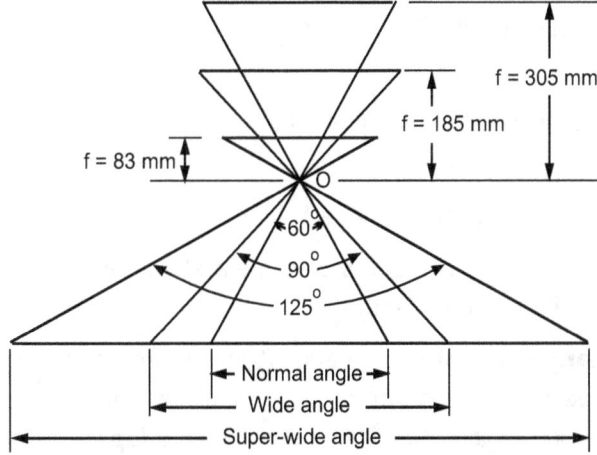

Fig. 3.1 (b) : Classification of camera lenses according to focal length

The shutter speed varies from $1/100^{th}$ to $1/1000^{th}$ of seconds.

The essential component parts of aerial camera may thus be specified as follows :

(i)　Lens assembly which is a combination of lenses, diaphragm shutter and filter.

(ii)　Camera cone

(iii)　Focal plane

(iv)　Body of camera

(v)　Camera drive mechanism

(vi)　Magazine (to hold required number of film rolls)

The size of the negative plate may be 10 cm × 10 cm, 18 cm × 18 cm and 23 cm × 23 cm, the 23 cm × 23 cm being in common use.

(ii)　Aircraft :

The aircraft to be used in aerial surveying should have sufficient space inside for accommodating the aerial camera and also for free movement of the air crew.

It should be capable of flying at high altitude (depending on the scale of the photograph) and at great uniform speed in a given horizontal direction. It is generally equipped with an *Altimeter* which records the height at which the aircraft is flying and an *Intervalometer* which automatically controls the exposure time and a *view finder* providing clear view of the ground below and ahead of the aircraft.

(iii)　Plotting Machines :

These are automatic highly precise plotting machines which are used for plotting directly from the stereo-pairs. Such machines are capable of reproducing the spatial relationship (three dimensional picture) of the ground covered by a stereopair of aerial photographs.

3.4.3 Classification of Aerial Photographs

The aerial photographs may be classified as follows :

(i)　Vertical

(ii)　Tilted (or nearly vertical) (unintentional tilt)

(iii)　Oblique (Intentionally tilted)

(iv)　Combination of vertical and oblique.

(i)　Vertical photographs : If the axis of camera at the time of taking photograph is vertical, the photograph is said to be vertical.

(ii)　Tilted (or nearly vertical) : If the aircraft at the time of taking photograph is not perfectly horizontal due to formation of air pockets, navigation difficulties etc., the axis of the camera may not remain vertical but will be slightly tilted (upto 3°) and the photograph is then called as *tilted* or *nearly vertical photograph*.

(iii) Oblique photographs : If the axis of camera at the time of taking photographs is not vertical but intentionally tilted, the photograph is called an *oblique photograph* which is further divided into *low oblique* and *high oblique*.

(a) In case of low oblique, the angle of tilt may be upto 30° with the vertical and the image of the horizon is not included; whereas,

(b) In case of a high oblique the tilt may be greater than 30° (but less than 90°) to the vertical and the image of the horizon is also included.

(iv) Combination of vertical and oblique : Such photographs are sometimes taken to obtain more details of the ground.

3.4.4 (a) Comparison of Vertical and Oblique Photographs

Vertical photographs	Oblique photographs
1. Used where high degree of precision is required and scale is large.	1. Mainly used for gathering information about the territory e.g. for military intelligence purposes.
2. More number of horizontal and vertical controls are required.	2. Used chiefly for small scale mapping.
3. Identification and interpretation of the object is somewhat difficult.	3. Identification and interpretation of the object is easy.
4. The area covered is less as compared to oblique photographs.	4. More area is covered.
5. It is somewhat difficult to take truely vertical photographs because of navigation difficulties.	5. Oblique photographs can be taken easily.

3.4.4 (b) Aerial Photo v/s Map

Vertical aerial photo	Map
1. Photograph is a perspective/conical projection.	1. Map is an orthographic projection.
2. Air photograph shows each and every detail available on earth at an instant of photography.	2. Map shows only pre-decided details essential from planning point of view.
3. Scale changes from point to point on photograph.	3. Scale is constant throughout on a map.
4. Photograph is distorted due to tilt and relief.	4. There are no such distortions on map.

... Contd.

5. Contrast air photographs shows lot of confusing details, such as bushes, trees, crops, varied ground tones, vehicle on road etc.	5. Map is a scaled plot of land showing possible prominent man made and artificial features.
6. Essential attributes such as place names, symbols, heights etc. do not appear on the photograph.	6. Place name, symbols, heights etc. are readily available on map.
7. Things are seen in their top view in aerial photo to which most of the user are not familiar, hence they find it difficult to use aerial photo.	7. Most people are familiar with maps and find them easy to use because they show those details which are essential for the particular purpose.
8. A photo takes almost no time to shoot. It can be taken at whenever desired. Frequent updating of data extracted from aerial photo is not very difficult.	8. As maps take time to produce, they become out of date by time they are published. Their frequent revision is not possible.

3.4.5 Definitions of the Terms (Used in Aerial Surveying)

(1) **Optical axis or camera axis (OpP) :** It is a line passing through the centre of the lens and intersecting the photographic plane at right angles.

(2) **Principal distance (or focal length) :** Focal length i.e. Op = f is the distance measured from the lens centre to the plane of photograph i.e. f.

(3) **Vertical axis (OvV) :** It is the axis of direction of gravity.

(4) **Angle of tilt (θ) :** It is the angle formed by the optical axis with the vertical line.

(5) **Plumb point (v) :** It is a point of intersection of the vertical axis with the photographic plane.

(6) **Principal point :** It is a point of intersection of optical axis with the photographic plane and generally coincides with the origin of X and Y axis.

(7) **Isocentre :** It is the point where the bisector of angle of tilt intersects the photograph. i.e. point i.

(8) **Tilt (θ) :** It is the angle between the vertical axis and optical axis of camera.

(9) **Principal line (vip) :** It is the line of intersection of the principal plane and the plane of photograph.

(10) **Height of flight or flying height :** It is the vertical distance of the lens measured above the ground level and is equal to height of the camera lens above m.s.l. minus the average height of the terrain = $H - h_a$

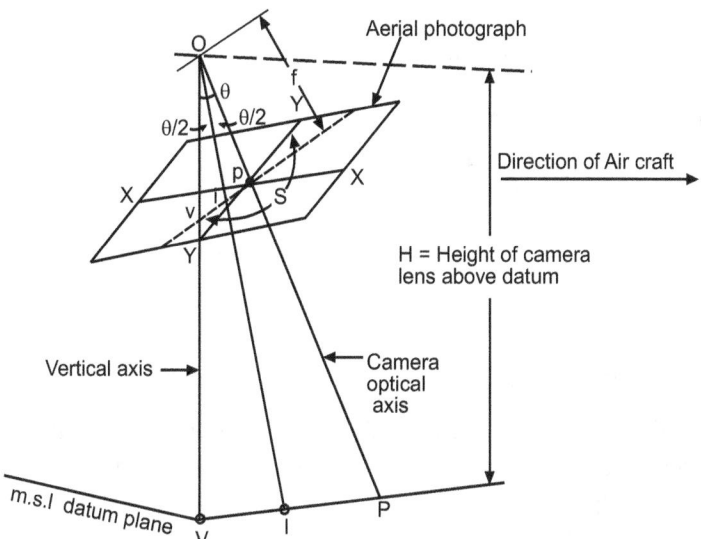

Fig. 3.2 : An unintentionally tilted aerial photograph with the optical axis tilted at an angle θ to the vertical

(11) Swing : It may be defined as 'the angle measured clockwise in the plane of photograph from the positive Y-axis to the nadir or plumb point, shown as angle S.

(12) Ground plumb point or Ground Nadir point : It is a point on the ground vertically below the lens centre O i.e. point V and its image v on the photographic plate is called *plate plumb-point* or *plate nadir point*. If the optical axis of the lens is vertical, the plate plumb point and the principal point will coincide.

3.4.6 Scale of the Vertical Photograph

Datum Point and Average Scales :

Scale of the vertical photograph is defined as 'the ratio of the distance between two points on the photograph to the corresponding distance between the same points on the ground', as seen from the Fig. 3.3.

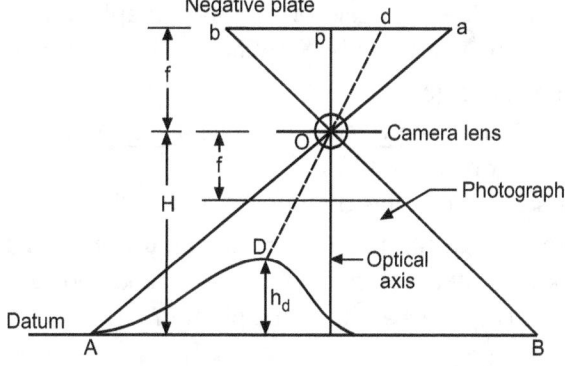

Fig. 3.3

$\therefore$ Scale $= \dfrac{ab}{AB}$

As the two triangles AOB and aob are similar,

$$\dfrac{ab}{AB} = \dfrac{f}{H} ;$$

where,   f = Focal length of the camera lens and

                              H = Height of aircraft above the datum level

$\therefore$ Datum scale $= \dfrac{ab}{AB} = \dfrac{f}{H}$,   the equation is true provided all the ground

points are lying at the datum plane. But as all the ground points are not lying at the datum plane, the equation needs modification. For example, for the ground point D, lying h_d metre above the datum plane, its scale will be,

$$S_{point\ d} = \dfrac{f}{H - h_d} = \text{Point scale for ground point D.}$$

Thus, it is obvious that the scale varies from photograph to photograph and also for the different points on the same photograph. Alternatively if h_{av} is the average elevation of the ground over which the aircraft flies, the average scale of the photograph will be,

$$\text{Average scale} = \dfrac{f}{H - h_{av}}$$

Thus, it can be stated that the scale of the photograph varies from point to point due to ground relief and hence average scale as stated above may be taken for computation purposes. Computation work carried out with such approximate average scale will obviously be less accurate and thus computations of distances etc., will not be cent per cent correct.

Various Methods of Determining Scale :

(a) Scale from topographic maps : If the topographic maps of the area surveyed by aerial photography are available, the scale of the photograph can be calculated by taking two points on the photograph which can be identified on the toposheet.

Thus, the scale of the photograph

$$= \dfrac{\text{Distance between two points on photograph}}{\left(\substack{\text{Corresponding distance between} \\ \text{the same two points on toposheet}}\right) \times \text{Scale of toposheet}}$$

(b) Scale from the ratio of photo-distance to the ground distance : In this method, a horizontal line AB of known length is marked on the ground and vertical aerial photograph of this line is taken so that it appears as ab on the photograph.

Then   Scale of photograph $= \dfrac{\text{Photo distance}}{\text{Ground distance}} = \dfrac{ab}{AB}$

(c)　Scale by making use of the formula : In this method, scale of the photograph is obtained by the formula –

$$\text{Scale of photograph} = \frac{f}{H - h_{av}}$$

where,　　　　　　　　f　=　Focal length of the aerial camera lens

　　　　　　　　　　　　H　=　Height of the flight of aircraft above datum

　　　　　　　　　　　　h_{av}　=　Average ground elevation in the area under consideration

The height of the flight (H) is determined by an altimeter or Air borne profile recorded (A.P.R) placed inside the aircraft.

3.4.7 Relief Displacement or Distortion due to Height

Introduction :

If the axis of the aerial camera at the time of exposure is vertical and the ground covered is perfectly horizontal, an orthographic projection of the ground is obtained on the vertical photograph, the scale of the photograph being same throughout. However, in practice, such conditions are never met with. Due to the variation in the ground elevation, the scale of the photograph varies and the image positions of the objects are displaced radially outwards from their true orthographic positions, the phenomenon being known as 'Relief Displacement'. Due to the relief displacement, any object standing above the ground (i.e. terrain) is seen to lean away, from principal point of the vertical photograph, radially outwards.

The 'Relief Displacement' varies directly to the height of the object, and to the radial distance of the object from the principal point and varies inversely to the flying height above the selected datum.

Relief Displacement or Distortion due to Height (on Vertical Photograph) :

(a)　Definition : Let PQR be the datum plane (Fig. 3.4) and let T be the point on the ground at an elevation h above the datum. Let B be the foot of the perpendicular from T to the datum plane line i.e. B is the orthogonal projection of the point on the datum line. Let O be the position of the camera lens at the time of exposure and let t and b be the points on the picture plane (at a distance equal to the focal length f of the camera lens), corresponding to the ground points T and B, the point B lying at the datum plane. Thus, the ground point T appears as 't' on the photograph. If this point was to lie at the datum plane, it would have appeared as 'b' on the photograph. In other words, the point T is displaced from its position b to t due to its relief or height above the datum plane and is called as "*Relief Displacement*". i.e. bt.

(b)　Derivation of expression for relief displacement : Referring to the Fig. 3.4, we have by the principle of similar triangles, Okt and OK'T,

$$\frac{kt}{K'T} = \frac{f}{H-f} \text{ but } K'T = QB$$

$$\therefore \quad \frac{kt}{QB} = \frac{f}{H-h} \text{ or } kt(H-h) = f \cdot QB \qquad ...(3.1)$$

Now, for the triangles Okb and OQB, we have,

$$\frac{kb}{QB} = \frac{f}{H}$$

$$\therefore \quad QB = \frac{kb \cdot H}{f} \qquad ...(3.2)$$

Putting the value of QB obtained in (3.2) in (3.1) above we have,

$$kt(H-h) = f \cdot \frac{kb \cdot H}{f} = kb \cdot H$$

But $\qquad kb = kt - bt$

$\therefore \qquad kt(H-h) = (kt - bt)H$

or $\qquad ktH - kth = ktH - btH$

Cancelling ktH, we get,

$$kth = btH$$

or $\qquad bt = \dfrac{kth}{H}$

but $\qquad bt = \text{Relief displacement} = d$

and $\qquad kt = \text{Displacement of the point T from the principle point (k)} = r$

$\therefore \quad \text{Relief displacement} = \dfrac{kth}{H} \text{ or } d = \dfrac{rh}{H} \qquad ...(3.3)$

where,

$\qquad d = $ Relief displacement

$\qquad h = $ Height of the object T above datum plane

$\qquad r = $ Radial distance measured on the photograph from the principal point to the displaced image t and

$\qquad H = $ Flying height measured above the datum

From the equation (3.3), the following conclusions can be drawn :

(i) Relief displacement increases directly with the

　　(a) increase in the radial distance (r) and

　　(b) elevation of the object above the datum (h).

(ii) Relief displacement decreases with the increase in flying height (H) above the datum.

Further, it can be seen that relief displacement will occur radially outwards for the points lying above the datum and radially inwards for the points lying below the datum.

Rearranging the equation (3.3) for relief displacement,

Vertical height of the object TB $= h = \dfrac{dH}{r}$.

Thus, relief displacement helps in determining the height of the object above the selected datum plane.

The formula derived above is valid for a photograph which is truely vertical.

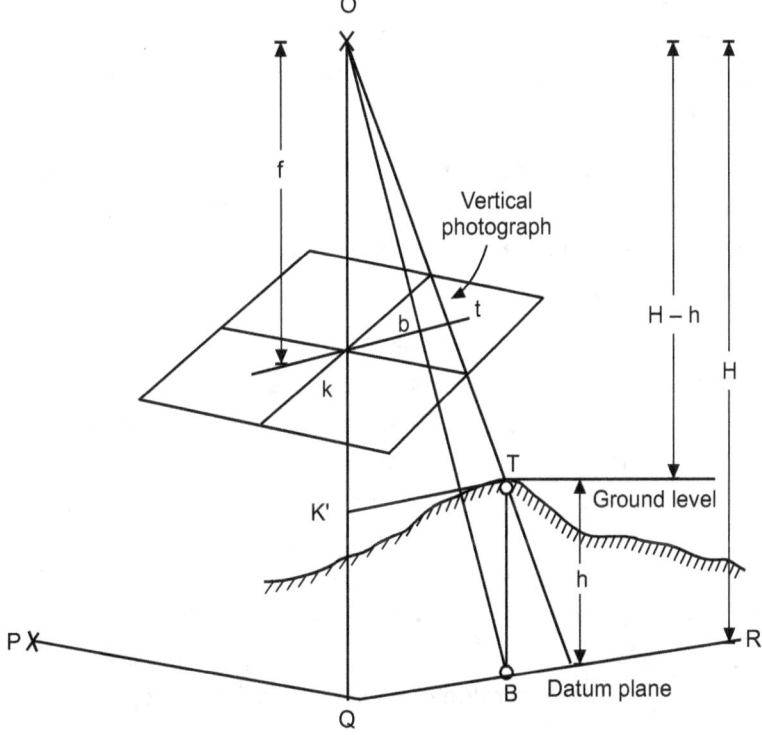

Fig. 3.4 : Relief displacement of distortion due to height

3.4.8 Flight Planning

Introduction :

In order to achieve complete success in the execution of any Civil Engineering project, it is to be preceded by proper planning. After a particular area has been specified, the first step in carrying out aerial surveying is to plan the photography so as to serve the desired purpose. A 'flight plan' clearly indicates 'where' and 'how' the photographs are to be taken to achieve the desired goal.

Flight Planning Considerations :

In flight planning, the following important points need thorough consideration :

(i)　Purpose of aerial survey : The purpose of aerial survey may be either metric or interpretative. For the preparation of topographic maps, aerial photos should possess good metric qualities, whereas for interpretative purposes, they should have good pictorial qualities, whereby identification of an object and judging its significance becomes easier.

(ii)　Scale of the photograph : This depends upon the purpose the aerial photographs are going to serve. For the preparation of topographic maps, the scale of the photograph depends upon the required map scale whereas for air photo interpretation, the scale of the photograph will depend upon the size of the smallest object that can be recognised on the photograph. Thus, the flight specifications for any particular project will vary with the purpose of the project.

(iii) Directions of the flight lines : The aircraft always flies parallel to the longest side of the area so that the number of strips required are kept to minimum. If there is abrupt change in the ground elevation, the aircraft should fly across such ground to avoid sudden variation in the scale of the photograph.

Vertical aerial photographs are always taken in such a way that when used in pairs and viewed under a stereoscope, a three-dimensional picture of the ground is obtained. For this, each photograph in a strip should overlap the previous one at least by 50 %, 60% being the most common. This overlap in the direction of flight is called as fore and after overlap or forward overlap or End lap. In order that no portion of the ground should be left unphotographed because of drift, crab, tilt etc., it is necessary to have overlap of adjacent flight strips. This is known as 'side lap' or ' transverse lap' and is generally 25 % to 30 %. An instrument called as 'Intervalometer' installed in the aircraft automatically controls the required overlapping. With 60 % end lap, the same object appears on three successive photographs which helps in the extension of controls. [Fig. 3.5 (a), (b) and (c)].

(iv)　Flying height : Knowing the focal length of the camera lens and the desired scale of the aerial photograph, the flying height may be computed by using the equation,

$$\text{Scale of photograph} \; = \; \frac{\text{Focal length of camera lens}}{\text{Flying height} - \text{Average ground level}}$$

i.e. $$S \; = \; \frac{f}{H - h_{av}}$$

The area covered by each photograph varies directly with the height of flight. An instrument known as Alimeter (a barometric instrument) installed in the aircraft enables the pilot officer to control and maintain the required height of flight. Considering all the aspects, it can be stated that the flying height of the aircraft depends mainly on the focal length of the camera lens, desired scale of the contour map and contour interval, the nature of the ground over which the aircraft flies and the plotting equipment available.

$a_1\ b_1\ c_1\ d_1$ is the first photograph in the direction of flight.

$a_2\ b_2\ c_2\ d_2$ is the second photograph with 60 % overlap in the direction of flight.

$a_3\ b_3\ c_3\ d_3$ is the third photograph with 60 % overlap in the direction of flight.

$a_2\ b_1\ c_1\ d_2$ is (60 %) overlap in the first two consecutive photographs.

p_1, p_2 and p_3 are the principal points of the photographs 1, 2 and 3 respectively.

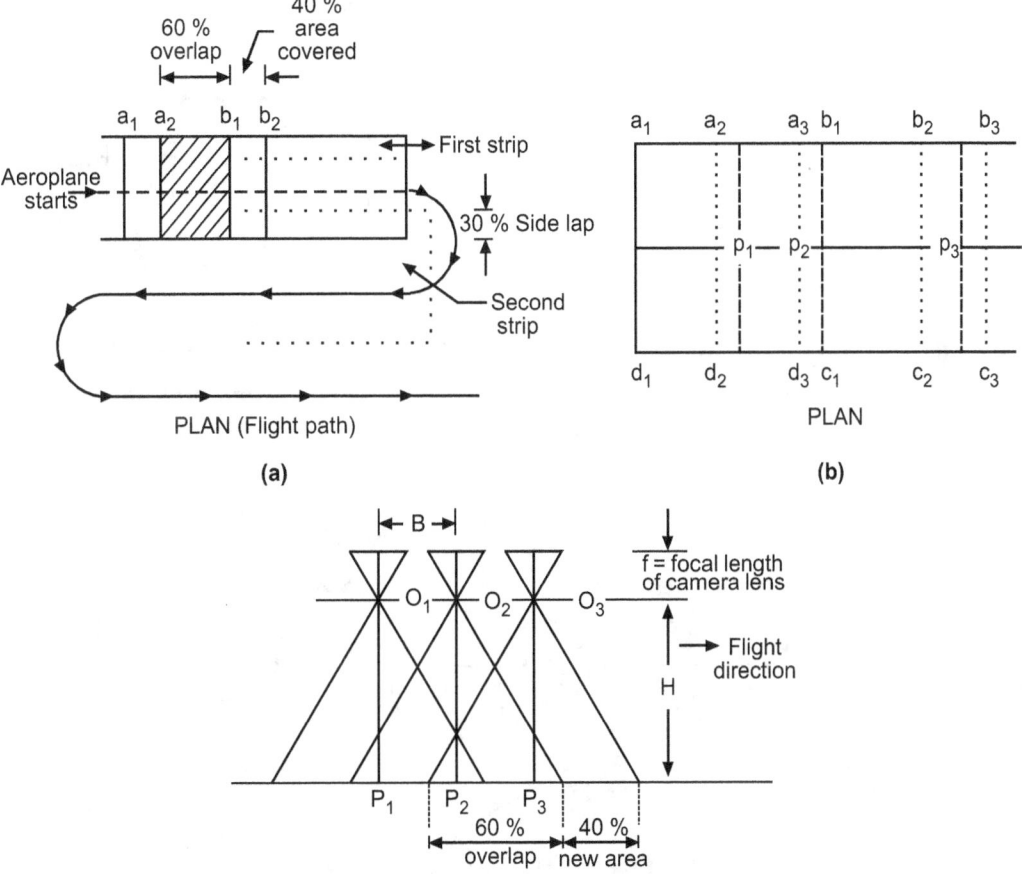

(a)

(b)

(c) 60% overlap in the direction of flight

Fig. 3.5

O_1, O_2, and O_3 are the three successive positions of aerial camera during flight path.

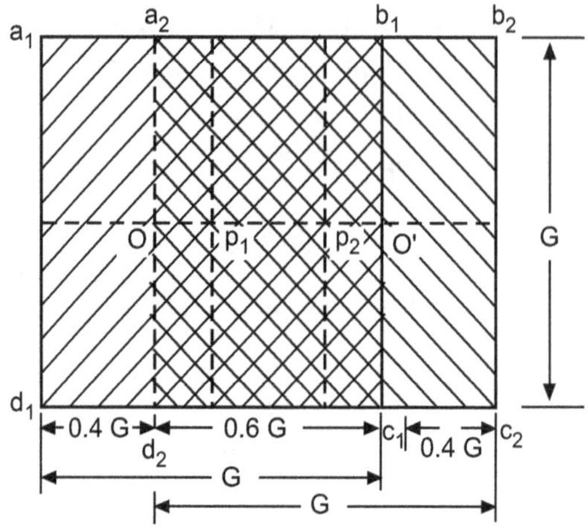

Fig. 3.5 (d)

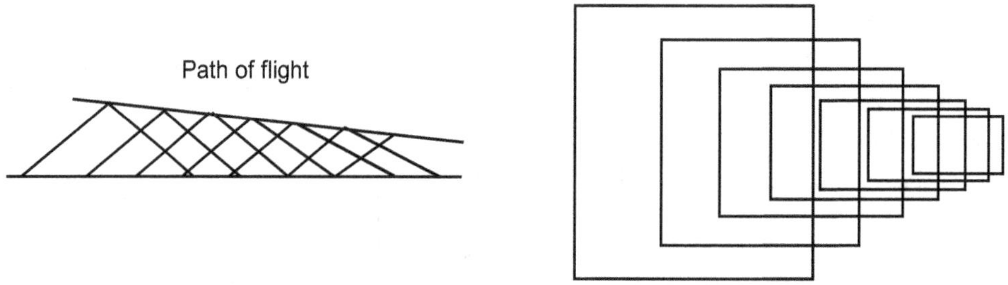

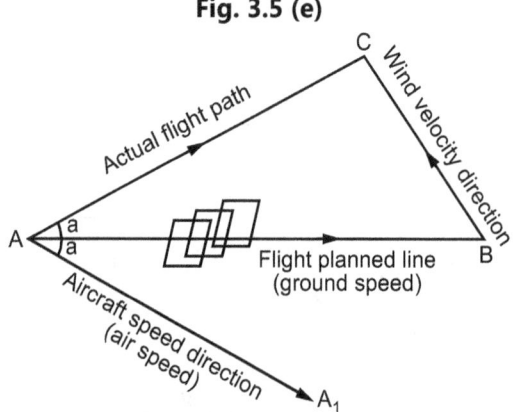

(i) Gradually rising ground

(ii) Area covered on the ground varies (in case of rising ground)

Fig. 3.5 (e)

Fig. 3.5 (f) : Effect of cross-wind

Referring to Fig. 3.5 (d), a_1 b_1 c_1 d_1 is the first photograph with principal point p_1 and a_2 b_2 c_2 d_2 is next photograph with principal point p_2 with 60 % end lap and 30 % side lap. a_2 b_1 c_1 d_2 is the common overlapped area.

Minimum Number of Photographs Required to Cover a Specified Area
(say L km × B km) :

The aerial photography is a highly specialised branch of surveying and requires proper planning. As the cost of the survey is directly proportional to the number of photographs, it is to be completed with a minimum number of photographs that will cover the specified area. Aerial photographs commonly used are 23 cm × 23 cm square in section. The longitudinal overlap generally adopted is 60 % so that the same object will appear on three successive photographs, the side lap being 30 %. The Fig. 3.5 (d) shows two such photographs $a_1 b_1 c_1 d_1$ with principal point p_1 and $a_2 b_2 c_2 d_2$ with principal point p_2, the end and side overlaps being 60 % and 30 % respectively.

$$\therefore \qquad OO' = 0.6\, G$$

where, $\qquad G$ = Length (or width) of square photograph in cm

But $\qquad p_1O' = 0.5\, G$

$$\therefore \qquad Op_1 = OO' - O_1O' = 0.1\, G$$

But $\qquad Op_2 = 0.5\, G$

$$\therefore \qquad p_1 p_2 = 0.4\, G$$

i.e. the distance between centre to centre of the adjacent photographs in the direction of flight (with 60 % overlap) is equal to 0.4 G.

i.e. $(1 - 0.6)$ G or $(1 - r_1)$ G; where r_1 = end overlap in percentage.

Similarly if the side lap is say 30 %, the distance between centre to centre of adjacent parallel strips will be 0.3 G i.e. $(1 - 0.7\, G)$ or $(1 - r_2)$ G, where r_2 = side lap in percentage.

If $L_{km} \times B_{km}$ ground area is to be covered, then the number of photographs required in the direction of flight (length wise) will be equal to

$$= \frac{\text{The total length to be covered on the ground}}{\left(\begin{array}{c}\text{Distance between c/c} \\ \text{of successive photograph}\end{array}\right) \times \text{Scale of photograph}}$$

$\therefore$ With 60 % overlap in the direction of flight, and S as the scale of the photograph expressed as 1 cm on the photograph (as S metres on the ground), then the above expression can be written as,

$$\begin{bmatrix}\text{Number of photographs required in} \\ \text{the direction of flight per strip}\end{bmatrix} = \frac{L_{km} \times 1000}{0.4\, G \times S} = N_1$$

Adding 1 extra for the end photographs $= N_1 + 1$

Similarly, the total number of photographs in the transverse direction

$$\text{assuming 30\% side lap} = \frac{B_{km} \times 1000}{0.7\,G + S} = N_2$$

$$\text{Adding 1 extra for the end strips} = N_2 + 1$$

$$\therefore \quad \begin{bmatrix} \text{Total minimum number of the photographs} \\ \text{required to cover the specified area} \end{bmatrix} = (N_1 + 1)\,(N_2 + 1)$$

If 2 extra photographs are added for end coverages, then

$$\begin{bmatrix} \text{Total number of minimum} \\ \text{photographs required} \end{bmatrix} = (N_1 + 2)\,(N_2 + 2)$$

Interval Between Exposures :

To determine the interval between successive exposures, it is necessary to know the speed of the aircraft and the distance between two successive exposures to be covered on the ground.

$$\text{Let,} \quad V = \text{Speed of aircraft in km/hour} = \frac{V \times 1000}{60 \times 60} \ \text{m/sec}$$

$$\text{Now,} \quad \begin{bmatrix} \text{The distance between centre to centre of} \\ \text{two photographs in the direction of flight} \end{bmatrix} = 0.4\,G \ (cm) = (0.4\,G \times S) \ \text{metres}$$

where S = Scale of the photograph

$$\therefore \quad \text{Interval between two successive exposures} = \frac{0.4\,G \times S}{\dfrac{V \times 1000}{3600}}$$

$$\therefore \ \text{Interval between two successive exposures} = \frac{0.4\,G \times S \times 3600}{V \times 1000} = \frac{0.4\,G \times S \times 3.6}{V}$$

Air Base Distance (B) :

The aerial photography is a highly specialised skilled branch of surveying and requires proper planning. As the cost of the survey varies directly with the number of photographs, it is to be completed with a minimum number of photographs. The distance between two successive exposures of camera lens in the air is called as 'Air Base Distance' (B) [Fig. 3.6 (a)] and the corresponding distance between two such points on the photographs being called as the 'photo base distance' (b).

The procedure of computing the air base distance for a given pair of aerial photographs is as follows [Fig. 3.6 (b)].

(1) Mark the principal point of each photograph say p_1 and p_2 and arrange them in the direction of flight.

(2) Fuse the two photographs under a stereoscope so that a three dimensional picture of the ground is obtained.

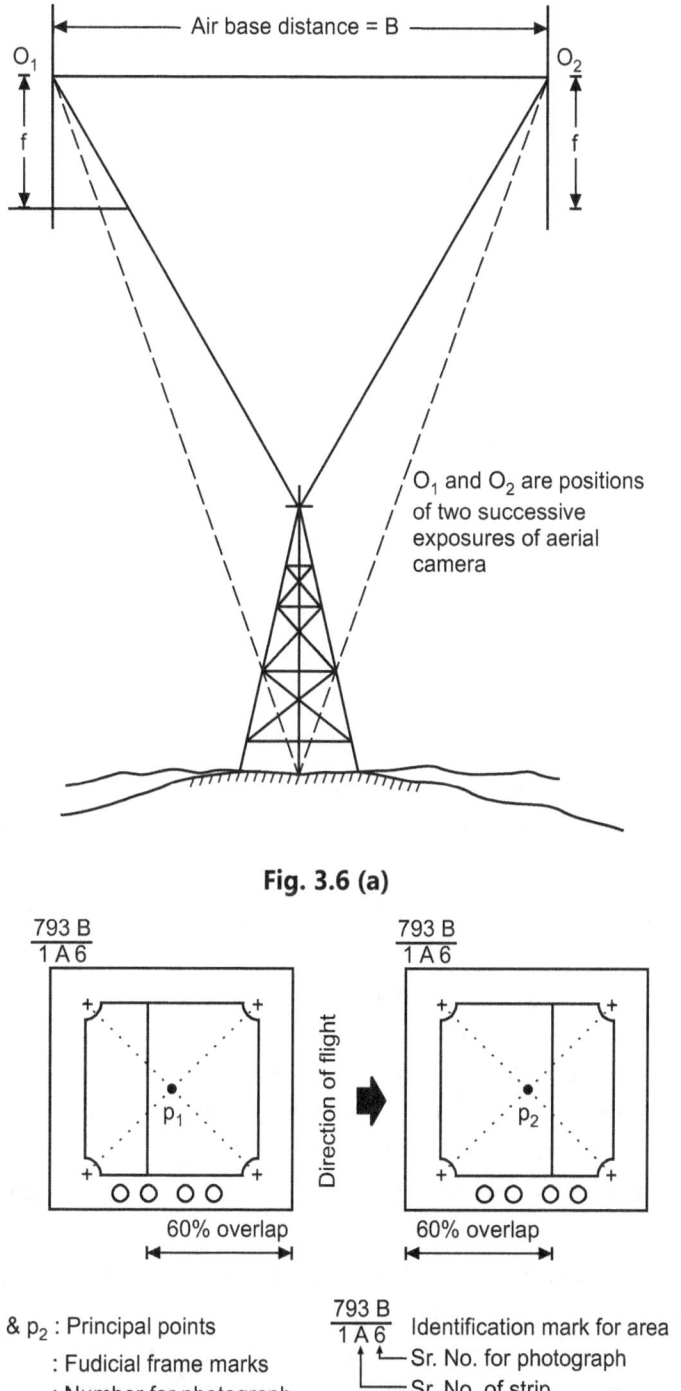

Fig. 3.6 (a)

Fig. 3.6 (b) : Typical sketch showing pair of aerial photographs

(3) Transfer the principal point (p_1) of the first photograph to the second and that of second (p_2) to the first. Let the transferred principal points be denoted by p_1' on the second photograph and by p_2' on the first photograph.

(4) Join $p_1 p_2'$ and $p_2 p_1'$. Theoretically $p_1 p_2'$ must be equal to $p_2 p_1'$ and is called as photo-base distance. If not, find the mean of $p_1 p_2'$ and $p_2 p_1'$ i.e. $\dfrac{p_1 p_2' + p_2 p_1'}{2} = b_m$ and is known as mean photo-base distance, (b_m).

(5) Determine the scale of the photograph as already explained above in Article 3.4.6. The mean photo base distance, b_m when multiplied by the scale of the photograph gives the 'air base distance' i.e. Distance between two successive exposures of camera lens.

General Hints on the Flight Planning :

1. Usually the aeroplane should fly parallel to the longest side of the area to be covered to reduce the number of strips to minimum.

2. While covering mountaneous ranges, where large difference of level exists, the aeroplane flies parallel to such ranges, to avoid rapid scale variations.

3. The overlap in the direction of flights is usually taken as 60 % so that the same object appears on three successive photographs. When such overlapped photographs are viewed under a stereoscope, a three dimensional view is obtained.

4. Each strip overlaps the previous strip by about 30 % so that no portion of the ground is left unphotographed.

5. As the aeroplane fuel is very costly, the number of turns and run-ins that amounts to non-productive expenditure should be kept to just minimum required.

6. The height of flight (H) of aircraft depends upon the nature of the ground to be covered, the scale of the photograph, the aircraft capabilities and the method of plotting to be used.

7. Depending upon the purpose of aerial photography (e.g. interpretative or metric), the flight specifications will vary.

8. The interval between two successive exposures of camera etc. depends upon the wind velocity at the time of actual flight.

9. The flight planning should be such that the entire area is covered with minimum number of photographs with required overlap and no portion of the ground to be covered should be left unphotographed. It is to be noted that the cost of the survey varies directly with the number of photographs.

10. While flying over a gradually rising ground [Fig. 3.5 (e)] maximum care should be taken to see that there is no loss of the minimum overlap required in the direction of flight and at right angles to it. The loss of overlap in the direction of flight in such cases is avoided by reducing the exposure interval. For side lap (i.e. overlap in the direction at right angles to the direction of flight) in such cases also called as lateral overlap, the flight lines should be arranged on minimum side-lap (i.e. usually 30 %) over the highest ground.

11. Effect of cross winds. The aircraft during its flight along the planned course may be drifted (say by an angle α) causing it 'crab' due to cross-winds (along BC) [Fig. 3.5 (f)] from AB to AC. This can be contoured by aligning the aircraft along the AA_1 inclined at angle α, so that due to the velocity of the cross-wind it will be flying along the planned flight line AB at a different velocity known as ground speed.

3.4.9 Plotting (Maps) From the Aerial Photographs

There are two methods of plotting plans from aerial photographs. One is Graphical Method and other is Stereoscopic Method. The graphical method is further divided into two types viz. Radial Line Method and Slotted Template Method.

(a) The Graphical Method :

1. The Radial Line Method (Arundel's Method) :

The radial line plot, often called as photo-triangulation. It is the graphical means of plotting planimetric map from vertical aerial photographs and does not require use of expensive instruments like stereo-plotter or multiplex projector. The scale of the map produced by this method is same as like that of the photographs from which it is produced. To use this method to produce map one should know the plan position of at least three points in each photograph.

This method assumes that the distortions due to relief are radial from the principal point. And the elevations of the points are less than about one tenth of the flying height. The procedure in short consists of plotting points by intersecting radials drawn from principal points. This method is more suitable when several ground points are known and when the old maps are to be revised.

Procedure of Radial Line Method :

(1) Determine the scale of photograph by comparing distance between two points on photograph and distance between them on ground. Two points chosen for scaling shall lie nearly equidistant on either side of principal point.

(2) Plot in advance the fixed (control) points say Q, R and S on the map paper to the same scale of photo worked out in step 1.

(3) Join diagonally opposite fudicial frame marks on photo and mark their point of intersection as principal point. These ways get marked principal points p_1 and p_2 of left and right photo.

(4) Place a tracing paper named as tracing paper A_1 on first (left) photo. Trace the principal point p_1 on it as p_1' and draw on this tracing paper A, radiations from the principal point p_1' to images of three fixed (control) points Q, R and S on photo.

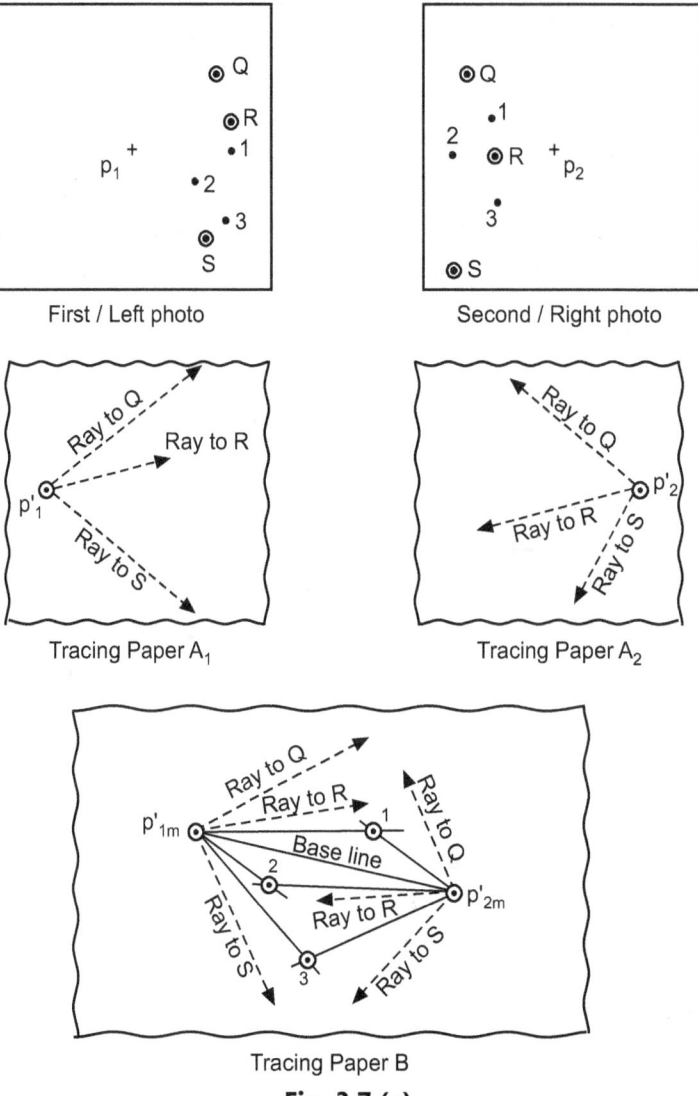

Fig. 3.7 (a)

(5) Place the same tracing paper A_1 on the map paper and adjust it by trial and error so that all the three radiations pass through corresponding fixed (control) points Q, R and S already available on the map paper. The point p_1' where these radiations meet is pricked through the tracing paper on the map. This gives location of principal point p_1 of first (left) photo on the map paper and it can be named as p_{1m} on map.

(6) Locate the principal point p_2 of second (right) photograph on the map paper in similar way and name it as p_{2m}. Tracing paper used for this, can be named as A_2.

(7) Trace from the map paper the base line formed by joining the principal points p_{1m} and p_{2m} on another tracing paper, say tracing paper B, along with the radiation drawn towards the fixed (control) points Q, R and S. This base line will be named as p'_{1m} - p'_{2m}.

(8) Impose this tracing paper B on first (left) photograph. Coincide the position of principal point p'_{1m} of this photo on tracing paper B with its actual principal point p_1 and orient the tracing paper B by matching the radiations drawn to corresponding fixed (control) points Q, R and S. Draw the radiations on the tracing paper B from the principal point p'_{1m} towards the objects 1, 2, 3 etc. on photo.

(9) Shift the same tracing paper B to second photograph. Coincide the position of principal point p'_{2m} on tracing paper B with its actual principal point p_2, and orient the tracing paper B by matching the radiations drawn towards the corresponding fixed (control) points Q, R and S. Draw the radiations on the tracing paper B from the principal point p'_{2m} towards the same objects 1, 2, 3 etc. on photo.

(10) The same tracing paper B is then again placed on map paper, displaced and rotated so that principal point p'_{m1} and p'_{m2} on tracing paper coincides with principal point p_{m1} and p_{m2} on map. The points of intersection of radiations p'_{1m}-1 and p'_{m2}-1 is transferred on map as object 1, that of radiations p'_{1m}-2 and p'_{2m}-2 is transferred on map as object 2 and that of radiations p'_{1m}-3 and p'_{2m}-3 is transferred on map as object 3.

(11) This way we can transfer all required objects/details from photo to map paper and can produce a map.

2. Slotted Template Method :

This is a mechanical extension of the radial line method. In this method, the tracing paper B is replaced by dimensionally stable transparent celluloid sheet template.

On this template, principal points p'_{m1} and p'_{m2} are replaced with punch holes, diameter of these punch holes will be same as that of the pins pricked at the photo and map principal points. Slots few mm long and having width equal to that of the pins pricked at photo fixed (control) points are created along all three radiations drawn towards the fixed (control) point

Q, R and S from each of the principal points p'_{1m} and p'_{2m} in such a way that the corresponding photo control point will fall at centre of the slot when the template is imposed on the photo. These slots allow easy orientation of the template on each of the photo to pick up the detail from photo to plot it on map.

(b) Stereoscopic Method :

In this method, the plotting is carried out with the help of the opto-mechanical machines. Such machines include vertical sketch master, radial line plotter and the multiplex. Amongst these, the multiplex was used extensively even upto the end of 2000. The multiplex which is also known as stereo-plotter works on the principle of stereoscopy. It is used to produce precise three dimensional maps. Third dimension is brought into play by drawing the contours on map. It create a precise three dimensional scaled optical model of the terrain seen in overlapped area and provides the means to view and measure this spatial model and also to plot its orthographic or preferred map projection. Such stereo-plotters are becoming obsolete. The Digital Photogrammetric Workstations (DPWs) almost have replaced the use of almost all types (regular, computer assisted and analytical) of conventional stereo-plotters.

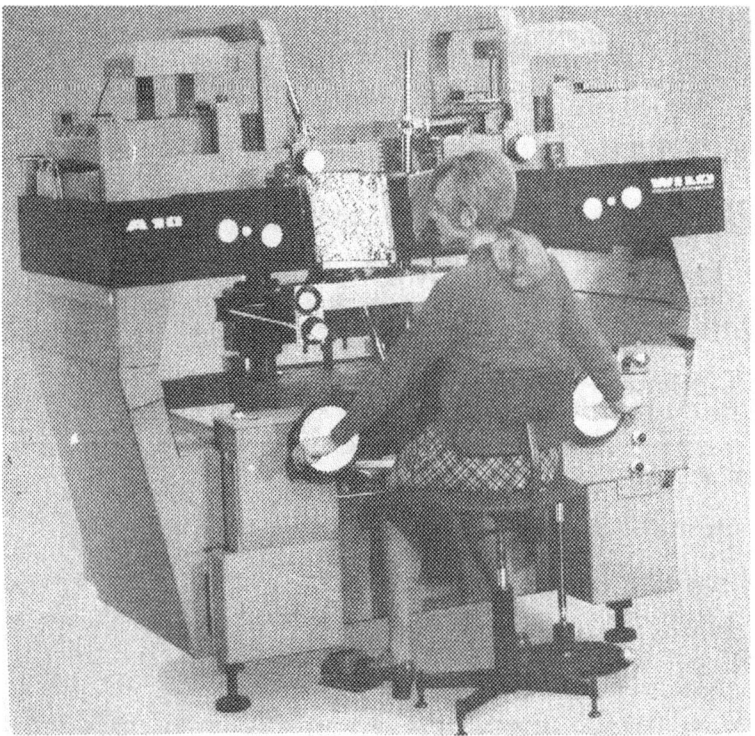

Fig. 3.7 (b) : Opto-mechanical stereo plotter – wild A10 autograph

3.4.10 Stereoscopy

(a) Binocular Stereoscopic Vision :

Stereoscopy is the process by means of which an individual can see the object in three dimensions by making use of his both eyes. Viewing an object with one eye enables to see a two-dimensional view (i.e. flat perspective), the depth perception not being possible. Normally, an individual sees the object with his two eyes. The left eye and right eye forming two different images of the same object fuse together on retina and the brain gets a three dimensional (i.e. depth perception) view of the object. This is known as 'Binocular or stereoscopic vision'. The process of viewing the object with human eyes is similar to that of an aerial camera taking overlapping pairs of aerial photographs.

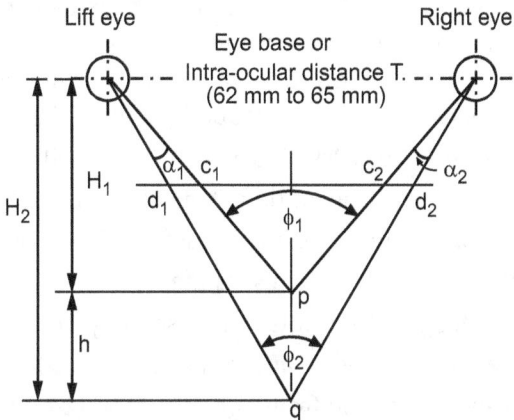

Fig. 3.8

In the Fig. 3.8 a vertical object pq is shown to be seen simultaneously from the two different positions of the eyes, their corresponding images of the top and bottom of the object as seen from left and right eyes being denoted by c_1, c_2 and d_1, d_2 respectively. The combined fused image of c_1 and c_2 as seen with both the eyes appears to be at p whereas that of d_1 and d_2 appears to be at q.

(b) Stereoscopic Depth :

The distance pq is then said to be 'Stereoscopic depth' and enables to determine the difference in elevation of the top and bottom of the object. ϕ_1 and ϕ_2 are the angles of convergence of the two rays, one passing through the left eye and the other passing through the right eye, and are known as **"parallax"** or **"parallatic angles"**. It is obvious that the 'stereoscopic depth' depends upon :

(i)　intra-ocular distance and

(ii)　the difference between the parallactic angles.

i.e. $\phi_1 - \phi_2$ is known as *differential parallax.*

But　　　　　　　　　$\phi_1 = \phi_2 + \alpha_1 + \alpha_2$

∴　　　　　　$\phi_1 - \phi_2 = \alpha_1 + \alpha_2$

It can further be seen that the "stereoscopic depth" increases with shorter eye base and smaller $(\alpha_1 + \alpha_2)$, whereas it increases with larger eye base and larger values of $(\alpha_1 + \alpha_2)$. ϕ_1 being greater than ϕ_2, the point p will appear closer than point q and h depends upon $(\alpha_1 + \alpha_2)$.

The lower limit of $(\phi_1 - \phi_2)$ or $(\alpha_1 + \alpha_2)$ for depth perception varies between 10 to 20 seconds.

(c) Stereoscopic Fusion :

The practical application of binocular or stereoscopic vision is the 'stereoscopic fusion' obtained by viewing a pair of overlapping aerial photographs under a stereoscope. The two photographs, taken from two different camera stations, with sufficient overlap between them, are viewed under a stereoscope, in such way that the left eye sees the left photograph and the right eye, the right photograph and then the two images of the objects on the overlapped portion will fuse together on the retina and the brain gets a three dimensional picture of the objects appearing on the overlapped portion. The principle of stereoscopic fusion can best be understood by the following simple illustrations :

(i)   Let a_1, a_2 and b_1, b_2 be two pairs of dots drawn in such a way that the distance $a_1\ a_2$ is less than distance $b_1 b_2$ [Fig. 3.9 (a)]. Now, hold a cardboard or a note-book vertically in the centre of the dots in such a way that left eye sees the left dots a_1, b_1 and the right eye sees the right dots a_2 and b_2. At first, all four dots will be seen by both the eyes and after some time it will be noticed that the images a_1 and b_1 as seen from left eye coincides with the corresponding images a_2 and b_2 as seen from right eye. It will be seen that the fused dot of a_1 and a_2 say 'a', appears nearer than the fused dot of b_1 and b_2 say 'b', which explains the phenomenon of 'stereoscopic' fusion.

a_1 ●   ● a_2

b_1 ●   ● b_2

Fig. 3.9 (a)

(ii)   As shown in the Fig. 3.9 (b), draw two equilateral triangles, the distance between their centres being about 5 cm. Shift the centre of each triangle slightly towards the other triangle and let such shifted centre points be denoted by O_1 and O_2. From O_1 and O_2, draw lines to the vertices of the triangles. Now, hold a cardboard or a note-book in between these triangles and view them as already explained in (i) above. After some time, the two triangles will fuse together and a solid pyramid with the apex standing above the base, can be clearly seen illustrating the phenomenon of stereoscopic fusion.

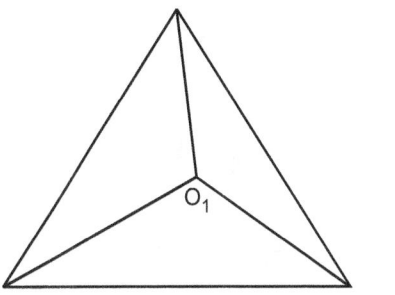 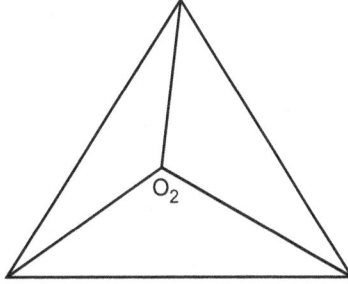

Fig. 3.9 (b)

(d) Stereo Viewing Systems :

The stereo viewing systems most commonly used are :

(1) Stereoscopic system and

(2) Anaglyphic system

(1) Stereoscopic system : In this system, an optical device called 'stereoscope' is used to obtain stereoscopic fusion and to get a three dimensional view for the overlapped portion of the stereopairs. The stereoscope was first invented by Mr. Wheatstone in 1838.

The basic functions of the stereoscope are :

(i) To accommodate wide separation of the object appearing on the left and right photographs to the fixed eye base length; and

(ii) To magnify the depth perception so that details can be seen more clearly.

The stereoscopes commonly used are :

(i) Lens stereoscope (or prism stereoscope) (or pocket stereoscope)

(ii) Mirror stereoscope.

(i) Lens stereoscope (or prism stereoscope) (Fig. 3.10) : The lens or prism stereoscope first constructed by Mr. Brewster in 1850 consists of two convex lenses or narrow small angled prisms, mounted on a frame which can be folded and kept in the pocket and are portable and ideally suited for field work. The spacing between the lenses is usually equal to the common human eye base called as intra-ocular distance (about 65 mm) and can be slightly varied to suit the individual. The height of the stereoscope is shorter than the focal length of lenses and thus rays of light coming from points on the photos converge while passing through each lens. The disadvantage of lens stereoscope is that stereopairs are to be placed close together as compared to their wide spacing under mirror stereoscope and thus they cause eye strain to the observer. They are usually used for small format images. If the images are large, they are to be folded.

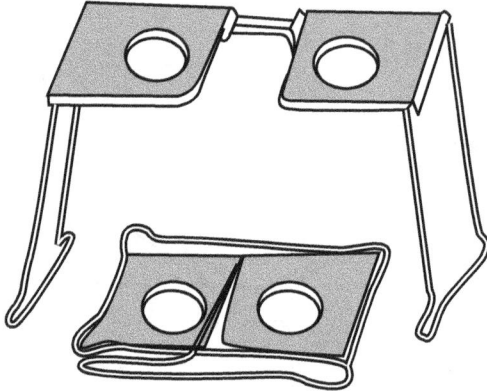

Fig. 3.10 : Lens stereoscope

(ii) Mirror stereoscope : It is used for larger image formats, as the visual base in this case is enlarged by system of double reflection.

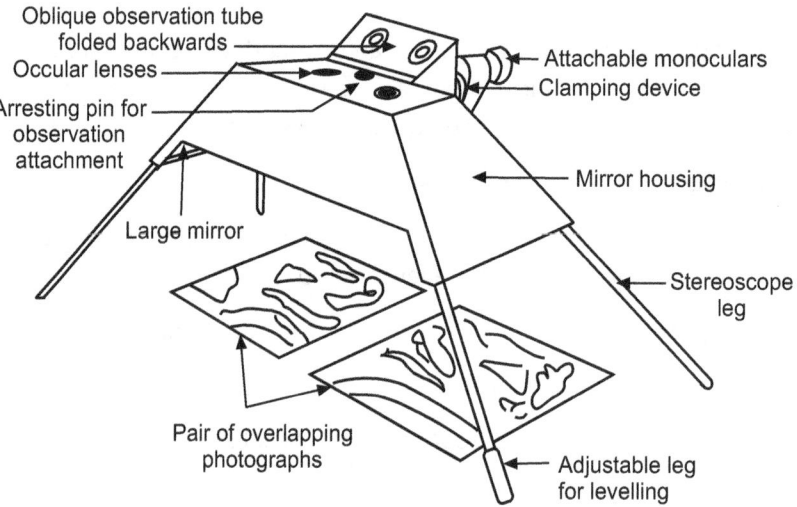

Fig 3.11 (a) : Mirror stereoscope

In this stereoscope, mirrors are used to bring the images together and permits the stereo pairs to be completely separated when viewing stereoscopically and thus the possibility of one photo obscuring part of the overlap of the other as experienced in lens stereoscope, will not arise. The stereoscope consists of two large mirrors and two small eye piece mirrors adjusted at 45° to the horizontal.

The mirror stereoscope is supported on four legs, the length of one of the leg being adjustable enables its setting even on an uneven base. The stereoscope consists of two large outside mirrors and two small ocular mirrors. All the mirrors have plane aluminised surfaces that can produce very bright clear images.

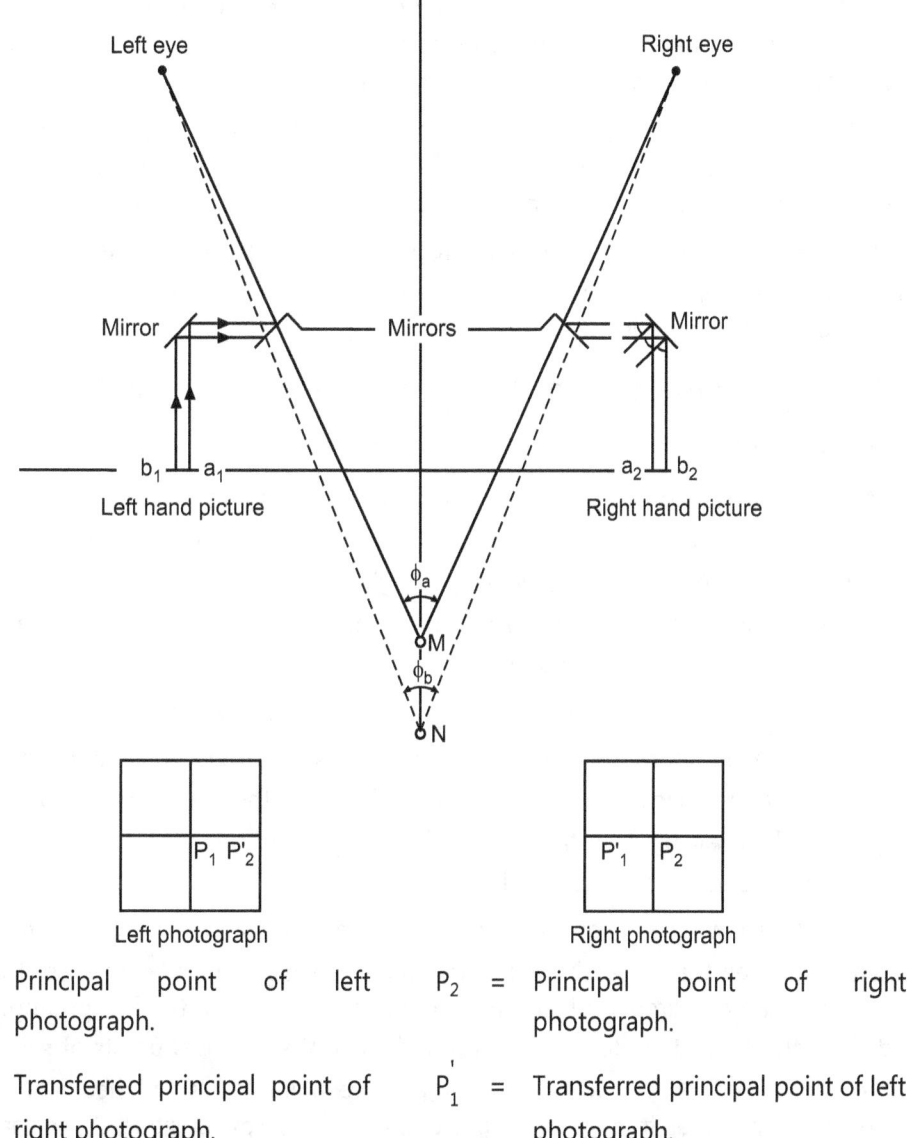

P_1 = Principal point of left photograph.

P_2 = Principal point of right photograph.

P'_2 = Transferred principal point of right photograph.

P'_1 = Transferred principal point of left photograph.

Fig. 3.11 (b) : Mirror stereoscope and pair of aerial photographs

In combination with the small ocular mirrors, the large mirrors deflect the path of rays in such a way that the interpupilliary base (natural eye-base) can be extended upto 260 mm. The image area is magnified by about 3.5 times. Ocular lenses at about 65 mm are also placed on the top of ocular mirrors to eliminate visual defects. Rays of light coming from the image points on the stereopairs, say a_1 and a_2, will be reflected from mirror surfaces and reach the eyes to form parallactic angle ϕ_a. Similarly, b_1 and b_2 will be forming another parallactic angle ϕ_b. With these parallactic angles the depth perception can be achieved.

Once the stereopairs are fused properly under a stereoscope, their positions are not to be changed. It is the stereoscope that can be moved about to see the stereo-model of the overlapped portion of the stereopairs. [Fig. 3.11 (b)].

When pair of overlapping photographs are viewed stereoscopically through a stereoscope, one gets a three-dimensional picture of the overlapped area. This enables the observer in only ascertaining the nature of the ground in the overlapped area.

For reliable quantitative measurements, the concept of parallax, differential parallax and its measurement and its applications in determining the difference in elevation by using stereometer is explained in detail hereafter.

3.4.11 Difference in Elevation by Differential Parallax

(i) Parallax of a Point :

As explained earlier, the stereoscopic depth depends upon the parallactic angle ϕ. But as the parallatic angle is formed in the space, it cannot be measured directly on the stereopairs of aerial photographs. However, parallatic angle ϕ being a function of horizontal parallax, the stereoscopic depth can be measured in terms of horizontal parallaxes, which are linear measurements on aerial photographs.

Parallax of a point or object is defined as 'the displacement of the image of an object on two successive photographs'. The parallax increases with the larger parallactic angles and such objects appear closer to the exposure stations. For the measurement of parallaxes, the projection of the air base on the planes of photographs (called as photo-base) is taken as X-axis and a line at right angles to it is called Y-axis.

Fig. 3.12 shows two exposure camera stations O_1 and O_2 lying at same height, the distance between the successive exposure stations being termed as Airbase distance B. Let M and N be the two ground objects appearing as m_1 and n_1 on the first photograph and m_2 and n_2 on the second photograph. Let p_1 and p_2 be the principal points of successive aerial photographs. Further it is assumed that positive plane is also carried along with aerial camera while it moves from its initial position O_1 to the next position O_2, so that m_1 and n_1 (on the first photograph) appears as m_1' and n_1' on the second photograph taken from O_2. Thus, it can be seen that there is an apparent movement or displacement of the image of ground object M relative to aerial camera from m_1' to m_2 and that of the object N from n_1' to n_2. i.e. the distance m_1' m_2 (the displacement of the image of the object M on two successive photographs) is known as 'parallax or absolute parallax' of the ground object M and similarly the distance n_1' n_2 is the 'parallax or absolute parallax' of the ground object N.

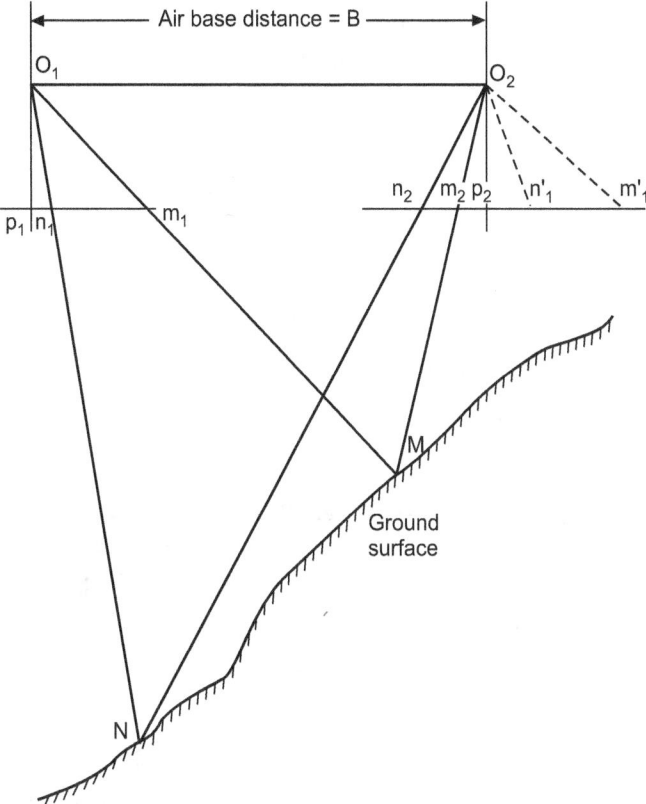

Fig. 3.12 : Illustration of parallax of a point and differential parallax

(ii) Differential Parallax :

Parallax or Absolute parallax of M $= m_1'm_2 = p_1 m_1 + p_2 m_2$

But $p_1 m_1$ and $- p_2 m_2$ are the co-ordinates in X direction of the ground point M on the successive photographs 1 and 2 respectively. Denoting these co-ordinates as x_1 and x_1', we can write,

Parallax of the ground point   M $= m_1' \, m_2 = p_1 m_1 + p_2 m_2$

$\qquad\qquad\qquad\qquad = p_1 m_1 - (-p_2 m_2)$

$=$ the algebraic difference of the x co-ordinates of the ground object M appearing on the pair of overlapping aerial photographs, say $(x_1 - x_1')$.

Similarly,

Parallax on the ground point N $= n_1' \, n_2 = p_1 n_1 + p_2 n_2$

$\qquad\qquad\qquad\qquad = p_1 n_1 - (-p_2 n_2)$

$=$ the algebraic difference of the x co-ordinates of the ground object N appearing on the pair of overlapping aerial photographs say $(x_2 - x_2')$.

And the differential parallax of the ground objects M and N

$$= \text{Parallax of M} - \text{Parallax of N}$$

$$= (x_1 - x_1^{'}) - (x_2 - x_2^{'})$$

and this difference in parallax of the two ground objects M and N is useful in measuring their difference in elevation. It can be seen that higher the ground object, higher will be its parallax and vice versa.

(iii) Parallax in Y-direction :

Further, it can be proved that if there is no parallax in a direction perpendicular to X - axis i.e. if y_1 and $y_1^{'}$ are the co-ordinates of the ground object P on two successive photographs perpendicular to X direction, then

$$y_1 - y_1^{'} = 0$$

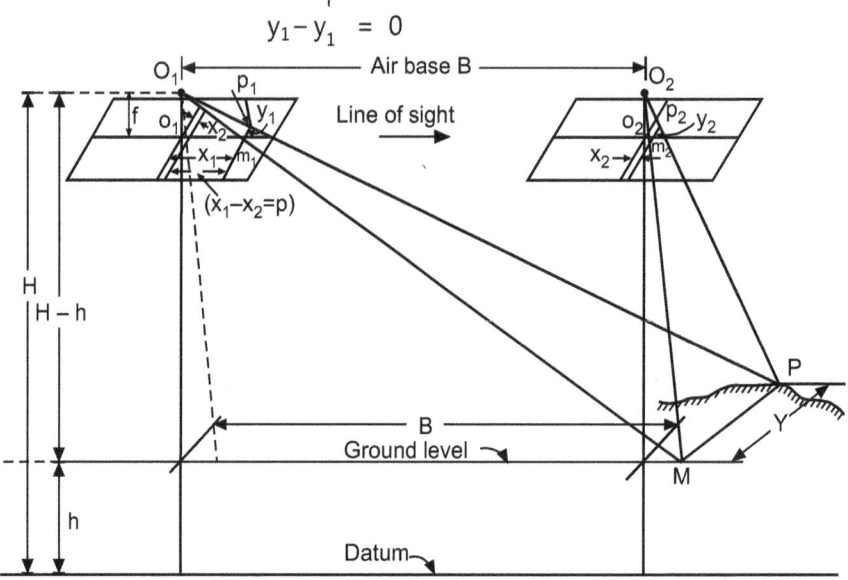

Fig. 3.13

Referring to the Fig. 3.13, let the O_1 and O_2 be the positions of the two successive aerial camera exposures at the same height H above datum, and the X - axis of each such aerial photograph is in the same vertical plane that contains the two successive camera exposures. Let x_1 and $x_1^{'}$ be the x co-ordinates of the ground object appearing on two successive photographs and their corresponding y co-ordinates be y_1 and $y_1^{'}$.

Then as per definition,

(i)   Parallax or absolute parallax of the ground object in X-direction $= x_1 - x_1^{'}$.

(ii)   Parallax of the ground object in Y-direction $= y_1 - y_1^{'}$.

Now, it remains to be shown that $y_1 - y_1' = 0$.

i.e. parallax in Y-direction is zero.

Proof : Consider triangles, $O_1 m_1 p_1$ and $O_1 MP$.

As these triangles are similar,

$$\frac{m_1 p_1}{MP} = \frac{O_1 m_1}{O_1 M}$$

or $\qquad m_1 p_1 = \frac{MP \cdot O_1 m_1}{O_1 M}$ ... (3.4)

But $\qquad \frac{O_1 m_1}{O_1 M} = \frac{f}{H - h}$

where, $\qquad\qquad f = $ Focal length of the camera lens

$\qquad\qquad H = $ Height of flight

and $\qquad\qquad h = $ Elevation of ground above datum

$\therefore \qquad\qquad m_1 p_1 = MP \times \frac{f}{H - h}$ ... (3.5)

Similarly in triangles $O_2 m_2 p_2$ and $O_2 MP$,

$$\frac{m_2 p_2}{MP} = \frac{O_2 m_2}{O_2 M}$$

or $\qquad m_2 p_2 = MP \times \frac{O_2 m_2}{O_2 M}$ ... (3.6)

but $\qquad \frac{O_2 m_2}{O_2 M} = \frac{f}{H - h}$

$\therefore \qquad\qquad m_2 p_2 = \frac{MP \times f}{H - h}$ ... (3.7)

Thus, from equations (3.5) and (3.7) above,

$$m_1 p_1 = m_2 p_2$$

i.e. $\qquad\qquad y_1 = y_1'$

or $\qquad\qquad y_1 - y_1' = 0$

i.e. There is no parallax in Y-direction for a pair of overlapping aerial photographs.

(iv) Computations of Space Co-ordinates :

Let the space co-ordinates of any ground object with respect to the left hand camera station O_1 be X_1, Y_1 and $H - h$. The expression for these space co-ordinates in terms of known co-ordinates can be derived as follows :

From the principle of similar triangles,

$$\frac{X_1}{x_1} = \frac{\text{(Ground co-ordinate)}}{\text{(Photo co-ordinate)}} = \frac{H - h}{f}$$

But

$$\frac{H - h}{f} = \frac{B}{x_1 - x_1'}$$

where

$$(x_1 - x_1') = \text{Parallax of the point } P = p$$

$\therefore$

$$\frac{H - h}{f} = \frac{B}{p}$$

$\therefore$

$$X_1 = \left[\frac{B}{p}\right] x_1 \qquad \qquad \dots (3.8)$$

Similarly,

$$\frac{Y_1}{y_1} = \frac{H - h}{f} = \frac{B}{x_1 - x_1'} = \frac{B}{p}$$

$\therefore$

$$Y_1 = \left[\frac{B}{p}\right] y_1 \qquad \qquad \dots (3.9)$$

and

$$H - h = \frac{B}{p} f \qquad \qquad \dots (3.10)$$

The expressions (3.8), (3.9) and (3.10) written above enables to compute the three space co-ordinates. Thus, the relative positions of the various ground objects in the overlapped portion of pair of aerial photographs can be easily computed.

(v) Difference in Elevation (Δh) by Differential Parallax (Δp) :

In the Fig. 3.14, let MN be a T.V. tower whose difference in elevation between the top and bottom is to be determined. Let O_1 and O_2 be two camera stations from which stereopairs of photographs are taken from an altitude of H metres above the datum.

Let m_1 and n_1 be the images of the top and bottom of TV tower with their x co-ordinates as x_2 and x_1 respectively appearing on the left photograph and similarly let m_2 and n_2 be the images with their x co-ordinates ax x_2' and x_1' appearing on the right hand photograph.

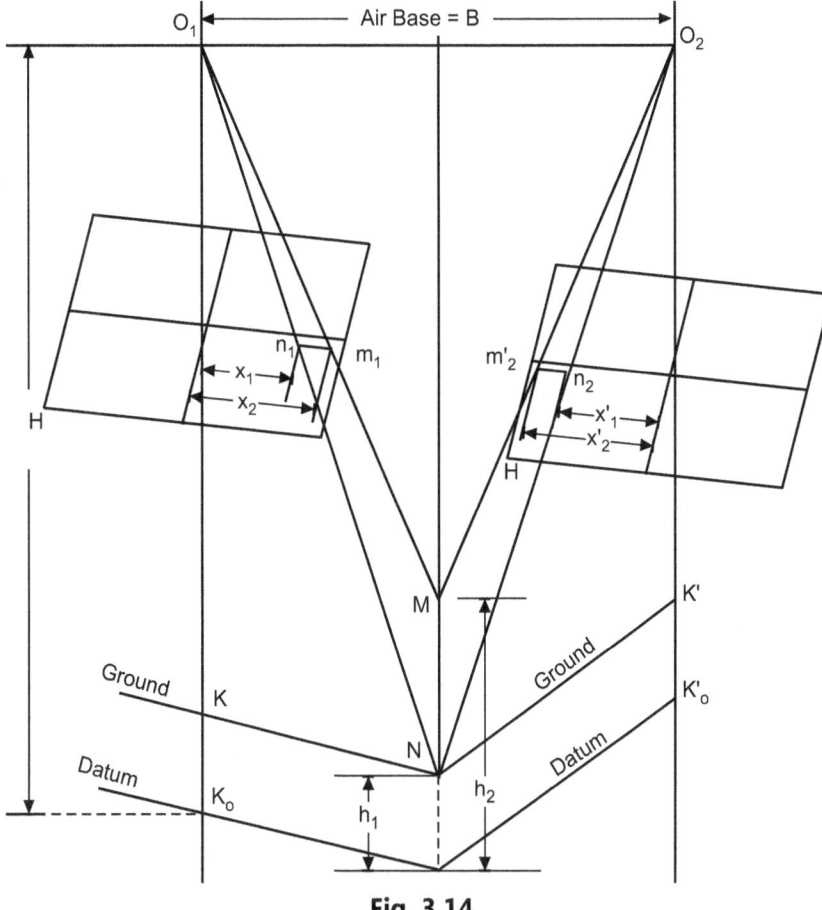

Fig. 3.14

Then $\qquad$ $p_1 = x_1 - x'_1$ = Parallax of bottom of T.V. tower

and $\qquad$ $p_2 = x_2 - x'_2$ = Parallax of top of T.V. tower

and $\qquad$ $(p_2 - p_1)$ = Differential parallax = Δp

As already derived above, the co-ordinate

$$H - h = \frac{Bf}{p}$$

$\therefore$ $\qquad$ $h = H - \dfrac{Bf}{p}$ $\qquad\qquad$ (General formula)

or $\qquad$ $h_1 = H - \dfrac{Bf}{p_1}$

and $\qquad$ $h_2 = H - \dfrac{Bf}{p_2}$

where h_1 and h_2 are the heights of the bottom and top of the T.V. tower above the datum level.

∴   Elevation difference between top and bottom of T.V. tower,

$$\Delta h = h_2 - h_1$$

$$= \left(H - \frac{Bf}{p_2}\right) - \left(H - \frac{Bf}{p_1}\right)$$

$$= \frac{Bf}{p_1} - \frac{Bf}{p_2}$$

∴ $$\Delta h = Bf \frac{(p_2 - p_1)}{p_1 p_2}$$

But $p_2 - p_1$ =   Differential parallax between the top and bottom of the T.V. tower.

∴   Writing Δp for $p_2 - p_1$,

$$\Delta h = \frac{\Delta p}{p_1 p_2} B.f$$

But $$p_2 = p_1 + \Delta p$$

∴ $$\Delta h = \frac{\Delta p}{p_1 (p_1 + \Delta p)} Bf$$

But $$\frac{b}{B} = \frac{f}{H}$$

∴ $$B = \frac{H}{f} \cdot b$$

∴   Putting this value of B in the above equation, we get,

$$\Delta h = \frac{\Delta p}{p_1 (p_1 + \Delta p)} \times \frac{H}{f} \cdot b \cdot f$$

$$= \frac{\Delta p}{p_1 (p_1 + \Delta p)} \times H \cdot b$$

Now, if the bottom of the T.V. tower N and both the principal points p_1 and p_2 are supposed to lie at the datum level, then we have,

$$p_1 = b \text{ (the photo base distance)}$$

∴   Writing this value of p_1 in the above equation, we get,

$$\Delta h = \frac{\Delta p \times H \cdot b}{b(b + \Delta p)} = \frac{H \cdot \Delta p}{b + \Delta p}$$

However, if the value of b_1 obtained from one photograph is not the same as b_2 obtained from the second photograph, then $\dfrac{b_1 + h_2}{2}$ will be the mean photobase distance b_m.

Thus, the above formula modifies to

$$\Delta h = \left(\frac{H \cdot \Delta p}{b_m + \Delta p} \right)$$

Now, since
$$H - h = \frac{Bf}{p}$$

$\therefore$
$$p = \frac{Bf}{H - h} \qquad \text{(General form of equation for parallax)}$$

$\therefore$
$$p_1 = \frac{Bf}{H - h_1} = \text{Parallax of bottom of T.V. tower}$$

$$p_2 = \frac{Bf}{H - h_2} = \text{Parallax of top of T.V. tower}$$

$\therefore$
$$p_2 - p_1 = \frac{Bf}{H - h_2} - \frac{Bf}{H - h_1}$$

$\therefore$
$$p_2 - p_1 = \frac{Bf \, [(H - h_1) - (H - h_2)]}{(H - h_2)\,(H - h_1)}$$

$\therefore$
$$p_2 - p_1 = \frac{Bf \, (h_2 - h_1)}{(H - h_2)\,(H - h_1)}$$

$\therefore$
$$(h_2 - h_1) = \frac{(p_2 - p_1)}{Bf} \, \{(H - h_2)\,(H - h_1)\}$$

$\therefore$
$$\Delta h = \frac{\Delta p \,(H - h_1)}{p_2}$$

$\therefore$
$$\Delta H = \frac{\Delta p \,(H - h_1)}{p_1 + \Delta p}$$

Neglecting the values of h_1 and h_2 (on the right hand side of the expression) which are very small as compared to height of flight H and writing $h_2 - h_1 = \Delta h$ and $p_2 - p_1 = \Delta p$,

$$h_2 - h_1 = \Delta h = \frac{\Delta p \cdot H^2}{Bf} \quad \text{(approximately)}$$

The equation can also be written as follows :

$$h_2 - h_1 = \left\{ \frac{(p_2 - p_1)}{\left(\dfrac{Bf}{H - h_2} \right)} \right\} \times (H - h_1)$$

But
$$\frac{Bf}{H - h_2} = p_2$$

and
$$h_2 - h_1 = \Delta h$$

$$p_2 - p_1 = \Delta p$$

$$\therefore \quad \Delta h = \frac{\Delta p \ (H - h_1)}{p_2}$$

$$= \frac{\Delta p \ (H - h_1)}{(p_1 + \Delta p)} \qquad (\because \ p_2 - p_1 = \Delta p)$$

(vi) Parallax Measurement by a Stereometer or Parallax Bar :

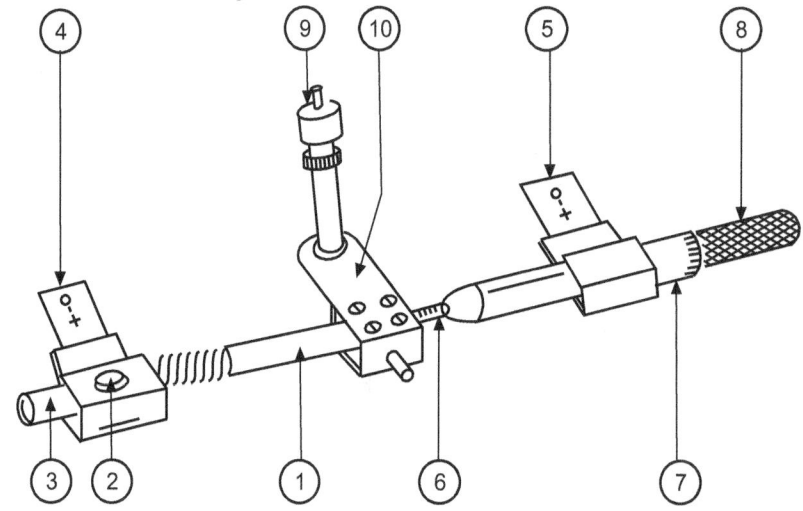

(1) Scale Rod, (2) Clamping Screw, (3) Adjustment Screw, (4) Left Hand Glass Graticule,
(5) Right Hand Glass Graticule, (6) Coarse Main Scale, (7) Fine Scale, (8) Micrometer Screw, (9) Weight, (10) Carrier

Fig. 3.15 : Stereometer or Parallax bar

In order to obtain the difference in elevation of two given points, it is necessary to determine the differential parallax of the two points. This differential parallax is obtained by the difference between the parallaxes of the two points, which are measured by an instrument called as stereometer or parallax bar. (Fig. 3.15)

The instrument consists of a rigid circular rod (1) graduated in mm (6) provided with two glass graticules or plates (4) and (5) with very fine dots engraved on them. The left hand glass graticule, which is adjustable, can be clamped (2) in any desired position along the bar. The right hand glass graticule can be moved along the bar by the micrometer screw (8) provided at the right hand corner of the bar. The provision of main scale (6) and fine scale (7) enables the readings to be taken upto $\frac{1}{100}$th mm. i.e. the least count of the instrument is 0.01 mm.

Measurement of Parallax :

(1) After marking the principal points on a given pair of aerial photographs, fuse them under a stereoscope so that a three-dimensional picture of the ground is obtained. Then base line the photographs.

(2) Let A be a ground point of known elevation and let it be required to determine the difference in elevation between this known point A and another unknown point B. Let the images of the two points A and B appearing on the first photograph be a_1 and b_1 and that appearing on the second photograph be a_2 and b_2.

(3) With the stereometer reading set to its middle, adjust the right hand dot mark of the right hand glass graticule (5) exactly over the image point a_2 on the second photograph by using only the right eye. Unclamp the left hand glass graticule and adjust the left hand dot mark (4) exactly over the image point a_1 on the first photograph by using only the left eye.

(4) On looking with both the eyes through the stereoscope, the two images a_1 and a_2 appear to fuse into one and a floating mark is said to be obtained. Now, by operating the micrometer screw (8), the floating mark is made to coincide with the ground point A. The reading on the stereometer is then to be recorded as the parallax of the point A, say p_1.

(5) Without altering the position of the left hand glass graticule (4), the left hand dot is now placed over the image b_1 appearing on the first photograph and on looking through the stereoscope, the micrometer screw is rotated till the floating dot appears to coincide with ground point B. The reading on the stereometer is the parallax of the point B, say p_2.

(6) The difference between the above two parallaxes is the required differential parallax of the two points i.e. $\Delta p = p_2 - p_1$.

(7) Knowing the value of Δp, and using any one of the appropriate equation for the difference in elevation i.e. Δh, derived above, the elevation difference can be computed.

3.4.12 Comparison between Aerial Photograph and Map

	Aerial photograph		Map
1.	It is a photograph of terrain at the time of exposure and depicts all the details of the terrain.	1.	Maps are prepared by actually carrying out linear and angular measurements of the ground.
2.	There is distortion of details due to tilt and relief displacement.	2.	No such distortion due to tilt or relief, as the map is prepared after carrying out necessary measurements.

... Contd.

3. The views obtained on aerial photographs are not familiar to our eyes.	3. Maps are common and familiar to people. Various details such as roads, rail-lines etc. are shown by conventional signs and symbols.
4. Elevation of the various objects cannot be obtained directly.	4. A contoured map enables to determine the elevation of the required objects directly.
5. Aerial photographs depict confusing details and are not easily recognisable. Revision of existing maps can be carried out with the latest aerial photographs of the terrain.	5. Preparation of map takes long time and as such by the time it is made available to its user, it becomes outdated.
6. Aerial surveying is a highly skilled job and for the preparation of maps from such photographs one needs costly automatic plotting machines.	6. Such maps can be prepared by carrying out conventional methods of surveying. They do not need any costly plotting equipment for preparation of maps.

3.4.13 Practical Applications of Aerial Photography

1. **Route survey :** Whenever a narrow width of a long length is to be surveyed (e.g., for highways, railway lines, canals etc.) and maps are to be prepared to a scale of 1 : 500 to 1 : 2500, aerial survey is the most convenient method of carrying out this job.

2. Aerial photography has important application in the town and country planning and in the preparation of regional and master plans for such projects.

3. Calculation of large quantities of earthwork, stock piles of materials etc. can very well be carried out by aerial surveys and viewing such stereo-pairs stereoscopically or by making use of automatic stereo-plotters.

4. Soil classification, geological investigation of dam and reservoir sites can be carried out satisfactorily by aerial surveys.

5. Flood absorption and flood control studies can be prepared by aerial photography. Flood affected areas can also be studied.

6. Reconnaissance survey of large difficult open hilly terrain can be carried out successfully by aerial photography.

7. Healthy growth of trees in the forests, diseases of the forest trees etc. can be studied by aerial surveys. Earthquake or cyclone devastation studies can also be carried by aerial surveys.

8. Catchment area and command area studies for irrigation projects can be carried out by aerial surveys.

9. Erosion of soil, land drainage, siltation of reservoirs studies can be accomplished by aerial photograph.

10. Concentration of enemy troops on the border area can be ascertained by aerial photography and military operations can be planned accordingly.

SOLVED EXAMPLES

Example 3.1 : If the distance between the images of the two objects appearing on a photograph is 10 cm and the corresponding distance between them on the ground is 1 km, calculate the scale of the photograph.

Solution :
$$\text{Scale} = \frac{\text{Distance between the objects on the photograph}}{\text{Distance between the objects on the ground}}$$

$$= \frac{10 \text{ (cm)}}{1 \times 1000 \times 100 \text{ (cm)}} = \frac{1}{10000}$$

Example 3.2 : A vertical photograph was taken from a height of 1500 m above mean sea level. If the elevation of the ground covered varies from 100 m to 500 m, and the focal length of the camera lens is 150 mm, calculate :

(i) Datum scale,

(ii) Average scale and

(iii) Point scale for an elevation of 500 m.

Solution : (i) Datum scale $= \dfrac{f}{H} = \dfrac{150}{1500 \times 1000} = \dfrac{1}{10000}$

(ii) Average scale $= \dfrac{f}{H - h_{av}}$

$$h_{av} = \frac{100 + 500}{2} = 300 \text{ m}$$

∴ Average scale $= \dfrac{150}{1000 \times (1500 - 300)} = \dfrac{150}{1200 \times 1000}$

$$= \frac{1}{8000}$$

(iii) Point scale (at 500 m) $= \dfrac{f}{H - 500} = \dfrac{150}{1000 \times (1500 - 500)}$

$$= \frac{150}{1000 \times 1000}$$

$$= \frac{1.5}{10000} = \frac{1}{6666.7} \approx \frac{1}{6667}$$

Example 3.3 : If the point scale for an object P lying at an elevation of 600 m above m.s.l is $\dfrac{1}{10000}$, calculate the scale for a point lying at an elevation of 400 m. The focal length of camera lens is 180 mm.

Solution : $\qquad$ Point scale $= \dfrac{f}{H - h_s}$

$\therefore \qquad$ Point scale @ 600 m $= \dfrac{180}{(H - 600) \times 1000}$

$\therefore \qquad \dfrac{1}{10000} = \dfrac{180}{(H - 600) \times 1000}$

$\therefore \qquad H = 2400 \text{ m}$

$\therefore \qquad$ Point scale @ 400 m $= \dfrac{180}{(2400 - 400) \times 1000}$

$\qquad = \dfrac{180}{2000 \times 1000} \approx \dfrac{1}{11111}$

Example 3.4 : Calculate the aeroplane flying height to obtain the average scale of photograph equal to $\dfrac{1}{9000}$. The ground surface elevation varies from 125 m to 325 m. Focal length of camera lens is 150 mm.

Solution : $\quad$ Scale of photograph $= \dfrac{f}{H - h_{av}}$

where, $\qquad\qquad\qquad\qquad f = $ Focal length of camera lens $= 150 \text{ mm}$

$\qquad\qquad\qquad h_{av} = $ Average ground elevation

$\qquad\qquad\qquad\qquad = \dfrac{125 + 325}{2} = 225 \text{ m}$

$\therefore \qquad\qquad \dfrac{1}{9000} = \dfrac{\dfrac{150}{1000}}{H - 225} = \dfrac{0.15}{H - 225}$

$\therefore \qquad\qquad H - 225 = 0.15 \times 9000 = 1350$

$\therefore \qquad\qquad H = 1350 + 225 = 1575 \text{ m}$

Example 3.5 : An object 20 m high appears in a vertical photograph taken at a flight altitude of 1000 m above the mean sea level. The distance of the image of the object from the principal point is 5 cm. Find the displacement of the image of the top of the object with respect to the image of its bottom. The elevation of the bottom of the object is 500 m.

Solution : Relief displacement, $d = \dfrac{rh}{H}$

where,

h = Height of object = 20 m

H = Flight altitude = 1000 cm

r = distance of image of object from principal point = 5 cm

$\therefore$ $d = \dfrac{5 \times 20}{1000} = 0.1$ cm

= displacement of the image of top w.r.t. its bottom

Example 3.6 : A line PQ measures 12 cm on a photograph taken with an aerial camera having a focal length of 20 cm. The same line measures 4 cm on a map drawn to a scale of 1/50,000. Calculate the flying height of the aircraft if the average altitude of the ground is 300 m.

Solution : Using the formula for the scale of photograph

$$\text{Scale} = \frac{f}{H - h_{av}}$$

$$= \frac{20 \times 10^{-3}}{H - 300} \qquad \dots \text{(i)}$$

Also $\text{Scale} = \dfrac{\text{Length of PQ on photograph}}{\text{Length of PQ on the ground}}$

and   Length of PQ on the ground = (Length of PQ on a map) $\times$ 50000

= 4 $\times$ 50000

= 200000 cm

= 2000 m

$\therefore$ Scale of photograph $= \dfrac{0.12}{2000}$ $\qquad \dots \text{(ii)}$

$\therefore$ Equating (i) and (ii),

$$\frac{0.20}{H - 300} = \frac{0.12}{2000}$$

$\therefore$ $400 = 0.12\,H - 36$

$\therefore$ $0.12\,H = 436$

$$H = \frac{436}{0.12} = \frac{43600}{12}$$

$\therefore$ $H = 3633.34$ m

$\therefore$ Flying height of aircraft is 3633.34 m.

Example 3.7 : A line AB appears to be 11.07 cm on a photograph taken with a camera of focal length 20 cm. The corresponding line measures 2.82 cm on a map whose R.F. is 1/60000. The terrain has an average elevation of 320 m above m.s.l. Determine the flying altitude of the aircraft at the time of exposure.

Solution :

$$\left(\begin{array}{c}\text{Length of the line 2.82 cm}\\\text{on a map of scale 1/60000}\\\text{on the ground}\end{array}\right) = 2.82 \times 60000 \text{ cm}$$

$$\therefore \qquad \text{Scale of photograph} = \frac{\text{Photo distance}}{\text{Ground distance}}$$

$$= \frac{11.07}{2.82 \times 60000}$$

$$= \frac{1}{15284.55}$$

Now, using the relation,

$$\text{Scale of photograph} = \frac{f}{H - h_{av}}$$

where,

$$\text{Scale} = \frac{1}{15284.55}$$

$$f = 20 \text{ cm} = 0.20 \text{ m}$$

$$h_{av} = 320 \text{ m}$$

$$\therefore \qquad \frac{1}{15284.55} = \frac{0.20}{H - 320}$$

$$\therefore \qquad H - 320 = 3056.91 \text{ m}$$

$$\therefore \qquad H = 3376.91 \text{ m}$$

Example 3.8 : A line 2400 m long lying at an elevation of 600 m above the datum measures 9.4 cm on a vertical photograph. If the focal length of the camera which has taken this photograph is 20 cm, calculate the flying height of the aircraft above the datum and also the scale of the photograph in an area, the average elevation of which is 800 m.

Solution :

$$\text{Scale (for 600)} = \frac{ab}{AB}$$

$$= \frac{9.4 \text{ cm}}{2400 \times 100 \text{ cm}}$$

$$= \frac{1}{25532}$$

Using the relation,　　　Scale $= \dfrac{f}{H - h_{av}}$

$$\dfrac{1}{25532} = \dfrac{20 \text{ cm}/100}{H - 600}$$

$\therefore$　　　　　　　$H = 5706 \text{ m}$

Now,　　　Scale (for 800) $= \dfrac{f}{H - h_{av}}$

$$= \dfrac{20/100}{5706 - 800}$$

$$= \dfrac{1}{24530}$$

Example 3.9 : Calculate the length of the air base from the following data, obtained in aerial surveying :

(i)　Height of flight = 3000 m;

(ii)　Focal length of camera lens = 150 mm

(iii)　Size of photograph = 23 cm × 23 cm.

(iv)　Overlap in the direction of flight = 60%.

Solution :　Scale of photograph $= \dfrac{f}{H - h_{av}}$

where,　　　　　　$f = 150 \text{ mm} = 0.15 \text{ m}$

　　　　　　　$H = 3000 \text{ m}$

　　　　　　$h_{av} = $ Assumed as zero

$\therefore$　　　　Scale $= s = \dfrac{0.15}{3000} = \dfrac{1}{20000}$

Now with 60% overlap in the direction of flight,

$\begin{bmatrix} \text{The distance between centre to} \\ \text{centre of consecutive photographs} \end{bmatrix} = (1 - 0.6) \times (\text{Width of photograph})$

　　　　　　$= 0.4 \times 23 = 9.2 \text{ cm}$

$\therefore$　　Air base distance $= 9.2 \times$ Scale of the photograph

　　　　　　$= 9.2 \times 20000 \text{ cm}$

$\therefore$　　Air base distance $= 1840 \text{ m}$

Example 3.10 : The line AB measures 7.5 cm on a photograph taken with a camera having focal length of 23 cm. The same line measures 3 cm on a map drawn to a scale of 1/25000. Calculate the flying height of the aircraft if the average elevation of the ground is 440 m.

Solution : (i) Scale of photograph $= \dfrac{\text{Length of line AB on photograph}}{\text{Length of line AB on the ground}}$

$$= \frac{7.5 \text{ cm}}{\left(\begin{array}{c}\text{Length of} \\ \text{line on map}\end{array}\right) \times \text{Scale of map}}$$

$$= \frac{7.5 \text{ cm}}{3 \times 25000 \text{ cm}}$$

$$= \frac{7.5}{75000}$$

$$= \frac{1}{10000}$$

(ii)   Now,   Scale $= \dfrac{f}{H - h_{av}}$

$\therefore$ $\dfrac{1}{10000} = \dfrac{0.23}{H - 440}$

$\therefore$ $H - 440 = 2300$

$\therefore$ $H = 2300 + 440 = 2740$ m

Example 3.11 : Vertical photographs were taken from height of 3048 m, the focal length of camera lens being 15.24 cm. If the prints were 22.86 × 22.86 cm square and the overlap 60%, what was the length of air base ?

Solution :

(i)   Scale of photograph $= \dfrac{f}{H} = \dfrac{15.24/100}{3048}$

$$= \frac{0.1524}{3048}$$

$$= \frac{1}{20,000}$$

(ii)

$\left[\begin{array}{c}\text{Distance between centre to centre} \\ \text{of photographs with 60\% overlap} \\ \text{in the direction of flights}\end{array}\right] = 0.4 \times$ Length of each photograph

$= 0.4 \times 22.86 = 9.144$ cm

(iii)   Length of air base $= 9.144$ cm $\times$ Scale of photograph

$= 9.144 \times 20000$ cm $= \dfrac{9.144 \times 20000}{100}$

$= 1828.8$ m

$\therefore$ Length of the air base $= 1828.8$ m

Example 3.12 : Calculate the flying height and area covered by the camera on the ground from the polling :

(1) Scale = 1 : 10,000

(2) Size of photograph = 23 cm × 23 cm

(3) Focal length, f = 180 mm.

(4) Average height of the ground, h_a = 450 m.

Solution : (1) Flying height :

$$\text{Scale} = \frac{f}{H - h_a}$$

$$\frac{1}{10000} = \frac{0.18}{H - 450}$$

$$H - 450 = 1800$$

$$\therefore \quad H = 1800 + 450$$

$$= 2250 \text{ m}$$

(2) Area covered by camera :

$$\text{Size of photograph} = 23 \text{ cm} \times 23 \text{ cm}$$

$$\text{Area of photograph} = 0.23 \times 0.23 = 0.0529 \text{ cm}^2$$

$$\therefore \quad \text{Area covered on ground} = 0.0529 \times 10000 \times 10000 \text{ cm}^2$$

$$= 529 \text{ m}^2$$

(3) To find out the scale of point on the photograph whose elevation is 600 m,

$$\text{Scale} = \frac{f}{H - h}$$

$$= \frac{180/1000}{2250 - 600}$$

$$= \frac{180/1000}{1650}$$

$$= \frac{0.18}{1650}$$

$$\therefore \quad \text{Scale} = \frac{1}{9167}$$

Example 3.13 : A section line AB appears to be 10.16 cm on a photograph for which the focal length is 16 cm. The corresponding line measures 2.54 cm on a map which is to a scale of 1/50000. The terrain has an average elevation of 200 m above the mean sea level. Calculate the flying altitude of the aircraft above mean sea level, when the photograph was taken.

Solution :   Scale of photograph $= \dfrac{\text{Length of line AB on photograph}}{\text{Length of line AB on the ground}}$

$$= \dfrac{10.16 \text{ cm}}{2.54 \times 50000}$$

$$= \dfrac{1}{12500}$$

$\left\{\textbf{Note :} \text{Length of line AB on the ground} = \begin{pmatrix}\text{Centre of line} \\ \text{AB on map}\end{pmatrix} \times \text{Scale of map}\right\}$

Now, $\text{Scale} = \dfrac{f}{H - h_{av}}$

$\therefore$ $\dfrac{1}{12500} = \dfrac{16 \text{ cm}}{H - 200}$

$$= \dfrac{0.16}{H - 200}$$

$\therefore$ $H - 200 = 12500 \times 0.16$

$$= 2000$$

$\therefore$ $H = 2200 \text{ m}$

$\therefore$ Flying altitude of aircraft $= 2200 \text{ m}$

Example 3.14 : Calculate the relief displacement from the following :

(i)   Distance of the image of the top of an object from the principal point = 70 mm.

(ii)   R.L. of top of object = 500 m.

(iii)   Height of flight = 3500 m.

Solution : Using the relation :

$$d = \dfrac{rh}{H}$$

$$= \dfrac{(70 \text{ mm}) \times 500 \text{ m}}{3500 \text{ m}}$$

$$= 10 \text{ mm}$$

Example 3.15 : An image of the top of an object is 60 mm from the principal point of the photograph. The elevation of top of the object is 400 m and the flying height is 3000 m above datum. Calculate the relief displacement.

Solution : Using the formula,

Relief displacement, $d = \dfrac{rh}{H}$

where,   r = Displacement of the image of top of object from the principal point = 60 mm

                                         h = Elevation of top of the object = 400 m

                                         H = Flying height = 3000 m

$\therefore$ Relief displacement, d $= \dfrac{60 \text{ mm} \times 400 \text{ m}}{3000 \text{ m}}$

                                         = 8 mm

Example 3.16 : An aerial survey was planned for a terrain having average elevation of 210 m above datum. A road strip 432 in length was measured as 7.2 cm in one of the vertical photographs of this survey. The radial distances to the top and foot of tower in this photograph were 7.4 cm and 6.7 cm respectively. Focal length of the camera was 200 mm. Compute the height of the tower.

Solution :   Scale of photograph $= \dfrac{\text{Photo distance}}{\text{Ground distance}}$

                                      $= \dfrac{7.2}{432 \times 100}$

                                      $= \dfrac{1}{6000}$

Now,   Scale $= \dfrac{f}{H - h_{av}}$

                 $\dfrac{1}{6000} = \dfrac{0.2}{H - 210}$

$\therefore$ H = 1410 m

Now using the relation,

                              d $= \dfrac{rh}{H}$

where   d = Relief displacement

                                = 7.4 – 6.7

                                = 0.70 cm

                              r = 7.4 cm

                              H = 1410

$\therefore$ h $= \dfrac{dH}{r}$

                                $= \dfrac{0.70 \times 1410}{7.4}$

                                = 133.37 m

Example 3.17 : The image of the top of the object is 46 mm from the principal point of the photograph. The elevation of the top of the object is 230 m and the flying height is 2000 m above datum. Calculate the relief displacement.

Solution : Using the formula,

$$d = \frac{rh}{H}$$

where,

d = Relief displacement to be found out

h = Elevation of top of object = 230 m

H = Flying height = 2000 m

r = Distance of the image of the top of object from the principal point = 46 mm

∴ $d = \dfrac{46 \text{ mm} \times 230 \text{ m}}{2000} = 5.29 \text{ mm}$

Example 3.18 : The scale of an aerial photograph is 1 cm = 200 m and the size of the photograph is 23 cm × 23 cm. Determine the minimum number of photographs required to cover a given area of 30 km × 20 km, if the overlap in the direction of flight is 60% and the side lap is 30%.

Solution : Length covered by one photograph in the direction of the flight

$$= 23 \times 200 = 4600 \text{ m}$$

∴   Distance between centre to centre in the direction of flight with 60% overlap

$$= 0.4 \times 4600 = 1840 \text{ m} = 1.840 \text{ km}$$

∴   Number of photographs required for a length of 30 km

$$= \frac{30}{1.84} \approx 17.00$$

∴   Adding 1 extra for end coverage, total number

$$= 17 + 1 = 18$$

Similarly, width covered by one photograph in lateral direction

$$= 23 \times 200 = 4600 \text{ m}$$

∴   Distance between centres of centre of adjacent strips with 30% side lap

$$= 0.70 \times 4600 = 3120 \text{ m} = 3.12 \text{ km}$$

∴   Number of strips required $= \dfrac{\text{Width of area}}{3.12} = \dfrac{20}{3.12} = 6.41 \approx 7$

∴   Adding 1 extra for end strips,

Total number of strips $= 7 + 1 = 8$

∴   Total number of photographs required to cover the given area

$$= 18 \times 8 = 144$$

Example 3.19 : The parallax difference of the two objects on a pair of aerial photographs is 3 mm and the mean base distance was found to be 90 mm. Calculate the difference in elevation of two objects, if the height of flight is 3000 m.

Solution : Using the formula for the difference in elevation of the two objects,

$$\Delta h = \left(\frac{H \cdot \Delta p}{b_m + \Delta p} \right)$$

where,　　　　　　　　H = Height of flight = 3000 m;

　　　　　　　　　　b_m = Mean base distance = 90 mm

and　　　　　　　　Δp = Parallax difference of two objects or differential parallax = 3 mm

∴　　　　　　　　$\Delta h = \dfrac{3000 \text{ m} \times 3 \text{ mm}}{(90 + 3) \text{ mm}}$

　　　　　　　　　　$= \dfrac{9000}{93}$ m

　　　　　　　　　　= 96.77 metres

Example 3.20 : The flight map shows the base position of 1500 m mountain peak at 10 cm from the flight line at the anticipated scale of photography. If the flying altitude is 6000 m above datum, estimate the relief displacement of the peak.

Solution :

$$\frac{\text{Displacement of the top of peak}}{\text{Displacement of the bottom of peak}} = \frac{H}{H-h}$$

∴　　Displacement of top of peak　$= \dfrac{6000}{6000 - 1500} \times 10$

　　　　　　　　　　$= \dfrac{6000}{4500} \times 10$

　　　　　　　　　　= 13.33 cm

∴　　　　Relief displacement　= 13.33 − 10.00

　　　　　　　　　　= 3.33 cm

Example 3.21 : A tower appears in two successive photographs taken at an altitude of 1500 m above datum. The focal length of camera lens is 150 mm and the length of air base is 250 m. The parallax for the top of the tower is 47.54 mm and that for the bottom is 42.32 mm. Compute the height of the tower.

Solution : Using the formula for the difference in elevation of the two points :

$$\Delta h = \frac{(p_2 - p_1)}{p_1 \, p_2} \, B.f$$

where, p_1 and p_2 = Parallaxes of the top and bottom of the tower in mm

B = Air base distance in m

f = Focal length of the camera lens in mm

$\therefore$ Δh = $\dfrac{(47.54 - 42.32)}{(47.54 \times 42.32)} \times 250 \times 150$

= $\dfrac{5.22 \times 250 \times 150}{47.54 \times 42.32} \left[\dfrac{mm \times m \times mm}{mm \times mm} \right]$

= 97.296 m

$\therefore$ Difference in elevation of top and bottom.

i.e.   Height of tower = 97.296 m $\approx$ 97.30 m

Example 3.22 : The scale of the aerial photograph is to be 1 cm = 100 m. The photograph size is 23 cm × 23 cm. Determine the number of photographs required to cover an area of 14 km × 10 km, if the longitudinal lap is 60% and the side lap is 30%.

Solution : With 60% overlap, the distance between centre to centre of the photograph

= 0.4 × 23 cm

= 9.2 cm on photograph

= 9.2 × 100 = 920 m on the ground

Now,   Length of the strip = 14 × 1000 m

$\therefore$ $\left(\begin{array}{c} \text{Number of photographs} \\ \text{required in one strip} \end{array} \right)$ = $\dfrac{14000}{920}$

= 15.2 say 16.00

Add 1 for end lap = 17

Similarly, the distance between centre to centre of photographs in the lateral direction (with 30% overlap)

= 0.7 × 23

= 16.1 cm

= 16.1 × 100 metres

= 1610 m on the ground

Now,   Width covered = 10 × 1000 m = 10000 m

$\therefore$ $\left(\begin{array}{c} \text{Number of photographs} \\ \text{required in the lateral direction} \end{array} \right)$ = $\dfrac{10000}{1610}$ = 6.21 say 7

Add 1 extra for end lap = 7 + 1 = 8

$\therefore$ Total number = 17 × 8

= 136

Example 3.23 : The parallax difference of the images of two objects on a pair of aerial photographs is 2.15 mm and an average photograph base of 85.48 mm. Calculate the difference in elevation of the two objects if the height of flight is 3200 m above the average ground level.

Solution : Using the formula,

$$\Delta H = \left(\frac{H \cdot \Delta p}{b_m + \Delta p} \right)$$

$$= \frac{3200 \text{ m} \times 2.15 \text{ mm}}{(85.48 + 2.15) \text{ mm}}$$

$$= \frac{3200 \times 2.15}{87.63} = 78.51 \text{ m}$$

Example 3.24 : In a pair of overlapping vertical photographs the distance between two principal points, both of which lie at datum, is 6.40 cm. The aircraft flying height was 600 metres above the datum and the camera focal length was 152 mm. Determine the scale of the photograph and the height of chimney, the bottom of which lies at the datum level, if the difference of parallaxes between top and bottom of the chimney was 15.90 mm.

Solution : (i) Scale of photograph $= \dfrac{f}{H} = \dfrac{0.152}{600}$

$$= \frac{1}{3947.4}$$

(ii)   The height of chimney $= \dfrac{H \cdot \Delta p}{b_m + \Delta p}$

$$= \frac{(600 \times 15.90)}{(64 + 15.90)}$$

$$= 119.40 \text{ m}$$

Example 3.25 : The parallax difference between the top and bottom of a tree is measured as 1.32 mm on a stereo pair of photographs taken at 900 m above the ground. Average photobase is 88 mm. How tall is the tree ?

Solution : Using the equation,

$$\Delta H = \frac{H \cdot \Delta p}{b_m + \Delta p}$$

where, ΔH = Difference in elevation of top and bottom of tree

H = Height of aeroplane above ground

b_m = Average photo base distance

Δp = Difference in parallax between top and bottom of the tree

∴ $\Delta H = \dfrac{900 \text{ m} \times 1.32 \text{ mm}}{(88 + 1.32) \text{ mm}}$

$= \dfrac{900 \times 1.32}{89.32} = 13.30 \text{ m}$

Example 3.26 : A radio tower appears on a pair of overlapping vertical air photographs taken with a 200 mm focal length camera. The flying height was 2000 m above the base of the tower and the distance between the two exposures was 870 m. Following measurements were recorded on the photographs, positive direction being in the direction of flight.

		Photo 1	Photo 2
(i)	Distance of top of tower from the principal point	+ 96.52 mm	− 1.05 mm
(ii)	Distance of the bottom of tower from the principal point.	+ 90.49 mm	0.98 mm

What is the approximate height of the tower ?

Solution :

(i)   Scale of photograph $= \dfrac{f}{H} = \dfrac{0.200}{2000}$

$= \dfrac{1}{10000}$

(ii)   Air base distance = Distance between two successive exposures

= 870 m (given)

∴   Photo base distance = 870 × Scale of photograph

$= 870 \times \dfrac{1}{10000}$

= 0.087 m

= 87 mm

(iii)   Height of tower = $\Delta h = \left(\dfrac{H \cdot \Delta p}{b_m + \Delta p} \right)$

Now, $\Delta p = p_1 - p_2$

$p_1 = 96.52 - (-1.05)$

$p_1 = 97.57$

$p_2 = 90.49 - 0.98$

$= 89.51$

$\therefore$

$$\Delta p = p_1 - p_2$$

$$= 97.57 - 89.51$$

$$= 8.06 \text{ mm}$$

$\therefore$ Height of tower $= \dfrac{2000 \times 8.06}{87 + 8.06} \left(\dfrac{m \times mm}{mm} \right)$

$$= \dfrac{2000 \times 8.06}{95.06}$$

$$= 169.58 \text{ m}$$

Example 3.27 : In determining the height difference between two points p_1 and p_2 by parallax bar from stereo-pair photographs the following data were available :

(i)   Focal length of the aerial camera = 200 mm.

(ii) Flying height = 1,100 m (average).

(iii) Air base = 380 m.

(iv) Difference in parallax between p_1 and p_2 = 4.18 mm.

Calculate the difference in height between p_1 and p_2.

Solution : $\Delta h = \dfrac{H \cdot \Delta p}{b_m + \Delta p}$

where, $H = 1100 \text{ m (given)}$

$$\Delta p = 4.18 \text{ mm}$$

and $b_m = \text{Mean photo base distance}$

$$= \dfrac{\text{Air base}}{\text{Scale of photograph}}$$

But,   Scale of photograph $= \dfrac{f}{H}$

$$= \dfrac{0.200 \text{ m}}{1100}$$

$$= \dfrac{1}{5500}$$

$\therefore$ $b_m = \dfrac{380}{5500} \times 1000 \text{ mm}$

$$= 69.09 \text{ mm}$$

$\therefore$ $\Delta h = \dfrac{1100 \text{ m} \times 4.18 \text{ mm}}{69.09 \text{ mm}}$

$\therefore$ $\Delta h = 66.55 \text{ m}$

Example 3.28 : An area of 120 km by 60 km is to be covered by aerial photographs, the size of photograph being 23 cm square. The height of aeroplane above m.s.l. is 3600 m and the longitudinal and side lap are 60% aerial photographs and 30% respectively, and focal length of camera lens is 18 cm. Calculate the following :

    (i)   Minimum number of photographs required to cover the given area.

    (ii)   The required interval between successive exposures, assuming the speed of aircraft as 120 km/hour.

    (iii)   The image movement (or blur) if the shutter speed is $\dfrac{1}{333}$ seconds.

Solution : (i)   Using the formula for the scale of photograph $= \dfrac{f}{H}$

$$\therefore \qquad\qquad \text{Scale} \;=\; \frac{\dfrac{18}{100}}{3600}$$

$$=\; \frac{18}{360000}$$

$$=\; \frac{1}{20000}$$

Now, length covered by one photograph on the ground with 60% overlap

$$= (0.4 \times \text{Length of photograph} \times \text{Scale})$$
$$= (0.4 \times 23 \times 20000) \text{ cm}$$
$$= \frac{9.2 \times 20000}{100}$$
$$= 1840 \text{ m}$$
$$= 1.840 \text{ km}$$

The given length of the area $= 120$ km

$$\therefore \qquad \binom{\text{Number of photographs}}{\text{required in each strip}} = \frac{120}{1.840}$$

$$= 65.21 \text{ Nos.}$$
$$\approx 66 \text{ Nos.}$$

Add 1 extra for end coverage.

$\therefore$ The total number per strip $= 66 + 1 = 67$ Nos.

Similarly, the distance between centre to centre of adjacent strips with 30% side lap

$$= 0.70 + 23 \times 20000 \text{ cm}$$
$$= \frac{0.70 \times 23 \times 20000}{100}$$
$$= 3220 \text{ m}$$
$$= 3.22 \text{ km}$$

and the width of the area to be covered = 60 km

$\therefore$ Number of strips required $= \dfrac{60}{3.22} = 18.63 \approx$ 19 Nos.

Adding one extra for end coverage = 19 + 1 = 20

$\therefore$ $\begin{pmatrix}\text{Total number of} \\ \text{photographs required}\end{pmatrix} = 67 \times 20$

$= 1340$ Nos.

(ii)   The speed of aircraft = 120 km/hour

$= \dfrac{120 \times 1000}{60 \times 60}$

$= 33.33$ m/sec

Now, $\begin{bmatrix}\text{Length covered by each} \\ \text{photograph on the ground}\end{bmatrix} = 1840$ m

Required interval between exposures $= \dfrac{1850}{33.33} = 55.20$ seconds

(iii)   The speed of aircraft = 33.33 m/sec

$\therefore$ Ground covered in $\dfrac{1}{333}$ seconds $= \left[\dfrac{33.33}{333}\right]$

$= \dfrac{1}{10}$ m

$= \dfrac{1000}{10}$

$= 100$ mm on the ground

$\therefore$ $\begin{pmatrix}\text{Corresponding image} \\ \text{movement (or blur)}\end{pmatrix} = 100 \times \text{Scale}$

$= \dfrac{100}{20000} = 5 \times 10^{-3}$ mm

$= 0.005$ mm

Example 3.29 : If in the previous problem, the number of such photographs taken in a strip are 10. Calculate the total area covered, the longitudinal overlap being 60%.

Solution : Area covered by one photograph on the ground

$= (23 \times 23) \times (20000)^2$ sq.cm.

$= \dfrac{529 \times 20000 \times 20000}{100 \times 100 \times 1000 \times 1000}$ sq.km.

$= 5.29 \times 4$

$= 21.16$ sq. km.

$$\therefore \quad \begin{pmatrix} \text{Total area covered by} \\ \text{10 photographs with} \\ \text{60\% overlap} \end{pmatrix} = 21.16 \times (1 + 9 \times 0.4)$$

$$= 21.16 \times (4.6)$$

$$= 97.34 \text{ sq. km.}$$

Example 3.30 : In a pair of overlapping photographs the mean distance between principal points, both of which lie on the datum, is 6.5 cm. At the time of photography, the aircraft was 800 m above the datum. The camera has a focal length of 150 mm. In the common overlap a tower 125 m high with its axis at datum level is observed. Determine the difference of parallax of the top and bottom of tower.

Solution : Using the formula for scale of photograph $= \dfrac{f}{H}$

$$= \frac{150}{800 \times 1000}$$

$$= \frac{1}{5333.34}$$

Now,   Mean base distance $= b_m = 6.5$ cm

$$\therefore \quad \text{Air base distance, B} = \frac{6.5 \times 5333.34}{100}$$

$$= 346.667 \text{ m}$$

Now, parallax for the top and bottom point of the tower can be calculated by the formula :

$$p = \frac{B.f}{H - h} \qquad (\because h = 0 \text{ at the datum})$$

$$\therefore \quad p_{1 \text{ (for bottom)}} = \frac{346.667 \times 0.15}{800 - 0}$$

$$= 0.065 \text{ m or } 6.5 \text{ cm}$$

and $p_{2 \text{ (top)}} = \dfrac{Bf}{H - h}$

$$= \frac{346.667 \times 0.15}{800 - 125}$$

$$= 0.07703 \text{ m}$$

$$= 7.703 \text{ cm}$$

$$\therefore \quad \text{Difference in parallax, } \Delta p = p_2 - p_1$$

$$= 7.703 - 6.5$$

$$= 1.203 \text{ cm}$$

$$= 12.03 \text{ mm}$$

$$\text{As a check, } \Delta h = \frac{H\Delta p}{b_m + \Delta p}$$

$$= \frac{800 \times 12.03}{65 + 12.03} \approx 125 \text{ m}$$

Example 3.31 : Two points A and B which appear in a vertical photograph taken from a camera having focal length of 220 mm and from an altitude of 300 m, have their elevations as 400 m and 600 m respectively. Their corrected photo co-ordinates are as under.

Point	Photo co-ordinates	
	X (mm)	Y (mm)
a	+ 23.8	+ 16.4
b	− 13.6	− 29.7

Determine the length of ground line AB.

Solution :

$$X_a \text{ (x co-ordinate of A on ground)} = \frac{H - h_a}{f} \cdot x_a$$

$$= \frac{(3000 - 400)}{220} \times 23.8 = + 281.27 \text{ m}$$

$$Y_a \text{ (y co-ordinate of A on ground)} = \frac{H - h_a}{f} \cdot y_a$$

$$= \frac{3000 - 400}{220} \times 16.4 = + 193.82 \text{ m}$$

$$X_b \text{ (x co-ordinate of B on ground)} = \frac{H - h_b}{f} \cdot x_b$$

$$= \frac{3000 - 600}{220} \times (- 13.6) = - 148.36 \text{ m}$$

$$Y_b \text{ (y co-ordinate of B on ground)} = \frac{H - h_b}{f} \cdot y_b$$

$$= \frac{3000 - 600}{220} \times (- 29.7) = - 324 \text{ m}$$

$$\therefore \quad \text{Length of line AB on ground} = \sqrt{(281.27 + 148.36)^2 + (193.92 + 324)^2}$$

$$\therefore \quad AB = 672.92 \text{ m}$$

Example 3.32 : An aerial survey of a particular area is to be carried out with the following details :

(i)   Ground area to be covered = 30 km × 12 km.

(ii) Scale of photography is 1 : 20,000.

(iii) Focal length of camera lens = 152 mm.

(iv)   Size of photographs = 23 cm × 23 cm.

(v)   Speed of aeroplane = 200 km per hour.

(vi)   Longitudinal overlap = 60%.

(vii) Side lap = 25%.

(viii) Assume 2 photos extra for end coverage.

Calculate :

(i)   Height at which aeroplane should fly.

(ii)   Minimum number of photographs required to cover the area.

(iii)   Interval between two exposures of camera.

Solution : (i) Scale of photograph $= \dfrac{f}{H}$

where f = 152 mm and H is not given

$\therefore$ $\dfrac{1}{20000}$ $= \dfrac{152}{H}$

$\therefore$ H = 152×20000 mm

$\therefore$ H = Height of flight = 3040 m

(ii)   Interval between exposures :

b_m = Mean base distance   = 0.4 W,

where,   W = Width of photograph

                                              = 230 mm

and overlap in the direction of flight = 60%

$\therefore$ b_m = 0.40×230 = 92 mm

$\therefore$ Air base distance $= \left(\dfrac{92 \times 20000}{1000}\right)$ m = 1840 m

{$\because$ Air base of distance = (Mean base distance × Scale of photograph)}

Now,   Speed of aeroplane = 200 km.h.

                                    $= \dfrac{200 \times 1000}{60 \times 60}$ = 55.55 m/sec

$\therefore$ Interval between exposures $= \dfrac{1840}{55.55}$ = 33.12 seconds

(iii)   Minimum number of photographs required :

$\left(\begin{array}{c}\text{Distance between c/c of}\\ \text{consecutive photographs}\end{array}\right)$ $= 0.4 \times 230$ = 92 mm

$\therefore$ $\left(\begin{array}{c}\text{Corresponding distance}\\ \text{on the ground}\end{array}\right)$ $= 92 \times 20000$ mm = 1840 m

$$\left(\begin{array}{c}\text{Number of photographs}\\ \text{required in the}\\ \text{direction of flight}\end{array}\right) = \frac{30 \times 1000}{1840} = 16.30 \approx 17$$

∴ Adding 2 extra for end coverage = 17 + 2 = 19

Similarly, number of photographs required in the lateral direction of flight

$$= \frac{12 \times 1000}{0.75 \times 230 \times \dfrac{20000}{1000}} = 3.84 \approx 4$$

∴   Add 2 extra = 4 + 2 = 6

∴   Total number of photographs = 19 × 6 = 114

Example 3.33 : The distance between principal points on two consecutive photographs is 8.1 cm, the scale of the photograph being 1 : 10000. If the focal length of the camera lens is 200 mm and the parallax of the object M is 90 mm, calculate the height of the aeroplane above M. Drive the formula if you use any for space co-ordinates.

Solution : Distance between principal points = 8.1 cm = Photo base distance.

∴   Air base distance, B = 8.1 × Scale of photographs

= 8.1 × 10000

= 81000 cm

= 810 m

Now using the relation,

$$\frac{H-h}{f} = \frac{B}{P}$$

∴ $$H - h = \frac{B \cdot f}{P}$$

$$= \frac{810 \times 200 \text{ mm}}{90 \text{ mm}}$$

= 1800 m

Example 3.34 : A tower appears on a pair of overlapping vertical air photographs taken with a camera having focal lens of 150 mm. The flying height was 2500 m above the base of the tower and distance between the two exposures was 900 m. Following measurements were recorded on the photographs, positive direction being in the direction of flight.

	Photo 1	Photo 2
Distance of top of tower from the principal point	+ 96.52 mm	−1.05 mm
Distance of bottom of tower from the principal point	+90.49 mm	+0.98 mm

Calculate the height of tower.

Solution : (i) Scale of photograph $= \dfrac{f}{H} = \dfrac{0.15}{2500} = \dfrac{1}{16666.67}$

(ii)   Air-base distance $=$ Distance between two successive exposures

$= 900$ m (given)

$\therefore$ Photo-base distance $= 900 \times$ scale of photograph

$= 900 \times \dfrac{1}{16666.67}$

$= 0.054 = 54$ mm

(iii)   Height of tower $= \Delta h = \left(\dfrac{H \cdot \Delta P}{bm + \Delta P} \right)$

Now, $\Delta P = P_1 - P_2$

$P_1 = 96.52 - (-1.05) = 97.57$

$P_2 = 90.49 - 0.98 = 89.51$

$\therefore$ $\Delta P = P_1 - P_2 = 97.57 - 89.51 = 8.06$ mm

$\therefore$ Height of tower $= \dfrac{2500 \times 8.06}{54 + 8.06} \left(\dfrac{m \times mm}{mm} \right)$

$= \dfrac{2500 \times 8.06}{62.06} = 324.68$ m

$\therefore$ Height of tower $= 324.68$ m

Example 3.35 : An area is to be surveyed with the aerial photographic survey with the following data :

(i)   Ground area to be covered $= 40$ km $\times 18$ km

(ii)   Scale of photograph $= 1 : 20,000$.

(iii)   Focal length of camera lens $= 152$ mm.

(iv)   Size of photograph $= 23$ cm $\times 23$ cm.

(v)   Speed of aeroplane $= 180$ km/hr.

(vi)   Longitudinal overlap $= 60\%$.

(vii) Side lap $= 20\%$.

(viii) Assume two extra photos for end coverage.

Calculate height at which aeroplane should fly ? Minimum number of photographs required to cover the area and interval between two exposures of camera.

Solution : (i)   Scale of photograph $= \dfrac{f}{H}$

$\therefore$ $\dfrac{1}{20000} = \dfrac{152}{H}$

$\therefore$ $H = 152 \times 20000$

$\therefore$ Height of flight $= H = 3040$ m

(ii)   Interval between exposures :

b_m = Mean-base distance = 0.4 W

where,   W = Width of photograph = 230 mm

and   overlap in the direction of flight = 60%

$\therefore$ $b_m = 0.40 \times 230 = 92$ mm

$\therefore$ Air-base distance $= \left(\dfrac{92 \times 20000}{1000}\right)$ m $= 1840$ m

Now,   Speed of aeroplane = 180 km/hr

$= \dfrac{180 \times 1000}{60 \times 60} = 50$ m/sec

$\therefore$ Interval between exposures $= \dfrac{1840}{50} = 36.8$ seconds

(iii)   Minimum number of photographs required :

Distance between c/c on consecutive photographs = $0.4 \times 230 = 92$ mm.

$\therefore$ Corresponding distance on the ground $= \dfrac{92 \times 20000}{1000} = 1840$ m.

Number of photographs required in the direction of flight

$= \dfrac{40 \times 1000}{1840} = 21.74 \cong 22$

Adding two extra for end coverage $= 22 + 2 = 24$

Similarly, number of photographs required in the lateral direction of flight

$= \dfrac{18 \times 1000}{0.75 \times 230 \times \dfrac{20000}{1000}} = 5.2 = 6$

Adding two extra for end coverage $= 6 + 2 = 8$

$\therefore$ Total numbers $= 24 + 8 = 32$ numbers

Example 3.36 : A camera having focal length of 200 mm is to be used to take a vertical photograph of a terrain having an average elevation of 2000 m. At what height above datum, the air craft should fly to have a photograph at a scale of 1 : 5000 ?

Solution : Given : Focal length of camera = f = 200 mm

Average elevation of a terrain = 2000 m

Scale of photograph = 1 : 5000

We know,   Scale of photograph $= \dfrac{f}{H - h_{av}}$

$\therefore$ $\dfrac{1}{5000} = \dfrac{\dfrac{200}{1000}}{(H - 2000)}$

$\therefore$ $\dfrac{1}{5000}(H - 2000) = \dfrac{200}{1000}$

$\therefore$ $(H - 2000) = \dfrac{200 \times 5000}{1000}$

$\therefore$ H = Flying height = 3000 m

Example 3.37 : A pair of photographs is taken with a camera having focal length 15 cm. The scale of photography is 1:10000 and photo base is 5.65 cm. The measured parallax of a vertical control point having an elevation 140 m is 87.28 mm. Compute the elevation of another point P whose measured parallax is 84.18 mm.

Solution : We know scale of photography, $s = \dfrac{f}{H}$

                f = focal length of camera lense = 15 cm = 0.15 m

and   H = height of flight

Here scale (s) of photography is given as 1:10000.

            $\dfrac{1}{10000} = \dfrac{0.15}{H}$

$\therefore$ Height of flight = 0.15 × 10000 = 1500 m

We also know difference of elevation between two points, $h = \dfrac{H \cdot \Delta p}{(b_m + \Delta p)}$

Here   H = Flying height = 1500 m

Δp = Difference parallax = Parallax for control point − Parallax for another point

                    = 87.28 − 84.18

                    = 3.1 mm

        b_m = Mean photo scale = 5.65 cm = 56.5 mm

∴　Difference of elevation between control point and another point

$$= h = \frac{1500 \times 3.1}{(56.5 + 3.1)} = 78.020 \text{ m}$$

But elevation of the control point is 140 m.

∴　Elevation of another point = Elevation of the control point + Difference in elevation

$$= 140 + 78.020$$

$$= 218.020 \text{ m}$$

Example 3.38 : Two points P and Q have elevation 280 m and 650 m above the datum respectively. The co-ordinates of P and Q measured from photograph taken with camera having focal length of 15 cm are tabulated blow.

Point	Co-ordinates	
	X	Y
P	+ 35.4 mm	+ 17.5 mm
Q	− 25.8 mm	+ 39.6 mm

Calculate length PQ. Flying height is 3000 m above datum.

Solution : Given :

$$\text{Elevation of P} = h_P = 280 \text{ m}$$

$$\text{Elevation of Q} = h_Q = 650 \text{ m}$$

$$\text{Focal length of Camera lense} = f = 15 \text{ cm}$$

$$\text{Height of flight} = H = 3000 \text{ m}$$

$$\text{Photo X co-ordinate of P} = X_P + 35.4 \text{ mm} = 3.54 \text{ cm}$$

$$\text{Photo X co-ordinate of Q} = X_Q = -25.8 \text{ mm} = -2.58 \text{ cm}$$

$$\text{Photo Y co-ordinates of P} = Y_P = 17.5 \text{ mm} = 1.75 \text{ cm}$$

$$\text{Photo Y co-ordinates of Q} = Y_Q = +39.6 \text{ mm} = 3.96 \text{ cm}$$

We have to calculate length of line PQ on ground.

We know, Length of line PQ $= L_{PQ} = \sqrt{[(X_Q - X_P)^2 + (Y_Q - Y_P)^2]}$

where,

$$X_P = \text{Ground X co-ordinate of P}$$

$$X_Q = \text{Ground X co-ordinate of Q}$$

$$Y_P = \text{Ground Y co-ordinate of P}$$

$$Y_Q = \text{Ground Y co-ordinate of Q}$$

We know, Ground X co-ordinate of nth station $= X_n = (H - h_n) * x_n/f$

∴

$$X_Q = (H - h_Q) * x_Q/f$$

$$X_Q = (3000 - 650) * 3.58/15$$

$$X_Q = -404.20 \text{ m}$$

and

$$X_P = (H - h_Q) * x_P/f$$

$$X_P = (3000 - 280) * 3.54 /15$$

$$X_P = 641.92 \text{ m}$$

We know, Ground Y co-ordinate of nth station = $Y_n = (H - h_n) * y_n/f$

$\therefore$

$$Y_Q = (H - h_Q) * y_Q/f$$

$$Y_Q = (3000 - 650) * 3.96/15$$

$$Y_Q = 620.4 \text{ m}$$

and

$$Y_P = (H - h_P) * y_P/f$$

$$Y_P = (3000 - 280) * 1.75/15$$

$$Y_P = 333.33 \text{ m}$$

$\therefore$

$$L_{AB} = \sqrt{[(X_Q - X_P)^2 + (Y_Q - Y_P)^2]}$$

$$L_{AB} = \sqrt{[(-404.20 - 641.92)^2 + (620.4 - 333.33)^2]}$$

$$L_{AB} = 1049.158 \text{ m}$$

Example 3.39 : The scale of photograph is 1:10000, effective at an average elevation of terrain of 500 m. The size of photograph is 230 mm × 230 mm. Focal length of camera lense is 20 cm. Speed of aircraft is 180 kmph, longitudinal overlap is 60% and side overlap is 30%.

Determine the number of photographs required to cover an area of 30 km × 22.5 km. Also determine exposure interval and flying height.

Solution : Given :

Length of area, L = 30 km

Length of photo, L_P = 0.23 m

Width of area, W = 22.5 km

Width of photo, W_P = 0.23 m

Side overlap, O_W = 30%

Longitudinal overlap, O_L = 60%

Scale of photograph = 1 : 10000, effective at an average elevation,

h_{avg} = 500 m.

Speed of aircraft = 180 kmph = (180 × 5/18) m/s = 50 m/s

Distance between two consecutive exposures (i.e.) Air base

$$= L_g = \frac{(100 - O_L)}{100} \times \frac{L_P}{S} = \frac{(100 - 60)}{100} \times \frac{0.23}{1/10000}$$

$$= 920 \text{ m}$$

No. of photos per flight line $= \dfrac{L}{L_g} + 1 = \dfrac{30000}{920} + 1 = 33.61$ say 34 photos

Distance between two adjoining flight lines

$$= W_g = \frac{100 - O_W}{100} \times \frac{W_P}{S} = \frac{100 - 30}{100} \times \frac{0.12}{1/10000} = 1610 \text{ m}$$

Number of flight lines $= \dfrac{W}{W_g} + 1 = \dfrac{22500}{1610} + 1 = 14.98$ say 15 flight lines

Total No. of photos = N = Number of photos per flight line × Number of flight lines

$$= 34 \times 15$$

$$= 510 \text{ photos}$$

We know exposure interval $= \dfrac{\text{Air base}}{\text{Speed}} = \dfrac{L_g}{v} = \dfrac{920}{50} = 18.4$ Seconds

3.5 GROUND CONTROL POINTS AND THEIR IMPORTANCE

Ground Control Points (GCPs) are the points on the surface of the earth of known positions. These are used to geo-reference aerial photographs or satellite images or scanned maps. To geo-reference something means 'to define its existence in physical space'. To geo-reference a photo or image, we must know the external orientation of the camera or sensor. The external orientation determines position and orientation of camera in absolute co-ordinate system.

Thus, establishment of ground control points, which are clearly distinguishable on the aerial photographs, is very important. The GCP must be a clearly and sharply visible object on the photograph which can be easily identified on the field of survey. The number of control points depends upon the scale and accuracy expected on final plan/map. The minimum number of GCPs required per photo is two plan points to control positions, scale and orientation and three height points to control elevations.

The ground survey for establishment of such control points can be divided into two categories viz. basic control survey and photo control survey. The basic control survey consists of establishing the network of triangulation stations, azimuth marks (marks to refer North direction), bench marks etc. The photo control consists of establishing the positions on ground of some clearly visible points on photograph with respect to basic control points. These controls can be established by triangulation and traversing with a theodolite or total station instrument or with help of space based positioning systems like GPS. The co-ordinates of GCPs shall preferably be referred to 'National Spatial Reference Frame', so that the data you are extracting from aerial photograph can be referred to national grid.

There are two types of GCPs viz. Pre-marked GCPs and Post-marked GCPs. The pre-marked points are selected on the ground first and then included in the photographs. In production of large scale engineering plans the GCPs are generally pre-marked. Their locations are usually finalized from initial (reconnaissance) photography, and when actually marked on the ground area is re-photographed. A popular type of pre-mark is a large white cross with arm length about 2 m long and 0.25 m wide. The post marks are the points selected on the photo after the aerial photography is over.

In digital photogrammetry, GCPs play a very important role in image rectification. Random distortions and residual unknown systematic distortions are corrected by analyzing well distributed Ground Control Points (GCPs) occurring in an image. The number and distribution of the GCPs and the accuracy of their co-ordinates, are the most important factors determining the overall accuracy of the image rectification process.

THEORETICAL QUESTIONS

1. What do you mean by photographic survey ?

2. What is stereo-photogrammetry ? Explain how the position and elevation of an object can be determined by this method. What are the special advantages of this method ?

3. Explain the field method of determining the focal length of the camera lens of a photo theodolite.

4. Explain the procedure of carrying out field work for ground photogrammetry.

5. Explain clearly the procedure of determining the elevation of an object in terrestrial photogrammetry.

6. In case of aerial surveying, explain the following :

 (i) Ground control

 (ii) Principal point

 (iii) Plumb point

 (iv) Floating mark.

7. Distinguish between longitudinal and side overlap.

8. Derive an expression for computing the difference in elevation by stereoscopic parallaxes.

9. What is meant by stereoscopic fusion ?

10. Draw a neat sketch to explain the development of stereoscopic depth in case of mirror stereoscope.

11. What do you mean by parallax of a point and the differential parallax ?

12. Show that there is no parallax in Y-direction in case of vertical aerial photograph.

13. Explain clearly the Arundel's method of plotting.

14. Describe with neat sketches the procedure of Radial line method of plotting.

15. Explain clearly the use of mirror stereoscope and parallax bar in aerial photogrammetry.

16. An aerial survey of a given area is to be carried out. Explain clearly, with neat sketches, the procedure of flight planning and derive an expression for the minimum number of photographs required to cover the above area.

17. What is meant by 'Parallax measurement' in connection with an air survey ?

18. Derive an expression for parallax of a point 'h' metres above the datum taking focal length as 'f' centimetres, air base 'B' metres and flying height of air craft above datum 'H' metres. State clearly the assumptions made.

19. What is meant by 'Horizontal parallax' of a point in aerial photographs ? Derive an expression for determining the difference in elevation by differential parallax.

20. State the merits and demerits of aerial photogrammetry. Under what circumstances you will recommend its use ?

21. Distinguish clearly between :

    (i) Vertical,

    (ii) Tilted and oblique aerial photograph.

22. Differentiate between high oblique and low oblique aerial photographs.

23. Write a short note on aerial camera used for aerial photogrammetry.

24. Define with a neat sketch the following terms :

    (i)   Ground plumb point and photo-plumb point.

    (ii)   Principal point.

    (iii) Iso-centre

    (iv)   Nadir point

    (v)   Tilt of photograph.

25. What are the different types of aerial photograph ?

26. Explain clearly the procedure of determining the minimum number of aerial photographs required to cover a given area.

27. What do you mean by relief displacement in case of aerial photographs ? Derive an expression for the relief displacement.

28. Also state how the height of an object can be determined by the relief displacement.

29. Explain how you will determine the height of an object by 'Relief displacement'.

30. What are the applications of photogrammetry ? Explain any one of them in details.

31. Explain with neat sketches the following terms :
    (i)   Fiducial marks
    (ii) Isocentre
    (iii) Principal point
    (iv) Nadir.

32. Explain briefly the following :
    (i)   Aerial photogrammetry
    (ii) Space photogrammetry.

33. Compare a map with aerial photograph.

34. What is meant by parallax of a point and differential parallax in case of aerial photographs ? Explain the procedure of computing the difference in elevation of two objects by means of parallax bar and stereoscope. Draw neat sketches to illustrate your answer.

35. Define :
    (a) Principal point.
    (b) Plumb point
    (c) Isocentre.

Ground Control Points :

36. What is ground control points ? Discuss in brief their importance in photogrammetry.

37. Define GCP, state their role in photogrammetry and bring out the difference between pre marked and post marked GCPs.

38. Why GCPs are required in photogrammetry ? Comment in brief on ground survey for establishment of GCPs.

NUMERICAL PROBLEMS

1. The ground points A and B are at elevations 455 m and 546 m respectively above datum. The photo was taken from 3333 m above the datum with 209.55 mm focal length camera. The camera axis was vertical. The photo-co-ordinates of the points were as given below :

Ground point	Co-ordinates on photograph	
A	+ 68.72 mm	+ 32.37 mm
B	– 87.44 mm	+ 26.81 mm

Determine :

(i)   Ground co-ordinates X and Y of the points A and B; and

(ii) Ground distance AB and its direction.

2. Calculate the value of focal length of the photo-theodolite from the following data :

(i)   Horizontal angle AOB = 30°.

(ii) The co-ordinates of the objects appearing on the photographs being 60 mm and 50 mm.

   Ans. : 205 mm.

3. A section line AB appears to be 10.16 cm on a photograph for which the focal length is 16 cm. The corresponding line measures 2.54 cm on a map which is to a scale of 1/50,000. The terrain has an average elevation of 200 m above mean sea level. Calculate the flying altitude of the aircraft above mean sea level, when the photograph was taken.

   Ans. : Scale of photograph = 1/12500, H = 2200 m.

4. Vertical photographs were taken from height of 3048 m, the focal length of camera lens being 15.24 cm. If the points were 22.86 cm × 22.86 cm and the overlap 60%, what was the length of the air base ?

   Ans. : Scale = $\dfrac{1}{2000}$, Air base = 1828.8 m.

5. An area of 224 sq. km is to be photographed at a scale of 1 in 8,000 from the air using a camera of focal length 150 mm, the photograph being 23 mm × 23 cm square. A longitudinal overlap of 60% and a lateral overlap of 25% must be provided. If the operating speed of the aircraft is 224 km per hour, find (i) the flying height of the air craft and the interval between exposures, (ii) the number of prints required if the flying strips are 16 km long.

   Ans. : 1200 m, 11.78 sec (22 + 1) (11 + 1) = 276 nos.

6.   In an aerial survey, if the speed of the aeroplane is 160 km per hour, and the size of the photograph is 18 cm × 18 cm and scale adopted is 1/10,000, find the vertical between the exposures if the end overlap is 55%.

$$\left(\textbf{Hint :} \text{ Air base distance } = \frac{0.45 \times 18 \times 10000}{100} = 810 \text{ m}\right)$$

$$\left(\therefore \quad \text{Interval between exposure } = \frac{810}{44.44} = 18.23 \text{ seconds}\right)$$

7.   In a pair of overlapping photographs (mean photo base length 89.84 mm), mean ground level is 170 m above datum. Two nearby points are observed and the following information is obtained :

Point	Height above datum	Parallel bar reading
X	155 m	9.54 mm
Y	?	11.66 mm

If the flying height was 2300 m above datum and focal length of camera lens was 15 cm, find the height of Y above datum.

8.   Determine the number of photographs required to cover an area of 250 sq. km. from the following data :

   (i)   Scale of photograph : 1 cm = 100 m.

   (ii)   Photograph size = 23 cm × 23 cm.

   (iii) Longitudinal overlap = 60% and side overlap = 30%.

   Ans. : 169 Nos.

9.   An image of an object is 90 mm from the centre of a photograph. The elevation of the object above the datum (sea level) is 600 m. What is the relief displacement of the point if the datum scale of the photograph is 1/20,000 and focal length of camera lens is 21.5 cm ?

   Ans. : H = 4300, Displacement = 12.558 mm.

10. Determine the minimum number of aerial photographs required to cover an area of 40 km × 30 km, with the following :

   (i)   Size of aerial photograph = 23 cm × 23 cm

   (ii)   Scale of aerial photographs : 1 cm = 150 m.

   (iii) Longitudinal overlap = 60%

   (iv)   Side overlap = 30%.

   Ans. : (29 + 1) (13 + 1) = 420 Nos.

11.   The scale of an aerial photograph is 1 cm = 200 m and the size of photograph is 23 cm × 23 cm. Determine the minimum number of photographs required to cover a given area of 30 km × 20 km if the overlap in the direction of flight is 60% and the side lap is 30%.

12.   In an aerial survey, a line PQ measures 12.40 cm on a photograph taken with a camera having a focal length of 16 cm. The same line measures 3.1 cm on a map drawn to a scale of 1/40000. Calculate the flying height of aircraft if the average elevation of the ground is 400 m.

       Ans. : Scale of photograph = 1 : 10,000, Flying height   = 2000 m.

13.   An aerial survey was planned for a terrain having average elevation of 210 m above datum. A road strip 432 m in length, was measured as 7.2 cm in one of the vertical photographs of the survey. The radial distances to the top and foot of the tower in this photograph were 7.4 cm and 6.7 cm respectively. Focal length of the camera lens was 200 mm. Compute the height of tower.

       Ans. : Scale = 1 : 6000, H = 1410 m, Height of tower = 133.77 m.

14.   An image of the top of a T.V. tower is 85 mm from the principal point of the photograph. If the flying height is 3200 m above the datum and the elevation of top of the T.V. tower is 420 m, calculate the relief displacement.

       Ans. : 1.195 mm.

15.   A line 2400 m long lying at an elevation of 600 m above the datum measures 9.4 cm on a vertical photograph. If the focal length of the camera which has taken this photograph is 20 cm, calculate flying height of the aircraft above the datum and also the scale of the photograph in an area the average ground level of which is about 800 m.

16.   An image of the top of the object is 60 m from the principal point of the photograph. The elevation of top of the object is 400 m and the flying height is 3000 m above datum. Calculate the relief displacement.

       Ans. : $d = \dfrac{rh}{H} = \dfrac{60 \text{ mm} \times 400 \text{ m}}{3000 \text{ m}} = \dfrac{60}{7.5} = 8$ mm.

17.   The parallax difference of the images of two objects on a pair of aerial photographs is 3 mm and the mean base distance was found to be 90 mm. Calculate the difference in elevation of the two objects if the height of flight is 3000 m.

       Ans. : $\Delta h = \dfrac{H \cdot \Delta p}{b_m + \Delta p} = \dfrac{3000 \times 3}{90 + 3} = \dfrac{3000 \times 3}{93} = 96.774$ m.

18. Determine the minimum number of aerial photographs required to cover an area of 40 km × 20 km from the following data :

    (1) Size of aerial photographs   =   23 cm × 23 cm

    (2) Scale of aerial photograph   =   1 : 1000

    (3) Overlap in the direction of flight   =   60%

    (4) Side overlap   =   30%

    Ans. : 45×14 = 630 Nos.

19. Determine the minimum number of aerial photographs required to cover an area of 50 km × 30 km from the following data :

    (1) Size of photograph   =   23 cm × 23 cm

    (2) Scale of photograph   =   1 : 15000

    (3) Overlap in the direction of flight   =   60%

    (4) Side overlap   =   30%

    Ans. : 38×14 = 532 Nos.

20. Photographs were taken from P and Q, two camera stations, 200 m apart. The focal length of the camera was 150 mm. The axis of the camera made an angle of 65° and 40° with the base line at stations P and Q respectively. The image of a point A appears 20.2 mm to the right and 20.4 mm above the hair lines on the photograph taken at P. The image of same point appears 35.2 mm to the left on the photograph taken at Q. Calculate the distance PA and QA and elevations of point A, if the elevation of instrument axis at P is 526.845 m.

    Ans. : PA = 90.625 m, QA = 169.249 m, R.L. of A = 526.845 + 12.21 = 539.055 m.

21. A section line AB appears to be 10.16 cm on a photograph taken with a camera of focal length 16 cm. The corresponding line measures 2.54 cm on a map which has a scale of 1/50000. The terrain over which the photograph is taken has an average elevation of 300 m above mean sea level. Calculate the flying altitude of the aircraft above mean sea level when the photograph was taken.

    Ans. : 2300 m.

22. From the following data, obtain the number of photographs to cover the area measuring 30 km × 20 km.

    (i) Scale of the photograph   =   1 : 50,000

    (ii) Longitudinal overlap   =   66%

    (iii) Side overlap   =   33%

    (iv) Size of the photograph   =   23 cm × 23 cm

    Ans. : 560, assuming 1 extra for end overlaps.

23. An image of an object is 90 mm from the centre of a photograph. The elevation of the object above the datum (sea level) is 600 m. If the datum scale of the photograph is 1/20,000, and the focal length of camera is 21.5 cm, what is the relief displacement of the point ?

24. Two points P and Q whose elevations above the datum are 400 m and 200 m respectively, appear on the aerial photographs having a focal length of 20 mm and flying height of 2000 m above datum. The co-ordinates of P and Q on the photographs are as follows :

Point	Photo-co-ordinates	
	x	y
P	+ 3.00 cm	+ 1.5 cm
Q	− 2.00 cm	+ 4.00 cm

Calculate the length of the line joining PQ on the ground.

25. The consecutive air photographs were taken with a camera having lens of 40 cm focal length at a height of 7300 m above datum. The overlap was exactly 60% and the prints were 22.5 cm × 22.5 cm. The ground was almost flat and was approximately 2500 m above mean sea level. Determine the scale of the photograph and length of the air base. Find out also the exposure interval, if the speed of the aircraft was 200 km/hour.

26. Co-ordinates of three points P, Q and R on a photograph were observed to be :

Point	x	y
P	− 37.50 mm	+ 20.40 mm
Q	+ 12.15 mm	− 18.22 mm
R	+ 40.38 mm	+ 16.72 mm

Focal length of the lens was 150 mm. Azimuth of the line OR was 2° 20'. Axis of camera was level at the time of exposure at station O, while taking the photographs. Determine the azimuth of the lines OP and OQ.

27. For a flight planning mission, the following data was obtained.

　(i)　Area to be photographed　　　　=　8 km wide and 12 km long

　(ii)　Focal length of the camera lens　=　20 cm

　(iii)　Speed of the aeroplane　　　　=　200 km p.h.

　(iv)　Scale of photograph　　　　　=　1 : 12000

(v)　　Average elevation of ground　　　=　400 m

(vi)　　Size of photograph　　　　　　=　22 cm × 22 cm

(vii)　Longitudinal overlap　　　　　　=　60%

(viii)　Lateral overlap　　　　　　　　=　30%

Find :

　　(i)　　Height of aircraft above terrain.

　　(ii)　　Effective longitudinal and lateral coverage.

　　(iii)　Approximate time between exposures.

❑❑❑

HYDROGRAPHIC SURVEYING

4.1 INTRODUCTION

The survey carried out on the surface of water that may be static (e.g. lake) or dynamic (e.g. rivers) is known as **'Hydrographic surveying'**. It may be carried out for :

(i)   measurement of tides, ascertaining mean sea level.

(ii)   determination of depth of water, velocity, discharge.

(iii)   fixing the shore line.

(iv)   determining the areas subjected to scouring and silting and to compute the quantities of material dredged.

(v)   preparation of navigational charts and submarine contours.

(vi)   planning of Civil Engineering works e.g. harbour and dock construction, bridges, dams, underwater tunnels, disposal of sewage etc.

4.2 ESTABLISHMENT OF HORIZONTAL AND VERTICAL CONTROLS

Hydrographic survey differs from the conventional land surveys as regards the following :

(i)   Determination of depth of the bed below the water surface which is termed as 'sounding' and

(ii)   Locations of the points on the surface of water, where soundings are made.

Thus, it is a job of establishing a point on the surface of water for which horizontal controls are necessary and for determining the depth of water i.e. sounding, vertical controls are required.

(a)   Horizontal control : It may be established by triangulation where high degree of precesion is required or by transit and tape survey for second order work. The location of the points on the surface of water where soundings are made, can thus be done with reference to the above horizontal controls established on the shore.

(b)   Vertical control : It consists of series of bench marks established along the shore line. These bench marks serve the dual purpose of setting and checking the tidal gauges that further serve as control points for the soundings. As the level of water in lake or river goes on varying with respect to time, it is absolutely essential to ascertain the exact level of water at the time of soundings by recording the gauge readings.

4.3 SHORE LINE SURVEY

This survey includes the following :

(i)   Determination of shore line.

(ii)   Location of details of shore line and prominent nearby topographical features to which soundings may be referred; and

(iii)   Establishing high and low water lines for average spring tides.

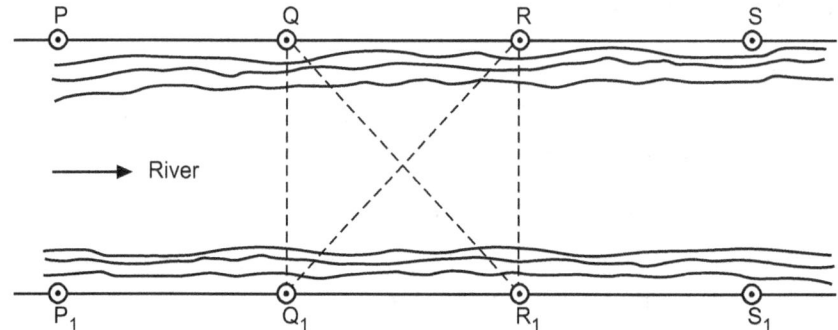

Fig. 4.1 : Shore line survey of wide river

For the determination of the shore line of a river, a theodolite traverse is run along the shore line, suitable offsets being taken to the water boundaries by a tape or plane tabling or tacheometry. In case of a narrow river, a single traverse on one bank of river is run and both the banks are located. However, in case of wide river, theodolite traverse on both the banks may be necessary. In order to check the accuracy of traverse, it is necessary to have check lines at regular intervals. The Fig. 4.1 shows a wide river, the traverse being run on both the banks. i.e. PQRS on the left bank and $P_1Q_1R_1S_1$ on the right bank. QR_1 and RQ_1 serve as check lines i.e. with the theodolite set up at Q_1 and R_1, the angles QQ_1R, RQ_1R_1 and RR_1Q, QR_1Q_1 can be measured. With these measured four angles and the length Q_1R_1 already measured as a traverse line, the length QR can be computed which should agree with its measured length QR. When it is inconvenient to run a theodolite traverse, a triangulation survey may be carried out as usual.

Location of high water line in tidal rivers, may be done approximately from the water marks on the bank rocks and shore deposits. For exact location of points along high water line, the usual direct method of contouring can be adopted. The same procedure may be followed for the location of low water line. However, in view of limited time available for carrying out such survey, it may be located by interpolation technique from available soundings.

4.4 SOUNDINGS

The measurements of vertical depths below the water surface upto the bed level are called **'soundings'**. The purpose of soundings is to know the nature of the bed level of the water bodies. The procedure of soundings is somewhat similar to levelling. In levelling, depths are measured below the horizontal line of collimation by a levelling instrument, whereas in soundings the depths are measured below the level of water surface, that goes on varying with respect to time. The soundings are generally made for :

(i)   preparation of up-to-date navigational charts.

(ii)   for ascertaining the scouring and silting in the water body.

(iii)   to compute the volume of material to be dredged.

(iv)   design of off-shore structures such as break water, sea wall etc.

(v)   under water investigations required for the construction of and development of ports.

4.5 SOUNDING EQUIPMENTS

The following equipments are required for the direct method of soundings :

(i)   Sounding boat,

(ii)   Sounding poles,

(iii)   Lead lines or sounding line,

(iv)   Sounding chain and sounding machine,

(v)   Echo sounding apparatus known as fathometer.

(i)   Sounding Boat : A roomy (i.e. spacious), stable row boat should be round-bottomed for rough waters, whereas for quiet water, a flat-bottomed one is preferred. In case of strong water currents accompanied by fast wind, a motor or steam launch may be suitable.

(ii)   Sounding Poles or Rods : It is a pole or rod made of sound, well seasoned timber usually 4 to 8 cm in diameter and about 4 to 8 m long. For easy transportation, they may be manufactured in pieces of 1 to 1.5 m length and easily joined to each other at the time of soundings. An iron or lead shoe provided at the bottom of the rods enables to hold them vertical in the water. The sufficient area provided at their bottom helps in preventing the sinking of the rod in the mud, sand etc. accumulated at the bottom of water body. The sounding pole or rod being graduated from its bottom upwards in metre, tenths of metre and hundredth of metre, the reading on the rod (i.e. where the uppermost surface of water touches the sounding rod or pole) is the required sounding to be recorded.

(iii) Lead Line (or Sounding Lines) : It is usually a line of hemp, or cotton or a brass chain provided with lead at the bottom. Due to the prolonged use of cotton or hemp line in water, it is likely to be stretched and will not maintain its original length. To guard against this error, it should be thoroughly stretched in wet condition and graduated afterwards. To be on safer side, its length should be compared before use with the standardized tape. Lead lines are generally used for water depths exceeding 6 m. The weight made up of lead attached to end of the lead line is known as sounding lead. It is conical in shape and weighs from 20 to 120 N depending upon the depth and strength of water current. A cup shaped cavity provided at its bottom is filled with fallow for picking up the samples at the bottom of the water body. An eye provided at its top enables it to be fastened to the lead line.

(iv) Sounding Chain or Machine : When extensive sounding is to be done, a sounding machine is used. The machine may be operated manually or automatically. It consists of a wire, wound round a drum with a lead weight of about 80 N, attached at its end. It is provided with two dials, one reading the depth in metres and the other reading to tenths of a metre. This sounding machine, which is mounted in a sounding boat, is used for depths upto about 33 m.

(v) Echo-sounding Apparatus i.e. Fathometer (Fig. 4.2) : For deep ocean soundings, an apparatus, called as *Fathometer,* is used. It consists of a transmitter, receiver and a recording unit. The depth of water can be ascertained by sending the sound waves from a point near the surface of water to the bottom of the water surface and back. The apparatus automatically records the depth of water according to the velocity of sound in a water where the observations are taken. The required depth may be read visually or graphically on a revolving roll, thus providing the real existing profile of the ocean.

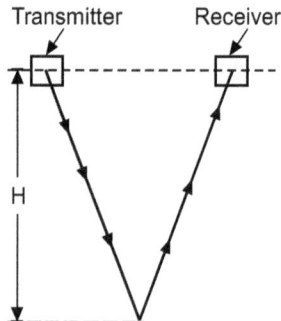

Fig. 4.2 : Echo-sounding

The apparatus, as shown in the figure, consists of a transmitting unit that sends the sound impulse to the bottom and a recorder or receiver that denotes the time required for the reflected sound impulse to return to the surface. Knowing the velocity of sound through the water medium v m/sec and the total time required for the travel say t seconds, the required depth H will be equal to $\left(\dfrac{v \times t}{2}\right)$ metres. As the transmitter and receiver are not installed at the same point but are separated slightly, the depth H computed will not be the required true depth. Therefore the computed depth is to be corrected suitably by using the property of a right angled triangle. It may be noted that echo sounding is an indirect method of sounding. The following are the merits of Echo-sounding system as compared to the conventional methods of sounding :

(a) Automatic recording of sounding and continuous plotting of profile.

(b) Ideally suited for strong water currents, where other conventional methods fail.

(c) The time required is comparatively less.

(d) The method is more accurate as compared to other methods.

Additional Equipments :

In addition to the above sounding equipments, the following equipments are also required for soundings :

(1) Shore signals,

(2) Buoys,

(3) Direction measuring instruments such as sextant or a theodolite.

(a) Shore signals : These are necessary for marking the range lines along which the soundings are to be taken. The signals should be conspicuous so that they can be seen from a long distance. If these signals are erected on the shore, they are known as shore signal. They are generally 10 cm square in section and are painted white and properly braced at the bottom to avoid wind effects. Flags of various colours may be used to distinguish these signals from each other. For shallow water, the shore signals may be used to mark the range line. However, in deep water, generally 'buoys' are used to mark the range line along the surface of water.

(b) Buoy : It is a float and consists of either a hollow air-tight vessel with increasing weight at the bottom, anchored properly so that it floats in vertical position. The buoy is made conspicuous by fixing a short flag pole in the hole bored from its top. The approximate length of the buoy may be upto one metre.

(c) **Instruments for the measurement of directions (sounding sextant) :** In order to measure the exact direction of the range line from the shore, a theodolite is used, but when such measurements are to be made from the sounding boat, a sounding sextant may be used with advantage.

Sextant [Fig. 4.3 (a)] :

It is a small portable, handy, precise instrument used for measuring horizontal and vertical angles from a sounding boat. It also measures oblique angles between two objects which are not lying in the same horizontal plane. It is similar in principle to the box sextant.

Referring to the Fig. 4.3 (b), aOb (H) and cO'd (I) are two mirrors. The mirror aOb which is half silvered, and fixed is known as *Horizon glass*, while the mirror cO'd, which is fully silvered and movable is called the *Index glass*.

MN is a one-sixth arc of circle (60°) graduated in degrees and one-sixth of degree. Let AEB be the angle to be measured, E, being the position of the observer's eye. As usual, the left hand object A is located by looking through the unsilvered portion of the horizon glass. The image of the right hand object B as seen through the silvered index glass is made to coincide exactly with left hand object A in the half-silvered portion of the horizon glass aOb, by gradually rotating the index arm O'P. It is evident from the figure that,

The exterior angle $OO'B = W + 2\alpha$

where W = the required horizontal AEB

i.e. $$2\phi = W + 2a$$

$$\angle AEB = W = 2\phi - 2\alpha = 2(\phi - \alpha) \qquad \text{... (4.1)}$$

Similarly from triangle OO'R,

$$\angle OO'G = \theta + \alpha$$

and $$\angle O'RO = \theta = \angle PO'Q$$

∴ $$\phi = \theta + \alpha$$

or $$\theta = \phi - \alpha \qquad \text{... (4.2)}$$

From (4.1) and (4.2), $$W = 2(\phi - \alpha) = 2\theta$$

∴ The required horizontal angle, $AEB = W = 2\theta$

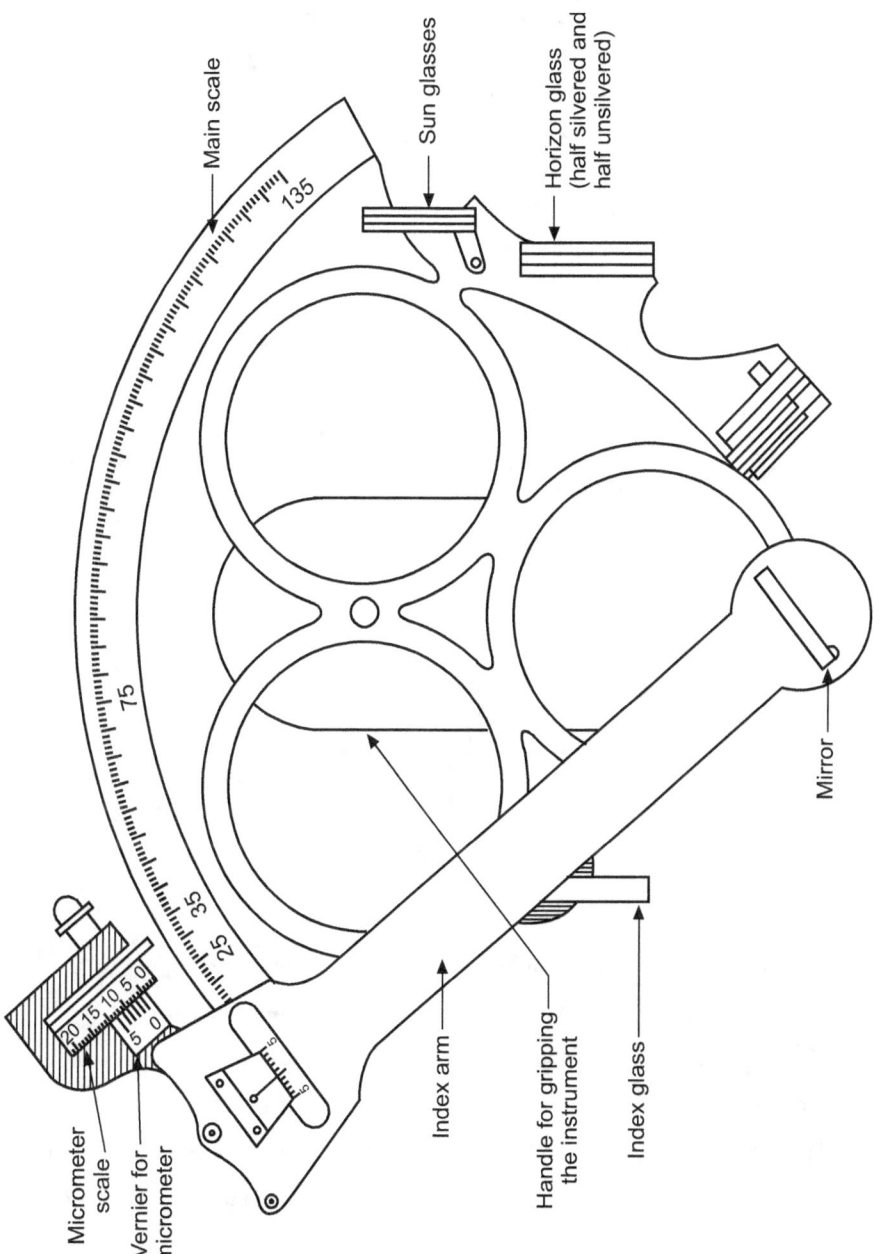

Fig. 4.3 (a) : Nautical sextant

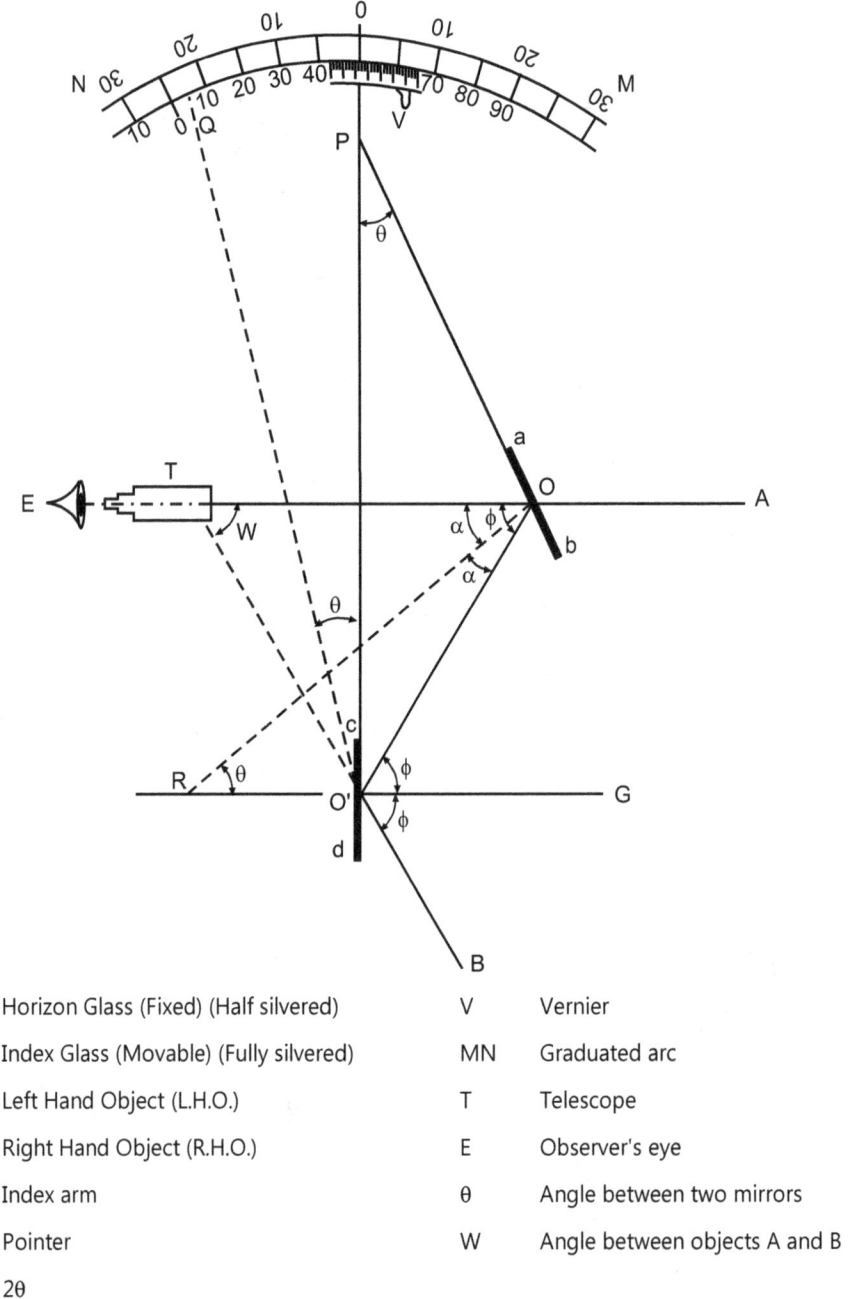

aOb	Horizon Glass (Fixed) (Half silvered)	V	Vernier
cO'd	Index Glass (Movable) (Fully silvered)	MN	Graduated arc
A	Left Hand Object (L.H.O.)	T	Telescope
B	Right Hand Object (R.H.O.)	E	Observer's eye
O'P	Index arm	θ	Angle between two mirrors
P	Pointer	W	Angle between objects A and B

W = 2θ

When angle between mirrors is θ, the angle between objects is 2θ which is directly read against the pointer along the arc length.

Fig. 4.3 (b) : Principle of nautical sextant

Thus, even if the graduations on the arc of circle sextant are upto $60°$ $\left(\text{i.e. } \frac{1}{6} \times 360°\right)$, it can very well be used for measurements of angles upto $2 \times 60°$ i.e. $120°$.

As already stated, the arc of the sextant is graduated in degrees and $\frac{1}{6}^{th}$ of degree and by means of vernier attached it can read upto 1' or 10". The instrument is also provided with coloured glasses to be used when bright objects are to be bisected.

The following adjustments should be satisfied by the sextant. :

(i)   Both the index glass and the horizon glass should be perpendicular to the plane of graduated arc i.e. plane of the sextant.

(ii)   When both the horizon and index glasses are parallel to each other, the reading under the vernier should be zero. If not, the small reading can be recorded as an Index error. If the zero of the vernier is on the scale or off the scale, the index error will be treated as negative or positive respectively.

(iii) The line of sight of telescope of the sextant should be parallel to the plane of sextant or plane of the graduated arc.

4.6 PERSONNEL REQUIRED FOR SOUNDING

The sounding party required consists of the following :

(i)   **Surveyor in charge of the work** who is overall responsible for the speedy completion of work.

(ii)   **Instrument man (or men)**, may be on the shore if the angular observations are taken by theodolite or will be on the boat, if the observations are taken with sextant.

(iii) **Record keeper :** Responsible for making immediate record of all the soundings, angular observations and the exact time of observation.

(iv)   **Leads man :** Responsible for making soundings and reading them loudly so as to enable the recorder to enter them in the field book.

(v)   **Boat men :** Responsible for rowing the boat along the desired ranges and to make boat stationary at the time of taking soundings.

(vi)   **Signal man :** Required when the angular observations are made from the shore. His job is to give signals to see that observations of soundings from the boat and the angular observations from the shore are done simultaneously.

4.7 RANGE LINES

Prior to making soundings, it is necessary to establish range lines along which the soundings are to be taken. Generally, they are laid on the shore, at right angles to the shore line and are therefore parallel to each other (Fig. 4.4). However, for irregular shore lines, they may be arranged radiating from a prominent shore object (Fig. 4.5). To make the shore line well defined, it is necessary to fix at least two shore signals on such lines. Each shore line should be accurately located either by triangulation, theodolite traversing or transit and stadia surveys. Depending upon the site conditions, the spacing of range lines may vary from 5 m to 25 m.

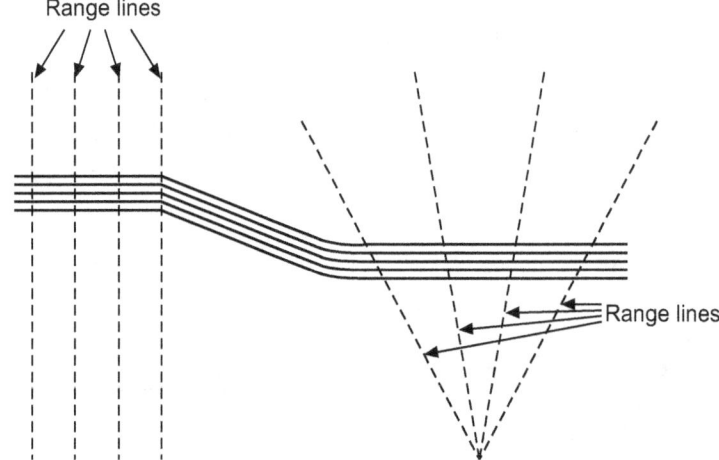

Fig. 4.4 : Parallel ranges   **Fig. 4.5 : Intersecting ranges**

4.8 OBSERVATION OF SOUNDINGS

For depths of water from 20 to 25 m, soundings may be observed from the moving boat.

(i) **Soundings with sounding rod :** If the sounding rod is used for sounding, the leadsman standing at the bow of boat plunges the rod in the water in the forward direction at such an angle that by the time the boat reaches the point at which sounding is to be taken, the rod touches the bottom and is vertical. The reading on the rod is the required depth of sounding. The leadsman will then read out this reading loudly so as to enable the recorder to enter it in the field book.

(ii) **Sounding with lead line :** When the sounding is carried out by lead line or sounding line, the leadsman standing at the bow casts the lead forward at such a distance, that by the time the boat reaches the point of sounding, the lead touches the bottom and the lead line becomes vertical. The reading is then taken and the lead is then withdrawn from the water. However, if the depth of water is greater than 10 m, the lead is not withdrawn from the water but simply lifted inbetween the soundings so as not to cause any obstruction to the movement of the boat in forward direction.

4.9 METHODS OF LOCATING SOUNDINGS

Whenever soundings are taken, it is necessary to locate the position of sounding with reference to some fixed known point on the shore established either by triangulation, theodolite traversing or tacheometry. The various methods employed for locating the sounding positions may be classified according to the place of observation which may be :

(i)   Exclusively from the shore observations.

(ii)   Exclusively from the boat observations.

(iii)   Shore cum boat observations.

Another method is, method of locating soundings using GPS.

4.9.1 Location of Soundings Exclusively from the Shore Only

The various methods are :

(a)   Location by tacheometry (i.e. transit and stadia).

(b)   By range and one shore angle.

(c)   By two angles from the shore.

(a) Location by Tacheometry i.e. Transit or Stadia Method (Fig. 4.6) :

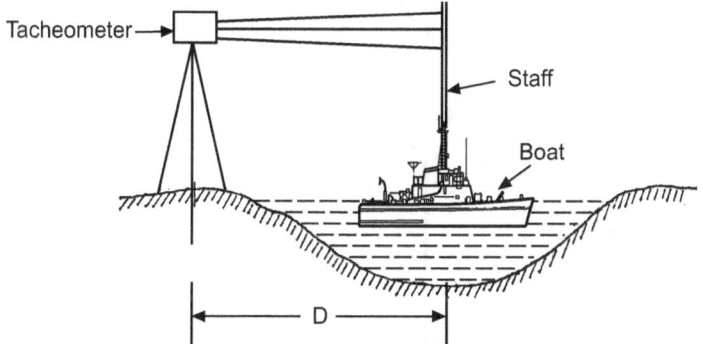

Fig. 4.6 : Transit and stadia or tacheometric method

The method, mostly adopted for smooth and shallow depths of water, is rapid and fairly accurate. A tacheometer is set up along the range line on the shore and readings are taken, on the stadia rod or staff held vertically on the sounding boat, at the instant of making soundings. The line of sight of the tacheometer placed near the water level should be kept horizontal so that it will not be required to read the vertical angle. Thus, horizontal distance of the position of soundings,

i.e.
$$D = \left(\frac{f}{i}\right) s + (f + d)$$

where $\left(\frac{f}{i}\right)$ and $(f + d)$ are multiplying and additive constants of the tacheometer and s is the staff intercept. In order to know the direction of sounding from the tacheometer, it is necessary to observe its direction by theodolite.

(b) By Range and One Shore Angle (Fig. 4.7) by Theodolite :

In this method, the sounding boat is rowed along the range line say BB' and the first point on the water where sounding is taken say B_1, is located by observing the angle with a theodolite set up at shore station A, established on the base line BA, set out at right angles to the range lines. Thus knowing the base distance 'd' (which can be actually measured on the shore) and the horizontal angle say α_1 to the position of boat B_1 at the time of first sounding, the horizontal distance $BB_1 = d \tan \alpha_1$. Similarly for the next positions of the sounding boat i.e. B_2, B_3, ... etc., the corresponding horizontal angles α_2, α_3, ... etc. are observed and the required distances computed.

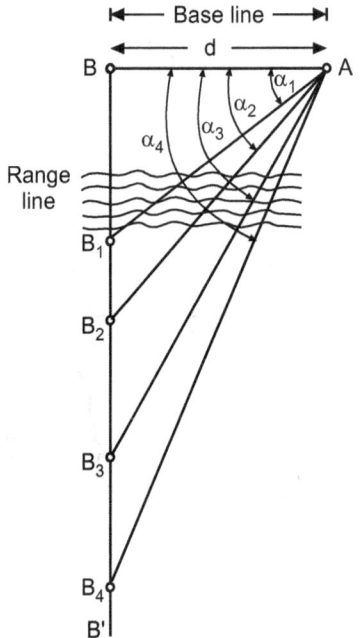

Fig. 4.7 : One angle from shore

It is an accurate method of locating soundings and also very convenient for plotting. The only drawback of this method is that the instrument man being on the shore and rest of the personnel on the boat, there is no better control of the surveyor, over the work. It is advisable to see that observed horizontal angles are greater than 30°, to avoid errors of plotting.

(c) By Two Angles from the Shore (Fig. 4.8) :

As the name suggests, the position of the boat at the time of soundings is located by angular observations taken from two shore stations say A and B, distance d metres (to be measured on the shore) apart. Both the stations A and B are connected to the horizontal controls established on the shore, by triangulation or traversing. For better accuracy in plotting, the two lines of sight of theodolites should intersect preferably at 90°. The procedure in short is to set up one theodolite at A with its line of sight directed towards B and the other at B, with its line of sight directed towards A, the horizontal circle reading on each being clamped at zero. When the boat comes to the point O, where the sounding is to be made, the lines of sight of both the theodolites are directed towards O, till the vertical hair of cross wires of theodolite exactly bisects the sounding rod or lead line held vertical from the boat for making soundings. The instant the sounding is taken, both the instrument men on the shore after getting necessary signal from the surveyor will observe the angle and record it in the field book. The point of intersection of the two lines of sight automatically fixes the position of the boat to be located.

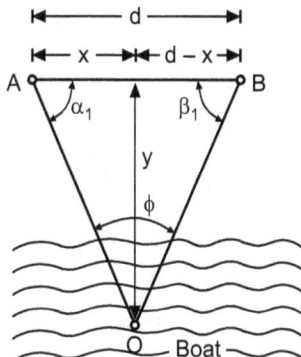

Fig. 4.8 : Two angles from shore

From the figure, knowing the horizontal distance 'd' between the two theodolite stations A and B and the observed horizontal angles α_1 and β_1, the two co-ordinates x and y required for plotting the position of boat O, at the time of soundings, can be calculated by the following relations :

$$x = \frac{d \tan \beta_1}{\tan \alpha_1 + \tan \beta_1}$$

and

$$y = \frac{d \tan \alpha_1 \tan \beta_1}{\tan \alpha_1 + \tan \beta_1}$$

Merits and Demerits of this Method :

Merits :

(i)　No necessity of setting out range lines and thus signals are not required.

(ii)　Very convenient for locating the soundings at the isolated points and also where strong current in water makes rowing difficult along a range line.

Demerits :

(i)　Method is laborious.

(ii)　No better control over the work by the surveyor.

(iii)　Two theodolites and two instrument men are required, thus increasing the cost of survey.

4.9.2 Location of Soundings Exclusively from the Sounding Boat Only

In this method, the soundings are located either :

(a)   By range and one boat angle or

(b)   By two (simultaneous) angles from the boat.

(a) By Range and One Boat Angle :

The method is similar to the "range and one angle from shore" with the difference that the angular observation in the present case is made with the help of sextant from the boat. The instrument man standing on the boat will observe the angle between the range line say BB_1 and some fixed known point on the shore, say A by sextant, the instant the sounding is observed. Thus, the required distance of the sounding boat at the time of sounding will obviously be equal to $d \cot \alpha$, where d = distance AB measured at right angles to the shore line, and α = observed angle from the boat with a sextant. Some of the advantages of this method over "range and one angle from the shore" are :

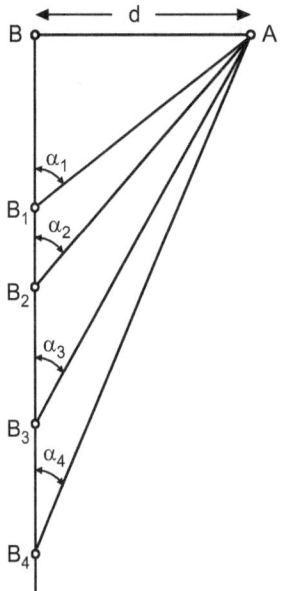

Fig. 4.9 : One angle from boat

(i)   As all the sounding party is on the boat, the surveyor has better control over the entire work.

(ii)   Mistakes in recording are also avoided as they are recorded immediately.

(b) By Two (Simultaneous) Angles from the Boat :

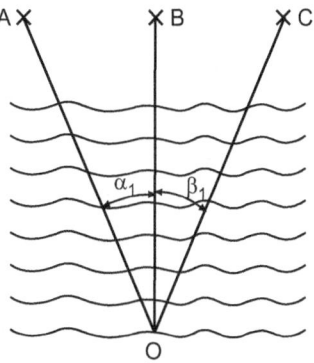

Fig. 4.10 : Two angles from boat

This method is similar to the "method of two angles from the shore". In this case instead of observing the angles from the shore, they are observed simultaneously from the boat with the help of sextants, to three well-defined known points on the shore, such as light houses, flag poles, church spires, towers etc. In the absence of such points, shore signals or range poles may be taken as reference points. Referring to Fig. 4.10, O is the position of the boat (at the time of sounding) to be located with reference to three well-defined known points A, B and C on the shore, by observing the angles AOB i.e. α_1 and BOC i.e. β_1 simultaneously with the help of two sextants preferably by two instrument men (one of them may be surveyor). If both the observations i.e. α_1 and β_1 are to be taken by the surveyor, very little time should be lost between the two observations, the respective angles being read afterwards.

The method is mostly used for location of soundings of isolated points, which are not connected by range lines.

4.9.3   Shore cum Boat Observations for Locating Soundings

A judicious combination of observations taken from the shore as well as boat enable the exact location of boat at the time of sounding.

The various methods are :

(a)   By range and time interval.

(b)   By one angle from the shore and other angle from the boat.

(c)   By intersection of ranges.

(d)   By cross-rope or wire.

(a) By Range and Time Interval :

After setting the range line by erecting shore signals, the boat is rowed at a constant known speed along the range line, the soundings being taken at regular decided intervals of time. Obviously, the distance of the point of sounding i.e. $D = v \times t$, where v is the velocity of the boat and 't' is the time required for the boat to reach the point of sounding. The method is most convenient for static water bodies having small depth and short distances. However, the accuracy obtained is less as it is difficult to row the boat along a range line at constant speed.

(b) By One Angle from Shore and the Other from the Boat (Fig. 4.11) :

To start with, the points A and B are selected on the shore, theodolite being set up at A and signal at B. When the sounding is taken at S, its position is located by observing angle α_1 with theodolite at A and angle β_1 i.e. $\angle$ ASB, observed from the boat with the sounding sextant. From the measured distance AB i.e. d, and with the observed angles α_1 and β_1, the co-ordinates x and y can be computed and the position of the boat located. The method is usually used for locating isolated sounding points.

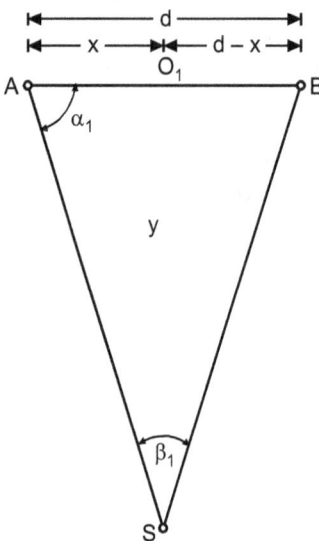

Fig. 4.11 : One angle from shore and other angle from boat

(c) By Intersection of Ranges (Fig. 4.12) :

The method is adopted when repeated periodic soundings are to be taken at the same points to ascertain the rate of silting or scouring in reservoirs, harbours etc. The ranges, which intersect each other automatically, locate the position of the boat at the time of sounding, no angular observation being required. The sounding boat starts moving along a range, at right angles to the shore line, the sounding being taken at the points of intersection of perpendicular and inclined range lines. All such intersecting points should be numbered and displayed by different flag colours to avoid confusion in identifying them from the shore.

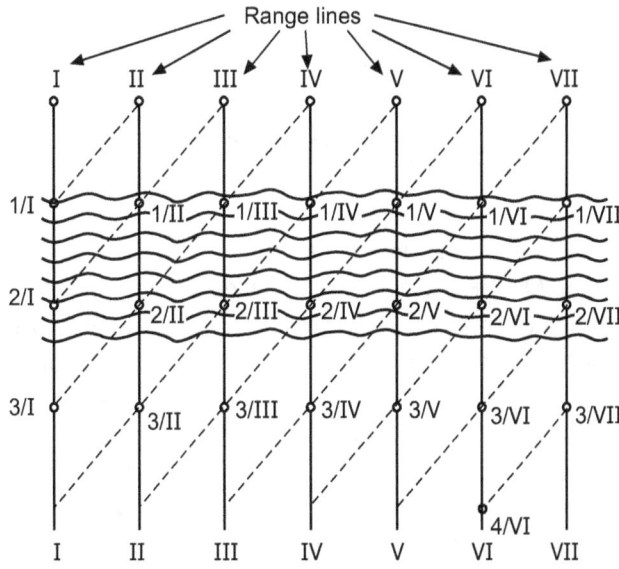

Fig. 4.12 : By intersecting ranges

(d) By Wire Rope Stretched Across a River (Fig. 4.13) :

A rope or wire with metal tags attached at regular interval is stretched across two fixed supports erected on the opposite banks of the water body e.g. river, harbours etc. The boat is rowed to these points whose distances are known from the beginning and soundings are observed by a weighted pole. The method, besides being accurate, is very expensive and is generally used when the cross-sections of the water bodies are to be plotted. The method can also be used for computing the quantity of material removed by dredging with two sets of sounding, one carried before and another after the dredging work.

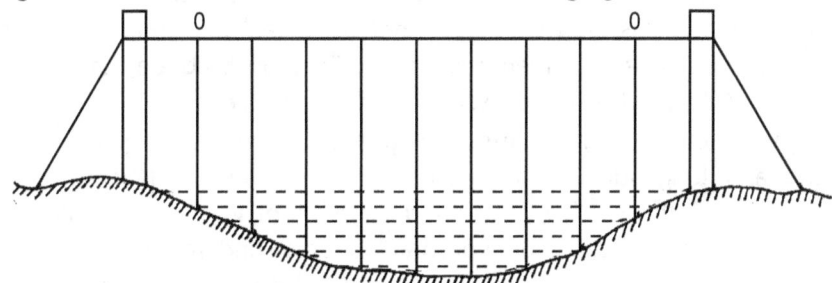

Fig. 4.13 : By wire rope stretched across a river

"Reel boat and sounding boat" method is usually adopted for harbour soundings. With the zero end of the wire (or rope) fastened to the one end of the shore, the reel boat starts moving towards the other end of shore, thus unwinding and stretching the wire rope. On reaching the other shore, the (other) end of the rope is firmly anchored and stretched. Then another boat called as a sounding boat, starts moving from the previous shore, along the wire (or rope) stretched and soundings are taken at the required interval. After the completion of sounding work, the reel boat is rowed back along the same wire-line, thus winding the rope again.

4.9.4 Method of Locating Sounding Using GPS

GPS is a system to define position of the points on earth's surface with respect to the reference points, the special purpose being navigational satellites in a space. While reducing position with GPS one does not requires collecting any kind of angular or linear measurement.

To determine the position of a sounding station with a GPS one will require holding the pre-initiated and switched ON GPS unit for the specified time at that station.

The position of sounding station may be determined in absolute positioning mode when very high positional accuracy is not expected. Positional accuracy of absolute positioning method may be enhanced by going for Precise Positioning System (PPS) than for Standard Positioning System (SPS). If still higher accuracy is expected, it is better to get incorporated the Differential Positioning System instead of Absolute Positioning System. It should be noted that, to determine position by Absolute Positioning we will require only one receiver unit; but in differential positioning one will require two units, one unit (Rover) on boat and other stationary unit (Base) on bank, at a point of known position and these two units shall be radio linked. If correction parameters for system wide errors are readily available through the radio link of an agency providing such data on commercial basis then one may eliminate the Base station on bank in differential positioning.

The planimetric position of sounding station is usually reduced in kinematic mode if fathometer is used to measure the depth of sounding. If depth of sounding is measured by sounding rod or sounding rope or sounding machine then position of a sounding station can also be worked out in static mode, provided sufficient time is available for GPS observations.

The accuracy offered by real time processing is sufficient to work out position of sounding station, but in case if system does not allow real time positioning and higher accuracy in positioning is desired, then it will be better to incorporate the post processing method to work out the position correctly.

The GPS gives the positions of the sounding in geographic co-ordinate system (i.e. in terms latitude and longitude) on imaginary datum 'World Geodetic System of 1984 (WGS 84)'. If required, this shall be converted in terms of local co-ordinate system and datum selected for plotting the data of hydrographic survey undergoing.

Locating position of the sounding station with GPS is much simple than conventional methods. It saves time and labour to considerable extent. It does not require any reference/control station/signal to be established on bank or within water body. Again the strength of fix achieved with GPS is much better than that by conventional method. Once upon time location of sounding with GPS was affordable only in ocean sounding, but with easy availability of GPS receiver at reasonable cost, now-a-days GPS can be used in hydrographic survey of rivers or reservoirs, harbourage or coastal areas.

4.10 REDUCTION OF SOUNDINGS

Whenever soundings are taken, they are with respect to the water level existing at the time of sounding i.e. these are the depths of bed measured below the water line and not with respect to the common datum. Thus, if the gauge reading at the time of soundings (i.e. actual water level) is also recorded, a necessary correction may be applied to the sounding to reduce the common datum.

i.e.
$$\begin{bmatrix} \text{Correction to the} \\ \text{observed sounding} \end{bmatrix} = \begin{bmatrix} \text{Gauge reading at the} \\ \text{time of sounding} \end{bmatrix} \pm \begin{bmatrix} \text{Gauge reading} \\ \text{of datum} \end{bmatrix}$$

+ve sign to be used if the gauge reading of datum is greater than the gauge reading at the time of soundings and vice versa.

The datum usually adopted is mean level of low water of spring tides and written as M.L.W.S. or as mean low water level of ordinary spring tides (i.e. L.W.O.S.T.).

e.g. if the M.L.W.S. = 2.00 m, and the mean gauge reading of the time of sounding is say 3.5 m, and the respective sounding recorded are say 1, 2, 3 and 4 metres, then the reduced sounding will be worked out as follows : Correction = 3.50 − 2.00 = 1.50 m. As the value of datum reading (i.e. 2.00) is less than the gauge reading at the time of sounding (i.e. 3.50), the sign of correction is negative. Thus, the reduced sounding would be :

(1.00 − 1.50); (2 − 1.50); (3 − 1.50); (4 − 1.50).

i.e.   − 0.50 m ; +0.50 m ; +1.50 m and +2.50 m respectively.

4.11 PLOTTING OF SOUNDINGS

(i) Conventional Method :

The routine plotting work is done in the following steps :

Step (i) : Plotting the shore survey : The entire shore survey carried either by triangulation, traversing or tacheometry is plotted on the plan to suitable scale.

Step (ii) : Next, range lines, reference points and the instrument stations selected on the shore are plotted on the above plan.

Step (iii) : The positions of the reduced soundings are then plotted with the help of observed angles, computed distances etc. and their numerical values (i.e. reduced soundings) are written against those points and as usual the underwater contours are drawn by interpolation technique.

(ii) Special Methods :

However, when the soundings are located by two angles from the boat with reference to three well-defined known points on the shore, the plotting can be done with any one of the following methods, that leads to the solution of three point problem.

Three point problem : Given three points A, B, C on the shore whose positions on the plan are known, and the two angles APB (i.e. α) and BPC (i.e. β), it is required to plot the position of the sounding boat P at the time of sounding. The problem is solved by any one of the following methods.

    (a)   Mechanical method,

    (b)   Graphical method, or

    (c)   Analytical method.

(a) Mechanical Method :

(1) Tracing Paper Method (Fig. 4.14) :

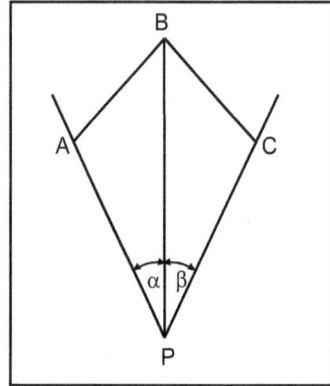

Fig. 4.14 : Tracing cloth paper method

On a tracing paper point P is arbitrarily taken and three lines PA, PB and PC are drawn so that ∠ PAB = α and ∠ BPC = β, α and β being actually observed by sextant from the boat. The positions of well-defined points A, B and C on the shore are then plotted on the plan to a convenient scale. The above tracing paper is then placed on the plan and adjusted in such a way that the lines PA, PB and PC drawn on the tracing paper simultaneously pass through the plotted points on the plan A, B and C respectively. The apex of the angles i.e. P is the required position of boat at the time of sounding and is to be pricked through by a needle.

(2) By Station Pointer (Fig. 4.15) :

A 'station pointer' also known as 'three arm protractor' consists of a graduated circle, in both the directions, from 0 to 360°, provided with three arms having a common centre, concentric with the centre of the graduated circle. The fiducial edge of the fixed middle arm coincides with zero reading on the graduated circle. The other two arms placed to the either side of the fixed arm are adjustable and can be clamped to any desired reading on the graduated circle. With the verniers and slow motion tangent screws provided, they can be set accurately to read upto 1'. The arms can be extended, if necessary, with extra lengthening pieces provided. In order to plot the position of boat P (at the time of sounding), the two movable arms are adjusted very precisely to the observed angles α and β and clamped. The station pointer is then placed on the plan and oriented so that the three bevelled or fiducial edges simultaneously pass through the plotted positions of A, B and C (on the plan). The centre of the station pointer is then the required position of P which can be marked on the plan by a pricker.

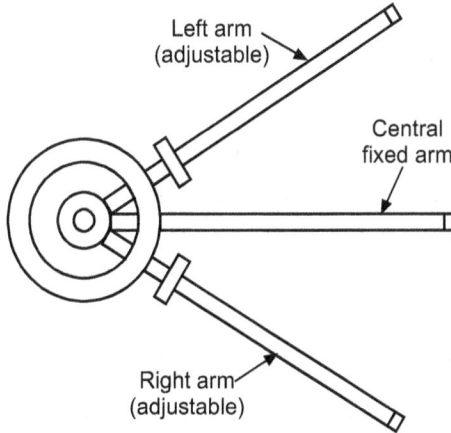

Fig. 4.15 : Station pointer

(b) Graphical Method :

The various methods of graphical solution are :

(1)   Circle method,

(2)   Intersecting circles method,

(3)   Cyclic quadrilateral method.

(1) Circle Method (Fig. 4.16) :

A, B, C represent the plotted positions of the three known points on the shore and α and β the observed angles by sextant from the position of the boat P.

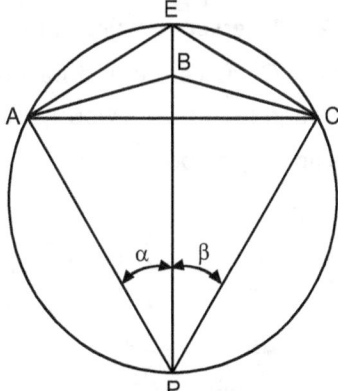

Fig. 4.16 : Circle method

Procedure :

(i)   Join A to C.

(ii)   From A and C draw lines AE and CE making angles equal to β and α respectively, intersecting at point E.

(iii)   Now, draw a circle passing through the three points A, E and C.

(iv)   Join E to B and produce it cutting the circle at P, which is the required position of the boat at the time of sounding.

Proof : Using the circle property,

$$\angle APE = \alpha = \angle ACE$$

and $\angle EPC = \beta = \angle EAC$

Thus, satisfying the required condition for solution.

(2) Intersecting Circles Method (Fig. 4.17) :

Let A, B and C be three given known points on the shore. Now, join A to B and B to C and from A and B, draw lines AO_1 and BO_1 towards P such that $\angle BAO_1 = (90 - \alpha) = \angle ABO_1$. Similarly from B and C, draw lines BO_2 and CO_2 such that $\angle CBO_2 = (90 - \beta) = \angle BCO_2$.

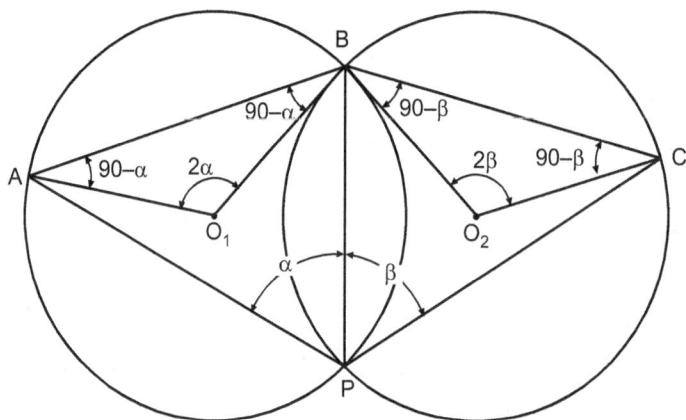

Fig. 4.17 : Intersecting circles method

Now draw two circles, one with O_1 as centre and passing through A and B and other with O_2 as centre and passing through B and C. Obviously the point at which the two circles intersect i.e. P is the required position of the boat P.

Proof : By the property of circles,

$$\angle AO_1B = 180 - [(90 - \alpha) + (90 - \alpha)]$$

$$= 2\alpha$$

and $\angle APB = \dfrac{1}{2} \angle AO_1B = \dfrac{2\alpha}{2} = \alpha$

Similarly, $\angle BO_2C = 180 - [(90 - \beta) + (90 - \beta)]$

$$= 2\beta$$

and $\angle BPC = \dfrac{1}{2} \angle BO_2C = \dfrac{2\beta}{2} = \beta$

Thus, $\angle APB = \alpha$ and $\angle BPC = \beta$ satisfy the given conditions for angles at P.

(3) Cyclic Quadrilateral Method (Fig. 4.18) :

(i)   Join AB and BC and at A and C draw perpendiculars AM and CN at A and B as shown in the figure.

(ii) Now, draw lines BM and BN so that $\angle ABM = 90 - \alpha$ and $\angle CBN = 90 - \beta$ and join MN.

(iii) From B, draw perpendicular to MN, the foot of the perpendicular being the required position of boat P at the time of sounding.

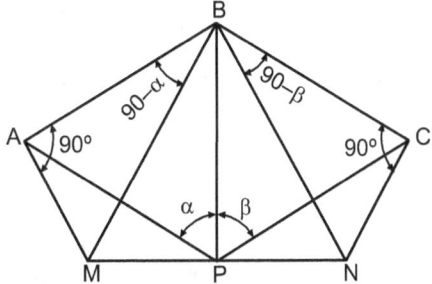

Fig. 4.18 : Cyclic quadrilateral method

Proof : $\angle BAM = 90° = \angle BCN$, the quadrilateral AMPB and BPNC are cyclic.

∴ $\angle APB = \angle AMB = \alpha$

and $\angle BPC = \angle BNC = \beta$

It may be noted that the problem becomes insoluble i.e. indeterminate when all the points A, B, C and P are concylic.

(c) Analytical Method :

Where high degree of precision is required, the analytical method is always preferred. Referring to the Fig. 4.19, let A, B and C be well-defined known points on the shore. It is required to determine the position of boat point P by taking observation to the above three points. Let the observed angles APB and BPC at P be α and β respectively. The points A, B and C are known and also the angle ABC and sides AB (i.e. c) and BC (i.e. a) are known :

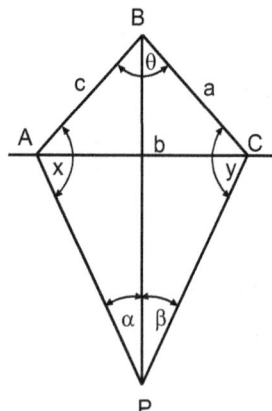

Fig. 4.19 : Analytical solution of three point problem

Let $\angle$ BAP = x

$\angle$ BCP = y

$\angle$ ABC = θ

x + y = ϕ = 360 – (α + β + θ)

As α, β and θ are known by actual measurements, value of ϕ can be calculated.

Consider triangle ABP.

Applying sine rule,   PB = $\dfrac{AB}{\sin \alpha} \times \sin x$

= $\dfrac{c \sin x}{\sin \alpha}$ ... (4.3)

Also, from triangle BPC,

PB = $\dfrac{BC}{\sin \beta} \times \sin y$

= $\dfrac{a \sin y}{\sin \beta}$ ... (4.4)

$\therefore$ Equating equations (4.3) and (4.4), we get,

$\dfrac{c \sin x}{\sin \alpha}$ = $\dfrac{a \sin y}{\sin \beta}$

or $\sin y$ = $\dfrac{c \sin x \sin \beta}{a \sin \alpha}$

But, ϕ = x + y

$\therefore$ y = $\phi - x$

∴   Putting $y = (\phi - x)$ in the above equation,

$$\sin(\phi - x) = \frac{c \sin x \sin \beta}{a \sin \alpha}$$

or $$\sin \phi \cos x - \cos \phi \sin x = \frac{c \sin x \sin \beta}{a \sin \alpha}$$

or dividing both the sides of the equation by $\sin \phi \sin x$, we get,

$$\frac{\cos x}{\sin x} - \frac{\cos \phi}{\sin \phi} = \frac{c \sin x \cdot \sin \beta}{a \sin \alpha} \times \frac{1}{\sin \phi \sin x}$$

or $$\cot x - \cot \phi = \frac{c \sin \beta}{a \sin \alpha \sin \phi}$$

∴   Rearranging the terms,

$$\cot x = \cot \phi + \frac{c \sin \beta}{a \sin \alpha \sin \phi}$$

$$= \cot \phi \left(1 + \frac{c \sin \beta \sec \phi}{a \sin \alpha} \right)$$

It can be seen that all the terms on the right hand side of expression being known, the value of cot x is known i.e. $\angle x$ is known and the value of $y = \phi - x$ is also known. Thus angles x and y being computed, we can now apply sine rule to the triangles ABP and BPC to compute the lengths of the sides PA, PB and PC, thus determining the position of the boat P.

i.e. In triangle ABP, applying sine rule,

$$PA = \left[\frac{c \sin(180° - \alpha - x)}{\sin \alpha} \right]$$

$$PB = \frac{c \sin x}{\sin \alpha}$$

and from triangle BPC, applying sine rule,

$$PC = \frac{a}{\sin \beta} \times \sin(180° - \beta - y)$$

$$PB = \frac{a}{\sin \beta} \times \sin y$$

It may be noted that the two values of PB obtained by above equations should fairly agree with each other which serves as a check over computations.

Depending on the position of boat P with respect to three known points A, B, C on the shore, the following cases are possible.

Case (i) : (Fig. 4.20) : Stations B and P lying on opposite sides of AC.

Here, $\qquad x + y \;=\; 360 - (\alpha + \beta + \theta) \;=\; \phi$

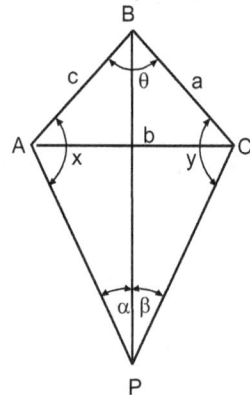

Fig. 4.20 : Case (i)

Case (ii) : (Fig. 4.21) : Stations B and P lying on the same side of AC.

In this case, $\qquad x + y \;=\; \theta - (\alpha + \beta) \;=\; \phi$

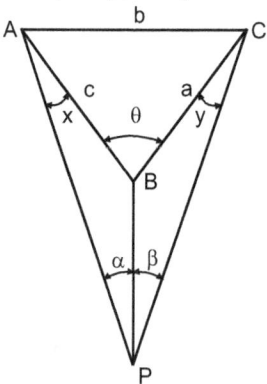

Fig. 4.21 : Case (ii)

Case (iii) : (Fig. 4.22) : When the station P lies within the triangle ABC.

Here, $\qquad x + y \;=\; 360 - (\alpha + \beta + \theta) \;=\; \phi$

Thus once the value of $x + y = \phi$ is known, the value of angle x can be computed by the equation for 'cot x' derived above.

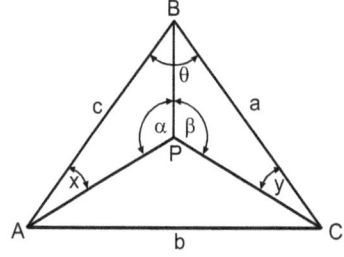

Fig. 4.22 : Case (iii)

4.12 TIDES

Introduction :

The tides, which are periodical variations in the level of water bodies, are generated mainly due to the gravitational attraction of the moon and the sun, the former being about 2.35 times greater than the latter. The attractive force always.

(i)   varies directly with the mass of the attracted and attracting bodies and

(ii)   inversely to the square of the distance between the bodies.

The tides are further classified as :

(i)   Solar tides generated due to the gravitational attraction between the earth and the sun and;

(ii)   Lunar tides generated due to the gravitational attraction between the earth and the moon. As the moon is comparatively nearer to the earth than the sun, the gravitational attraction from the moon is much more than the sun and it is a major force that produces tide.

Tidal Day :

The mean interval between two successive crossings i.e. transit, over a meridian is called Tidal day and is equal to 24 hours and 50.05 minutes. The mean interval between two successive high water tides is taken as 12 hours and 25 minutes.

Definitions of Terms :

(i)   Spring tide : It is the highest tide that occurs in a month and is generated on new or full moon when the combined attraction due to the moon and the sun is maximum.

(ii)   Age of the tide : The time lag between the theoretical spring tide and actual spring tide (that occurs somewhat late) is known as age of tide.

(iii) Neap tide : It is the lowest tide that occurs in a month and is generated when the gravitational attraction of the moon and sun are opposing each other. The interval between such successive tides is not constant, but each tide occurs 50 minutes later than the corresponding tide on the previous day.

(iv)   Astronomical lowest tide : The lowest possible tide is taken as a datum for reduction of soundings and is also known as astronomical lowest tide.

(v)   Equinoctial spring tides : When the sun and moon are vertically over the terrestrial equator, such tides occur and are very high.

4.13 TIDAL GAUGES

Introduction :

In sounding, the bed level of the water body is determined with respect to the existing water level at the time of making soundings. These soundings are to be further reduced to certain datum level. i.e. the existing level of water at the time of soundings must be related to some common datum whenever soundings are taken and this is achieved with the help of 'Tide gauges' installed at the sounding site. The datum commonly adopted may be either :

(i)   Levelling datum i.e. bench marks established by Central or State Govt. agencies generally used for all civil engineering projects, or

(ii)   Mean low water ordinary spring tides (M.L.W.O.S.T.) i.e. tidal datum commonly adopted for preparing navigational charts.

Classification of Tide Gauges :

The tide gauges are classified as : (a) Non-self registering tide gauges and (b) Self registering tide gauges, an observer being required to note down the gauge reading in the former, whereas the latter are automatic and are self registering, thus eliminating the observer.

(a) Non-self Registering Tide Gauges :

Some of the non-self registering tide gauges commonly used are as follows :

(1)   Simple staff gauge.

(2)   Float gauge.

(3)   Weight or chain gauge.

(1) Staff gauge :

It is the simplest form of tide gauge and consists of vertical staff about 15 to 20 cm broad graduated suitably in metres and tenth or twentieth of a metre of such a height that its top end is always above the water level and the bottom end remains below the water level. The zero of the staff gauge need not be at the bottom level (i.e. M.L.W.O.S.T.) but it may be at a convenient pre-determined level obtained by connecting it to the nearest standard bench mark. The location of staff gauge should be such that it indicates the level of the undistributed water surface and allows visual observations to be made from certain distance. These are generally used where the intensity of tides is low.

(2) Float gauge :

The generation of high waves in the water body may create difficulties in accurate reading of the staff gauge. In such cases, a float gauge is recommended. The gauge consists of a simple float supporting a graduated vertical staff, surrounded by a wooden box, 35 cm square in section. The box which serves as a stilling chamber, is open at the top. The holes provided at the bottom of the box, allow the water to enter inside and thus lifts the float. An index mark seen through the slit window, enables the accurate reading of the float gauge.

(3) Weight or Chain gauge :

A weight gauge consists of a weight attached to the graduated chain or wire, passing over a pulley. In order to measure the level of water, it is just necessary to lower the weight to touch the water surface, the reading being taken against the fixed index mark against the chain. In order to obtain the reduced level of the water surface corresponding to zero reading of the scale, it is necessary to hold the foot of the staff opposite to the bottom of the suspended weight and to observe its reading with a levelling instrument.

(b) Self-Registering Tide Gauges :

As the name suggests, it is a self-registering automatic gauge and is used where continuous records of water surface for a long time are required. It consists of a float, suspended in a chamber or well, connected to a wire passing over wheel kept under constant tension. The movements of the float are directly recorded by suitable gear arrangement by a pencil on the graph paper passing over a drum that rotates at constant speed by some clock mechanism. Thus a continuous automatic recording of changes in the level of water surface is available on a graph paper.

4.14 DATUM MEAN SEA LEVEL

In order to determine the exact mean sea level, it is necessary to have hourly observations extending for about 19 years and its average is taken as mean sea level. For all ordinary purposes, where high degree of precision is not required, mean of the observations taken during one lunar month will suffice the purposes. Thus, after the gauge of the m.s.l. is known, the reduced level of the bench marks established on the shore can be determined.

SOLVED EXAMPLES

Example 4.1 : In order to locate the position O of a boat, observations were made to three points A, B, C on shore.

The angles AOB and BOC were found to be 48°35' and 30°29' respectively. From the map, AB was scaled as 600 m and BC as 350 m, while the angle ABC measured is 158°39'. What were distances of O from A, B and C respectively ?

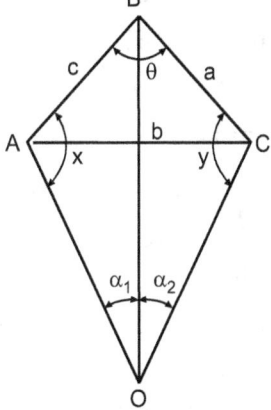

Fig. 4.23

Solution :

Data :   (1) $\angle AOB = \alpha_1 = 48° 35'$

            (2) $\angle BOC = \alpha_2 = 30° 29'$

            (3) $\angle ABC = \theta = 158° 39'$

            (4) $AB = c = 600 \text{ m}$

            (5) $BC = a = 350 \text{ m}$

            (6) $\phi = 360° - (\alpha_1 + \alpha_2 + \theta)$

                       $= 360° - (237° 43')$

                       $= 122° 17' = x + y$

$\therefore$ $\cot x = \cot \phi + \dfrac{c \sin \alpha_2}{a \sin \alpha_1 \sin \phi}$

$$= \cot 122° 17' + \frac{600 \times \sin 30° 29'}{350 \times \sin 48° 35' \times \sin 122° 17'}$$

$\therefore$ $\cot x = \cot (90° + 32° 17') + \dfrac{600 \times \sin 30° 29'}{350 \times \sin 48° 35' \sin (90° + 32° 17')}$

$$= -0.6318 + \frac{600 \times \sin 30° 29'}{350 \times \sin 48° 35' \times \sin 57° 43'}$$

$$= -0.6318 + 1.3720$$

$$= 0.7402$$

$\therefore$ $\cot x = 0.7402$

$\therefore$ $x = (90° - 36° 30')$

$\therefore$ $x = 53° 30'$

            $x + y = 122° 17'$

$\therefore$ $y = 68° 47'$

In Δ AOB, $\angle BAO = x = 53° 30'$

                 $\angle AOB = \alpha_1 = 48° 35'$

$\therefore$ $\angle ABO = 180° - x - \alpha_1$

                    $= 77° 55'$

$\therefore$ Distances OA and OB : By sine rule,

$$\frac{OA}{\sin \angle ABO} = \frac{AB}{\sin \alpha_1}$$

$\therefore$ $OA = \dfrac{AB \sin ABO}{\sin \alpha_1}$

$$= \frac{600 \times \sin 77° 55'}{\sin 48° 35'}$$

$\therefore$　　　　　　$OA = 782$ m

$$\frac{OB}{\sin x} = \frac{AB}{\sin \alpha_1}$$

$\therefore$　　　　　　$OB = \dfrac{AB \sin x}{\sin \alpha_1}$

$$= \frac{600 \times \sin 53° 30'}{\sin 48° 35'}$$

$\therefore$　　　　　　$OB = 643.00$ mm

In $\triangle$ BOC,　　$\angle OBC = \angle ABC - \angle ABO$

$$= 158° 39' - 77° 55'$$

$\therefore$　　　　　$\angle OBC = 80° 44'$

(i)　$\therefore$　　　　$\dfrac{OB}{\sin y} = \dfrac{BC}{\sin \alpha_2}$

$\therefore$　　　　　　$OB = \dfrac{BC \sin y}{\sin \alpha_2}$

$\therefore$　　　　　　$OB = \dfrac{350 \times \sin 68° 47'}{\sin 30° 29'}$　　　　　　$(\because \angle y = 68° 47')$

$\therefore$　　　　　　$OB = 643$ m

(ii)　　　　　　$\dfrac{OC}{\sin OBC} = \dfrac{BC}{\sin \alpha_2}$

$\therefore$　　　　　　$OC = \dfrac{BC \sin OBC}{\sin \alpha_2} = \dfrac{350 \times \sin 80° 44'}{\sin 30° 29'}$

$\therefore$　　　　　　$OC = 680.5$ m

$\therefore$　　$OA = 782$ m,　$OB = 643$ m,　$OC = 680.5$ m

Example 4.2 : The $\angle APB = 30° 25'$ and $\angle BPC = 45° 25'$ are measured with a nautical sextant at a sounding station P with respect to three control stations A, B and C on bank. Stations B and P being on opposite side of line AC. AB = 4 km, BC = 4.99 km and AC = 8.169 m. Work out distance of the sounding station P from stations A, B and C.

Solution : Given :　$\angle APB = 30° 25' = \alpha$　　　　$\angle BPC = 45° 25' = \beta$

　　　　　　　　　$AB = 4$ km = c　　　　　　$BC = 4.995$ km = a

　　　　　　　　　　　　　　　　　　　　$AC = 8.169$ km = b

B and P being on opposite side of line AC.

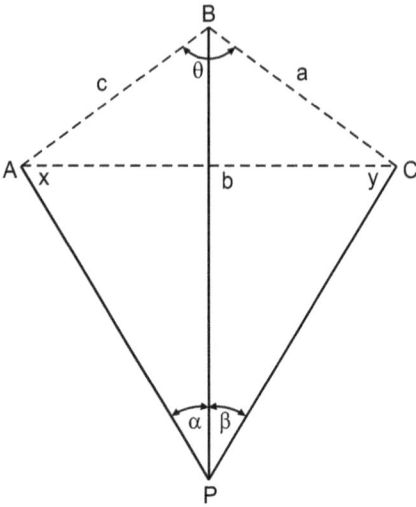

Fig. 4.24

Let us first workout $\angle ABC = 0$

We know, $\qquad b^2 = c^2 + a^2 - 2 \cdot c \cdot a \cdot \cos \theta \ldots$ (cosine rule)

∴ $\qquad 8.169^2 = 4^2 + 4.995^2 - 2 \times 8.169 \times 4 \times \cos \theta$

∴ $\qquad 2 \times 8.169 \times 4 \times \cos \theta = 4^2 + 4.995^2 - 8.169^2$

∴ $\qquad \theta = \cos^{-1} \left[\dfrac{(4^2 + 4.995^2 - 8.169)^2}{(2 \times 8.169 \times 4)} \right] = 113° \ 14' \ 9''$

We know, $\qquad (x + y) = \phi$ and when B and P are on opposite side of AC,

$\qquad \phi = 360 - (\alpha + \beta + \theta)$

∴ $\qquad \phi = 360 - (30° \ 25' + 45° \ 25' + 113° \ 14' \ 9'') = 170° \ 55' \ 51''$

We also know, $\qquad \cot x = \cot \phi + \dfrac{c \cdot \sin \beta}{a \cdot \sin \alpha \cdot \sin \phi}$

∴ $\qquad \cot x = \cot 170° \ 55' \ 51'' + \dfrac{4 \cdot \sin 45° \ 25'}{4.995 \times \sin 30° \ 25' \cdot \sin 170° \ 55' \ 51''}$

$\qquad\qquad = 0.882$

But $\qquad \cot x = \dfrac{1}{\tan x}$

∴ $\qquad \dfrac{1}{\tan x} = 0.882$ or $\tan x = \dfrac{1}{0.882} = 1.134$

∴ $\qquad y = \tan^{-1} (1.134) = 48° \ 35' \ 16'$

∴ $\qquad y = \phi - x = 170° \ 55' \ 51'' - 48 \cdot 35' \ 16' = 122° \ 20' \ 35''$

Applying sine rule to $\triangle$ ABP,

$$PB = \frac{c \cdot \sin x}{\sin \alpha} = \frac{4 \times \sin 48' \, 35' \, 16'}{\sin 30° \, 25'} = 5.925 \text{ km}$$

$$PA = \frac{c \cdot \sin (\angle ABP)}{\sin \alpha} = \frac{c \cdot \sin (180 - \alpha - x)}{\sin \alpha}$$

$$= \frac{4 \times \sin (180 - 30° \, 25' - 48° \, 35' \, 16')}{\sin 30° \, 25'} = 7.756 \text{ km}$$

Applying sine rule to $\triangle$ CBP

$$PC = \frac{a \cdot \sin (\angle CBP)}{\sin \beta} = \frac{a \cdot \sin (180 - \beta - y)}{\sin \beta}$$

$$= \frac{4.995 \times \sin (180 - 45° \, 25' - 122° \, 20' \, 35'')}{\sin 45° \, 25'} = 1.487 \text{ km}$$

$$PB = \frac{a \cdot \sin y}{\sin \beta} = \frac{4.995 \times \sin 122° \, 20' \, 35''}{\sin 45° \, 25'}$$

$$= 5.925 \text{ km}$$

$\therefore$ PA = 7.756 km, PB = 5.925 km, PC = 1.487 km

THEORETICAL QUESTIONS

1. What is hydrographic survey ? State the various objects of carrying out hydrographic survey.

2. Describe how a shore line survey is conducted in hydrographic surveying.

3. State in brief the application of hydrographic surveying in the Civil Engineering field.

4. What are the various steps involved in conducting river survey ?

5. What is meant by 'Soundings' ? State the various methods of locating soundings and explain any two methods in details.

6. In case of hydrographic surveying, explain clearly the use of the following :

   (a) Tidal gauges,

   (b) Nautical sextant,

   (c) Station pointer,

   (d) Sounding chain.

7. Explain the various types of tidal gauges and their importance in hydrographic survey.

8. State the necessity and uses of tidal gauges. Explain any two types of tide gauges.

9. (i)   State the objects of carrying out hydrographic survey.

    (ii)   You are assigned the work of measuring the discharge of a river 60 m wide. Explain the procedure that you will adopt to accomplish this task.

    (iii) Define three point problem in hydrographic survey. Explain how you will solve it by using the station pointer.

10. Write short note on Echo-sounders.

11. Explain the following :

    (i)   Method of locating sounding by range and one angle from the boat.

    (ii)   Use of station pointer in locating the position of sounding.

    (iii) Locating the position of sounding with the help of nautical sextant.

    (iv)   Fathometer.

12. What is three point problem in hydrographic surveying ? When does it becomes indeterminate ? Show how the problem is solved by :

    (i)   Calculations and

    (ii)   Graphically.

13. Explain clearly the analytical method of determining the position of a boat, in hydrographic surveying, by the method of two angles from the boat.

14. Explain clearly how would you determine the levels of points on the river bed and fix the positions of the soundings of a navigation channel –

    (i)   by use of sextant in a boat.

    (ii)   by use of theodolite on the shore.

15. State the various methods of solving three point problems in hydrographic surveying and explain clearly the analytical method.

16. Explain clearly how you would determine the bed levels of river having flowing water depth upto 5 m and locate the positions of soundings –

    (i)   by use of nautical sextant in the boat.

    (ii)   by use of transit theodolite on the shore.

17. In case of hydrographic surveying explain clearly the following :

    (i)   Sounding,

    (ii)   Ranges,

    (iii)   Tidal gauges,

    (iv)   Station pointer.

18. With the help of neat sketch, explain how would you make the use of station pointer for location of the station in hydrographic survey.

19. Name the different methods of locating soundings. What are the relative merits and demerits ?

20. What is meant by three point problem in hydrographic surveying ? Explain how would you solve the same using a station pointer.

21. Explain how tides are produced. What are their effects on the mean sea level ?

22. How do you measure the velocity and discharge of the flowing water in a stream ?

23. Explain the following methods of locating soundings in hydrographic surveying giving the advantages of each method.

    (i)   Range and angle from shore.

    (ii)   Range and angle from boat.

    (iii)   Two angles from shore.

24. What are soundings ? How are they taken, reduced and recorded ? State the equipment and personnel required for taking the soundings.

25. (i)   What are the uses of hydrographic surveying ?

    (ii)   What do you understand by submarine contours ? What are the advantages ?

26. What do you understand by shore line survey ?

27. What do you understand by Echo-sounding ? Give its advantages.

28. Explain the following :

    (i)   Staff gauge.

    (ii)   Float gauge.

    (iii)   Weight gauge.

29. Describe the scope and purpose of multifarious work of hydrographic surveying which a civil is likely to encounter during his professional carrier.

30. Write short note on Tides.

31. What is meant by sounding and sounding rod ?

32. 'Location of shore points by the two angles from boat can be done'. Discuss this statement.

33. Explain the principle of echo sounding.

34. Write short note on current meter.

35. What is meant by sounding ? State the equipment and persons for locating soundings. Describe briefly the various methods of locating soundings.

36. Describe with the aid of sketches the following :

    (a) How the profile of a bed of a river approximately 100 m wide and having a minimum depth of 5 m may be determined ?

    (b) Three methods of locating soundings of shore.

37. (i) What is an echo sounder ? How it works ?

    (ii) Sextant is an instrument used in hydrographic survey.

        (a) What is the ethymology (or root or origin) of the word sextant ?

        (b) Why it is so called ?

        (c) Who is credited for developing this instrument ?

        (d) If sextant is to be used on land, it requires a companion. Name it.

38. Explain clearly how you would determine the levels of river bed and fix the positions of sounding –

    (a) by use of a sextant in a boat.

    (b) by use of a theodolite on the shore.

39. (i) Explain different objects of hydrographic survey. How are the surveys conducted ?

    (ii) Describe in detail the sounding party and the equipment for sounding in hydrographic surveying.

40. Given a small boat, current meter, sounding rod, ropes, poles, transit, floats and assistants, explain how would you determine the discharge of a small river of width about 40 m and maximum depth 4 m. Illustrate your explanation with a cross section, showing depth areas, velocities etc.

41. (i) How is mean sea level established at a place ?

   (ii) The m.s.l. of India before partition of 1947 was the m.s.l. of Karachi. What is it now ? Comment on it.

   (iii) What is a fathom ? Is it still in vogue ? Why ?

   (iv) What are the particulars furnished in a Nautical chart for use of sailors ?

42. What is an echo sounder ? Briefly explain how it works.

43. Distinguish between the following :

   (i) Flood tide and Ebb tide.

   (ii) High tide and low tide.

   (iii) Spring tide and neap tide.

   One method of locating soundings uses "three-point problem". What are the instruments used in the field and in the office ?

44. (i) What are tides ? How are they caused ? How are they predicted ?

   (ii) Define sounding. List four important methods of locating soundings in sea.

   (iii) Briefly describe how a stream discharge can be gauged.

45. Briefly discuss with neat sketches, how the velocity of a stream can be measured.

NUMERICAL PROBLEMS

1. Observations were made with a sextant at point A to three points P, Q and R on the shore, the point A being outside the triangle PQR and on the same side of PR as Q. The observed angles $\angle$ PAQ, $\angle$ QAR were 28° 47' and 47° 31' respectively. The lengths PQ, QR and RP were scaled from the map and found to be 1640 m, 2000 m and 3000 m respectively. Find the distances of 'A' from P, Q and R.

2. In order to locate the positions of a boat, observations were made with a sextant to three points A, B and C on shore. The angles AOB and BOC were found to be 50° 56' and 27° 23' respectively. From the map, AB was scaled as 394 m and BC as 198 m while the angle ABC measured 163° 18'. What were the distances of O from A, B and C respectively.

   Ans. : $\angle$ x = 51° 25' 14", OB = 396.2 m, OA = 495.70 m, OC = 429.7 m.

3. In order to locate the position of the sounding boat S_1, observations were made to three shore stations A, B and C. The available data are as follows :

   $\angle AS_1B = 50° 56'$, $\angle BS_1C = 27° 23'$, Distance AB = 343.3 m,

   Distance BC = 220.0 m, Angle ABC = 163° 18'.

   The boat position S_1 was on the opposite side of B with respect to AC. Find the distance S_1 from A, B and C.

4. The sides AB and BC of a triangle ABC with stations in clockwise order are 2001 m and 3144 m respectively and angle ABC is 120° 24'. Outside this triangle, a station O is established, the stations B and O being on the opposite sides of AC. The position of O is to be found by three point resection on A, B and C, the angles AOB and BOC being respectively 25° 10' and 34° 26'. Could you locate O with reference to A, B and C ?

UNIT V

REMOTE SENSING

5.1 INTRODUCTION TO REMOTE SENSING

In every situation a civil engineer as a project manager has to take technically sound and economically feasible decisions in planning, design and execution phases of the project in his charge. Effective decisions cannot be made in absence of adequate information. To generate such information lot of raw, descriptive and locational data about different items or phenomenon related with a project is required to be made available directly or indirectly. Such data when processed through an information system yields information required for decision making. Many times the size of such data is very large, and it is spread over a wide area, it does have lots of aspects and its collection in stipulated time and budget is almost not possible. Much of such data can be made available by the way of Remote Sensing.

Remote sensing is a technique of knowing about something without going in physical contact of it. It is a method used to study physical and/or chemical characteristics of objects from distance. Sight, smell and hearing are all basic forms of remote sensing. Another interesting example of remote sensing is the system which guides a bat while flying in night. However, the term remote sensing is restricted to the methods that make use of electromagnetic energy such as light, heat, microwave etc. for detection and measurement of the characteristics of the target objects remotely. Remote sensing is usually carried out with the help of sensors such as photographic camera, multi-spectral scanner, radar etc. mounted on platforms like balloon or aircraft or satellite. The idea of remote sensing came into existence in 19th century from interpretation of the objects or phenomenon from the photographs. In Remote Sensing the information about earth's environment and its natural and cultural resources is gathered through aerial photographs and satellite images.

5.2 DEFINITION OF REMOTE SENSING

Remote sensing is the science and art of obtaining information about an object, area or phenomenon through analysis of data acquired by a device which is not in physical contact of it.

5.3 NECESSITY AND IMPORTANCE OF REMOTE SENSING

With advancement in medical science population is increasing perpetually and with ever developing economy standard of living is rising day by day. This is putting increasing pressure on natural and artificial resources and infrastructure. Hence, it is necessary to manage the available limited resources and costly infrastructure effectively and economically and also plan for fulfilling the shortfall in both of them. This requires periodic preparation of accurate inventories of resources and schedules for the availability, performance and condition of the infrastructure. This can be achieved through Remote Sensing very effectively since it provides data spread over time about almost everything on surface of earth. This data if converted into information, will be useful for inventory, monitoring and management of resources and infrastructure.

5.4 APPLICATION AND SCOPE OF REMOTE SENSING

Remote sensing data (aerial photographs and satellite images) provides a record of topographical features of the area over time. The abundance of information in a photograph is much greater than that provided by any other cartographic device (cartography is an art and science of map making). The camera/sensor often exposes the ground information that would have been ordinarily missed by a human eye.

Developments in space technology have greatly enhanced the capabilities of resource survey and mapping. Remote sensing has found many applications in the study of Earth's resources, mainly on account of repetitive coverage of large area at a glance, to gather information in real time. Data acquired by remote sensing has been successfully used in the field of topographic mapping, mineral exploration, snow hydrology, reservoir sedimentation, river morphology, water resource management and assessment, watershed conservation, flood estimation, geological investigations, land use/land cover mapping, planning or development of human settlements and communication routes, crop growth monitoring and crop yield forecasting, natural hazard studies (such as that for earthquake, landslides, land subsidence, floods, tsunamis), metrological studies, archeological studies etc.

5.5 PRINCIPLE OF REMOTE SENSING

The reflected electromagnetic energy from everything on and around surface of the earth is different than the electromagnetic energy incident on it. This difference in energy is coming into play on account of interaction of the electromagnetic energy with the ground object/phenomenon. The degree of interaction is dependent on the characteristics of the objects. Hence, the reflectance from the objects can be used in their identification and quantification of their condition or status.

5.6 PROCESS OF REMOTE SENSING

The two basic processes involved in Remote Sensing are : (a) Data acquisition and (b) Data analysis.

1. **Data acquisition :** It involves source of energy (*Electro Magnetic Radiations, EMR*) propagated through atmosphere, the interaction of energy waves with the objects, the reflected energy waves sensed through a suitable sensing system.

2. **Data analysis :** It involves a suitable interpretation device/system to interpret data, compiling the interpretation in graphical or other forms and presenting the data for decision making.

5.7 THE ELECTROMAGNETIC SPECTRUM

All matter radiates a range of electromagnetic energy which travels at speed of light and propagates even through vacuum such as outer space. The EM spectrum is continuum of energy that ranges from most energetic γ rays having wavelength less than 0.03 nanometres to radio waves having wavelength greater than 0.3 metres.

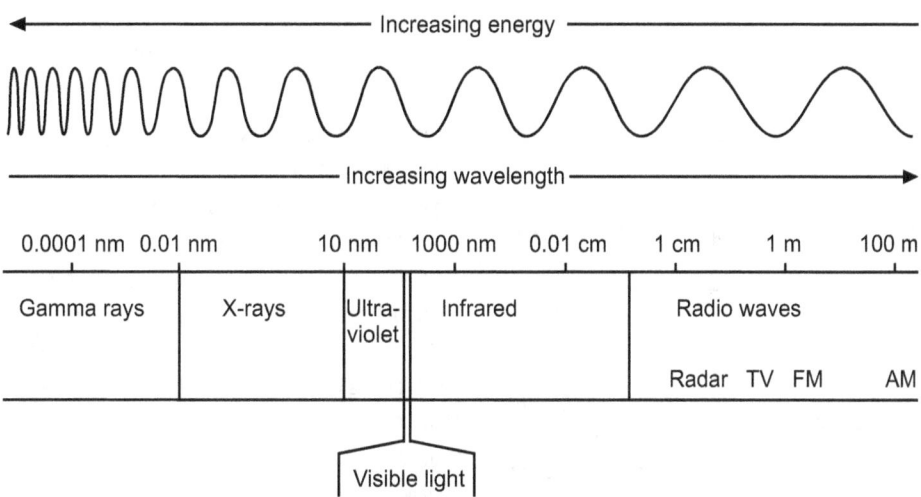

Fig. 5.1 : Electromagnetic spectrum

EM Spectral Regions, Their Suitability and Sensors Required to Sense Them :

1. Gamma Rays : Wavelength < 0.03 nm, such incoming radiations are completely absorbed by the upper atmosphere and are not available for remote sensing.

2. X Rays : Wavelength 0.03 to 3.0 nm, completely absorbed by atmosphere and is not employed in remote sensing.

3. Ultraviolet Rays : Wavelength 0.3 to 0.4 μm, incoming wavelengths less than 0.3 μm are completely absorbed by ozone in upper atmosphere.

4. Optical Region : The optical wavelength region (Wavelength 0.38 to 12.5 μm) is an important region for (passive) remote sensing applications, its further subdivision, principal applications, and sensors required to sense them are discussed in table below. Microwave region (1 mm to 1 m) is another portion of EM spectrum that is frequently used to gather valuable remote sensing information.

Table 5.1 : Optical Wavelength Region

Wavelength Region				Wavelength in μm	Principal Applications	Remark
Optical Region	Visible Region	Reflective Region	Blue	0.45 – 0.52	Coastal morphology and sedimentation study, soil and vegetable differentiation, coniferous and deciduous vegetation discrimination.	Only one of the many regions of EMS which is used maximum to acquire RS data for natural resource mapping. This wavelength band is usually referred to as light and may be sensed with films and photo detectors.
			Green	0.52 – 0.60	Vigor assessment, Rock and soil discrimination, Turbidity and bathymetry studies.	
			Red	0.63 – 0.69	Plant species differentiation.	
	Infrared Region		Near IR	0.76 – 0.90	Vegetation Vigor, Biomass, Delineation of water features, Land forms, Geomorphic studies.	The sensors operating in this region are Spectrometers, Radiometers, Polarimeters and Laser based active sensors.
			Mid IR-1	1.55 – 1.75	Vegetation moisture content, Soil moisture content, Snow and clod discrimination.	
			Mid IR-2	2.08 – 2.35	Differentiation of geological materials and soils.	
		Emissive or Thermal	Thermal IR-1	3.00 – 5.00	For hot targets i.e. fires and volcanoes	
			Thermal IR-2	10.4 – 12.5	Thermal sensing, Vegetation discrimination	

5. Microwave Region : Wavelength varies from 0.1 to 30 cm. Allows active form of remote sensing. The sensors operating in this region are radar, microwave radiometers, altimeters, scatterometers etc.

6. Radiowave Region : Wavelength 30 cm, longest wavelength portion of electromagnetic spectrum, not very greatly used in remote sensing.

5.8 AN IDEAL REMOTE SENSING SYSTEM

An ideal remote sensing system is a system which offers no flaws. Such system actually does not exist.

The basic components of an ideal remote-sensing system are as follows :

(a) A uniform energy source : This source will provide energy over all wavelengths, at a constant, known high level of output, irrespective of time and place.

(b) A non-interfering atmosphere : This will be an atmosphere that will not modify the energy from the source in any manner, whether that energy is on its way to earth's surface or coming from it. Again, ideally this will hold irrespective of wavelength, time, place and sensing altitude involved.

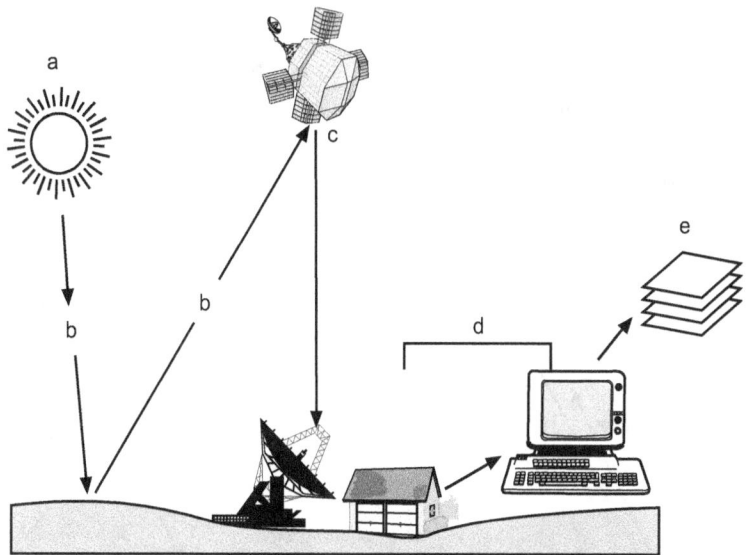

Fig. 5.2 : Idealised remote sensing system

(c) A super sensor : This will be a sensor, highly sensitive to all wavelengths, yielding spatially detailed data on the absolute brightness (or radiance) from a scene (a function of wavelength), throughout the spectrum. This super sensor will be simple and reliable, requires, virtually no power or space, and will be accurate and economical to operate.

(d) A real-time data handling system : In this system, the instant radiance versus wavelength response over a terrain element is generated; it will be processed into an interpretable format and recognized as being unique to the particular terrain element from which it comes (Radiance is the radiant flux per unit projected area and per unit solid angle, its unit is watts per m^2 per steradian). This processing will be performed nearly instantaneously (real time), providing timely information. Because of the consistent nature of the energy/matter interactions, there will be no need for reference data in the analytical procedure. The derived data will provide insight into the physical-chemical-biological state of each feature of interest.

(e) Multiple data users : These people will have comprehensive knowledge of both their respective disciplines and of remote-sensing data acquisition and analysis techniques. The same set of data will be used for various forms of information for different users, because of their vast knowledge about the particular earth resources being used.

5.9 TYPES OF REMOTE SENSING

Remote sensing can be classified as per source of energy and as per region of electromagnetic spectrum used.

(a) Types with Respect to the Energy Sources :

As per source of energy used in remote sensing it is divided into two types viz. (i) active remote sensing and (ii) passive remote sensing.

(i) Active Remote Sensing :

In this system, the sensing equipment emits radiation, which is reflected back from the object. An active sensor provides its own source of energy. Radar is typical example of such a system. The reflected radiations are analysed to determine the distance and presence of the object in the ranging area. Another common example of active remote sensing is flash photography.

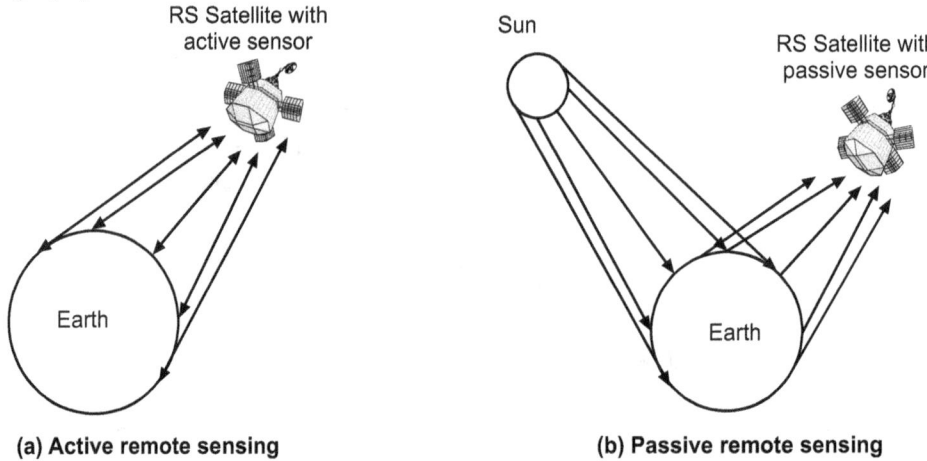

(a) Active remote sensing   (b) Passive remote sensing

Fig. 5.3 : Types of remote sensing with respect to the energy sources

(ii) Passive Remote Sensing :

In this system, the sensing equipment does not generates and emit radiation. The radiation from an external source is made available to the object. Passive system makes use of solar/natural radiations. The main advantage of passive sensors is that they are relatively simple, both mechanically and electrically, and do not have high power requirements. The disadvantage of passive sensor is that, particularly in wavebands where natural emittance or reflectance levels are low, high detector sensitivities and wide radiation collection apertures are necessary to obtain reasonable signal level. Another disadvantage of passive system is dependency on good weather conditions. Passive system is used more popularly than the active system. Still or motion picture or television cameras incorporate passive system of remote sensing.

(b) Types with Respect to Regions of Electromagnetic Spectrum :

As per regions of electromagnetic spectrum incorporated, remote sensing is divided in to following three types.

    (i)   Visible and Reflective Infrared Remote Sensing.

    (ii)   Thermal Infrared Remote Sensing.

    (iii)   Microwave Remote Sensing.

5.10 ATMOSPHERIC WINDOW

The region of the electromagnetic spectrum in which atmospheric absorption is minimum are called 'Atmospheric Windows'. It is through these 'Windows' that 'Remote Sensing' of the earth's surface takes place. Atmospheric windows used for remote sensing are 0.4 -1.3, 1.5-1.8, 2.2-2.6, 3.0-3.6, 4.2-5.0, 7.0-15.0 μm and 0.01 m - 0.1 m.

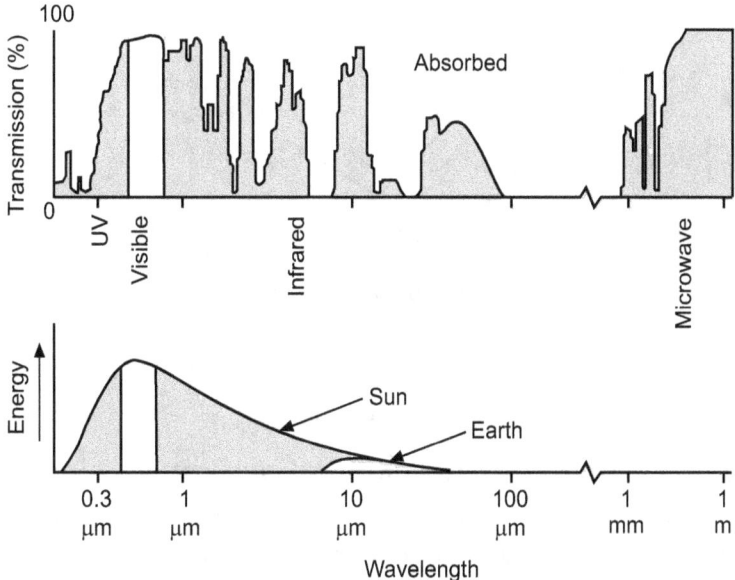

Fig. 5.4 : Atmospheric windows

These atmospheric windows are not totally free from atmospheric absorption. Even in atmospheric windows the gases and suspended particles in the atmosphere absorb the radiation from ground objects, resulting in decrease in radiation at the sensor and also emit radiation of their own, thus adding noise to the radiation at the sensor. The effects are very variable in space and time and often necessitates the atmospheric correction of remotely sensed data.

Some of the commonly used atmospheric windows are 0.38 to 0.72 μm (visible), 0.72 to 3.0 μm (Near and Middle IR), 8 to 14 μm (Thermal IR). Photography occurs through the visible window of 0.4 to 0.9 μm and thermal infrared sensing occurs through the two atmospheric windows at 3 to 5 μm and 8 to 14 μm.

5.11 INTERACTION OF EME WITH EARTH OBJECTS

Electro Magnetic Energy (EME) is perceived or sensed through its interaction with objects. When radiated EME strikes any object, it can interact with the object. The extent and manner of interaction of EME with a given object is dependent upon the physical and chemical nature of the object. The EME interacts with matter in any or all of following five ways.

(i)   Reflection,

(ii) Emission,

(iii) Scattering,

(iv) Transmission,

(v)   Absorption.

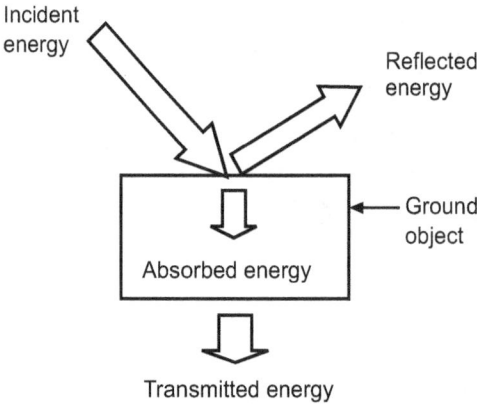

Fig. 5.5 : Interaction of EME with matter

Reflection, emission and scattering are called as *surface phenomenon*, as these are determined by properties at surface, viz. colour, roughness etc.

Transmission and absorption are called *volume phenomenon* because these are determined by the internal characteristics. Atmosphere selectively absorbs energy in different wavelengths with different intensity.

Different energy interactions result from different types of matter with different wavelengths. This can be differentiated by using different types of remote sensors which responds to different wavelengths. This enables different objects to be identified, discriminated and in some cases quantified.

Of all the interactions, reflection is most useful and helpful in remote sensing applications. Reflection occurs when a ray of light is redirected as it strikes a non-transparent surface. The type of reflection is dependent on the size of the surface irregularities relative to the incident wavelength. Whether a particular target reflects in specular or diffuse manner, or somewhere in between, depends on the surface roughness of the feature. Surface roughness is a function of the wavelength of incident radiation.

When a surface is smooth we get *specular or mirror-like reflection* where all (or almost all) of the energy is directed away from the surface in a single direction and the angle of reflection is equal to the angle of incidence. Radar instruments have a hard time identifying water bodies because the wavelength is much longer than the general character of the surface roughness. Specular reflectance helps and hinders remote sensing depending where the sensor is situated relative to the outgoing radiation.

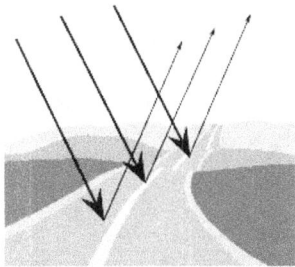 

(a) Specular reflection　　　　　**(b) Diffuse reflection**

Fig. 5.6 : Types of reflections

Diffuse reflection occurs when the surface is rough, relative to the incident wavelength and the energy is reflected (scattered) more or less uniformly in all directions. Diffuse reflection is also called as isotropic or lambertian reflectance. Many natural surfaces act as a diffuse reflector to some extent. A perfectly diffuse reflector is termed as a lambertian surface and the reflective brightness is the same when observed from any angle.

5.12 SPECTRAL SIGNATURE

Interaction of EMR with any object on earth's surface is selective by wavelength. Thus, same object will interact differently with different wavelengths of EME. Every object on the surface of the earth has its unique spectral reflectance at given wavelength of EM radiations. This brings ahead concept of spectral signature. The plot of spectral reflectance v/s wavelength is also unique for the given object and is known as 'spectral reflectance curve' or 'spectral signature'.

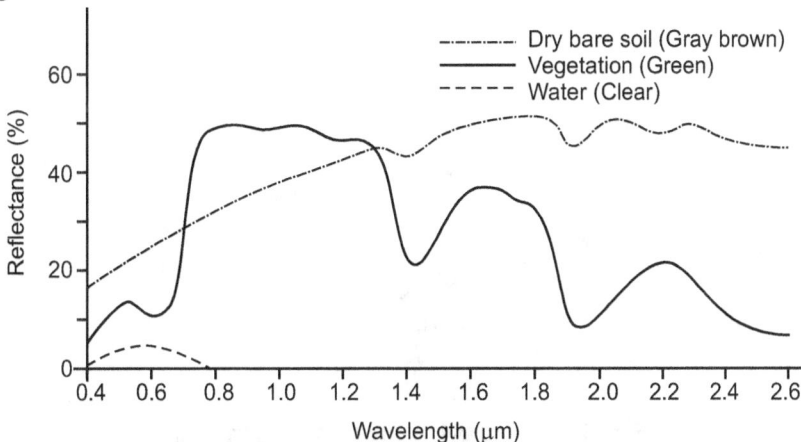

Fig. 5.7 : Spectral signatures or spectral reflectance curves

Everything in nature has a spectral signature. If we can detect that spectral signature we can separate features, and get an insight to the general size and shape of objects. Spectral signatures (spectral response patterns) change over time and space. Hence with available technology we cannot identify unique objects repetitively. We have to characterize surface targets based upon a spectral signature which allows for more error in identification.

5.13 PLATFORMS FOR REMOTE SENSING

Platforms are the devices on which the cameras or the sensors for the remote sensing can be mounted. The remote sensing platforms are broadly divided in two categories viz. (a) Air borne platforms and (b) Space borne platforms.

(a) Air Borne Platforms :

The air borne platforms mainly include balloons and aircraft.

(i) Balloons : These are suitable for specific projects of limited area. Its use is restricted by metrological factors, such as wind velocity, wind direction etc. Balloons can be free one or tethered one.

(ii) Aircrafts : These are suitable for regional coverage and large scale mapping. Flexibility in flying height and data acquisition as per need is the additional benefit. The RS aircraft should have capability to maintain maximum stability and to fly at uniform speed. In India Avro, Cessna and Canberra aircrafts are commonly used for aerial remote sensing.

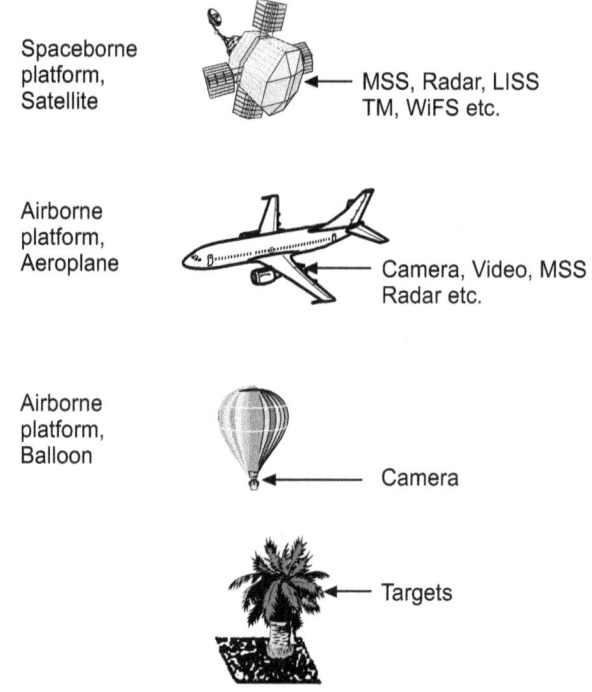

Spaceborne platform, Satellite — MSS, Radar, LISS TM, WiFS etc.

Airborne platform, Aeroplane — Camera, Video, MSS Radar etc.

Airborne platform, Balloon — Camera

Targets

Fig. 5.8 : Platforms for remote sensing

(b) Space Borne Platforms :

Space borne platforms (satellites) offer several benefits over airborne platforms. It allows observation of very large area in a single image (synoptic view) and systematic coverage repetitively. As they are situated in outer space, are less affected due to atmospheric drag allowing maintenance of orbit. Space borne platforms are further divided into two categories viz. (i) Geo-stationary satellites and (ii) Sun synchronous satellites.

(i) Geo-stationary Satellites :

These are positioned in equatorial plane at an altitude of 36000 km. They move with same velocity like that of earth. They are relatively in stationary position over equator with respect to earth. It continuously senses the earth and covers 1/3 part of the earth. About three geostationary satellites are sufficient to cover entire earth at a time. They are mainly used for meteorological, communication purposes but their use can be extended for natural resource assessment etc.　INSAT and GOES satellites are the example of geostationary satellites.

(ii) Sun Synchronous or Polar Orbiting Satellites :

They move in low earth orbit at 800 to 1000 km altitude over or near the earth poles. The orbit coincides with the plane of the sun, which means orbit remains in a constant plane relative to the Sun's position while the Earth spins below it. They visit/cross a particular place on the earth at a same local sun time within same season to ensure consistent illumination conditions and to provide repetitive coverage. These satellites provide global coverage with high resolution. Such data is primarily used for resource surveying and monitoring. LANDSAT, SPOT and IRS series satellites are the satellites of this category.

5.14 FEW REMOTE SENSING SATELLITE PROGRAMMES

(a) Landsat Satellite Programme :

National Aeronautical and Space Administration (NASA) of USA decided to launch a series of Earth Resource Technology Satellites (ERTS) and first satellite in the series was launched in 1972. Then after, NASA renamed ERTS programme as Landsat programme and the first ERTS satellite was renamed as Landsat 1, number of Landsat satellites have been launched so far. The images remotely sensed by Landsat satellites are finding useful natural resources management, land use and land cover analysis, civil engineering, cartography, environmental monitoring, agriculture, forestry, geology, oceanography, geography etc.

(b) SPOT Satellite Programme :

System Pourl Observation Dela Terre (SPOT) is the joint satellite programme for remote sensing of earth by three European countries viz. Sweden, Belgium and France. SPOT 1, the first satellite in the series was launched in early 1988. The SPOT is capable to supply high resolution image data. The SPOT data is specifically useful in transportation planning and urban planning in addition to natural resource management.

(c) Indian Remote Sensing (IRS) Satellite Programme :

India launched its first RS satellite Bhaskara I mid 1979 in co-operation with, then USSR. The second satellite in the series, the Bhaskara II was launched two years later Bhaskara I. Both of these satellites were under the programme "Satellites for Earth Observation (SEO)". Following the successful launching of Bhaskara series satellites, India began development of Indigenous remote sensing satellites known as IRS satellites. Until now, number of IRS series satellites viz. IRS 1A to 1E and IRS P1 to P6 have been launched followed by Resourcesat, Cartosat and Oceansat, series satellite. Data collected by this satellite is widely used in natural resource management, infrastructure planning, urban development, metrological applications etc.

5.15 REMOTE SENSORS

Remote sensor is an electro-mechanical device that sense in storable form, the electromagnetic radiations reflected or emitted by the objects on or around the earth, converts into signal that corresponds to the energy variations of different objects and present it in a form suitable for obtaining information.

The acquisition of data in remote sensing is dependent upon the sensor used. Various remote sensing platforms are provided with different type of sensors. A sensor simply record in selected spectral bands, the variation in amount of electromagnetic energy reflected or emitted by the earth objects. The signals from a sensor can be recorded and displayed in digital or image form. The strength of signal depends on different factors such as Instantaneous Field of View (IFOV), magnitude of energy recorded, spectral band width, altitude etc. A regular photographic camera is the most primitive and familiar type of remote sensor.

5.15.1 Types of Sensors

(i) Types of Sensors on the Basis of Energy Source :

On the basis of energy source, there are two types of the sensors, viz. passive sensors and active sensors.

An active sensor provides its own source of energy. Camera with flash or radar is the best example of an active sensor.

A passive sensor records the energy that naturally reflects or radiates from an object. Passive sensors cannot use at night time except Thermal Sensors. Passive sensors can be Optical imagers (works in visible band of EMS), Optical Infrared (OIR) Imagers, Thermal Sensors or Microwave sensors.

(ii) Types of Sensors on the Basis of Final Presentation of Signals :

On the basis of presentation of signals the sensors can be classified as imaging and non imaging sensors.

In case of *imaging sensors* the electrons released are used to excite or ionize a substance like silver (Ag) in film or to drive an image producing device like a TV or computer monitor or a cathode ray tube or oscilloscope or a battery of electronic detectors; since the radiation is related to specific points in the target, the end result is an image (picture) or a raster display (for example : the parallel horizontal lines on a TV screen).

The non-imaging sensors measures the radiation received from all points in the sensed target, integrates this, and reports the result as electrical signal strength or some other quantitative attribute, such as radiance.

(iii) Types of Sensors on the Basis of Recording the Scene :

On the basis of the way of recording the scene the sensors are classified as framing sensors and scanning sensors.

Sensors that instantaneously measure radiation coming from the entire scene at once are called *framing sensors*. The eye, a photo camera, and a TV camera belong to this group. The size of the scene that is framed is determined by the apertures and optics in the system that defines the *Field of View* (FOV).

If the sensor senses the scene point by point (equivalent to small areas within the scene) along successive lines over a finite time, it is called as *scanning sensor*. Most non-camera sensors operating from moving platforms image the scene by scanning.

The scanning sensors can further be divided in two categories viz. cross track scanner and framed scanners.

The *Cross Track* scanner normally uses a oscillating mirror to sweep the scene along a narrow line (few metres wide) traversing the ground that is very kilometres long. This is sometimes referred to as the Whiskbroom mode from the vision of sweeping a table side to side by a small handheld broom. The scan carried out by such a scanner is called as object plane scan.

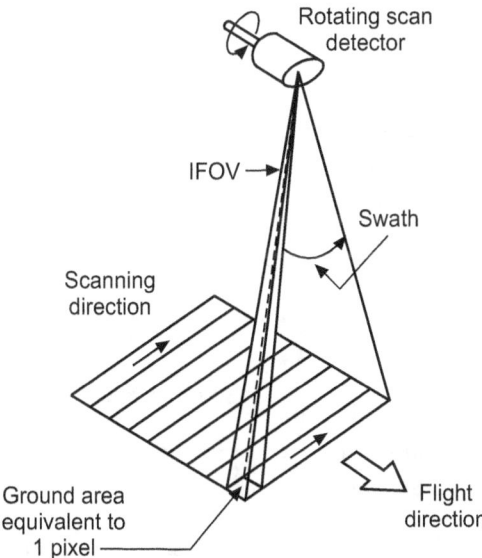

Fig. 5.9 : A cross track or whisk broom or object plane scanner

The *Along Track* Scanner has a linear array of detectors [Charge Coupled Device (CCD)] oriented normal to flight path. The Instantaneous Field of View (IFOV) of each detector sweeps a path parallel with the flight direction. This type of scanning is also referred to as push broom scanning from the mental image of cleaning a floor with a wide broom through successive forward sweeps. Scan carried out by such a scanner is called as *image plane scan*.

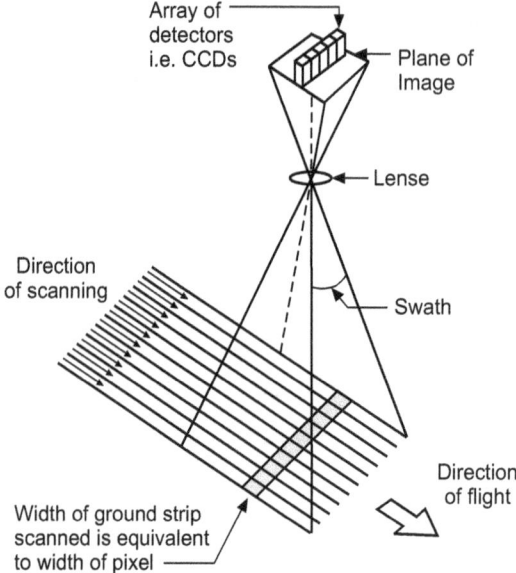

Fig. 5.10 : An along track or push broom or image plane scanner

Table 5.2 : Types of Sensors at a Glance

Sensors	Passive Sensors	Non-scanning Sensors	Non-imaging Sensors	Microwave Radiometer
				Magnetic Sensor
				Gravimeter
				Fourier Spectrometer
				Others (Resistivity meter etc.)
			Imaging Sensors (Cameras)	Monochrome Camera
				Panchromatic Camera
				Infrared Camera
				Colour Infrared Camera
				Other
		Scanning and Imaging Sensors	Image Plane Scanning	TV Camera
				Solid Scanner
			Object Plane Scanning	Opto Mechanical Scanner
				Microwave Radiometer
	Active Sensors	Non-scanning and Non-imaging Sensors		Microwave Radiometers
				Microwave Altimeters
				Laser Water Depth Meter
				Laser Distance Meter
		Scanning and Imaging Sensors	Image Plane Scanning	Passive Phased Array Radar
			Object Plane Scanning	Real Aperture Radar
				Synthetic Aperture Radar

5.15.2 List of Commonly Used Sensors

(i)   PAN - Panchromatic Camera

(ii)   LISS - Linear Imaging Self Scanning Camera Sensors

(iii)   WiFS - Wide Field Sensor

(iv)   AWiFs - Advanced Wide Field Sensor

(v)   MSS - Multi Spectral Scanning

(vi)   TM - Thematic Mapper

(vii)   ATM - Aerial Thematic Mapper

(viii)   RBV - Return Beam Vidicon

(ix)   MESS - Multi Spectral Self Scanning Radiometer

(x)   CSZS - Colour Zone Colour Scanner

(xi)   MSR - Microwave Scanning Radiometer

(xii)   VTIR - Visible and Thermal Infrared Radiometer

(xiii)   HRV - High Resolution Vidicon Camera

(xiv)   MOS - Modular Optoelectronic Scanner

(xv)   DMSV - Digital Multi-spectral Video

(xvi)   CASI - Compact Airborne Spectrographic Imager

5.15.3 Resolution of Sensors

Resolution can simply be defined as "the smallest magnitude of the parameter used in remotely sensed image for identification or characterization of the ground object'. In the design of an optimal remote sensor, an ideal set of resolutions is an essential requirement. In multispectral sensors, these resolutions have valid relationship with each other. There are main four types of resolutions viz. temporal resolution, spatial resolution, spectral resolution radiometric resolution".

(i) Temporal Resolution :

It refers to the time frequency of collection of data or the time interval between repetitive coverage of an area or simly it is a time of revisit of a particular satellite at a place. It is vital for monitoring changes over the time. Temporal resolution for LANDSAT is 18 days, for IRS satellites is 20 days and for SPOT satellites is 4 days.

(ii) Spatial Resolution :

It is the size of minimum detectable area on the ground by a detector placed on a sensor or it is the size of the smallest object on the ground identifiable in the image. It depends on the contrast ratio in that spectral region and IFOV (Smaller the IFOV, the better is the spatial resolution) and swath. Spatial resolution for LANDSAT MSS is 80 m, for TM is 30 m; for SPOT multispectral Channel is 20 m, for PAN is 10 m; for IRS 1A/1B LISS-I is 72.5 m, for LISS-II is 36.25 m, for IRS 1C/1D for PAN is 5.8 m.

IFOV is a measure of the spatial resolution of a remote sensing imaging system. It is defined as 'the angle subtended by a single detector element (CCD) on the axis of the optical system'. IFOV depends on solid angle through which a detector is sensitive to radiation and the distance from the target. A low altitude imaging instrument will have a higher spatial resolution than a higher altitude instrument with the same IFOV.

(iii) Spectral Resolution :

Spectral resolution refers to the band width and the number of bands used for collecting the data. On the basis of this, sensors can be classified as monochromatic (sensing is carried out only in one band of EMS), panchromatic (sensing is carried out in three bands of visible portion of EMS), multispectral (sensing is carried out in three bands of visible portion and few bands from infrared portion of EMS), hyper-spectral (sensing is carried out in so many bands of visible portion of EMS). Spectral resolution of IRS 1C/1D LISS III is 4 Bands, and that of LandSat MSS is - 7 Bands.

(iv) Radiometric Resolution :

Radiometric resolution is the number of levels of grey tones present in an image. The more are levels, better is the radiometric resolution. For example, in Landsat 8 BIT TM there are 2^8 i.e. 256 i.e. (0 - 255) grey levels and in 7 BIT, IRS LISS II the radiometric resolution is 2^7 i.e. 128   i.e. (0 - 127) grey levels. Radiometric resolution describes ability of sensor to discriminate very slight difference in energy and thus eases image interpretation process. Radiometric resolution is also referred as quantization level.

5.16 FEATURES OF SOME OF THE REMOTE SENSING SYSTEMS IN ACTION

Table 5.5

Characteristics of the System → Name of the system ↓	Altitude in km	Orbital Period in Minutes	Temopral Resolution in days	Sensor on Board	Number of Spectral Bands and Spectral Regions (Spectral Resolution)	Spatial Resolution in metres	Quantization BITs	Swath in km	Off nadir Viewing
Landsat 7 (USA)	705	103	16	ETM	6; Visible, NIR, MIR, 1 TIR, 1 PAN.	30 60 15	8	185	No
				HRMS I	1 PAN, 4 Visible, NIR	5 10	6 8	185	Yes No
SPOT 4 and 5	832	101	26/5	PLA	1; PAN	10	6	60	Yes
			26/5	MLA	4; Visible, NIR, MIR	20	8	117	Yes
			26/1	VMI	6; Visible, NIR, MIR	1000	8	2000	--
IRS 1A/1B 1988/1991	903	103.2	22	LISS I	4; Visible, NIR	72.5	8	148	No
				LISSII	4; Visible, NIR	36.25	8	75	No
IRS 1C/1D 1994 /1997	904	101.35	24	PAN	1; Visible	5.8	6	70 and 90	Yes
				LISS III	4; Visible, NIR, SWIR	23.5 in B2:4 and 70.5 in B5	7	141, B2:4; 148, B5	No
				WiFS	2; Visible, NIR	188.3	7	810	No
Resourcesat1 (IRS-P6) 2003	817	101.35	24	LISS IV	3, G, R, NIR	5.8	10	23.9 in MS mode, 70 in mono mode	Yes, ± 26°
				LISS III	4, Visible, NIR	23.5 in B2:4, 70.5 in B5	7	141 in B2:4, 148 in B5	No
				AwiFS	4, G, R, NIR, MIR	56 m	10	740-Combined 370-Under Each Head	No
Cartosat-1 (IRS-P5) 2005	618	97	5	PAN (Fore and Aft)	0.5 – 0.85 mm	2.54 m	10	29.42 - Fore 26.24 - Aft	--
Cartosat-2 India, 2008	--	--	4	PAN	0.45-0.85 m	0.8	10	9.6	--
Oceansat India, 2009	720	--	2	MSS	B1-B8, 40 - 885µ, Visible-NIR	50 km	12	1420	--

5.17 REMOTE SENSING DATA PRODUCTS

The data products used in remote sensing are :

(a) Aerial Photographs

(b) Mosaics

(c) Orthophoto

(d) Satellite imagery or digital image

(a) Aerial Photographs :

Aerial photograph is a photograph of the ground from an elevated position. The term usually refers to images in which the camera is not supported by a ground-based structure. The spectral range of a photographic film largely depends upon the type of emulsion used. Different emulsions have different spectral sensitivity. Some of the most common emulsions used for remote sensing, are discussed below.

(i) Black and White Panchromatic :

Panchromatic emulsion is a type of black and white photographic emulsion that is sensitive to all wavelengths of visible light. A panchromatic emulsion therefore produces a realistic image of a scene. Almost all modern photographic emulsions are panchromatic. The spectral sensitivity of this emulsion covers the spectral range from 0.4 to 0.7 μm. These emulsions provide good definition and contrast, wide exposure latitude, low cost and identification of minute textural variations. The limitation is that sometimes it is difficult to manually interpret ground features due to the ability of the eye to distinguish between minute differences in grey tones/shades. Digital panchromatic imagery of the earth's surface is produced by some modern satellites such as QUICKBIRD and IKONOS. This imagery is extremely useful, as it is generally of much higher spatial resolution than the multispectral imagery from same satellite. For example, the QUICKBIRD satellite produces panchromatic imagery having spatial resolution of 0.6 m while the spatial resolution of its multispectral sensor with same pixel configuration is 2.4 m.

(ii) Black and White Infrared :

The spectral sensitivity of this type of emulsion is from 0.4 to 0.9 μm which includes some part of reflected infrared portion of EMS to visible spectrum. Since infrared radiation tends to be strongly absorbed by water, the boundaries between water and land are very clearly identified. It is also possible to differentiate between different species of vegetation, such as between coniferous and deciduous trees.

(iii) Colour :

The human eye can differentiate only 20 to 30 shades of grey on a black and white aerial photograph, but same human eye can differentiate over 2000 shades of different colours. Thus a colour photograph will provide much more information than the equivalent black and white photograph.

Natural colour photography has advantages over panchromatic because the light has been bundled into different groups which can allow you to learn more about features on the ground. One typical use of colour photography is to map vegetation communities or land cover, tasks that benefit from colour separation.

Perception of colour depends largely on the relative amounts of the three primary colours, blue, green and red which are reflected by a particular object. Combining or adding the three primary colours in different proportions therefore, enables all possible colours to be produced.

An alternative approach to produce a particular colour is that of a subtractive colour mixing. In this case, rather than adding the three primary colours, the three subtractive primaries, yellow, magenta and cyan, are combined.

(iv) False Colour Composites (FCC) :

False Colour Composite is a method of displaying multi-band imagery. By assigning three of the spectral bands in visible portion of EMS to the fundamental colours red, blue and green, you can produce a colour image. The blue band in the original image is often affected by atmospheric effects such as haze, and is therefore usually left out and unlike normal colour emulsions, colour infrared emulsions are designed in order to record green, red and infrared energy. When the assigned image bands do not correspond to the frequencies of red, blue and green, the output image will appear in colours that are not natural. In false colour image, a blue image results from objects reflecting primarily green energy, green images result from objects reflecting primarily red images, and red images result from objects reflecting energy primarily in the near-infrared portion of the spectrum. Such an image is known as a False Colour Composite (FCC).

This emulsion has spectral sensitivity from 0.4 to 0.9 μm. The advantages are that it can penetrate through haze and it provides accurate identifiable data on vegetation, rocks, soils, water bodies and moisture distribution. It is useful for extracting information which is difficult to differentiate in the original imagery, variations in vegetation species or health. The disadvantages are that it has lower resolution than colour composite.

(b) Mosaics :

Already discussed in the chapter of Photogrammetry.

(c) Orthophoto :

Already discussed in the chapter of Photogrammetry.

(d) Satellite Imagery or Digital Image :

Satellite imagery consists of view of Earth or other planets made by means of artificial satellites. Satellite images are collected in digital form using sensors, and stored in digital form. This data in the digital form is usually termed as the 'imagery'. The photographic image as paper prints is called the 'hard copy'. The digital images are made up of picture elements called 'pixels'. A Pixel is having both spatial and spectral properties. The spatial property defines the "on ground" length and width and the spectral property defines the intensity of spectral response in a particular band in terms of Digital Number (DN). Thus, the image is a vast matrix of numbers ranging from 0 to 255 (in case of quantisation level 8). Satellite imagery covers a large area and allows multi-temporal and multi-spectral analysis. It minimizes field collection of data. Being in digital form, the satellite imagery allows digital image processing. The disadvantage of the imagery is that it requires expensive software and trained personnel for its analysis and interpretation.

5.17.1 Aerial Photograph versus Satellite Imagery

Sr. No.	Point of Comparison	Aerial Photograph	Satellite Image
1.	Data Format	Initially analogue, right now digital	Digital, right from beginning
2.	Visual perception	High, for all	Vary from low to high
3.	Cost	Relatively considerably costly	Relatively cost effective
4.	Procurement process	Cumbersome and time consuming	Easy and fast
5.	Relief displacement	More	Negligible
6.	Delineation of features (Conversion of photo or image into map/plan)	Easy	Not that easy
7.	Analysis	Were less computer compatible initially	Computer compatible right from beginning
8.	Stereoscopabilty	All of them are collected with an intention of stereoscopabilty. Stereo viewing is possible with all of them.	Possible only with those which are collected with an intention of stereoscopability.
9.	Effect of Earth's Curvature	Negligible	Significant
10.	Atmospheric error	Less	More

5.18 IMAGE INTERPRETATION

5.18.1 Introduction

Generally speaking, remote sensing works on the principle of the *inverse problem*. While the object or phenomenon of interest or it's state may not be directly measured, there exists some other variable that can be observed / measured, which may be related to the object of interest via some (usually mathematical) model. The common analogy given to describe this is trying to determine the type of animal from its footprints.

5.18.2 Steps In or Aspects of Photographic Interpretations

(i)   Detection : In this step an interpreter picks out an object from photo. e.g. There is a linear object uniform in features all along its length.

(ii)   Identification : In this step, the interpreter tries to identify the feature he had picked up in step of detection. e.g. the linear feature detected in step one seems to be a railway line.

(iii)   Analysis : In this step, the interpreter analyses the features of the object identified so that it can be grouped into different groups. e.g. There seems to be only one track and gauge seems to be about 1.7 m for the railway line identified in step two.

(iv)   Classification : In this step, the interpreter arranges the objects identified in step two into different groups on the basis of analysis carried out in step three. e.g. The railway line identified in step two seems to be a single broad gauge line.

(v)   Deduction : In this step, the interpreter deduces some references directly or indirectly about the object identified, analysed and classified through steps one, two and three respectively. Deductions shall firmly be confirmed by ground validation or ground truthing, so that the interpreter does not arrive at some wrong inferences. Transferring the details from an image to existing map or preparing the map from the image, or working out certain quantities from an image is also known as deduction. e.g. The alignment of railway line we have dealt with here upto is passing through stations A, B, C, D the length of this railway line from station A to D is 24 km etc.

(vi)   Idealisation : In this step, the interpreter draws some conclusion or takes some decision regarding the object (here a railway line) dealt so far in the context of study is being carried out from remotely sensed image. e.g. deciding set of symbols or colours to be adopted to represent this object in map; preparation and provision of attribute tables so that data will be readily available for inputting with the geographic information system or any other such a system.

5.18.3 Elements of Visual Interpretations

Size : The size of objects must be considered in the context of the scale of a photograph. The scale will help you determine if an object is a pond or a Lake.

Shape : Refers to the general outline of objects. Regular geometric shapes are usually indicators of human presence and use. Some objects can be identified almost solely on the basis of their shapes e.g. buildings, football fields, cloverleaf highway interchanges.

Tone or Colour (also called Hue) : Tone refers to the relative brightness or colour of elements on a photograph. It is, perhaps, the most basic of the interpretive elements because without tonal differences none of the other elements could be discerned.

Texture : The impression of smoothness or roughness of image features is caused by the frequency of change of tone in photographs. It is produced by a set of features too small to identify individually. Grass, cement and water generally appear smooth, while a forest canopy may appear rough.

Pattern (spatial arrangement) : The patterns formed by objects in a photo can be diagnostic. For example, the random pattern formed by an unmanaged area of trees and the pattern of evenly spaced rows formed by an orchard.

Shadow : Shadows aid interpreters in determining the height of objects in aerial photographs. However, they also obscure objects lying within them.

Location or Place or Site : It refers to topographic or geographic location. This characteristic of photographs is especially important in identifying vegetation types and landforms.

Association : Some objects are always found *in association with* other objects. The context of an object can provide insight into what it is. For instance, a nuclear power plant is not (generally) going to be found in the amidst of single-family housing.

5.19 ADVANTAGES OF REMOTE SENSING

(i) Accurate Positioning of Features : With availability of images with higher and higher spatial resolution it is possible to locate the position of features and phenomenon accurately.

(ii) Synoptic View : Synoptic view means view of relatively large area at a glance. Such synoptic view facilitates the study of various surface features of earth in their spatial relation to each other and help to delineate the required objects or phenomenon. A synoptic view gives regional coverage and allows study of entire region at a time in different context.

(iii) Real Time Data : The remotely senses show, within the limitation of a sensor, everything related with the object or phenomenon of interest available at the time of sensing.

(iv) Repitivity : Remote sensing provides consistent repeat coverage of area at relatively frequent intervals, making detection and monitoring of change feasible.

(v) Accessibility : Remote sensing process makes it possible to gather information about the area which is not physically or politically accessible.

(vi) Time Saving : Since information about a large area can be gathered quickly, the remote sensing technique saves time considerably.

(vii) Labour Saving : Remote sensing almost does not require any human effort for collection of field data. Even the labour requirement in interpretations of image is considerably less on account of use of computers in interpretation process.

(viii) Cost-effective : It is a cost-effective technique as again and again fieldwork is not required and also a large number of users can share and use the same data.

5.20 DISADVANTAGES AND LIMITATIONS OF REMOTE SENSING

(i) Although microwave sensors can image Earth through clouds, many other sensors cannot obtain data and information through cloud cover. This may break consistency in the data required in change studies.

(ii)   Spatial resolution which is achievable with many sensors is relatively low, which does not detect smaller objects required in micro level planning and also does not allow mapping of smaller areas.

(iii)   The remote sensing data needs to be corrected for atmospheric absorption and scattering and for the absorption of radiation through water on the ground and makes it difficult to obtain desired data and information on particular variables.

(iv)   Satellite remote sensing creates large quantities of data that typically require huge storage extensive cumbersome processing and analysis.

(v)   Data from satellite remote sensing are often costly if purchased from private vendors or value-adding resellers, and this initial cost, together with intellectual property restrictions, can limit the dissemination of products from such sources.

(vi)   Very huge costs are involved in building and operation of remote sensing data collection system, hence its establishment in individual/private capacity is out of thought and one will require to depend on data made available by the supplying agency.

(vii)   Data interpretation can be difficult because one needs to understand theoretically how the instrument is making the measurements one shall know about measurement uncertainties and also needs to have some knowledge of the phenomena you are sampling.

5.21 APPLICATIONS OF REMOTE SENSING

The remote sensing can be used for assessing and observing vegetation types, conducting soil surveys, carrying out mineral exploration, map making to facilitate easy study of information, construct thematic maps based on requirement, planning and monitoring water resources, carry out urban planning, assessing crop yields and other agriculture management, assessing and managing natural disaster etc. Some of the applications of the remote sensing are discussed at length here below.

5.21.1 Applications of Remote Sensing for Land Use and Land Cover Analysis

With growth of population at rapid rate, land use and land cover patterns all over the world are changing continuously. Agricultural land being used for development of human settlement and forest lands are getting converted into agricultural one. Land is a resource which cannot be created. Thus, land must be used in highly planned manner otherwise it will become scarce, making its cost to touch the sky, inviting the evil elements to interfere in the event of land use.

Thus, whatever is land available in the jurisdiction of concerned authority shall be used in optimum way. The authorities such as Municipalities, Municipal Corporations, New Town

Development Authorities (NTDA), Metropolitan Region Development Authorities (MRDA), must be well versed with current use of all land in their jurisdiction. For example, the land available in jurisdiction of urban local bodies may be used for variety of purposes, such as developing human settlement (housing), constructing communication routes such as roads; railways; canals etc., for developing recreational facilities like parks; playgrounds; gardens etc. or may be utilized for building the amenities such as schools; hospitals; banks; markets; clubs etc.

The authority must be known exactly the percentage of land utilized for such various purposes so that they may conclude whether that utilization is going in right or wrong directions. By marking use of remotely sensed images one can analyze land use and land cover by studying recent remotely sensed image of the area under study. The pattern of change in land use can also be studied by studying last few consecutive remotely sensed images.

Such land use and land cover analysis is unavoidable in process of preparation of town planning schemes (Micro level planning), development plans of cities and regional plans (Macro level planning).

Remotely sensed images can also be used to monitor the land use in the process of implementation of the master plans in form of a Development Plan (DP) for a city or a Regional Plan (RP) for an entire district.

The importance of remotely sensed images in the context of land use and land cover can also be extended to level of state or entire country because remotely sensed images needed for the purpose are available to those scales also.

5.21.2 Applications of Remote Sensing in Natural Hazard Mapping/Management

Cyclones, Tsunamis, Earthquakes, Volcanic eruption, Floods, Forest fires etc. are the common natural hazards happening continuously somewhere on earth's surface.

If one has the set of remotely sensed images immediately before and after such natural hazard, it is possible to predict the extent of damage and its distribution to various elements related with human life in that area. Rough estimation of damage in material/monitory terms is essential in planning and execution of rehabilitation program which is possible from remotely sensed images.

For example, In Earthquake damaged areas one may delineate the area affected by the earthquake; find out damages to the individual houses, damages to services, damages to aerobic culture. One can classify the area on the basis of intensity or scale of damage and can decide upon priorities of making available assistance or help.

In flood affected areas one may ascertain which settlements, fields were actually submerged or effected by the floods and also extent of effect. Such images will very much useful for insurance companies when it is not possible to physically verify damage by site visit, especially when very large area is getting affected and help is to be made available on war basis.

From regular studies of remotely sensed images of forest areas one may detect any irregularity in the forest such as unofficial cutting, forest fire etc. In case of forest fire one can understand the exact location, intensity, direction of progress, properties or settlements likely to come in its way etc.

The remotely sensing may be used to predict some of the disasters by making thorough studies of variations occurring either gradually or suddenly, over certain period, on past few consecutive images. By proper use of such images one may avoid considerably the loss of lives and related things.

5.21.3 Applications of Remote Sensing for Resource Inventory and Management

With growing population and rising standard of living pressure on natural resources has been increasing day by day. It is therefore become necessary to manage the available resources effectively and economically. It requires periodic preparation of accurate inventory of natural recourses both renewable and non-renewable. This can be achieved through remote sensing, since it provides multi-spectral and multi-temporal data useful for preparation of resource inventory as well for its planning, monitoring and management.

The natural resources include water resources, forest resources, geological resources (minerals, oils etc.), and crop resources. From remotely sensed images one can understand about the quantum of such resources available, condition of these resources, locations of these resources etc. From this, one may predict whether those are sufficient or deficient, locally available or not and accordingly the measures can be planned and executed for their utilization or their growth or their mobilization.

The remotely sensed images are popularly used in exploration of natural resources especially those which are in deficit.

In India there is a body NNRMA (National Natural Resource Management Agency), who looks after the inventory of natural resources in the context of the national population. Such agencies are also formed at state level for further planning of such resources at state level. Through remote sensing one may have effective control on the resources likely to be over utilized and are around to be vanish. Remotely sensed images can also be utilized in effective equitable distribution of the available resource.

The technology of remote sensing is being popularly used all over the world for managing forests, water bodies, gas cover surrounding the earth.

5.21.4 Applications of Remote Sensing in Mapping

The remotely sensed data is available to the spatial resolution of few hundred metres to few decimetres. It is as low as 0.6 m with QUICK BIRD and Cartosat images and is high as 1000 m with SPOT images taken using VMI sensors. The largest scale of the maps required as readily available with Survey of India for macro planning is 1 : 25000. If readability of naked eye is taken as quarter mm, the object of size 3.25 m × 3.25 m can be seen on such a map by a quarter mm thick dot.

Ground size of dot (pixel) on QUICK BIRD images is 0.6 m × 0.6 m and that on SPOT images with VMI sensors is 1000 m × 1000 m. That means it is possible to convert the remotely sensed images into maps required for micro planning to macro planning.

The images are conical projections and maps are orthographic projections. To convert the conical projections to into orthographic projections, it is essential to visualize the images in three dimensions and for this purpose images should be available as stereo-pairs. With advent of QUICK BIRD, IRS, 1D, 1E, 1F and Cartosat satellites, now the remotely sensed images are available as stero-pairs.

Such images can be converted into map of required scale using optomechanical or electronic digital stereo plotters. Before such conversions one will require to georeference the image, so that interpreter will know the co-ordinates of few points on the photograph to their correct geographical position. One may take the assistance of GPS in the process of georeferencing. Before attributing the features transferred from the image to map one must make ground verification.

Now-a-days, remotely sensed images are available in soft/digital form. Hence, map can also be prepared directly in digital form. Such digital maps can be attributed with much more information than conventional paper maps by integrating such digital maps with GIS. The data required for this detail attribution will be available from that remotely sensed image itself and its updation is regularly possible because of temporal collection of remotely sensed data on routine basis.

5.22 ELECTRONIC DISTANCE METER (EDM) AND ELECTRONIC TOTAL STATION (ETS)

5.22.1 Electronic Distance Meter (EDM)

5.22.1.1 Introduction

Electronic Distance Meter abbreviated as EDM is one of the latest and sophisticated invention in the field of survey. The EDM is actually an electronic device to measure distances. The range of EDMs varies from 0.5 km to 100 km or even more, and the accuracy obtained is from 1 : 10000 to 1 : 100000 and even more. Its introduction has made the work of measuring distances between two points very easy and precise. The first EDM instrument was developed by Eric Bergstrand in Sweeden in 1948, which was called 'Geodimeter' (geodetic distance meter) based on a modulated light beam. The second one was designed in South Africa in 1957, called 'Tellurometer' employs modulated microwaves.

5.22.1.2 Principle of Working of EDM

EDM instruments measures distance using Electro Magnetic (EM) waves (light or radio). The EDM works on the *principle of phase comparison* and not on SONAR (Sound Navigation and Ranging) as velocity of electromagnetic waves is very high about 3×10^5 km/sec. The electromagnetic waves are transverse periodic waves and follow the sinusoidal form.

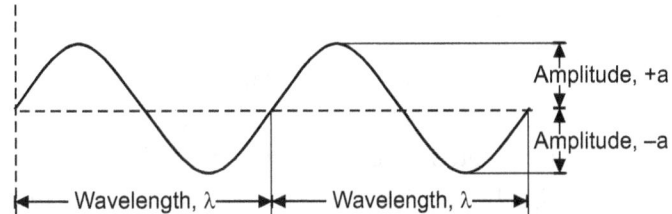

Fig. 5.11 : Sinusoidal form of electromagnetic waves

The electromagnetic waves are characterised by the equation "$= f \cdot \lambda$", where 'C' is velocity, 'f' is the frequency and 'λ' is the wavelength of the electromagnetic waves. Velocity of electromagnetic waves (C) is constant and its exact value is (299792.5 ± 0.4) km/s in vacuum. A correction will require to be applied to value of 'C' for temperature and pressure variations observed at the time of observations. Frequency is complete number of wave units crossing a particular section per unit of time. The energy possessed by wave is direct function of its frequency. From characterisation equation it is clear that frequency is inverse function of wavelength, waves with higher wavelength will have lower frequency and vice versa. Thus, waves with greater wavelength posses less energy and vice a versa. To transmit overdesired distance, wave should have sufficient energy otherwise it will face problem of interference and fading.

5.22.1.3 Pattern/Types of Electromagnetic Waves Used With an EDM

In the process of distance measurement EDM incorporates two kinds of waves, namely 'Measuring waves' and 'Carrier waves'. The waves with greater wavelength are suitable for measuring process. Those are known as 'Measuring Waves' and are unsuitable for transmitting over longer distance as their frequency and thus the energy is less. The commonly used measuring waves do have wavelength inbetween 40 m to 450 nm and frequency in between 500 to 7.5 MHz and face the problems like interference and fading while travelling over longer distance.

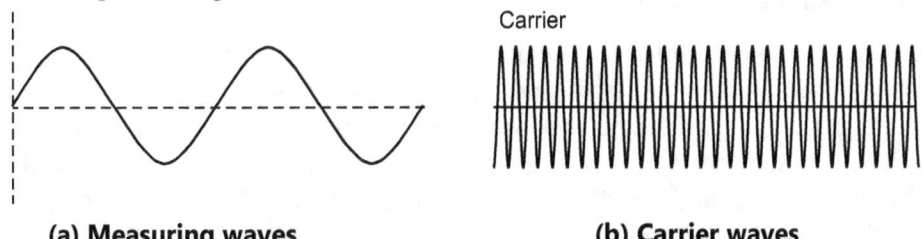

(a) Measuring waves　　　　**(b) Carrier waves**

Fig. 5.12 : Forms of measuring and carrier waves

The waves with higher frequency and thus higher energy are suitable for transmitting over longer distance. Those are known as 'Carrier Waves' and are unsuitable for measuring process as their wavelength is short. Carrier waves may be either Infrared light waves [λ = 450 to 1000 nm and f = 6.7 to 3 GHz] or Micro Waves [λ = 1 to 8.6 mm and f = 35 to 3 GHz].

Hence measuring waves needs to be superimposed on the waves suitable for transmitting over longer distance (Carrier waves) by the process of modulation. Modulation is the process whereby some characteristic (like amplitude or frequency or phase) of a high frequency wave is varied in accordance with instantaneous value intensity of low frequency wave. Measuring waves are modulated on carrier waves either by the process of Amplitude Modulation (AM) or Frequency Modulation (FM) or Phase Modulation (PM).

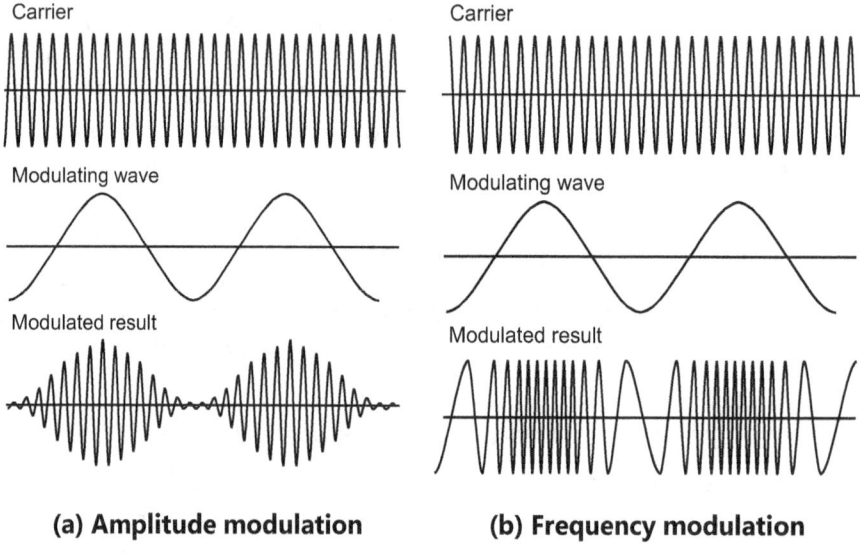

(a) Amplitude modulation   **(b) Frequency modulation**

Fig. 5.13 : Methods of wave modulation

Modulation allows generation of multiple wavelengths from same source of radiation and makes the unit smaller lighter and less power hungry.

5.22.1.4 Working of an EDM

The EDM instrument generates, modulates and transmits a pair of optical or micro-waves of specified frequencies, from one end of a line whose length is to be measured towards the prism reflector facing the instrument at other end of the same line. It then receives back the same pair of waves reflected from the prism reflectors, demodulates it, measures their phases and send it to the microprocessor within. The microprocessor compares the phases of these pair of the waves and reduces distance of reflector from EDM centre along the line of sight in specified system of units either MKS or FPS.

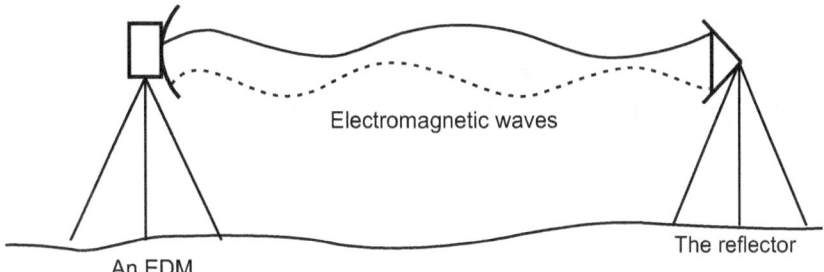

Electromagnetic waves

An EDM

The reflector

Fig. 5.14 : Working of EDM

If line of sight is inclined, the measured distance will be inclined one. Such inclined distance can be resolved into its horizontal and vertical components after supplying vertical angle made by inclined line of sight with the horizontal. The distances and other information are displayed on the LCD (Liquid Crystal Display) in digital form.

(a) NI 450 citation EODM mounted in yoke on index frame of a theodolite
(b) A single prism with target plate mounted on tribratch

Fig. 5.15 : EDM and reflector

The reflector is a corner cube of glass in which the sides are perpendicular to a very close tolerance. It has the characteristic that incident light is reflected parallel to itself, thus returning the beam to the source. This is called a retro-directive prism or retro reflector. Reflector might include a single prism or group of prism depending upon magnitude of distance to be measured. Reflector can be a simple reflecting paper sticker, they are called sheet prisms and are very useful at construction sites and in deformation monitoring of structures.

5.22.1.5 How an EDM Works Out a Distance?

Phase of a wave is an angle indicating the position of an electronic pulse along the wave. Phase is 0° at the beginning, 180° at mid and 360° at the end of a complete wave unit.

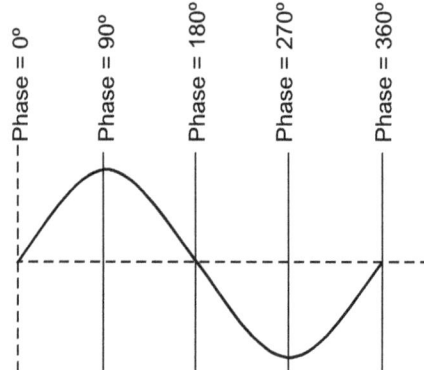

Fig. 5.16 : Illustrating phase of a wave

The distance between EDM and reflector is expressed as D and

$$D = (n\lambda + p) \div 2 \qquad \text{... (Refer Fig. 5.18)}$$

Where n is complete number of wave units in the forward and return travel of wave in between EDM and the reflector and p is the phase difference. Phase difference is the fraction of wavelength by which double length line exceeds the integral numbers of complete wave length. In above equation, since p is divided by 2, so is the λ, we will call, $(\lambda/2)$ as effective wavelength or half wavelength.

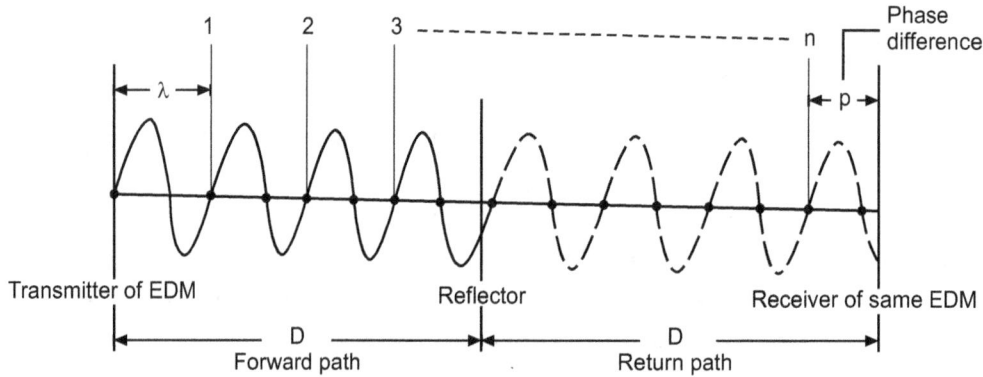

Fig. 5.17 : Working of an EDM

Counting the number of complete wavelengths "n" would require very accurate measurement of time, which is practically not possible. Hence, EDM calculates distance from the comparison of *'Phase Difference'* measured separately for each of the wave pattern from the pair of electromagnetic waves selected for distance measurement process.

Phase difference, p = (phase angle (ϕ) for fraction of wavelength by which double length line exceeds $\div$ 360°) × Wavelength (λ).

If only one frequency is used, the distance obtained will not be unique as same phase difference can be obtained with different distances. Thus, to remove ambiguity one more measuring wavelength is used which produce beat with basic frequency.

Let D is the distance between EDM station A and reflector station B, m_1 and m_2 are two measuring units and p_1 and p_2 are phase differences corresponding to waves with frequency f_1 and f_2 respectively.

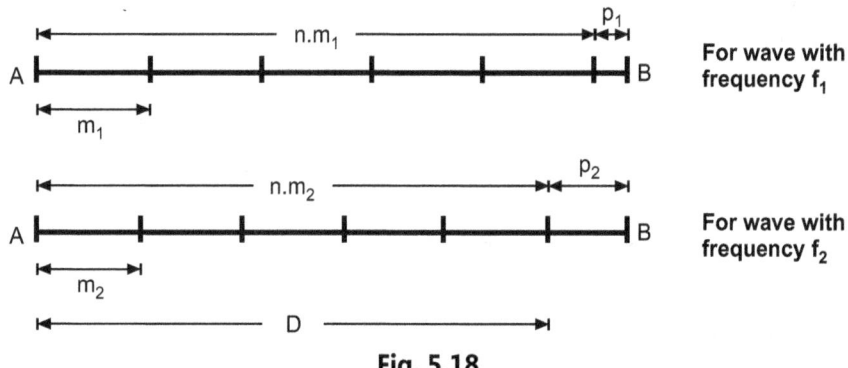

Fig. 5.18

Then $\qquad\qquad\qquad$ $D = n \cdot m_1 + p_1$ $\qquad\qquad\qquad\qquad\qquad$ ... (i)

and same way also, $\qquad$ $D = n \cdot m_2 + p_2$ $\qquad\qquad\qquad\qquad\qquad$ ... (ii)

Subtracting equation (i) from (ii), we get a relation,

$\qquad\qquad\qquad$ $(p_2 - p_1) = n \cdot [m_1 - m_2]$ $\qquad\qquad\qquad\qquad\qquad$ ... (iii)

Let m_1 and m_2 are related in such a way that

$\qquad\qquad\qquad\qquad$ $10 \cdot m_1 = 11 \cdot m_2$

Then $\qquad\qquad\qquad\qquad$ $m_2 = \left(\dfrac{10}{11}\right) \cdot m_1$

Putting this in equation (iii)

$\qquad\qquad\qquad$ $(p_2 - p_1) = n \cdot [m_1 - (10/11) \cdot m_1]$

$\qquad\qquad\qquad$ $(p_2 - p_1) = n \cdot m_1/11$ $\quad$ or $\quad$ $n \cdot m_1 = 11 \cdot (p_2 - p_1)$ $\qquad\qquad$ ... (iv)

Substituting equation (iv) in equation (i),

$\qquad\qquad\qquad\qquad$ $D = 11 \cdot (p_2 - p_1) + p_1$ $\qquad\qquad\qquad\qquad\qquad$ ... (v)

The equation (v) clearly indicates that the required distance D can be uniquely measured without knowing the number of full measuring units. There is limit to distance measurement with relation "10 m_1 = 11 m_2". Same phase difference could repeat for some higher distances. Thus, for large distances the relation could be changed to "100 m_1 = 101 m_2" or "1000 m_1 = 1001 m_2" and so on.

5.22.1.6 Component Parts of an EDM

The EDM consist of a wave generator, wave modulator, wave transmitter, wave detector/receiver wave demodulator, a small in-built computer required for calculating the distances and other such information.

5.22.1.7 Functions an EDM Needs to Perform While Measuring Distance

1. Generation of waves.
2. Modulation of waves.
3. Transmission of waves.
4. Detecting and receiving back the waves reflected from prism reflectors.
5. Demodulation of waves.
6. Phase measurement and comparison.
7. Reduction/calculation of distances.

5.22.1.8 Classification of EDM

1. As Per Wave Pattern :

(a) EODM : Electro Optical Distance Meter - makes use of optical/light waves – requires EDM transmitter/receiver unit at one end and reflector at other end.

(b) MDM : Microwave Distance Meter - makes use of microwaves – requires identical transmitter/receiver units at both ends.

2. As Per Ranges :

(a) Short Range EDM – Range ≤ 5 kms – usually an EODM.

(b) Medium Range EDM – 5km ≤ Range ≤ 100km - may be an EODM or a MDM.

(c) Long range EDM – Range >100km – usually a MDM.

3. As Per the Slave Required :

(a) Direct reading EDM - makes use of LASER, do not require reflector, range is short, usually not greater than 250 m.

(b) Indirect reading EDM/Reflector Based EDM - makes use of infrared light beam, requires a reflector, range may be in multiples of km.

5.22.1.9 Differentiating Features of an EDM
w.r.t. Conventional Linear Measures

Conventional measuring instruments require repeated interference by human beings and human beings are likely to cause errors. These conventional instruments have to be continuously adjusted. These instruments are also very time consuming and require great skill to obtain a high level of accuracy. Continuous attention has to be given to the temporary adjustments of the instruments.

The EDM, on the other hand, is very easy to use. It is a time saving, and highly precise instrument. Directing the instrument to the required direction/point and on just pressing a single button, distance even in multiples of km is worked out at a stretch to mm precision just in few seconds. The EDM can be used for control as well for detailing survey.

5.22.1.10 Advantages of EDM

(i)   Can measure distance even in multiples of km at a stretch.

(ii) Can measure such a long distance in just few seconds.

(iii) Can measure distance even to a mm accuracy with very high precision.

5.22.1.11 Disadvantages of EDM

(i)   Problem of misalignment when mounted on theodolite.

(ii) Measures distance along the line of sight.

(iii) Distance needs to be corrected for eccentricity of EDM axis and theodolite axis.

5.22.1.12 Errors and Mistakes in Measurements with an EDM

Refer article No. 5.22.2.15 and 5.22.2.16 from this chapter

5.22.1.13 The NI 450 Citation EDM

(a) Features of NI 450 Citation EDM :

This is an EDM manufactured by 'Cubic Precision' of USA, marketed in India through then National Instrument (NI) by 'Wild' of Switzerland presently known as 'Leika'. It's an electro-optical distance meter incorporating infrared light waves as carrier waves and amplitude modulation. Its range is about 4.3 km with a triple prism assembly. Its weight is around 2.5 kg. Its accuracy is about (± 5mm + 5 ppm). It can operate in a temperature in between −20°C to +50°C. Typical time of computing a distance is around 8 seconds in normal mode and 1 second in tracking mode. It can convert a distance measured along inclined line of sight to its horizontal and vertical equivalent, when provided with a vertical angle through which line of sight is inclined. It comes with 12 V – 7 Ah Ni-Cd battery capable to provide charge for around 500 observations but can also work on 12 V lead acid batteries. It can be mounted on theodolite either on its telescope or on in yoke on its index frame with help of a special accessories manufactured for the purpose. It can also be used independently by mounting in yoke on tribratch.

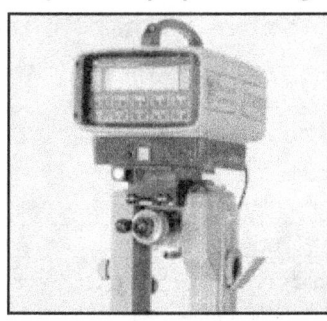 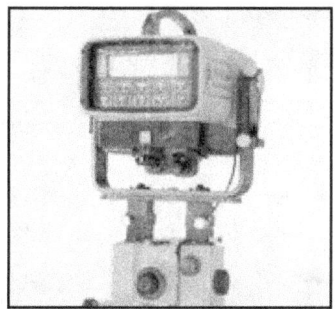 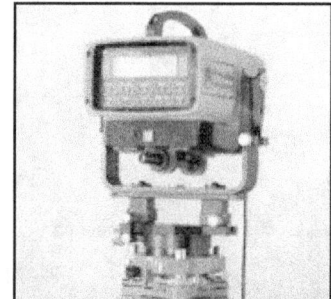

| (a) On telescope of a theodolite | (b) In yoke on index frame of a theodolite | (c) In yoke on tribratch |

Fig. 5.19 : Various types of mounts for NI 450 citation EDM

As electronic surveying total station instruments are very popular now-a-days and those invariably are fitted with EDM in their body, no body prefer independent EDM instruments, thus independent EDM instrument especially capable to measure longer distances are not easily available in the market.

(b) Control Panel for NI 450 Citation EDM :

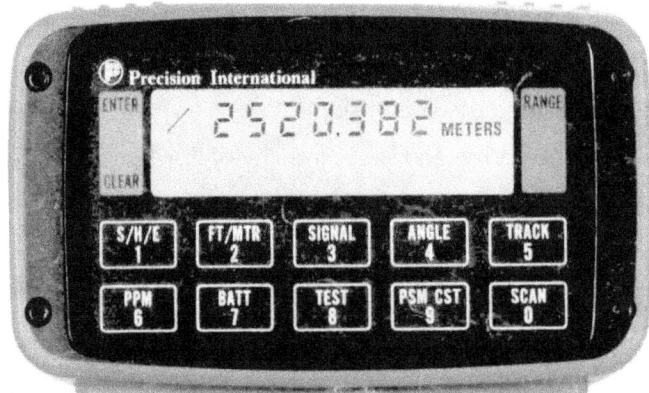

Fig. 5.20

ENTER **CLEAR**	This key is used to enter information into the microprocessor or into Citation's memory. It is also used to clear an incorrect entry.
RANGE	Touch RANGE once for the **standard measuring mode**. The distance is displayed in few seconds (usually not more than 8 seconds) to 5 mm ± 5 ppm standard deviation. Touching RANGE twice puts Citation in **repeat mode.** Measurements are repeated and displayed automatically every 8 seconds. Repeat mode is used when several measurements have to be taken for maximum accuracy for those critical distances.
S/H/E **1**	Changes the display from slope to horizontal distance to height difference. Simply touch the key to select whichever you need. A line (sloped/horizontal/vertical) at the left of the readout indicates which value is displayed.
FT/MTR **2**	Changes the display values instantly from metres to feet or from feet to metres.
SIGNAL **3**	Touching this key activates two fine pointing aids, the variable tone and the cursor.
ANGLE **4**	Needed for reductions. This key is used to display the vertical angle entered into Citation or to enter a new vertical circle reading. Angles are entered to 1″.
TRACK **5**	Activates the **tracking mode** for setting out or measuring to a moving target. After the 8 second time of initial measurement, updates at an interval of 1 second time are continuously displayed. Citation tracks slope distance like other EDMs, and if the vertical angle is entered it will also track horizontal distances and height difference. As Citation can track horizontal distances, it is particularly useful for staking out.

PPM **6**	With this key, ppm value upto 999 ppm in steps of 1 ppm can be entered into Citation's permanent memory. Atmospheric correction, reduction to sea level and projection scale factor can all be taken care of with ppm facility.
BATT **7**	Causes Citation to display a digital indication of the battery strength. If battery reading is above 600, it is fully charged. If battery is below 200, it is about to end and you have to stop use of Citation otherwise there is possibility of change of polarity of battery.
TEST **8**	Puts Citation into the pre-operational test mode. The display is checked and a complete internal measurement automatically controls all circuits and verifies that the unit is functioning perfectly.
PSM CST **9**	With this key, prism constants up to 999 mm in steps of 1mm can be entered in to Citations memory. Simply key in the value for the prism you are using.
SCAN **0**	A special feature unique to Citation. Touch SCAN to display in continuous sequences the slope distances, horizontal distance, height difference and vertical angle entered. Each is seen for 2 seconds. SCAN is an operator aid. The results can be written down and verified as they follow each other continuously through the display.

(c) Procedure for Use of an EDM (NI 450 Citation with Wild T2 – 1" Theodolite) :

Set up the Wild T2, 1" LC theodolite on tripod stand and get its all temporary adjustments done. Remove the EDM from its box and get it mounted on index frame of the theodolite with help of the yoke provided with it.

Get measured height h1 of EDM axis above GL. Power the unit. Hold a prism reflector prism at the other end of the line whose distance is to be measured. This prism shall reflect back the incident waves into its source without scatter. Get recorded height h_2 of the prism centre above the GL. Direct the object screen of the EDM instrument to the reflecting prism. Bring to the centre of the prism in line with the centre of the cross-hairs of the universal focusing telescope provided beneath the EDM body for sole purpose. Ascertain the bisection, with triple bisecting aids which consist of a bulls eye, a moving cursor and an audible signals. Then press the 'RANGE' switch and in no time the sloped distance L of prism centre from instrument centre along the line of sight, will be displayed on the LCD. If you requires horizontal component D and vertical component V of this inclined distance then read the vertical angle θ made by line of sight with the horizontal, with help of a theodolite on which the EDM is mounted and enter in this vertical angle to the theodolite. Instrument will give you now the required values of D and V. Using h_1, h_2 and V one can work out reduced level of the prism reflector station.

Error in measurement on account of EDM axis being eccentric from theodolite axis can be corrected with help of standard correction charts and tables available in the *Operation Manual* of the EDM.

5.22.2 Electronic Total Station

5.22.2.1 Introduction

While carrying out survey, either we are defining relative position of a control station with respect to other control station or we are defining relative position of a detail with respect to a control station. The station whose position is to be defined is called as 'object station' and the station with reference to which position is to be defined is called as 'reference station'.

The simplest way to define relative position of an object station with respect to a reference station in horizontal plane is to measure polar co-ordinates and in vertical plane is to measure differential elevation. Measuring polar co-ordinates means measuring distance between bearing of line joining reference station and object station. These polar co-ordinates can be easily converted into rectangular co-ordinates.

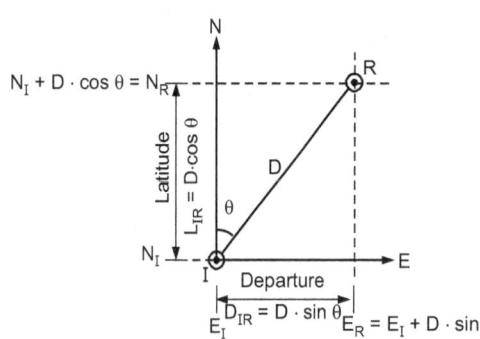

I is a reference station.

R is an object station.

(D, θ) are polar co-ordinates of R w.r.t. I

(E_I, N_I) are rectangular co-ordinates of I

(E_R, N_R) are rectangular co-ordinates of R

$E_R = E_I +$ Departure of line IR

$\qquad = E_I + D \cdot \sin \theta$

$N_R = N_I +$ Latitude of line IR

$\qquad = N_I + D \cdot \cos \theta$

Fig. 5.21 : Relation between polar and rectangular co-ordinates

Hence, we can say that carrying out survey means nothing but measuring distances and directions and doing some reductions. Upto very recent times this distance direction data was collected using conventional instruments like chain, tape, compass, theodolite sextants and levels etc.

Merits of Conventional Instruments/Methods :

1. Simple in construction.

2. Low capital cost.

3. Almost no operating cost.

4. On field repair/adjustment is easily possible.

5. Local Manufacture and Service.

6. Almost no computer awareness essential to work with them.

Demerits of Conventional Instruments/Methods :

1. Laborious and Fatiguing.

2. Constant or invariable precision.

3. Switching over from one system of units to other, especially for angular measurement is not possible.

4. Measurement, especially large linear measurements, needs to be done in parts.

5. Different instruments for different process of measurement.

6. More number of instruments for same process of measurement.

7. Manual reading, recording, corrections and reductions, no computer compatibility.

8. Achieving higher accuracies is relatively difficult.

9. Time consuming.

Necessity of a Total Station :

Majority of demerits of conventional instruments cannot be kept unattended in this era of shortage of time and manpower and requirement of faster and faster speed of work execution at higher precision and accuracy. The problems due to demerits of the conventional distance and direction measuring instruments were considerably lowered with the innovation of Electronic Distance Meter (EDM) and Electronic Digital Theodolite (EDT).

Fig. 5.22 : An EDT mounted with EDM and both connected to an EFB

(Courtsey : Sokkisha Instruments)

But again the surveyor was requiring operating two different units independently and distance-direction data collected with them was recorded and processed either manually or with help of one more unit called as Data Logger or Electronic Field Book (EFB). Even though each of this unit is more precise, accurate, speedy and easy to operate; handling, operating and maintaining such three units at a time was bit an awkward and cumbersome job. This necessitated bringing ahead the concept of an all in one instrument the Total Station.

The Electronic Total Station (ETS) :

It is an opto-mecha-tronic instrument used in modern surveying. This instrument is a combination of an Electronic Digital Theodolite [EDT], an Electronic Distance Meter [EDM] and compact limited capability microprocessor with appropriate solid state memory device.

5.22.2.2 Construction of a Total Station

Basically a total station is an electronic digital theodolite in whose telescope an EDM is mounted and in whose index frame a microprocessor is housed along with memory unit and power unit. In its simplest form total station broadly consists of following two main parts,

    (a) A Levelling head - The lower fixed part and

    (b) An alidade - The upper moving part.

(a) A Levelling Head :

It is three foot screw type for easy and quick levelling of the instrument. The bottom face of lower tribratch of the levelling head is machine planed, so that instrument can displaced during fine centering, over plane and smooth stand head top through a circle of about 25 mm diameter by loosening a instrument fixing screw. A levelling head usually incorporates an optical plummet or a laser plummet for fine centering of the instrument. In many of the instrument the levelling head can be detached from the alidade to exchange the target and alidade in precise surveying.

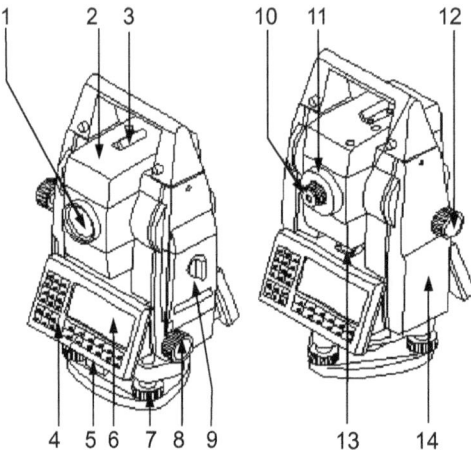

1. Object glass
2. Telescope with EDM
3. Collimator
4. Keyboard
5. Tribrach
6. LC Display
7. Foot screw
8. Horizontal tangent screw
9. Memory card drive
10. Eye piece
11. Focusing sleeve
12. Vertical tangent screw
13. Round bubble
14. Battery

Fig. 5.23 : Component parts of a typical total station

(b) An Alidade :

The alidade of a total station consist of the following main parts :

(i)   A horizontal circle and vertical circle along with their reading systems and control screw,

(ii) The telescope in a pair of index frame,

(iii) An EDM mounted within the telescope and

(iv) A microprocessor capable to establish character users interface (CUI) or graphical users interface (GUI) either on DOS based or Windows based operating system. Such microprocessor is usually accommodated in an index frame on opposite side of vertical circle.

(v)   Memory device – It is usually a solid state non-volatile type memory. The memory of a total station is measured in terms of points. Storing a point means storing its three co-ordinates, its description and its identification number. Many of the total stations in market have memory about 10000 points.

(vi) A Display unit – It is alpha numeric type and may support graphics also.

(vii) A battery unit – Usually total stations are furnished with NiMH standard camcorder type 6 Volt – 1.8 or 3.6 Ah rechargeable batteries, capable to provide power upto 4 to 6 hours at a stretch. Such batteries can be fully recharged over 1 to 2 hours.

(viii) A data exchange system – In old versions of total stations, it is usually a RS 232 type port. In recent versions of the total stations data exchange system consists of USB ports and data can be exchanged with help of pen drive. Such ports are usually provided at the bottom of the alidade. Sometimes total stations are provided with blue tooth system for data exchange.

The telescope of all total stations can be transited so that readings can be taken with both faces to eliminate or minimize errors due to faulty permanent adjustments of the instrument.

5.22.2.3 Types of Total Stations

Total stations can be classified in to different types on different basis as discussed below.

1. Classification Based on Type of Wave Pattern Used On EDM within Total Station :

EDM resolves the distance by phase comparison of the electromagnetic wave pattern used in it. Initially in addition to navigational EDM the surveying EDMs were also microwave based. Now days the surveying EDMs are optical/light wave based and are known as Electro Optical Distance Meters (EODM). The EODM can be either reflector based or direct reading, accordingly the total stations are divided in following two types.

(a) **Reflector Based Total Stations :** They make use of infra red light waves in the process of distance measurement. They need to hold, facing the total station, a prism reflector or reflector sheet at an object station to measure either distances up to it or co-ordinates of it.

(b) Direct Reading Total Stations : They make use of laser in working out distance. They do not require a prism reflector or reflector sheet to be held at an object station. You can directly sight the required point. But the surface on which this point is lying shall not be darker than Kodak grey. The range of direct reading total stations is very much limited and is very rarely more than 250 m.

2. Classification Based on Range of EDM within Total Station :

As per the range up to which an EDM within the total station can measure distance, the total stations are divided in following two types.

(a) Short Range Total Stations : Distance measuring range of such total stations is usually up to 250 m. They usually incorporate Laser based EODM and do not requires a prism reflector or reflector sheet.

(b) Medium Range Total Stations : Distance measuring range of such total stations is usually inbetween 250 m and 5 km. They incorporate infrared wave based EODM and invariably requires reflector sheet or single mini/regular prism reflector up to distance of 1 km and set of prism reflector consisting of usually not more than three regular prisms when distance is more than 1 km.

(c) Long Range Total Stations : Distance measuring range of such total stations is usually in between 5 km and 100 km. They also incorporate infrared wave based EODM and invariably requires a prism reflector consisting of usually more than three regular prisms.

3. Classification Based on Angle Resolution System on EDT within Total Station :

Most modern EDT measure angles on the basis of digital image processing technique, in which electro optical scanning of extremely precise digital bar code pattern etched on glass discs rotating within the instrument is carried out to resolve the angle. Depending upon type of scanning system used to resolve the angle from this bar coded pattern, the total stations can be divided in following two categories.

(a) Absolute Encoding Total Stations : They give angular output on the basis of unique digital response for each individual increment of displacement. Detection of 0° position is no longer needed. That means no indexing is required to begin with angular measurements. It gives stable and high accuracy angular measurements. All high end modern total stations are usually absolute encoding type.

(b) Incremental Encoding Total Stations : They give angular output based on the number of periods or counts between start and finish of the whole displacement. Thus start position has to be known for the determination of the measurement. That means indexing is required to begin with angular measurements.

5.22.2.4 Advantages of a Total Station

1. More accurate distance and angle measurements.
2. Elimination of manual errors.
3. Elimination of manual mathematical reductions.

4. Generation of data in digital format.

5. Zero error in plotting.

6. Reduction of labour, time and cost.

7. Professional quality output even with beginners.

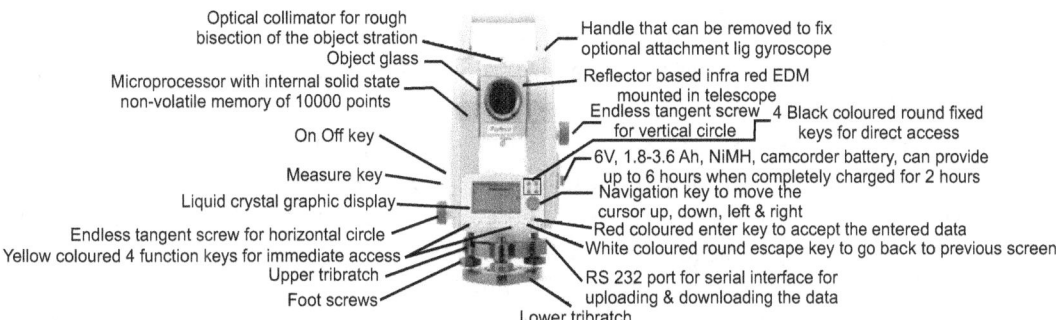

Fig. 5.24 : Display side view of Leica TPS 407 electronic total station
(Courtsey : Leika Instruments)

5.22.2.5 Features of ETS

(1) Effortless levelling through electronic digital bubble of variable sensitivity. Depending upon job requirements one may change sensitivity of the digital bubbles so that it will be easy to achieve desired precision.

(2) Vertical Axis Compensator either, single or double – Compensator keeps the vertical axis vertical within predefined limit of tilt usually not more than 15′. Single axis compensator keeps the vertical axis vertical in XZ plane and double axis compensator keeps the vertical axis vertical in XZ and YZ plane simultaneously. Here X-axis is assumed along horizontal line of collimation, Y-axis along transverse or trunnion axis and Z axis along the vertical.

(3) Effortless centering with help of a laser plummet whose intensity can be changed to match with ambient light condition.

(4) Automatic detection of true north : If fitted with an optional 'Gyro Attachment' the total station can detect itself, the true meridian.

(5) Effective control on work through : Laser guide or Track light or Lumi-guide or Voice communication type devices. These devices assist a reflector man to come in line or to occupy the point to be set out with minimum or no instructions from instrument man.

(6) Uniaxial Clamp tangent or Friction lock and Endless Drives: In case of instruments with uniaxial clamp tangent, there is no separate clamp and tangent screws, the clamp and tangent screw share the common axis. In case of instruments with friction locks, there are no clamping screws; the instrument locks itself by friction. The tangent screws on such a friction clamp instrument are limitless and never end on either side.

(7) Robotic operation – Means operating the instrument from remote location such as reflector station. Such instruments are motorized and are capable to rotate telescope itself in horizontal and vertical plane within predefined limits to search the reflector and are known as robotic total stations. Such types of total stations are fitted with automatic target recognition sensors. Reflector provided with robotic total stations is an active 360° reflector and emits electromagnetic radiations so that total station can detect it. Such reflector requires battery to operate them. In addition to display unit available with such total station, readings taken and reductions made by robotic total station can also be seen on remote display unit available with surveyor standing with reflector at object station. Such remote display can be a display that can be detached from robotic total station or an additional display unit. Robotic total station communicates data and reductions with such remote display with the help of wireless radio link. As robotic total station allow its controlling from the remote points, only one person is sufficient to carry out survey with robotic total stations.

(8) Automatic target recognition – Possible only in case of total station fitted with automatic target recognition sensors.

(9) Variable precision/accuracy – You can change precision/accuracy of the EDM or EDT on the ETS depending upon the requirement of job or time available or funds available.

(10) User friendly graphic display with functions like pan, zoom etc.

(11) Same unit is capable to measure direction in hexagesimal or centesimal or radian system either clockwise or anticlockwise and distance in meter and feet simultaneously. Magnitude of a circle is assumed 360° in hexagecimal system, 400 Gons in centesimal system and $2\pi^c$ in radian system.

(12) Vertical angle can be measured with respect to horizontal or vertical or in percentage mode.

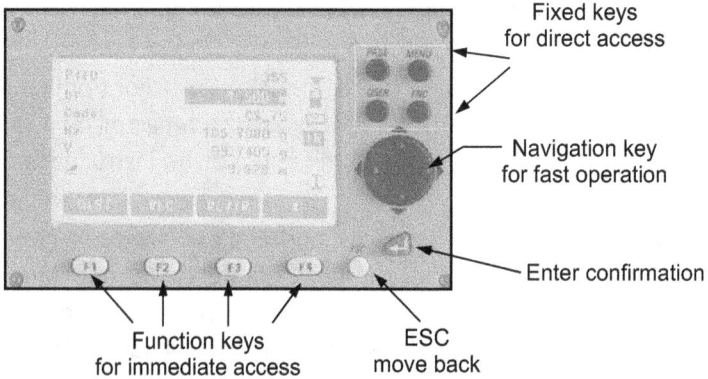

Fig. 5.25 : User friendly control panel of Leica TPS-407 electronic total station

(13) Automatic Correction For: Temperature and Pressure, Curvature, Refraction and Closing Error in traverse survey.

(14) Data Storage Facility: The instrument is capable to store the co-ordinates of the points along with their point number and point description either on on-board memory device or on built in extra drive or external drive.

(15) On board processing upto certain extent with the help of an on board computer and preinstalled programs like Remote Elevation Measurement (REM), Missing Line Measurement (MLM), Co-ordinate Geometry (COGO) etc.

(16) Card Drive (Optional) – To upload new or repair the old in-built programs and store the data in excess of in-built memory.

(17) Data Downloading and Uploading through RS 232 port and special purpose software known as communication/transfer software or USB port and pen drive system or Secured Digital (SD) card system or Blue tooth system.

(18) File Management – Open/Close/Edit/Delete/Rename/Upload/Download the job file.

It must be noted that only few of the feature listed above are available with many of the standard models marketed by many of the manufacturers. Features available with the total stations change from model to model and from manufacturer to manufacturer. If you are not satisfied with features available with standard models of ETS manufacturer of your choice, then it is possible to specify the features of your desire while ordering for ETS and get a custom built total station for you.

5.22.2.6 The Prism Reflector

The total stations provided with infra red waves based EODM requires to complete the distance measurement process, a retro-reflector. Retro-reflector is a device that reflects light or other radiations back to its source. These are trihedral prism manufactured from the glass (BK7 or equivalent) with excellent optical characteristics specifically the refractive index (Refractive index is the ratio of speed of light in vacuum and in substance; it is 1.5168 for BK7 glass). Such prisms are commonly referred as a corner cube in which the reflective surfaces are perpendicular to a very close tolerance. The diameter (ϕ) of such a regular prism is about 50 to 60 mm and thickness (T) is around 0.87 times the diameter.

This prism reflector reflects back in direction parallel to that of transmission, the optical waves transmitted by the EDM essential for reduction of distances by the principal of phase comparison. The incident and reflected will be parallel to within few minutes to seconds depending upon quality of prism. Such prisms are also called as retro directive prism or retro reflector.

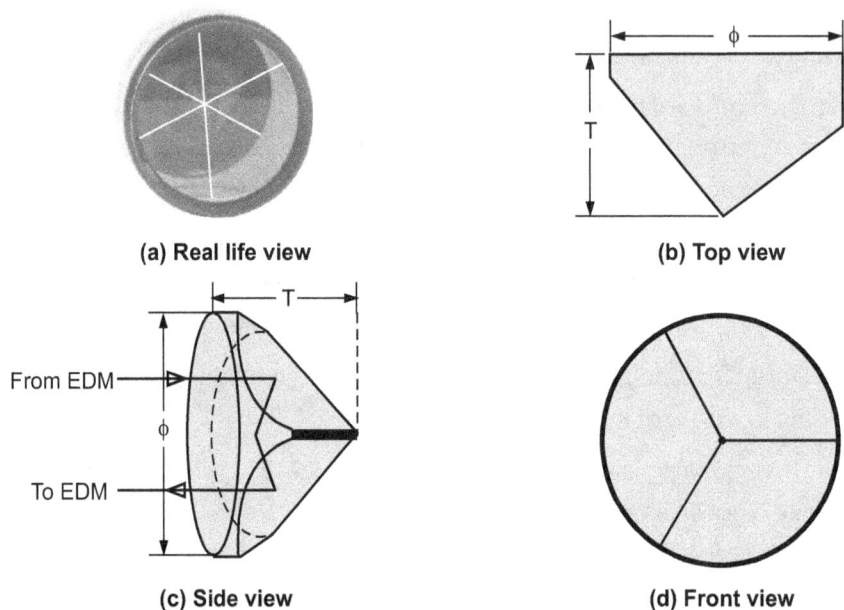

(a) Real life view   **(b) Top view**

(c) Side view   **(d) Front view**

Fig. 5.26 : Construction and working of a prism reflector

The distance that the user wants, is the distance from the vertical axis of the instrument to the vertical axis of the prism. However, the path of the beam includes the distance the beam must travel through the prism and must be corrected for this "extra" distance and the effect on the speed of light when the beam travels through the glass instead of air. This correction needs to be taken into account in the process of distance reduction and is called as *Prism Constant*.

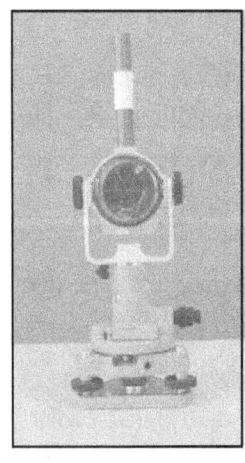
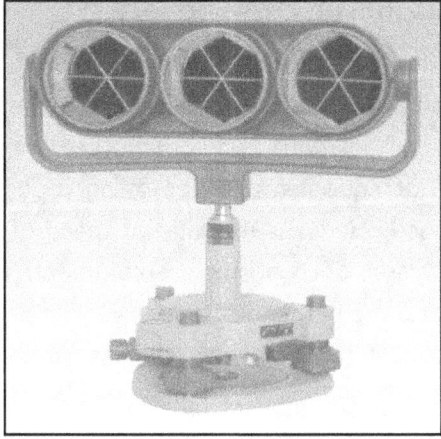

(a) Single prism reflector with target plate   **(b) Single prism reflector with target rod**   **(c) Triple prism assembly with horizontally arranged prisms**

Fig. 5.27 : The prism reflectors

This prism constant is usually few millimeters and may change from prism to prism. For a regular prism this constant is around 35 to 40 mm.

The prism is usually mounted on pole or tripod but may be held in hand if required. The distance measuring range of the EDM on ETS is directly influenced by number of prisms held together at a station and optical characteristics of the prisms. If very frequently the observations are required to be taken against a vertical surface, as in case of measurement of settlement of the buildings, then a reflector sheet may be pasted at the intended point on that vertical surface. The constant of a reflector sheet is zero.

5.22.2.7 Fundamental Measurements Made by a Total Station

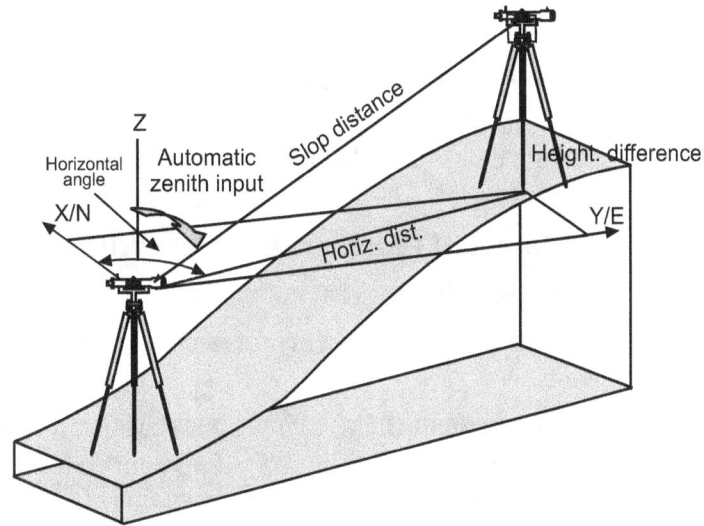

Fig. 5.28 : Fundamental measurements made by a total station

When aimed at an appropriate target station, a total station measures following three parameters :

1. The *rotation* of the instrument's line of sight from the meridian in a horizontal plane i.e. bearing (θ).
2. The *inclination* of the line of sight with respect to the horizontal i.e. *vertical angle (α).*
3. The distance between the instrument and the target along line of sight i.e. sloped distance (l).

Knowing sloped distance l and vertical angle α, instrument works out the horizontal distance say D (= $l \cdot \cos \alpha$) and vertical component V (= $l \cdot \sin \alpha$) to the reflector station say R.

Knowing horizontal distance (D) and bearing (θ), instrument works out Latitude (D $\cdot \cos \theta$) and Departure (D $\cdot \sin \theta$) of reflector station (R) with respect to instrument station (I).

Knowing North co-ordinate (N_I) and East co-ordinate (E_I) of the instrument station say I, and Latitude (D $\cdot \cos \theta$) and Departure (D $\cdot \sin \theta$) of reflector station (R), instrument works out the North co-ordinate N_R (= N_I + D $\cdot \cos \theta$) and East co-ordinates E_R (= E_I + D $\cdot \sin \theta$) of the reflector station R.

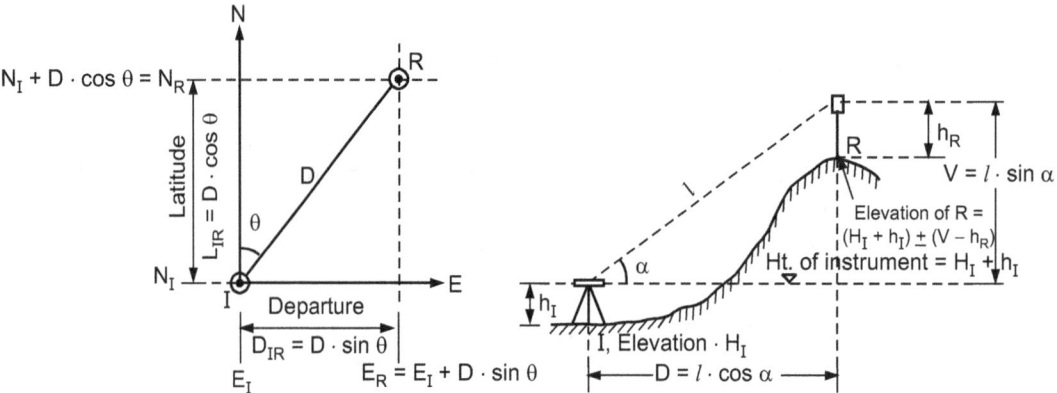

Fig. 5.29 : Reduction of co-ordinates from sloped distance, vertical angle and bearing

Knowing Elevation (say H_I) of the instrument station I, height (say h_I) of the instrument above ground, vertical component V and height of reflector (say h_R) above ground, instrument works out elevation $H_R = [(H_I + h_I) \pm V - h_R)]$ of the reflector station R.

5.22.2.8 Some Common Onboard Programs Available With ETS Instruments

(1) Reduction of Co-ordinates : Works out X, Y, Z or N, E, H for the point bisected.

(2) Area and Perimeter Calculation : Works out area or perimeter of the figure enclosed by given set of points.

(3) Remote Elevation Measurement (REM) : Works out elevation of inaccessible point whose base is accessible. To do so set up total station at a point from which that remote point is visible and its base is accessible. Activate the REM programme.

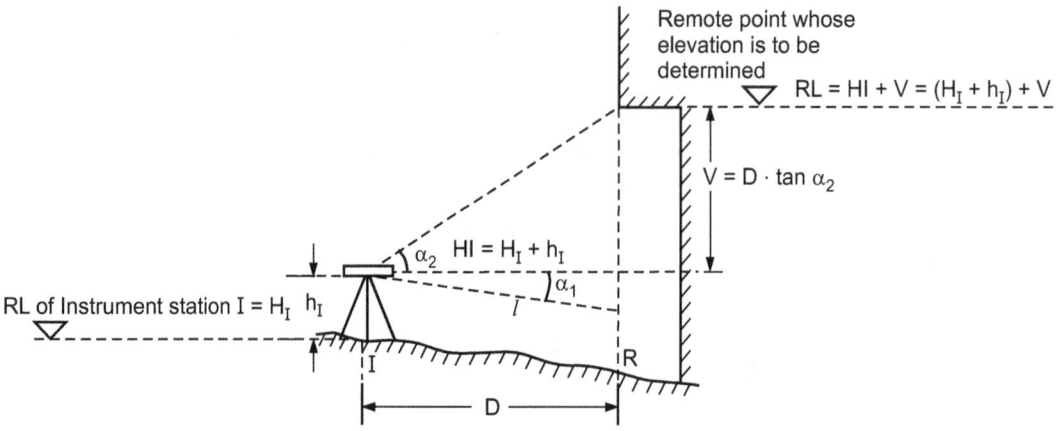

Fig. 5.30 : Remote elevation measurement

Hold a prism reflector on pole at a point exactly vertically below that remote point and bisect it with total station. Total station measures sloped distance (l) and vertical angle (α_1) to prism centre and reduces horizontal distance (D) of remote point from instrument station. Then bisect that remote station. The total station measures vertical angle (α_2) to remote station, works out vertical component V (= D . tan α_2), applies it to elevation ($H_I + h_I$) of the instrument axis and works out elevation (= $H_I + h_I \pm V$) of the remote station by taking +V if remote point is above the line of sight and by taking –V if remote point is below the line of sight.

4. Missing Line Measurements (MLM) : Many times vision between the terminal stations of a line whose length or bearing is required is obstructed or it is not possible to occupy terminal station/s of such a line. The MLM program works out length and bearing of such a line from a station other than its terminal stations. To do so set up total station at a point from which both of the terminal stations of that line are visible. Bisect the terminal stations one by one.

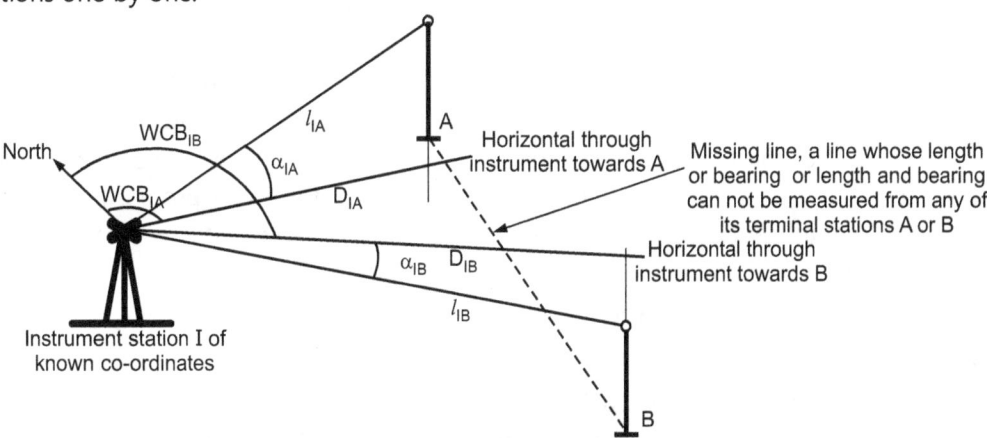

Fig. 5.31 : Missing Line Measurement (MLM) or Remote Distance Measurement (RDM)

Instrument will work out co-ordinates of the terminal stations and then will work out the lengths and bearing of a line joining those terminal stations from co-ordinate geometry.

5. Offset Measurements : Works out co-ordinate of the object when it is required to keep the reflector off the object on account of some limitations. This program is very useful to work out co-ordinates of the objects whose centre is inaccessible due to some reasons. It can be used to work out co-ordinates of a tree, well etc.

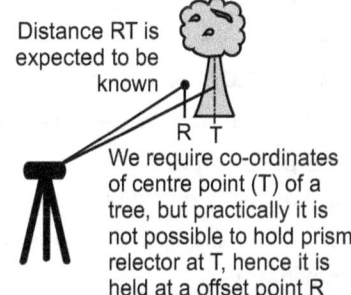

Distance RT is expected to be known

We require co-ordinates of centre point (T) of a tree, but practically it is not possible to hold prism relector at T, hence it is held at a offset point R

Fig. 5.32 : Offset measurement

6. COGO (Co-ordinate Geometry) : It is a special purpose program to work out point of intersection of - two lines, a line and a arc, two arcs etc.

7. Setting Out a Point : Using this program one can mark a point of known/required/given co-ordinate. This program will be useful to line out for foundations of the structures such as buildings, communication routes, dams, bridges etc. They can also be used to set out for curves.

8. Resection or Free Stationing or Floating Point Measurement : Using this program one can reduce the co-ordinates of the station occupied by taking back sight to two to three stations in nearby vicinity, whose co-ordinates are known by the operator.

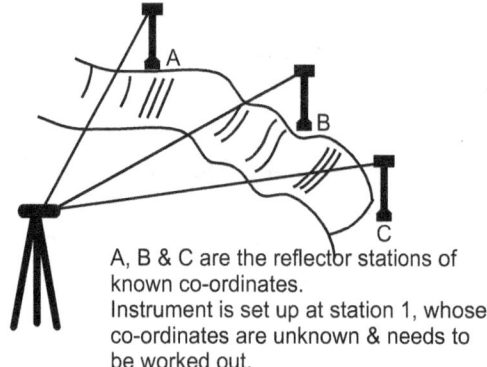

A, B & C are the reflector stations of known co-ordinates.
Instrument is set up at station 1, whose co-ordinates are unknown & needs to be worked out.

Fig. 5.33 : Resectioning or Free stationing

8. Traversing : This programme is exclusively developed to carry out traverse survey either open or closed or fixed. Fixed traverse is traverse run from a point of known co-ordinate to another point of known co-ordinates. Using the same programme we can correct the co-ordinates of the traverse stations as well as details located from all such traverse stations.

5.22.2.9 Uses of a Total Station

1. General purpose angle measurement.
2. General purpose distance measurement.
3. Provision of controls by traversing or triangulation or trilateration surveys.
4. Levelling and Contour survey.
5. Locating the details in property survey or topographical survey.
6. Fixing the alignment and setting out or lining out for buildings, roads, railways, dams, canals, bridges etc.

5.22.2.10 Factors Affecting Use of an ETS

1. A clear line of sight between the instrument and the measured points is essential.
2. The precision of the instrument is dependent on the raw repeatabilities of the angle and distance measurement.
3. A well defined measurement point or target/prism is required to obtain the maximum accuracy.
4. The accuracy of angle and distance measurement is subject to the same instrumental errors as electronic theodolites and EDM respectively.

5.22.2.11 Temporary Adjustments of a Total Station

The adjustments required to be performed at every instrument station in order to make the instrument ready for use at that station are called as the temporary adjustments. A total station is basically a theodolite; hence temporary adjustments of the total station are more over same as like that of a theodolite.

Following are the temporary adjustments of a total station.

1. Setting up of tripod, taking out instrument from box and fixing the instrument on tripod head.

2. Levelling up of the instrument :
   (a) Coarse levelling with spirit level by leg adjustment.
   (b) Fine levelling with digital bubble and foot screws.

3. Centering up of the instrument :
   (a) Coarse centering by leg adjustment.
   (b) Fine centering with laser plummet by shifting the instrument bodily on machine finished tripod head.

   Levelling and centering shall be done in succession to each other till both of them are satisfactory.

4. Setting up the station :
   (a) By inputting station name, instrument height and co-ordinates at first station and
   (b) By recalling the station occupied from memory at next stations.

5. Orienting the instrument :
   (a) By setting horizontal angle to 00 when instrument is directed toward the accepted meridian (usually North direction) at first station, and
   (b) By taking back sight to previously occupied traverse station (So that same meridian will be referred).

5.22.2.12 Recording Measurements with a Total Station

Some of the ETS models (like that of Pentax R326) are provided with two separate modes. One mode (e.g. Mode A) to use it as EDT or EDM to measure angles and distances, and other mode (e.g. Mode B) to use the special programs provided on it. Other ETS are not provided such separate modes (e.g. Leika's ETS model TPS-407).

1. Measuring Angles with a Total Station :

(a) Measuring Horizontal Angle :

1. To measure horizontal angle AOB with an ETS, set up instrument at station O and perform only first three temporary adjustments as enumerated above. Machine gets switched on in the process temporary adjustments. Keep face left, select a measurement screen/mode which displays the horizontal angle and ascertain that clamping screws (if any) are loose.

2. Look against optical collimator, rotate the telescope in horizontal and vertical plane and bisect approximately the peg at station A by vertical cross hair and tighten horizontal and vertical circle clamp screws if instrument do not have friction clamping arrangement.

3. Look through telescope, rotate the telescope in horizontal and vertical plane by making use of horizontal and vertical circle tangent screws and bisect exactly bottom of nail over peg at station A by point of intersection of cross hairs on diaphragm of telescope.

4. Set horizontal angle to 00 by pressing the appropriate key.

5. Bisect station B in the same way as like that for station A and read the reading in display against the horizontal angle.

6. Record this horizontal angle reading manually on your record/field book. Please note that ETS is usually not programmed to store in its memory, an individual angle or distance.

7. If required, repeat the steps 2 to 6 by changing face to right to obtain one more set of reading. This is highly essential, especially when A, O and B are at different elevation, to avoid error due to imperfect permanent adjustments.

(b) Measuring Vertical Angle :

Before starting with measurement of vertical angle with an ETS, one should borne in mind that many of the total ETS instruments are designed to measure the vertical angles either with respect to a vertical line or with respect to a horizontal line or in percentage mode. So first decide what way you have to measure the vertical angle, and accordingly carry out initial setting by following the appropriate procedure as suggested by the manufacturer of the instrument.

1. To measure from station O, a vertical angle to any object say E above or D below the horizontal line of sight, set up instrument at station O and perform only first three temporary adjustments as enumerated above. Machine gets switched on in the process of temporary adjustments. Keep face left, select a measurement screen/mode which displays the vertical angle and ascertain that clamping screws (if any) are loose.

2. Look against optical collimator, rotate the telescope in horizontal and vertical plane and bisect approximately the station E or D by horizontal cross hair and tighten horizontal and vertical circle clamp screws if instrument do not have friction clamping arrangement.

3. Look through telescope, rotate the telescope in horizontal and vertical plane by making use of horizontal and vertical circle tangent screws and bisect exactly the station E or D by point of intersection of cross hairs on diaphragm of telescope. Read the reading in display against the vertical angle.

4. Record this vertical angle reading manually on your record/field book. Please note that ETS is usually not programmed to store in its memory, an individual angle or distance.

5. If required, repeat the steps 2 to 4 by changing face to right to obtain one more set of readings. This is highly essential, especially when there is possibility of vertical index error.

2. Measuring Distances between Two Points :

(a) To Measure Horizontal Distance between Two Points :

1. To measure horizontal distance between two points say A and B, set up ETS at station A and perform only first three temporary adjustments as enumerated above. Machine gets switched on in the process of temporary adjustments. Select the measuring screen/mode ready to show the horizontal distance and ascertain that clamping screws (if any) are loose.

2. Hold vertically the prism pole at station B, so that face of the prism is directed towards the ETS at station A.

3. Look against optical collimator, rotate the telescope in horizontal and vertical plane and bisect approximately the prism at station B and tighten horizontal and vertical circle clamp screws if instrument do not have friction clamping arrangement.

4. Look through telescope, rotate the telescope in horizontal and vertical plane by making use of horizontal and vertical circle tangent screws and bisect exactly the centre of prism at station B by point of intersection of cross hairs on diaphragm of telescope.

5. Press the button (DIST or MEAS) exclusively created for carrying out distance measurement process. Within few seconds machine will display the results. Read the value against horizontal distance.

6. Record this horizontal distance reading manually on your record book. Please note that ETS is usually not programmed to store in its memory, an individual angle or distance.

(b) To Measure Vertical/Sloped Distance between Two Points :

1. To measure vertical/sloped distance between two points say A and B, set up ETS at station A, and

   For ETS model like Leika TPS 407 - Perform all of 5 its temporary adjustments as enumerated above. Machine gets switched on in the process of temporary adjustments. Select the measuring screen showing the vertical and sloped distances.

   For ETS model like Pentax R 326 – Perform only first 3 temporary adjustments enumerated above. Machine gets switched on in the process of temporary adjustments. While in mode A, select a measuring screen showing vertical and sloped distances.

2. Hold vertically the prism pole at station B, so that face of the prism is directed towards the ETS at station A.

3. Look against optical collimator, rotate the telescope in horizontal and vertical plane and bisect approximately the prism at station B and tighten horizontal and vertical circle clamp screws if instrument do not have friction clamping arrangement.

4. Look through telescope, rotate the telescope in horizontal and vertical plane by making use of both horizontal and vertical circle tangent screws and bisect exactly the centre of prism at station B by point of intersection of cross hairs on diaphragm of telescope.

5. Feed in height of prism centre above station occupied by it before proceeding ahead. If you are working with ETS like Pentax R 326 in mode A, feeding in prism height is not required.

6. Press the button (DIST or MEAS) exclusively created for carrying out distance measurement process. Within few seconds machine will display the Results.

    The vertical distance and sloped distances shown by ETS model like Leika TPS 407 are in between ground points A and B and those shown by ETS model like Pentax R 326 in mode A are in between centre of instrument and centre of prism.

    If you want these distances as distances between ground points with ETS model like Pentax R 326 ETS, you will require carrying out all 5 temporary adjustments and will require working in Mode B.

• Record these distance readings manually on your record book. Please note that ETS is usually not programmed to store in its memory, an individual angle or distance.

5.22.2.13 Generalized Procedure for Survey with a Total Station

1. Carry out reconnaissance survey of the area under consideration to finalize position of the control/traverse stations in the vicinity of the details to be located.

2. *Set up the total station* and carry out its *coarse levelling* with the help of round spirit level by leg adjustment and *coarse centering* with the help of plumb bob by leg adjustment.

3. *Switch on the instrument* and allow it to boot up and carry out *fine levelling* with help of digital bubble and foot screws and *fine centering* with help of laser plummet and shifting the instrument laterally on stand head.

4. *Set a new job or open the old/existing job* if you are continuing the old work.

5. *Set a station* by inputting station name, instrument height and co-ordinates of the station occupied.

6. *Set orientation* of the instrument by setting horizontal angle to 00 when instrument is directed toward north.

7. Start the process of *locating the details*. To locate a detail first enter in, the name or number for detailing station along with height of reflector to be held at detailing station and then shoot the detail (i.e. press measure and record key/s) to obtain its co-ordinates and store it in the memory.

8. Do not forget to *record the short description* of the detail either on the instrument or on the external record book, so that there will be no confusion when a drafting person is connecting these points in CAD software to prepare plan/map.

9. These ways get located all intended points from that instrument station. Finally *get located the next traverse station* to which the instrument is to be shifted.

10. Switch off and *shift the instrument* to next traverse station already located from previously occupied traverse station and set it up there.

11. As we are continuing the same job, *no need of setting the job* at this station.

12. *Set the station* at new traverse station by recalling back from the memory the co-ordinates traverse station occupied and inputting the new instrument height.

13. *Orient the instrument by taking back sight* to previously occupied traverse station so that same meridian will be referred.

14. Now *get located the details* from this station. Get located next traverse station and shift the instrument to next traverse station in switch off condition.

15. This way get occupied all the previously fixed control/traverse stations.

16. Do not forget to *locate first traverse station from the last traverse* station, so that closing error in the work can be evaluated.

17. *Data down loading*: Depending on the facility available with the instrument, the data down loading can be carried out by any one of the following way available with the instrument.

    (a) Connect the instrument to the off board computer which is installed with *the Communication/Transfer Software* and get downloaded the job data.

    (b) Insert a pen drive into USB port of the instrument and get copied the required job data on it.

    (c) Transfer the job data to blue tooth compatible off board device/gadget using a blue tooth system available with instrument.

To convert into required field book or drawing or report format, the data downloaded so is processed further using *the Post Processing Software/s*.

5.22.2.14 Softwares Essentially Required With a Total Station

In order to make more productive use of the total station, following two kinds of computer softwares are invariably required along with a total station.

1. The Communication/Transfer Software :

The work environment of the processor on board of the ETS instrument is usually different than your off board computer, the desktop or laptop etc. It is essential to establish interface between the computers on the board of the ETS and off the board, to have exchange of the data in between them. The software used for the purpose is the Communication/Transfer software. Such softwares are usually supplied along with the ETS instrument as an essential accessory. Leica Geo-Office, Nikon-Transit, Pentax DL30 are some of such softwares. The format of data downloaded with help of such softwares is such that it can support graphic based softwares like Autocad or spreadsheet type softwares like MS Excel or data base management softwares like Access for further processing of down loaded raw co-ordinate data to support the Management Information System (MIS).

The total stations making use of 'USB port – pen drive' system or 'Secured Digital (SD) card' system or 'blue tooth' system for data exchange will not require making use of such communication or transferring software.

2. The Post Processing Softwares :

These are the special purpose softwares installed on the off board computer and exclusively developed for converting data down loaded from electronic surveying instruments into useful information in form of plots, geometrical parameters, quantities etc. Such softwares may work on any regular CAD platform or work independently in any usual operating system (OS) like DOS, Windows, UNIX or equivalent. Using such software one can produce plans/maps, sections, contoured drawings etc. Generating the data required for lining out for building; road; dam; canal; pipeline; huge machines; assembly lines; etc. with desired geometry, reduction of earthwork quantities, finalizing control levels in reservoir planning, development of digital terrain model, tracing the grade contour, prediction of runoff and lot other such operations are possible with this software. Autocad, Leica Liscad, Pythagorous, Autocivil, Microsurvey, Eaglesoft, Road-Cal are some of such softwares.

5.22.2.15 Errors in Total Station Surveying

Errors are discrepancies in measurements which can be minimized by taking proper care of measuring instrument and by following proper process of measurement but their absolute elimination is almost not possible.

Total station is combination of electronic digital theodolite and electronic distance meter and principally is used to reduce rectangular co-ordinates (Northing, Easting and Elevation) from observed polar co-ordinates (radial distance, horizontal angle and vertical angle). Thus, error in final output (many times co-ordinates) of a total station is combined effect of errors caused by electronic digital theodolite and errors caused by electronic distance meter.

I.   Errors in Angular Measurement :

Errors in angular measurement are the errors due to digital theodolite incorporated in a total station. These can be broadly divided into three categories viz. instrumental errors, errors of manipulation and sighting and errors due to natural causes.

(a) Instrumental Errors :

1. Errors due to imperfect relationship between fundamental lines or principal axes of the total station : This includes error on account of

(i)   Axis of plate bubble not perpendicular to vertical axis,

(ii) Line of collimation not perpendicular to horizontal axis,

(iii) Horizontal axis not perpendicular to vertical axis, and

(iv) Line of collimation not horizontal when vertical circle is reading zero and plate bubble is centered.

The effects of these errors can be removed by carrying out permanent adjustment, calibration or by using suitable field procedures.

If the plate bubble is out of adjustment, the vertical axis remains tilted even when the bubble is centered. It is not possible to remove any error caused by this by taking observations with both faces. If the theodolite is levelled electronically, it will usually be fitted with a dual axis compensator and it can calculate corrections for any errors caused by vertical axis tilt and will apply these to displayed horizontal and vertical angles. However, the compensator itself may be out of adjustment. To correct for this, an on-board electronic calibration can be carried out in which the compensator index errors are measured and then automatically applied to all readings.

Error on account of line of collimation not perpendicular to horizontal axis or horizontal axis not perpendicular to vertical axis or line of collimation not horizontal when vertical circle is reading zero and plate bubble is centred are removed by taking the average of face left and face right readings, or by carrying out an electronic calibration on the instrument.

2. **Error due to eccentricity of the plates** *:* Occurs when vertical axis of instrument does not coincide with centre of plates. Can be eliminated or minimized by taking several pair of diametrically opposite readings all along the plates and averaging. This happens automatically in highly precise instruments.

3. **Error due to circle graduation errors** : Caused by erroneous or uneven marking of plates. Can be eliminated or minimized by many readings all along the plates and average. This happens automatically in highly precise instruments.

4. **Error due to peripheral instruments/accessories** : The line of collimation of an *optical or laser plummet* must coincide with the vertical axis of the total station. The clamping mechanism and circular bubbles in *levelling head* should be checked regularly. All of the parts of a *tripod stand* should also be inspected regularly to check that they have not become loose.

(b) Errors of Manipulation and Sighting :

1. Error due to limitations on levelling of the instrument and/or target.

2. Error due to limitations on centering of the instrument and/or target.

3. Error due to poor optical or mechanical condition of the instrument.

4. Error due to incorrect bisection of target (i.e. a pin or nail or tip of shoe of prism pole or ranging rod etc.) on account of ability of observer's eyes and poor environmental conditions limiting clear vision of the target. The best way to minimize pointing errors is to repeat the observation several times and use the average as the result.

(c) Errors due to Natural Causes :

1. **Error due to even/uneven settlement of tripod :** This leads to change in elevation of collimation plane and mis-levelling. Avoid this, by setting up of tripod on firm ground. If surveyor is compelled to set up instrument on marshes and swamps, insert long wooden pegs in it, flush with surface and set tripod on these pegs. Most total station instruments have provision to suspend observations when mis-levelling becomes too large.

2. **Error due to uneven heating of the instrument/tripod :** Uneven heating of the instrument/tripod can lead to instrument mis-levelling. Temperature differences between the instrument and the surrounding environment will result in changes to the characteristics of the instrument, in particular of the compensator over time. This can mostly but not totally be eliminated by taking measurements with both faces. Hence to minimize error on account of this, it is better to cover instrument with umbrella and allowing the instrument to adjust with ambient temperature before starting measurements, while working in hot sunshine.

3. **Error due to vibration of instrument or tripod due to wind :** Vibration due to speedy wind do not allow vertical axis to remain vertical. If inclination of vertical axis is likely to exceed the compensating limit of tilt compensator then it is better either to protect instrument from wind by using shield or discontinue the observations until wind speed reduces. Observing and setting out angles in windy conditions is not recommended.

4. **Error due to refraction :** Refraction causes bending of line of sight. Avoid line of sight close to objects such as the ground, cars, large trees that can create microclimates. When this cannot be done, postpone measurements until better conditions exist. Do not take observations when refraction is likely to be a problem.

II. Errors in Linear/Distance Measurements :

Errors in linear measurement are the errors due to electronic distance meter incorporated in a total station. Like that of errors in electronic digital theodolite, errors in electronic distance measurement can also be divided into three categories viz. Instrumental errors, errors of manipulation and sighting and errors due to natural causes.

(a) Instrumental Errors :

1. **Constant and Scalar error :** All total stations have a linear accuracy quoted in the form $\pm$ (p mm + q PPM).

   The constant error p is independent of the distance being measured and is governed by mechanisms within the instrument and are normally beyond the control of the user. It is an estimate of the individual errors caused by such phenomena as unwanted phase shifts in electronic components, errors in phase and transit time measurements.

   The scalar/systematic error b is proportional to the distance being measured, where 1 PPM (part per million) is equivalent to an additional error of 1 mm for every kilometre measured.

Specified constant + Proportional error for EDM in a total station may vary from ± (2 mm + 2 PPM) to ± (5 mm + 5 PPM).

The constant error is more significant over shorter distance. For very long distances the constant error becomes negligible. For example: ± (2 mm + 2 PPM), at 100 m the error in distance measurement will be ± [2 mm + (2 mm/km × 0.1 km)] = ± 2.2 mm

The systematic error is more prominent over longer distance. For example : ± (2 mm + 2 PPM), at 1.5 km, the error will be ± [2 mm + (2 mm/km × 1.5 km)] = ± 5 mm

Example 5.1 : Constant and scalar error for an EDM fitted within a total station is ± (5 mm + 5 PPM). Work out the possible value of distance of 2350 m measured with this total station.

Solution :

We know constant and scalar error for given instrument is ± (5 mm + 5 PPM)

$$\therefore \quad \text{Error over distance 2350 m} = \pm \left[5 \text{ mm} + \frac{5}{1000000} \times (2350 \times 1000) \text{ mm} \right]$$

$$= \pm [5 \text{ mm} + 11.75 \text{ mm}]$$

$$= \pm 16.75 \text{ mm, say} \pm 17 \text{ mm} = \pm 0.017 \text{ m}$$

$\therefore$ Possible value of distance of 2350 m measured = (2350 ± 0.017) m

$$= 2349.983 \text{ m to } 2350.17 \text{ m}$$

2. Error due to electrical centre of the EDM is being offset : EDM equipment should be checked against first order base line at regular time interval to assure its accuracy and reliability and to determine measurement constant (k) if any.

3. Error due to optical centre of the prism is being offset : The error may be minimized by accounting the reflector constant.

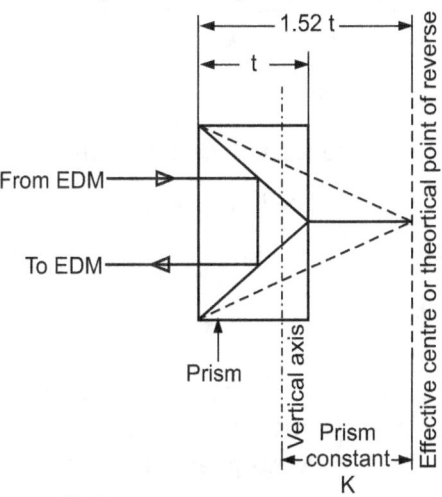

These reflectors have a so-called effective centre (theoretical point of reversal). Locating centre of prism purely from geometry is not possible because velocity of propagation of an electromagnetic wave as it enters a glass body is decelerated thereby the actual measured distance is extended. The effective centre will be behind the prism itself and is generally not over the station occupied. Thus, there is a reflector constant or prism constant to be subtracted from the measurement.

Fig. 5.34 Concept of prism constant

Practical Way to Determine Prism Constant :

Mark a straight line PR with a point Q approximately midway between the terminal stations P and R.

P   Q   R

Fig. 5.35 : Determining a prism constant

Measure with same EDM and same reflector distances PQ and PR from station P and distance QR from station Q.

Then $(PR + K) = (PQ + K) + (QR + K)$ ... (Here K is prism constant)

$\therefore$ $K = PR - (PQ + QR)$

Example 5.2 : A, B and C are three colinear points. Distances AB and AC measured with an EDM at A towards reflector set up at B and C are 114.514 m and 226.388 m respectively. Distance BC measured with the same EDM at B towards same reflector set up at C is 111.909 m. Work out constant of the prism reflector.

Solution :

Let K be constant of a prism.

Then $(AC + K) = (AB + K) + (BC + K)$

$\therefore$ Constant of prism, $K = AC - (AB + BC)$

Here AC = 226.388 m, AB = 114.514 m and BC = 111.909 m

$\therefore$ Constant of prism, $K = 226.388 - (114.514 + 111.909) = -0.035$ m

Here –ve sign indicates that absolute value of prism constant shall be subtracted from distance measured with an EDM, without considering the prism constant.

(b) Errors of Manipulation and Sighting :

1. Error due to limitations on centering and levelling of EDMs and reflector.

2. Error due to limitations on measurements of instrument and reflector heights.

3. Error due to poor optical and mechanical condition of the instrument.

4. Errors due to limitations on determination of metrological factors such as atmospheric pressure and temperature.

(c) Errors due to Natural Causes :

1. **Error due to variation in temperature and pressure :** Primary natural cause for error in electronic distance measurement is variations in atmospheric temperature and pressure at work site with respect to that at time of calibration. Atmospheric temperature and pressure affects the refractive index of crystal generating modulation and changes the wavelength of electromagnetic waves used in the process of distance measurements.

As a thumb rule, variation of 1°C in the atmospheric temperature affects the measured distance by about 1 PPM; similarly variation of about 2.5 mm (of mercury column) in atmospheric pressure affects the measured distance by 1 PPM. It should be noted that the atmospheric pressure in terms of mercury column drops by 1 mm of with every 11 m gain in height.

Many modern instruments can account for error due to variation in temperature and pressure after obtaining the values of temperature and pressure at work site either from built-in temperature and pressure gauge or from the operator. In older versions of EDMs, manufacturers provide charts or graphs to work out value of PPM constant against known values of site temperature and pressure at place of survey. The value of PPM constant determined from such charts and graphs shall be fed into the instrument.

Example 5.3 : If the temperature changes from 20°C in morning to 39°C in afternoon on a summer day, and the PPM correction of EDM within the ETS was not changed. How much could be a discrepancy in distance of 900 m measured in morning and afternoon?

Solution : We know, as a thumb rule, variation of 1°C in the atmospheric temperature affects the measured distance by about 1 PPM.

∴ Discrepancy over unit distance measured with ignorance to PPM correction for temperature variation from 20°C to 39°C = $\left[\dfrac{(39° - 20°)}{1°}\right]$ PPM = 19 PPM

∴ $= \dfrac{19}{1000000} = 0.000019$ units

∴ Discrepancy over distance of 900 m measured with ignorance of PPM correction for temperature = 0.000019×900 m = 0.0171 m = 17.1 mm

Example 5.4 : A surveying party achieved an altitude of 750 m from 200 m but PPM correction for an ETS within was not changed. How much could be a discrepancy in distance of 900 m measured at altitude of 200 m and 750 m ?

Solution : Gain in altitude = 750 – 200 = 550 m

We know atmospheric pressure drops by 1 mm of mercury column with every gain in height of 11 m, hence drop (variation) in atmospheric pressure over gain in height of 550 m will be $\left[\dfrac{550}{11} \times 1\right]$ mm = 50 mm.

We know, as a thumb rule, variation of 2.5 mm in the atmospheric pressure affects the measured distance by about 1 PPM.

∴ Discrepancy over unit distance measured with ignorance to PPM correction for pressure variation of 50 mm = $\left[\dfrac{50}{2.5}\right]$ PPM = 20 PPM = $\dfrac{20}{1000000}$ = 0.000020 units.

∴ Discrepancy over distance of 900 m measured with ignorance of PPM correction for pressure = 0.000020×900 m = 0.018 m = 18 mm

2. **Error due to line of sight too close to object :** Allowing the sight line to come too close (less than 0.5 m) to objects such as the ground, cars, large trees can create errors as large as 0.5 m at a time because there is a microclimate near these objects which will induce abnormal refraction.

5.22.2.16 Mistakes in Total Station Surveying

Mistakes are discrepancies in measurements which can be eliminated completely. Mistakes are mainly due to inattentiveness towards the work by the surveyor and the supporting staff. Some of the common mistakes in total station surveying are listed here below.

1. Inadequate levelling of the instrument.

2. Inadequate centering of the instrument.

3. Reading wrong temperature and pressure required to predict PPM correction factor.

4. Incorrect prediction of PPM constant from chart or graph provided, when value of PPM correction factor is to be evaluated and entered manually.

5. Referring wrong value of prism constant.

6. Entering wrong reference data such as name and/or co-ordinates of the station occupied and/or back sight station while setting up and/or orienting the instrument.

7. Referring incorrect value of instrument height or prism reflector height.

8. Pressing wrong number keys while making data entry into the instrument.

9. Prism pole not held vertically.

10. Incorrect bisection of the target (i.e. a pin or nail or tip of shoe of prism pole or ranging rod etc.) while measuring angles and incorrect bisection of centre of prism or reflector sheet while measuring distances or co-ordinates.

11. Improper focusing of eye-piece leading to dull view of cross hairs.

12. Parallax not eliminated completely due to inadequate focusing of the object glass.

13. Slippage of circle plates on account of insufficient tightening of related clamping screw (if any).

14. Incorrectly reading the values of angles or distances or co-ordinates from display of the instrument.

15. Forgetting to record or save the co-ordinates of the points which will require to be referred at next station.

16. Incorrectly recording the values of angles or distances or co-ordinates or description of the survey points in record/field book.

THEORETICAL QUESTIONS

1. Define remote sensing ? Bring out necessity and importance of remote sensing.

2. Differentiate between active and passive remote sensing.

3. Draw a neat sketch showing the components of idealized remote sensing system.

4. Enumerate various platforms for remote sensing and state where each of them will be more useful.

5. State characteristics of any one of the following remote sensing systems.

    (a) Resourcesat – 1, (b) SPOT 4-5, (c) LANDAT – 7, (d) Cartosat – 2.

6. Explain various kinds of resolutions used in remote sensing.

7. Discuss the types of sensors on the basis of recording the scene.

8. What do you mean by swath and IFOV ? Explain with sketch.

9. State and explain fundamental equation for conceptual design of remote sensing.

10. What is electromagnetic spectrum ? Explain with sketch.

11. Explain the concept of atmospheric window.

12. Comment brief on spectral signature as a tool to interpret the RS images.

13. Bring out difference between various RS data products and state with whom they are available in India.

14. Bring out difference between Aerial photograph and satellite image.

15. Discuss in brief the methods to study remotely sensed images.

16. What is photo interpretation key ? Explain its types.

17. State the advantages of remote sensing.

18. Enlist the limitations of remote sensing.

19. Comment on applications and scope of remote sensing.

20. Explain the application of remote sensing cartography / mapping.

21. Discuss the application of remote sensing in Resource Inventory and Management.

22. What is total station? State the classification based on range of total station.

23. Explain salient features of a total station.

24. What is total station? State the classification based on type of wave pattern used on EDM.

25. Write short note on a total station.

26. State the classification of EDM instruments.

27. What is total station? State any five functions available in a total station.

28. Write short note on basic principle of EDM instrument.

29. What is total station? Explain any six principal features of a total station.

30. What is difference between EDM and Total Station? State various special functions available in total station.

31. Explain the principal used in Total Station. State various special functions available in total station.

32. Explain the principal used in Total Station. Explain its advantages over 20" transit theodolite.

33. Enlist different functions available on total station. Out of it explain RDM (Remote Distance Measurement) in detail.

34. Give advantages of using total station to carry out road survey instead of the traditional instruments.

35. What are the advantages of using total station for surveying? Explain the use of special function RDM (Remote Distance Measurement).

36. Write a short note on total station and its applications in the field.

37. Explain any four special functions available on total station.

38. Define EDM, state principle of EDM and bring out difference between measuring and carrier waves.

39. Comment in brief on pattern/types of electromagnetic waves used with an EDM.

40. Explain in brief working of an EDM.

41. State and explain with sketch, how an EDM works out distance.

42. Discuss in brief classification of the EDM instruments.

43. List down the functions an EDM needs to perform while measuring distance.

44. Enumerate advantages and disadvantages of EDM.

45. Prepare brief note on ETS.

46. What is a total station? Explain any six principal features of a total station.

47. Enlist the programs available on ETS and explain one such programme.

48. State the merits and demerits of the ETS.

49. Enlist and explain the uses of ETS.

50. Explain the concept of REM, RDM and Resection in the context of ETS.

51. Define total station. List down commonly available programs/special functions with a total station and explain the program/special function MLM.

52. Comment in brief 'limitations/factors effecting use of a total station'.

53. Explain in brief temporary adjustment for a total station.

54. Explain in brief process of measuring horizontal angle with an ETS.

55. Explain in brief process of measuring vertical angle with an ETS.

56. Explain in brief process of measuring horizontal distance with an ETS.

57. Explain in brief process of measuring sloped/vertical distance with an ETS.

58. State stepwise the process to carry out survey with a total station.

59. Explain with neat sketches how a total station works out co-ordinates of a object station.

60. Discuss in brief various types of the total stations.

61. Prepare brief note on the prism reflector.

62. Discuss in brief the concept of constant of a prism reflector and explain in brief a method to determine it on field.

63. It is required to determine elevation of an inaccessible point whose base is accessible with a total station. Explain the procedure to do so.

64. There are three visible control stations in the vicinity of the area where topographic survey is to be carried out. Describe the process to work out the co-ordinates of the station occupied by the instrument from which the process of locating the details is likely to be started.

65. The client wants to determine the co-ordinates of an open well of known diameter with a total station. Describe the most appropriate process for the same.

66. Bring out difference between the communication software and the processing software in the context of a total station.

67. Explain the temporary adjustments of a total station.

68. Explain in brief errors in angular measurement in total station surveying.

69. Explain in brief errors in linear measurement in total station surveying.

70. List down common mistakes in total station surveying.

NUMERICAL PROBLEMS

1. Constant and scalar error for an EDM fitted within a total station is ± (3 mm + 3 PPM). Work out the possible value of distance over the distance of 1850 m.

2. If the temperature changes from 46°C in afternoon to 34°C in evening on a summer day, and the PPM correction of an EDM within the ETS was not changed. How much could be a discrepancy in distance of 1200 m measured in afternoon and evening?

3. A surveying party dropped an altitude to 195 m from 915 m but PPM correction for an EDM within the ETS was not changed. How much could be a discrepancy in distance of 1350 m measured at altitude of 195 m and 915 m?

❑❑❑

UNIVERSITY QUESTION PAPERS

March 2014

Time : 3 Hours   Total Marks : 80

Instructions to candidates:

(1) Do not write anything on question paper except Seat No.

(2) Answer sheet should be written with blue link only. Graph or diagram should be drawn with the same pen being used for writing paper or black HB pensile.

(3) Students should note, no supplement will be provided.

(4) Answer **any two** subquestions from each unit.

(5) Figures to the right indicate full marks.

(6) Assume suitable data if necessary.

UNIT – I

1.   What are the object and method of geodetic surveying.   **[8]**

2.   Explain different four correction to be applied to the base line measurement. **[8]**

3.   From an eccentric station E, 14.25 m to the wert of main station B following angle were measured.

$\angle BEC = 78° 25' 32''$ $\angle CEA = 56° 30' 20''$

The station E ϕ C are on the opposite side of the line AB. Reduce the angle centre B. if AB ϕ BC are 5368.2 m ϕ 4682.3 m respectively.   **[8]**

UNIT – II

4.   State and explain four law of weight.   **[8]**

5.   Explain the procedure of adjustment of a Geodetic quadrilateral by approximate method.

6.   In carrying a line of level across a river, the following eight reading were taken with a level under identical conditioned.

2.322, 2.346, 2.352, 2.306, 2.312, 2.300, 2.306, 2.326

Calculate :

(i)Probable error of single observation

(ii)Probable error of the mean.

UNIT – III

7.   Define relief displacement. Derive the expression for relief displacement. **[8]**

8.   The scale of an aerial photography is 1 cm = 100 m. The photograph size is 20 cm × 20 cm Determine the number of photograph required to cover an area 10 km × 10 km. if the longitudinal lap is 60% and the side lap is 30%. **[8]**

9. (a) Differentiate between map and vertical photograph. **[8]**

(b) Write a short note on Mirror stereoscope. **[8]**

UNIT – IV

10.   What is meant by sounding ? State various method of locating sounding ? Explain any one method. **[8]**

11.   Write a short Note on : **[8]**

(a) Nautical sextant

(b) Fathometer.

12.   Describe the classification of Tide Gauge. **[8]**

UNIT – V

13.   What is total Station ? State the classification base on range of total station.**[8]**

14.   Explain type of platform used in remote sensing. **[8]**

15.   State applications of remote sensing to civil Engg. **[8]**

✠ ✠ ✠

Dec. 2014

Time : 3 Hours   **Total Marks : 80**

Instructions to candidates:

    (1) Do not write anything on question paper except Seat No.

    (2) Answer sheet should be written with blue link only. Graph or diagram should be drawn with the same pen being used for writing paper or black HB pensil.

    (3) Students should note, no supplement will be provided.

    (4) Answer **any two** subquestions from each unit.

    (5) Figures to the right indicate full marks.

    (6) Assume suitable data if necessary.

UNIT-I

1. (a) Two stations A and B 120 km apart are 144 m and 556 above mean sea level. An intervening peak 70 km from A has RL of 160. As certain whether A and B are intervisible or not. If not find the height of the scaffold at B so that the line of sight has 2 clearance everywhere.   **[8]**

    (b) Explain in brief the various triangulation figures commonly adopted and compare its merit and demerits.   **[8]**

    (c) Explain about base line measurement. List the equipment used for base line measurement.   **[8]**

UNIT – II

2. (a) State and explain any five laws of weights.   **[8]**

    (b) Explain :

        (i) Delambres method.   **[4]**

        (ii) Adjustment of triangle with central station.   **[4]**

    (c) Explain method of adjustment of geodetic quadrilateral.   **[8]**

UNIT – III

3. (a) Explain crab and drift in aerial photogrammetry.   **[8]**

(b) Write short notes on following.

    (i) Aerial photograammetry. **[4]**

    (ii) Terrestrial photogrammetry. **[4]**

(c) Define photogrammetry, its objects and applications to various fields. [8]

UNIT – IV

4. (a) Explain methods of locating soundings. **[8]**

(b) Explain the principle of working of Nautical Sextant, Explain procedure of measuring horizontal angle with Nautical Sextant. **[8]**

(c) Explain the various methods of solving a three point problem in hydrographic surveying and explain clearly the analytical method. **[8]**

UNIT – V

5. (a) Explain with a sketch the components of a "Remote sensing" system. **[8]**

(b) State clearly the various practical applications of remote sensing to civil engineering field. **[8]**

(c) Explain principle of EDM. State the applications of EDM to civil engineering. **[8]**

✠ ✠ ✠

March 2015

Time : 3 Hours   **Total Marks : 80**

Instructions to candidates:

(1) Do not write anything on question paper except Seat No.

(2) Answer sheet should be written with blue link only. Graph or diagram should be drawn with the same pen being used for writing paper or black HB pensil.

(3) Students should note, no supplement will be provided.

(4) Answer **any two** subquestions from each unit.

(5) Figures to the right indicate full marks.

(6) Assume suitable data if necessary.

---

1. (a) What are the object and method of geodetic surveying.   **[8]**

(b) Explain in brief the various triangulation figures commonly adopted and compare it's merit and demerits.   **[8]**

(c) Explain signals and their classification.   **[8]**

UNIT – II

2. (a) Explain method of adjustment of Geodetic quadrilateral.   **[8]**

(b) In carrying a line of level across a river, the following eight reading were taken with a level under identical conditioned.   **[8]**

2.322, 2.346, 2.352, 2.306, 2.312, 2.300, 2.306, 2.326

Calculate :

(i) Probable error of single observation

(ii) Probable error of the mean.

(c) State and explain four lows of weight.   **[8]**

UNIT – III

3. (a) Explain crab and drift in aerial photogrammetry.   **[8]**

(b) Define relief displacement. Derive the expression for relief displacement.   **[8]**

(c) (i) Differentiate between map and vertical photograph.

(ii) Write short note on mirror stereoscope.   **[8]**

UNIT – IV

4. (a) Write short note on: **[8]**
   (i) Nautical sextant.
   (ii) Fathometer.
   (b) Explain methods of locating sounding.   **[8]**
   (c) Explain about hydrographic surveying in details.   **[8]**

UNIT – V

5. (a) Explain type of platform used in remote sensing.   **[8]**
   (b) State clearly the various practical applications of remote sensing to civil engineering field.   **[8]**
   (c) Explain principle of EDM. State the applications of EDM to civil engineering.   **[8]**

✠ ✠ ✠